About the Author

Keith West studied fine art, drawing and painting at Coventry College of Art. He exhibited at various London galleries and churches, such as St Martin-in-the-Fields and Westminster Abbey, among others. He was a lecturer and, later, head of arts at the Camden Institute. He was commissioned in 2008 by the Tate Gallery Archive to write a memoir about close friend and international art critic Barbara Reise and of his experience as an art student during the influence of a radical conceptualist philosophy at Coventry and its impact on British art and art education. The document was published in a narrative version, *Light Under a Bushel,* in 2020.

Caravaggio's Boy

Keith West

Caravaggio's Boy

Vanguard Press

VANGUARD PAPERBACK

© Copyright 2025
Keith West

The right of Keith West to be identified as author of
this work has been asserted by him in accordance with the
Copyright, Designs and Patents Act 1988.

A CIP catalogue record for this title is available from the British Library.

ISBN 978-1-83794-251-0

Vanguard Press is an imprint of
Pegasus Elliot Mackenzie Publishers Ltd.
www.pegasuspublishers.com

First Published in 2025

Vanguard Press
Sheraton House Castle Park
Cambridge England

Printed & Bound in Great Britain

Acknowledgements

I'd like to thank Josephine Powell for a lifelong friendship, teaching and mentoring; Peter Webb for his generous analysis and pages of invaluable notes; Jo Cammack for her enthusiastic support for the project; likewise, Barry Gurney at Barnet Waterstone for practical advice and guidance. Walther Friedlaender's *Caravaggio Studies,* the first analytical biography of Caravaggio, his paintings and known documents. Andrew Graham-Dixon's *Caravaggio: A Life Sacred and Profane* – heir to Friedlaender. Professor Gianni Papi's catalogue raisonnè of the paintings by Cecco del Caravaggio. Curatorial staff Apsley House, London, and the Ashmolean Museum, Oxford. Dušan, Buran Chief Curator, Slovenska Narodna Galerie Bratislava, Director Professor Lukasz Gawet, Muzeum Narodowe Warszawie, Warszawa. Curatorial team The Art Institute of Chicago. Mark Simpson's coinage of *Male Impersonators: Men Performing Masculinity.* Ever supportive partner Brendan. Finally, Marguerite Yourcenar's *Mémoires d'Hadrien*, inspiration for the form of the book and her goal – 'to reinterpret the past but also strive for historical authenticity'.

"Checco del Caravaggio tis calld among the painters twas his boy haire darke, 2 wings rare, compasses liute violin & armes & laurel, it was ye body & face of his owne boy or servants that laid with him"

Richard Symonds (1617 – 1660)

29th September 1620

A cacophony of syncopated chimes near and far – every bell in Rome rang the feast of Saint Michael, dissonant as memories. Recollections of good companions, laughter, wild nights and… the other… spilled wine and blood, grief and loss. Reaching the Ponte Sant'Angelo, I daren't look back in case my resolve crumbled and instructed the carter to turn the mules around. I stared ahead. My vision filled by the towering red-orange fortress surmounted by the marble statue of an angel sheathing his bronze sword indicating God's punishment of the plague was over. The white figure glowed gold in the early sun. An armed angel… Michael? Perhaps a sign I had finally abandoned the past. It was ten years since he died, a decade and nearly… three months. His name, if not forgotten, no longer spoken, but his paintings still drew the faithful. Truly faithful pilgrims who knelt before saints as familiar as family, friends and neighbours. I bore memories of the paintings like holy relics, having witnessed the creation of many: memories of the blessed, He who blesses and he—co-creator, Michelangelo Merisi from Caravaggio. I knew him as Michele in the eleven years I was his foundling, his model, assistant and, for a time, lover.

There were many things I witnessed and came to know about Michele but much I never knew or only gathered from rumour and gossip. I am Francesco Boneri, known as Cecco del Caravaggio – Caravaggio's boy, if you like.

Chapter 1

Cittadina di Caravaggio 1576

The child gazed at cracks in the ceiling above his bed. Lines that criss-crossed revealed to him an angel, perfectly formed – head, body, arms, legs and wings; the lines defined what was angel and what was not. It must be an angel because he was born on the feast of Holy Michael, prince of angels and mighty warrior, although his angel had no sword. He gazed up at the angel until his eyelids quivered and… He took a stick from the ashes in the fireplace, the end burnt to charcoal, then stretched up to rub his blackened finger on the plaster absorbing the cracks to give the angel form and life as he emerged from the void. The charcoal was as black as the cracks at the edges but lighter where an imaginary light from below caught the body, arms, legs and wings. His wet finger lightened areas of the chest, belly, upper thighs and nearest wing. A floorboard creaked; his mother stood silently, watching. For a moment, he thought she might be cross, but she simply stood, arms crossed, hip leant against the doorframe, her belly swollen. She smiled. His younger brother Battista clung to his mother's skirt and stared as ever sullen, finger in mouth. Michele grinned, pointed a black finger to the angel. She nodded and watched as he brought the angel to life. When satisfied, he stepped back, and his mamma came to sit on the bed and drew him down to rock him in her arms.

"Will Papa be cross?"

She laughed. "Fermo? Has Papa ever been cross with you?"

He grinned and shook his head. "Not very cross. I'll draw something for Papa too. I wonder what he would like… but when will he come home?"

She stroked his hair. "He has much work to do for the Marchese. You know how busy he is, but he will come back to us soon."

"And he will see my angel?"

"He will see your angel."

"Will he like it?"

"Of course." She licked the sleeve of her blouse and wiped the boy's face, turning the cuff dark grey.

Her eyes flicked between her sleeve and his streaked face and laughed. "I don't know which is dirtier." His younger brother, Battista, stood watching from the door.

Papa never saw the angel. He never returned nor Zio Ludovico the priest, Nonno Bernardino and Nonna Merisi. The plague ravaged the city, surrounding towns and villages, which even the devout Archbishop Borromeo could not stop with prayers as he walked barefoot, knelt before every church and holy statue until his robes were torn, caked in dirt, and his feet bled. Mamma was pregnant with her third son, so Papa sent her away from Milan to keep the children safe. He never cried for Papa but very much for his mother. She said they must think of Papa and everyone being in heaven but however brave she appeared during the day – hiding her grief from her chicks – he heard her muffled sobs in the night. She struggled to make things appear normal as possible, as though Fermo and the others might return any day.

As the oldest boy, Michele felt protective of his mamma but helpless when he saw tears in her eyes. In the night, the darkness pierced by the candle light by her bed, he hardly whispered and gently stroked her arm. She quickly wiped her eyes and drew him close.

An unexpected comfort for Mamma was the arrival at Caravaggio of the Marchesa Sforza-Colonna. She also left Milan as soon as the outbreak was known. She too was with child and delivered her first son just weeks after Mamma's fourth. The women became close despite the Lady Costanza's descent being one of the most illustrious families in Europe and Mamma Lucia being the obscure but respectable Aratori family. The last months and weeks of their confinements brought them ever closer.

Mamma shared her experience of her pregnancies to put the marchesa at ease and to ignore old wives' tales. Costanza was not much more than a girl of sixteen, whose upbringing sheltered her from the world, and, when she married, she was shocked by what she considered bestial demands of the marital bed. She had to be gently persuaded that what happened between her legs was what men and women did as an expression of love and creation.

When the marchesa delivered her firstborn son, Muzio, Lucia arranged her sister Margherita to wetnurse the child. High-born ladies did not breastfeed their offspring to ensure they were ready to conceive again as soon as possible. Mamma said Michele had met the marchesa several times in Milan, but he had no memory of the beautiful golden-haired lady before her arrival in Caravaggio. He was overwhelmed by the affection she showered on him, hugging and kissing, even lifting him up, never mind her huge belly. She called Michele her little warrior, saying he was a special child born around the time of her father Marcantonio Colonna's victory over the Ottomans at the Battle of Lepanto.

The prince was the hero of Europe, and his daughter's eyes shone with pride, referring to him with reverence as His Excellency but sometimes simply Papa. She often visited the Merisi house, arriving in her little carriage with the Colonna badge on the door. She and Mamma chatted like sisters as Margherita breastfed Muzio.

She called Michele her angel, stroked his hair and sat him on her lap. "I see wonderful things for you, my angelic Michele."

Once her son was born, the marchesa arrived more often at the house, which was a haven, surrounded by the soothing sounds of muttering chickens and buzzing bees around the house and yard and distant quivering maas of sheep in the fields. It was a stark contrast to her bustling household in Milan. There she was never alone, even when she visited, the coachman and bodyguard hovered nearby, but Lucia sent wine and bread, cheese, slices of boar and olives to where they waited in an outhouse.

Most mornings, Michele left the house soon after sunrise and wandered the fields, closely examining tall grasses, long oleander leaves, shiny basil leaves and leathery Verbascum Mullein that put out yellow florets during the Feast of the Baptist. He watched Mamma prepare Mullein when any of her brood had sore throats. The earthy brew was a specific remedy dedicated to the voice calling in the wilderness. Near a marshy area, he noticed a large rock he thought resembled the shape of a lamb. Several ewes regarded him from a few yards away. He selected a hard black stone and, staring intently at the lamb, traced its outline on the rock, its spindly legs scored down, hooves obscured by grasses. He chipped the rock with short strokes to emulate fleece. It took hours, scraping and chipping with occasional breaks to sip cool water from a nearby spring. In the late afternoon, Mamma came looking for him, his baby brother Pietro on her hip and Battista, as ever, clinging to her skirts. Sister Caterina tottered, barely walking, as she gathered field flowers.

"There you are."

He stood and turned to smile at her. She stared a few moments, then stepped closer. Michele moved aside to let her see his handywork. She laughed with delight, set Pietro down and stroked the image.

Battista stood beside her, head to one side and pointed his skinny finger. "Lamb."

She looked up at Michele. "It *is* a lamb... a perfect lamb, the lamb of God." She fetched bread and cheese for Michele and told Battista and Caterina to leave their brother alone as he worked. By the time the sky turned orange and the sun settled purple on the horizon, the lamb was finished.

He visited the lamb every day and made slight refinements until the afternoon someone came from behind and smacked his head. "What's this? Why aren't you helping your mother?" Michele wheeled around, to see a man he barely recognised. "She said you'd be here making pictures." The man was one of the half-brothers of his papa, whose generous loving likeness was marred by a scowl and creased brow.

"I do my chores before—"

He slapped Michele's face and pushed him over. "Don't answer me, boy." The uncle pushed him again and the boy fell beside a broken branch, which he seized, leapt up and hit the man hard in the chest. Winded, the man fell sideways, grasping his chest and Michele struck again, bringing the branch down even harder on his wrist to prevent him from hitting back.

Michele stood holding the heavy branch high and panting, his teeth clenched and voice an unexpected growl. "Don't ever hit me or my mother or I will *kill* you." The uncle gasped with pain, wide-eyed with shock at the vehemence of the boy's voice.

Mamma bandaged her brother-in-law's swollen wrist and dabbed salve on his chest but didn't look her son in the eye when she made him say sorry. She was unsettled by the violence of her son's seething rage. So out of control that she had to wrench the branch from his clenched fist and knew from his glare and set jaw that his grudging apology was insincere. The uncle left, threatening he and his brother would take everything from Lucia.

When he was gone, Mamma sent Michele to bed. He heard her weeping and went to put his arms around her. "What is it, Mamma? Why did he say such things?" He felt her tremble when she hugged him. It was several years before he learned Papa had not written a will, leaving his half-brothers with a claim against the house and land. The matter dragged on several years but, finally, the house was taken in exchange to settle Papa's debts. Lucia was left just a few hectares of land and a small house that, thankfully, Papa left in reasonably good repair. The frequent visits by the marchesa were certainly known to the brothers, who left Lucia in peace, although the strain of dealing with lawyers was expensive and exhausting. Mamma fought on despite the likelihood that much would be lost to lawyers and greed which Lucia surely could not afford.

Lady Costanza was fiercely loyal and generous to those whom she respected and who served her well. It was perhaps the lady's discreet support and persuasion that legal matters were eventually resolved, and Lucia moved to the smaller house at Porta Folceria. Despite their changed circumstances, Costanza continued to visit with her increasing brood.

The year after Muzio came Fabrizio, who from childhood looked angelic but was more than boisterous, and, on one occasion, he arrived with a sword. The marchesa said he was taking fencing lessons. He was six, about half Michele's age but already almost as tall and keen to show off his skill. Michele used a stick to defend himself but was barely able to fend off Fabrizio's vicious blows, whose sword, although forged for a boy, had a blade with a lethal edge.

His mother called out to him, "Not so hard, Fabrizio. Michele doesn't have your training."

He continued to hack Michele's stick until it was finally shredded and the game was over. Fabrizio stalked off and, later, there was a commotion, screeching and clucking in the yard behind the shed. Lucia and Costanza rushed to find the yard strewn with bloody feathers. Fabrizio stood proudly in the coop, hand on hip, having decapitated several chickens. Lady Costanza was cross, snatched the sword from him and sent him to sit in her carriage with the coachman to keep an eye on him. She insisted she replace the half dozen murdered fowl. The family ate chicken the rest of the week as though it was a festive season and, although they laughed, it was impossible to ignore something dark about Fabrizio. Michele's younger brother Battista said the family shouldn't indulge his evil with their mirth.

From an early age, Battista was determined to take holy orders and insisted on joining the junior seminary at age eight, where he seemed more devout each time he was permitted to visit the family. Michele grew to dislike him, always a sneak and thought Battista's ostentatious piety was a mask to attract attention. The final humiliation came when it was agreed Michele would be apprenticed to the painter Master Simone Peterzano in Milan and was furious when Battista, aged just twelve, signed the contract because he was a seminarian and Lucia was a mere woman. He made great play handing over the cash but worse was his smug piety and condescension in the presence of the lawyer. Signing the paper with a flourish, he clasped his hands as though in prayer. It was obvious that becoming a lowly priest would never satisfy his ambition. Michele was stony faced as papers were exchanged.

Despite his dour façade, Master Peterzano was a kind man. He encouraged Michele to make friends with other apprentices, but he remained aloof, being older than most of the other lads. From the moment he entered the workshop, he inhaled the intoxicating smell of walnut and linseed oil, paints, varnishes, sickly boiling rabbit-skin glue, vinegar-musty raw canvas and fresh wood for stretcher pieces or altar panels. There were also strainers on which canvases were strung and stretched in preparation for painting. Master Simone's wife Angelica often served rabbit, the white leg bones ground to powder mixed with chalk, gum Arabic and a little oil to make gesso, the barrier layer to prevent precious oil colour seeping into the canvas and becoming dull. In an adjacent locked storeroom, jars of powdered pigment were lined in rainbow order on shelves and an early task was to grind small stones of lapis lazuli to fine powder in a granite pestle and mortar. It was time-consuming and laborious, wrists and arms ached, but, by the end of the day, the powder was satisfyingly fine as flour. Master Simone said blue lapis was extravagantly expensive, mined in a distant country called Khorasan. Other rare colours came from distant lands, including haematite and cinnabar reds, and green stones from the Holy Land and beyond and Egypt too. Less expensive colours came from Sienna or Naples and some hues like verdigris was scraped from corroded copper, white from lead, chalk and marble dust and black from soot and tar, as Michele knew, from charcoal.

Michele was occasionally invited to visit the marchesa and her children. Muzio was a little distant and soon left to complete his education in Spain, but Fabrizio was always boisterous and insisted Michele share the young prince's fencing lessons. By now, Fabrizio was a highly skilled swordsman and taught Michele posture, balance, defence and attack manoeuvres but couldn't recall ever beating him and frequently returned to Master Simone's workshop with cuts which sometimes needed salve and bandages. He was not supposed to take the sword from the castle but occasionally managed to sneak it past the guards and practice in the yard behind the workshop.

Michele stayed past sunset at the castle one occasion and Fabrizio said he should stay the night. Over supper, the Lady Costanza agreed. In the bed chamber, Michele removed doublet and hose, but Fabrizio stripped unashamedly naked, climbed into bed and cuddled Michele, reverting to the boy he was. Michele slipped an arm 'round his shoulder, a protective older brother he never was for Battista until Fabrizio's hand slipped down and tugged Michele's underpants. "Let me see… you have hair." Michele pushed his hand away, but the sudden unexpected attention was arousing and Fabrizio was insistent. "Let me see you make manjuice…"

Chapter 2

Bergamo 1591

I overheard chatter about the Merisi family of Caravaggio and their connection to the grand Sforza-Colonna family. It was said the father, I never knew his name, died in the great plague before I was born. He was master of works for the Sforza and his wife was his second. I heard her name was Lucia. There were brothers, Michele and Battista, and sister, Caterina, all orphaned when Lucia was widowed. There may have been a third son who died young. The older brother apprenticed to a painter and the younger went to the seminary. Apart from that, I heard little else of the Merisi until I was older. I was about ten when rumours circulated about the painter brother running away from Milan with a price on his head.

People clucked with paper-thin indignation about an attack on a law officer – perhaps, one of Cardinal Borromeo's militia. But the scandal in Milan was soon overshadowed in Bergamo by the arrival of a new curate. The old priest was getting on, decent enough and easy on penances but the younger priest, Father Gennaro, was instantly popular and, from his well-tailored cassock, perhaps he was the younger son of a minor aristocrat. Because of his age, it was assumed he was one of Archbishop Borromeo's acolytes but, apart from declaiming the archbishop's missives, he was preoccupied with encouraging boys to join the choir and older lads to train as altar boys.

I was keen to be a chorister, but my pa said I had more important things to do in the workshop. Like his father and grandfather before him, Pa was a painter who worked in the same way they had done with little or no variation for generations. I swept and tidied the workshop, cleaned brushes, sanded poplar panels and coated them with layers of gesso until surfaces were smooth as ivory, Sometimes Papa told me to apply the reddish boule before he began painting a Madonna, a Jesus or a saint. I enjoyed the work, but Pa was brutal and his first son, my half-brother, even more so vicious to me but worse to Mamma, often beating her mercilessly for no reason other than she was not his mother.

My ambition was to be a painter but not in the old-fashioned style of pictures Pa sold to local dignitaries and churches. He was addressed as master but was hardly more than a journeyman, barely making enough to feed and clothe us. I believe he knew demand for his kind of devotional paintings was likely to die before he did and directed his ire at an engraving of a statue of David by the famous sculptor and painter Michelangelo. Pa called him a sodomite and took pains to criticise and ridicule the nude figure in the engraving. "It's out of proportion… the hands are too big and look— look at the cock… even your scrawny thing's bigger, and most of yours is foreskin…"

His son joined the mockery and goaded me until I punched him. His nose and mouth bled, his teeth pink as he growled and, fists flailing, beat me to the floor. When I was down, he started kicking me and, when Mamma rushed to help me, he turned on her, beat her around her head and punched her stomach. She gasped and crawled away, cradling her belly, but, with a howl, I swung around and hit him in the face with a cooking pan.

Pa came to see what the commotion was about, saw his son floored by the blow and attacked Mamma, battering and roaring at her. "Let that be a lesson. Never lay a finger on my son again."

Mamma lost several teeth, and her jaw was so badly broken she never spoke again without a hissing sound. She sent me to stay a few days with neighbours who lived at the edge of town until matters were calmer. Our neighbour's son, Paulo, was my friend. Mamma gave me a small sack of provisions to cover the cost of my stay, and I set off along the path. It was only a mile or so from the house when I met the young curate.

He smiled. "You're the younger, Boneri boy."

"Yes, Father. I'm Francesco."

"I thought so… Cecco, I suppose." He slightly frowned. "Have you been fighting? You're very bruised."

"It was a fall, Father."

"I think it's more than that… Who did this to you?" I looked down, not willing to make matters worse. "Let me see." He examined my swollen face and drew my jerkin and shirt off my shoulder. "You're bruised… everywhere. Come." He led me to a barn and told me to take off my shirt. He gently touched my bruises. "You poor boy."

At home, the atmosphere was tense as ever. Mamma's bruises were black and yellow, much worse than mine, and there were dark red-brown scabs on her lip and nose and her right eye was black and swollen. She glanced up at me with a wistful smile. Pa strutted about to cover his shame and his son was wary. Their brutality towards Mamma and me did not go unnoticed locally, and Pa was canny enough to realise this time he and son had gone too far. Their brutality was not good for the business of making devotional icons.

Although the house was calmer, the ghost of Mamma limped, quietly suffering the drudgery of sweeping and cleaning, washing, repairing, cooking, gathering vegetables and herbs and bartering her woven reed baskets for eggs, hens, scrag-ends of lamb and, occasionally, slivers of pancetta. It was as she sorted my washing, a coin fell from my breeches' pocket, tinkled on the stone floor and rolled across the room. Pa picked it up. It represented several day's wages. "Where did this come from?" Mamma stood in silence and apprehensive, my breeches in her hand. Pa glared at me. "Where did you get this?"

I didn't dare admit the curate gave it to me, seeing myself standing naked in the barn as he kissed and fondled me, his other hand fumbling under his cassock. "I found it."

"Liar!" He hit my head. "You stole it."

"No, I didn't, Papa. It was on the path near the barn." I was surprised he didn't pursue the matter but merely scowled and, of course, kept the coin. I avoided mentioning the curate and wondered as I did my chores in the workshop when I would next see him and lay awake at night, thinking of my protecting angel.

Days passed slowly until I was up early the following Sunday as the bells rang. I washed in the cold water and put on a fresh shirt, breeches and jerkin and ran to the church where altar boys dressed the altar and lit candles. Father Gennaro appeared, genuflected deeply to the host, arranged the missal on the south side of the altar, flicked the pages back and forth, marking passages with red ribbons. I stepped close to the choir and, as he turned, I smiled. He froze for an instant, then hurried from the sanctuary. I was confused by his reaction, and, whenever I could sneak away from the workshop, I loitered in the town near the church, but, whenever I saw Father Gennaro, he was never alone. He was popular with the congregation, his easy charm attracted people and, of course, he was tall and handsome with shiny dark hair and blue-grey eyes.

On a bright late autumn evening, Mamma sent me to the apothecary in the town for a remedy, and, on the way, I saw Father Gennaro coming towards me on the path. He stopped. "Francesco."

"Father, good evening. I hoped to see you."

"Why would you want to see me, boy?"

"I thought—"

"I know what you thought but, in future, stay away from me…"

"But why, Father, what have I done?"

"You don't need to ask."

"I don't understand, Father…"

"Your tears do you no good… you will no longer tempt me… keep away from me."

Chapter 3

Rome 1592

The stench wafting from the river made him cover his nose but he leaned further to watch men casting hooks in the river to catch a bundle of slimy rolls of fabrics. When landed on the narrow strand, the bindings were cut and spilled the silver-grey flesh and lolling head of a woman with red hair, the skin drawn back from a pouting gash in her throat. A young lad, stripped to the waist, leapt back, flinging his arms wide, his yelp heard across the river. An older man climbed down to comfort the younger who covered his eyes. Standing up to their calves in mud, the elder reverently covered the woman's nakedness.

A crowd had gathered on the bridge and chattered, pointed and resurrected the unknown woman with their certainties: as sure as an article of faith, she was a prostitute; her last client wouldn't pay full price or she was pregnant, killed by her pimp or on the order of some aristocrat or priest or cardinal. Women tutted, crossed themselves, shocked by the slander of a holy priest… At least that was the pretence. Each face revealed meanness, envy, pettiness, a bully, another leered at the naked corpse; grimaces and knowing looks leaked the state of their souls. Only the shocked half-naked youth and older man who comforted him had true compassion for the dead woman.

People dispersed, but Michele stayed to watch the sagging body secured by ropes and hauled up to the embankment where closeness to the lifeless body instilled reverence in the men above. Rather than cross the bridge to find the tenement where he hoped to lodge, he scanned the horizon for the dome of St Peter's obscured by a mesh of scaffolding. The urge to see *The Ceiling* was irresistible but, joining the queue of pilgrims on the stair to the chapel, he was unexpectedly anxious. Engravings he had seen at Master Simone's workshop hinted at their magnificence and, during a few days' stay in Florence, he saw the towering naked youth, David – three times the size of a normal man, perfectly still yet tense as though about to move. He feared such towering ambition, that he might be crushed by his namesake.

When the shuffling queue eventually entered the chapel, it was airier and much higher than expected. He hesitated before glancing up at what first appeared a jumble of figures and patchwork of shocking bright colours, pastel pinks, pale blues and greens. Engravings were no preparation for the effect of colour or sheer scale. He wandered to the far end of the chapel to follow the sequence from the creation: Adam brought to life and ending with Noah's drunkenness, the second fall painted directly above *The Last Judgement* on the altar wall.

The chapel was illuminated with searing blue light, and a crack of thunder shook the building. *The Last Judgement* covered the entire wall, seemingly blasted away, revealing the end of time, crowded with figures rising blessed or tumbling damned, swirling around the majestic figure of Christ, his mamma and entourage of saints. No gentle Gesù this but a sturdy man, hailing the blessed with a raised arm, the other shunning the damned. It was impossible not to be overawed by such a feat, but Michele was relieved the ceiling and altar wall were done with such apparent ease he was drawn into the act of making and apprehension waned as he contemplated the frescos. As he might silently mouth the words of a poem, his looking shared the activity of painting, each brushstroke, colour and tone guided by the master's hand.

After several hours, his neck and shoulders ached and amber sunlight raked through the high windows. Engrossed by the frescos, he could not tell if the storm had broken or simply passed over, leaving a legacy of golden light. Sated for the moment, he hitched the saddle bags on his shoulder and quickly left the Vatican.

The sun burned yellow-orange as he hurried to locate the tenement where he hoped to find lodgings, following a rough sketch map made by Lorenzo, someone he met in Venice many months earlier. The journey to Rome had been exhausting, and the mule Master Simone gave him was sold days ago to buy food. The journey was arduous and longer than expected. He was ill several days and the soles of his boots were worn through, his feet blistered and bled.

The first distant glimpse of the Holy City was disappointing, cowering under sagging purple-grey thunder clouds, and the humidity was unbearable. Unlike Milan or Florence, Rome had seen better days, many times fought over like a bitch in heat by foreign powers. Imperial troops devastated the city decades earlier, leaving many of the palaces as shabby as tenements that affronted them cheek by jowl. Here and there were splendid new palaces and churches that stood out from older down-at-heel buildings. Away from the river, hot breezes wafted the stink of piss from the walls of buildings whether grand or dismal and desiccated dog shit crumbled in corners.

He became lost in the narrow streets and dark alleys. No one wasted a second to help, some vaguely pointed as they rushed by. It was dusk by the time he found the tenement. The windows blank with oil cloth. The jagged teeth of the ancient door gnawed the high step and shrieked as he shoved it open to enter a cool passage leading to a small dim courtyard. Above a rectangle of fading orange sky was framed by the overhanging roof.

"Lorenzo!" His call echoed in the narrow shaft. "Lorenzo! Sicilian Lorenzo… Lorenzo!"

A head appeared from a window on the third floor. "Who is it…? Who wants Lorenzo?"

"It's me… from Venice… Michele."

"Michele!" They met halfway up the turning staircase and embraced. "You're here at last… Come up, come in."

The apartment comprised two large rooms that stank of adolescent spoor with soiled straw mattresses, grimy blankets and underclothes, rags, bags, empty wine flagons and other personal possessions strewn around. A chest served as a makeshift table with an oil lamp and several thick candle stubs filched, no doubt from churches, embedded in layers of wax in cracked earthenware dishes. "Put your bags there."

Michele hesitated, loathe to let his few possessions out of his sight, but put them down by the open door to the second room. The familiar oily scent blossomed as he followed Lorenzo into the other room, where a young man sat at an easel, working on a quarto, concentrating on a still life before him. He didn't turn until Lorenzo made introductions. "Filippo… Filippo Triesegni. This is Michele… from Caravaggio."

"Painter?" He nodded and glanced around the room. There were two other easels with work in progress, pedestrian stuff.

He turned to Lorenzo. "How many live here?"

"Seven, eight… sometimes more."

Filippo laughed. "We take turns sleeping."

"Where is everyone?"

"Some work for Master Cesari. He's a bad-tempered bastard but has lots of work. Others find work where they can."

The apartment was in a quarter south of the ruins of the Roman Forum where mainly Lombard artists congregated. By nightfall, the apartment became noisy, young bucks bragged about successes of the day, mainly lies about girls.

Lorenzo took him to a nearby tavern. "Any money, Michele?"

"A little…"

"It's all right. Everyone's skint. I'll pay for the meal; it won't be much" – he grinned – "but enough for wine."

"I'll pay you back when—"

"Listen, Michele. I'll speak to Cesari in the morning; he's not that bad and always on the lookout for good assistants. Do you have anything I can show him?"

"A few small pictures, a still life. Lombard style."

"Good, he likes fine, detailed work for his backgrounds. Now tell me what have you been up to since Venice. Nothing bad, I hope?"

Lorenzo's approach to Cesari was unsuccessful. "Not another Lombard…" Instead, Michele presented himself to the Colonna palace despite apprehension about the kind of reception he might receive since his flight from the authorities in Milan with a price on his head. He was relieved the Lady Costanza immediately rose to greet and embrace him and likewise his aunt Margherita who had suckled the marchesa's many children. There was no mention of Milan nor his mother but the sight of the marchesa was startling; for the first time he saw a resemblance to his mamma, Lucia.

His aunt asked how he fared in Rome, and, when he mentioned the tenement where he lived among rowdy young men, arrangements were made for him to lodge with a priest, Father Pandolfo Pucci, who had unspecified connections to the Colonna. In exchange for household work, he was given a room where he slept and painted. Among other duties, he shopped in the market where he bought cheap pitted apples, lemons and stole better quality grapes, quinces and vegetables. The cook served only salad, day after day, and, when Michele raised the matter, Pucci said eating meat aroused carnal desires and bestial aggression. Behind his back, Michele called Pucci *Signor Insalata*.

He spent free daylight hours painting fruit in a basket perched on a ledge at eye level. He outlined the general forms by scratching through the base layer prepared earlier, then overlaid true colour. Using small brushes, he worked up each object in fine detail, staring a long time at the still life before quickly rendering each wind-burned vine leaf, bruised and pock-marked apple as precisely as seen and without artifice.

When domestic duties allowed, he roamed the city, visiting churches and often returned to the Vatican to spend hours in the Sistine Chapel, lying on the floor to imprint the images on his memory and drew several of the major scenes, concentrating on the *Creation of Adam*. He also made detailed studies of some of the ignudi, one in particular close to the scene of *The Flood*, a nude that twisted, close arm forward, legs splayed, head thrown back with a downwards wide-eyed glance of terror at the long drop from the ceiling. Overcome one afternoon by the heavy heat of the chapel, he was woken by a young priest who gently rocked him with his slipper-clad foot.

"Wake up, ruffian; this isn't a dosshouse." Michele roused and blinked, his small portfolio clutched to his chest, broken chalk and charcoal sticks lay in pieces all around. He rubbed his eyes. The priest pulled his arm, coaxing him to stand, then took the portfolio and read *Michelangelo Merisi* in fine script on the cover. "A second Michelangelo…" He leafed through the sheaves. "You have talent Master Merisi; you don't copy… you steal." He winked and glanced up at the ceiling. "Such perfection, the frescos were the only way Michelangelo could realise his ambition to sculpt the slaves for Pope Julius' tomb. It would have been impossible to complete his ambition in stone in a single mortal lifetime, even a life as long as his."

"Not perfection, Father. Some of the figures twist in impossible positions and the one closest to the first day of creation is poorly done."

The priest followed the line of Michele's pointing finger, hesitated a moment, then shrugged. "Even the greatest artists are faint echoes of the prime Creator." He gently tapped his cheek. "Bless you, Michele… but now I must lock the doors."

"You're different from priests I've known in the past, Father."

"We're only human, bad in the good and good in the bad but you must go now."

"Father, what's your name?"

The young priest observed him a while, then gripped his shoulder. "If you're looking for goodness, Michele, or guidance, go hear Father Filippo Neri. He's old now but if you have the opportunity, I believe you'd find his words inspiring. And since you ask, my name is Giacomo—*Father* Giacomo to you. Now, bless you, but piss off."

Chapter 4
Leaving Bergamo

Father Gennaro's cold accusation was a shock. What had I done? Did he say get thee behind me, Satan…? Maybe not his words, but I heard an echo… For days, I struggled to hold back tears and barely spoke as I completed my tasks in the workshop and helped Mamma whenever I could. She knew I was in misery and, when Pa was out of sight, she gently hugged and kissed me. She stroked my hair, but I couldn't tell her I felt sinful, not because of anything I had done but because Father Gennaro's words made me so. I only made confession to the old priest but omitted my sin of tempting the curate. Whenever my chores were done, I wandered the fields, paid close attention to grasses, trees and listened to birdcalls, sparrows' chirps, a goldfinch and lark twittering in the dome above and occasionally a cuckoo.

The first time I laughed in a long time was hearing the second Merisi son was called Michelangelo. I glanced at Pa's creased engraving of David, the youthful Old Testament hero who slew Goliath, and was thankful Pa was not in the workroom as my sniggers erupted into laughter. This Merisi Michelangelo was apprenticed to a painter in Milan, starting late age thirteen so they said. According to gossip, his widowed mother sold what little land they had left to raise the money.

Most apprentices started about age eight, and, when I asked Pa if I would be apprenticed, he tapped me on the head. "Why would I pay someone else to tell you what I've already shown you? Good money after bad." What he meant was money we didn't have, even Lucia Merisi had to sell valuable land for her son to study with a half-decent master. I know nothing of his years as an apprentice but it was said that when he left his master, he went to Venice. I assumed he must have been very talented, but his stay was short and, on his return to Milan, chatter told how he almost killed one of Archbishop Borromeo's private guard and fled an outlaw. We heard he fetched up in Rome. For me, this Michelangelo… Michele, was no longer a shadowy figure but suddenly real, fascinating, even glamourous. I pictured him tall, shiny black hair, grey eyes and handsome.

Since the beating Mamma suffered from Pa and his son, public shame meant the house thereafter was less violent if no less miserable. Mamma was a whisp of smoke, silently moving about the house, no more than a servant. I helped her as much as I could when not in the workshop. Pa's son was sent to work with a local farmer which made life tolerable. There was tension when I made better preparatory drawings than Pa. He shouted I should only draw the way he did but for once didn't hit me. On my own initiative, I cut leather templates of Madonnas, saints and the Holy Child to trace basic silhouettes onto prepared surfaces. Certain characteristics could be added as necessary – the palm for a martyr, for instance, or Santa Lucia's eyes on a golden platter. Pa merely grunted when he saw what I had done. I knew he was surprised, even impressed how I saved time and effort in future by simply tracing outlines.

Whenever I was in the town or at the church, I kept my distance from Father Gennaro. If he saw me, he glared. The excitement I took for love soon evaporated not only by his rejection and angry guilt but thoughts about Father Gennaro were gradually replaced by imaginings of Michele Merisi and his life in Caravaggio, Milan and Venice. I heard it said Venice was a floating city with palaces covered in beaten gold and towers of glass – domes of lapis lazuli and boats with banners flying, draped in costly fabrics woven with gold and silver thread. Such fantasies, the allure of Venice and now Rome, were attached to Michele who in my imagination became a mythical creature with the aura and glamour of a prince... a prince of painters.

The week I was eleven, I took the path to town and saw Father Gennaro walking towards me. I stepped off the path to allow him to pass, expecting him to ignore me but, instead, he smiled. "Cecco. I haven't seen you in a while..."

I nodded, looked down at the dry stones, weeds and my scuffed orange-brown leather shoes. "I attend Mass every Sunday, Father." It was the answer the old priest would have expected. Assuming the conversation was over, I nodded again. "Good day, Father." I walked crab style to pass the curate but he caught my arm.

"How are the bruises?"

"It's been a nearly a year, Father..."

He smiled. "I suppose so. You've not been telling tales, I hope?"

"About what?"

"You know very well." He caught me by the neck and dragged me back along the path to the barn. Hens and swifts fluttered out of the gaps in the wood plank walls when he pushed open the door and shoved me to the ground.

When he was done with me, he buttoned his cassock and hissed, "Not a word to anyone… you understand?" I wiped tears on my sleeve as I slowly dressed. "Do you understand?" I nodded. "You understand?"

"Yes, Father."

"You've kept your distance like a good boy, let it stay that way and always remember… God is watching you." I went on to town to buy preparations that eased the pain of Mamma's badly set jaw and fresh bread because she had not found time to bake that day.

When I slipped into the house, she stopped me, gently caught me by the chin and tilted my head and saw the redness of my eyes from weeping.

"Pappa?"

"No."

"The son?"

"No, Mamma."

"Then who?"

I shook my head and went to the bedroom. There was a throbbing pain deep inside and I pulled down my breeches to see if there was blood. I knew there was no escaping Gennaro now that he had come to an accommodation with his conscience and would always shift the blame onto me. The following Sunday I caught up with my friend Paulo and persuaded him to walk with me instead of attending Mass. We slowly trod in step and in silence until he caught my arm. "What's wrong, Cecco?"

"I can't say." I stood and as my mouth gaped. I covered my face. "I can't tell you."

Paulo tucked his thumbs in his belt and looked away, embarrassed that I wept. Eventually he squeezed my shoulder, half-hearted but a welcome gesture. "It can't be that bad… unless you killed somebody… not that bastard brother?"

I laughed, wiped snot on my sleeve. "No…" He didn't press further. I glanced over his shoulder, suddenly aware the breeze from the distant hills was chilly and I shuddered. I looked him in the eyes. "If I said I was going to run away, would you come with me?"

"What?" He stared wide-eyed. "Leave… where… where would you go?"

I was about to say Rome but hesitated, unwilling to give away my true goal. "Milan… maybe, Florence."

Chapter 5

Fr Filippo Neri

As the Mass began, the old priest sat to the left of the sanctuary in profile, upright with his head bent in deep contemplation. A young priest began the service: *Commixtio salis et aquae panter fiat in nomine Patris et Fili...* Michele, as everyone, instinctively touched his forehead, chest and shoulders as the familiar litany was delivered at a stately pace which heightened expectation so the Epistle and even the Gospel readings were heard against increasing murmurs of anticipation as the moment approached when the old man would address them.

The ancient knelt in prayer, his lips slightly moved, then crossed himself and stood with some effort but waved away a deacon who stepped forward to offer help. He crossed to the altar steps, genuflected deeply, then turned. The entire congregation burst out laughing. He slowly made his way from the choir, down the steps to the nave, stroking his beard, half of which was clean shaved. He shrugged, gave the most seraphic unashamed gap-tooth smile, then giggled. It was a while before gales of laughter ebbed and he raised his arms.

At first, his voice was thin and reedy. "My dear brothers and sisters... my barber left on an urgent errand early this morning..." More laughter... "Be sure a joyful heart is more easily made perfect than a downcast one, so let us never forget those wonders with which our Lord God has blessed us." He walked slowly along the nave, stroking faces of those who strained to be close to him. "At the time I am speaking of, I lived at one of the great universities and a young man bright and clever came up to me, beaming with delight because his family had given leave for him to study for the law and went on at great length about how he would study unstintingly and with great attention until he was more than competent in the law." He yawned.

"You know what students are like. When the young man eventually finished his rather long speech, I said, 'And when you have finished your studies... what then?' The student replied, 'Well... then I shall take my doctorate and I will attract many cases and my success will attract attention and my learning and zeal will build my reputation.'"

By now the old priest's voice rang from the rafters. "'And then?'"

"'Well, I shall be promoted to some great office and I will make money and become rich.'"

He raised his eyebrows. "'And then?'" There were ripples of laughter. "'Well, I will live comfortably and with great honour, in health and respect and look forward to a quiet and venerable old age.'"

He raised his arms and the congregation joined him. "'And then?'" And then… "'And then, I suppose I shall die…'" The old man stroked his chin, beamed, then raised his arms again. "'And then?'"

The congregation laughed and repeated, "And then?"

The old man nodded until laughter subsided. "And then… the young man had no answer, except that his answer was to go away and contemplate his life and, eventually, he gave up his ambition to be a famous lawyer and devoted himself to follow Christ in the pursuit of good works." He smiled.

"Brothers and sisters, I ask you all, as you go about your daily toil and aim to satisfy all your hopes and wishes… what will you do then? If your brother or your sister is in need, pain or sorrow… what then? And if you meet a beggar, a stranger, someone fallen from grace, in trouble or in sickness… what then? Hungry, thirsty or dying, what then? Are not all these, sick in body and soul, hungry, thirsty, naked, prisoner, prostitute or beggar… Are they not known to us? Are they not one with us? Is it not Our Lord we see? Is it not Our Lord's words we hear? *In as much as you have done it unto one of these my brethren, ye have done it unto me*… Amen. Now, dear brothers and sisters, let us share our dear Lord's Supper and then… go in peace. In nomine Patris et Fili et Spiritus Sancti. Amen…"

The inspiration and spiritual joyfulness of Father Filippo's words were at odds with the tedium and bizarre regime living with Pandolfo Pucci… With only lettuce to eat, Michele again presented himself to the Colonna palazzo. Although the Lady Costanza was not in residence, he was told to return a few days later when he was advised to introduce himself to Master Antiveduto Gramatica, a painter originally from Sienna. He was hardly older than Michele, his work was popular mannered devotional paintings, with banal sharp outlined figures posed against unconvincing perspective backgrounds. He also produced what he called *head paintings* of famous men but Michele was impatient to collaborate with a master from whom he could learn necessary lessons to fill the glaring gaps in his technique.

In the following weeks, Michele received little money for his efforts and Gramatica required assistants paint backgrounds and other details from his preparatory drawings. For one picture, Michele was told to paint foliage as background for a small image of the Madonna. The cartoon suggested only vague leaf-shapes he assumed was shorthand for recognisable leaves so he gathered laurel, oleander and vine leaves with tendrils. The following day, Gramatica came from behind and slapped his head. "Who told you to paint leaves like that?"

Michele snatched the knife from his belt. "Don't touch me, bastard…"

Gramatica was shaken and hesitated before he cautiously pushed the knife from his chest. "Look at it." He gestured to the painting; his hand visibly trembled. "This leaf is curled and that has brown spots; you've painted what they look like, not the way they *should* look."

"But that's how they do look." Michele nodded to the bunch of leaves in a small pottery jug on the far side of the work bench but Gramatica swept the jar from the bench where it smashed on the floor. He raised his voice a little to regain some semblance of authority. Aware other lads were watching, he dare not lose face.

"Don't argue, Michele, paint out what you did and start again following my design."

"Up your arse." Michele grabbed his doublet from under the workbench and strode to the door.

"If you leave, Michele, you'll never work in Rome again." Gramatica stood with his hand on his hip. "What are you thinking?"

"Ha. I painted real leaves instead of—you're pissed off because what I can do shows how shitty the rest of the painting is."

"Who do you think you are? Your Lombard friends think you're another Leonardo, bragging you can paint as well as nature but it won't sell. This is Rome. We supply what patrons want, not what's good for them. They want what they know, nothing too new and, unless you understand that, Michele, you're finished before you started… and don't delude yourself that talent alone will bring success; your technique is pedestrian, you're not that good, quite a shitty painter, really. Perhaps Master Simone threw you out?"

Michele spat, kicked the door open and stepped into the blinding light. He returned to the tenement and slinging his sack of tools in the corner, slumped onto his mattress.

He was woken by Lorenzo. "Good news, Michele. Master Cesari wants to meet you. I took your latest – the painting of the basket of fruit – and he is impressed."

Cesari's workshop was busy. There were many assistants and several apprentices. One of Cesari's assistants, Prospero Orsi, known as Prosperino because he was short, gave him special attention and technical advice and guidance. Michele was about ten years younger than Prosperino, who with occasional demonstrations from Cesari, taught him more in a few months than Simone taught him in years. Although bad tempered, Cesari was fair and, within reason, gave Michele a free hand rather than expect rigid adherence to his designs, recognising the value his work added to his paintings. He encouraged Michele to paint foliage, fruit and vegetables in his own way, capitalising on his careful attention to fine detail in Lombard manner, much influenced by the Germans and Flemings. It was a profitable exchange. Cesari got quality work and Michele received sound technical advice and instruction.

Cesari encouraged Michele to paint side-lines, some he sold or kept in lieu of commission. Several still lives were sold to an artist dealer called Fantino Petrignani who probably passed them off as his own. Michele worked hard painting fruit and vegetables but was desperate to paint figures since they were a more highly regarded subject matter.

Frustrated that Cesari only gave him fruit and vegetables to paint, Michele persuaded Lorenzo to model, that is until Mario joined the rag-tag community. Mario Minniti, from Syracuse, said he was eighteen but looked boyish. Lorenzo was rather shy when modelling because of his obvious attraction to Michele, but Mario was not in the least reserved and, even though he preferred girls, shamelessly flirted with Michele.

They became firm friends and collaborated on a painting; the subject suggested when Michele watched Mario absorbed, peeling a green pear. "Bet you can't peel it without breaking the skin." Another more profitable subject occurred when an Albanian girl offered to tell Mario's fortune for a few coins.

He fell for her roguish glances and she tickled his palm. "Watch her; she'll rob you blind."

The girl spat at Michele and shouted, "I am no thief; you are very bad man for thinking so."

He made amends by offering to pay her to model and, after much haggling, she agreed with the proviso: "I take not off the clothes."

"*Puttana sciocca*, I want to paint you in the clothes you're wearing." Michele borrowed props from Cesari's workshop, a smart doublet and a hat with a feather. Mario and the girl were flirtatious so neither complained about the hours they posed. Mario brought her home several nights. The lads sniggered, aroused by the murmurs and fumbling from behind the thin curtain.

Cesari was impressed with the painting, recognised a novel subject and gave it the title *The Fortune Teller*. It sold within days and Cesari took a fair percentage. He suggested Michele make copies and paint other low-life stuff popular with the high-ups. Michele also began another ambitious subject he called *Cardsharps*. A lodger at the tenement, Lionello Spada, whom Michele had not met before, returned and reclaimed his mattress. Lorenzo said Spada was light-fingered but Michele was intrigued by his pale sharp features and attracted to his braggadocio, restless energy and shameless flirtation. He bragged about his family name, or the name he claimed was Spada (sword). Michele suspected it was a nickname bolstered by a collection of weapons, including several daggers and an illegal sword he claimed he stole from a man who paid him for sex.

Meeting Spada was the suggestion for the subject of *Cardsharps*. Lorenzo, Mario and others mocked Spada behind his back and were instinctively wary but Michele was reminded of Fabrizio Sforza when he was a youth although Spada lacked his charm and finesse. With the instinctive opportunism of a streetwise ruffian, Spada recognised Michele's obvious talent and, when he asked if he would model, his response was instant. "I'll model, so long as you have the spondulix."

The subject told a simple cautionary tale in a gambling tableau of a con-artist – an aristocratic youth dressed in black, modelled by Mario, played cards with Spada in the role he was born to play: a cheat. Spada introduced a friend, a shady individual, to play the part of the cheat's accomplice who signalled the cards held by Mario. Spada wore a yellow doublet with narrow black stripes; the older rogue also wore yellow with black wasp-striped sleeves – the colour assigned to the treacherous Judas in religious paintings.

Like The *Fortune Teller*, the *Cardsharps* was snapped up within days of going up in Cesari's workshop. Michele's work was becoming technically more sound and fluent thanks to the influence of Cesari and Orsi and the novelty of his subjects attracted attention, depicting the Roman underbelly of ragamuffins and crooks, girls and boys on the game, anybody for spare change, a drink, cheap meal or just a bed for the night. None at the tenement needed reminding they were only a few days' pay from the streets.

Another coincidence suggested what was to become Michele's most accomplished painting to date. Cesari suggested he paint another, larger basket of fruit, but Michele dragged his feet until he noticed a lad in the market selling fruit well past its best and going cheap. He bought the fruit and basket and had Mario pose with them in his arms. The general outlines were drawn in sgraffito through the wet base. He yanked down Mario's shirt to expose his right shoulder and chest and tilted his head backwards, prompting the roguish look he wanted and painted a recognisable portrait, lavishing a great deal of time and effort on the basket of fruit, producing a highly polished finish.

Cesari paid a decent price, confirming the painting's worth and called it *Boy with a Basket of Fruit*. Michele assumed Cesari would sell it to turn a quick profit but, surprisingly, he kept the painting on display in the workshop and refused all offers. By now, he treated Michele with special regard, which irritated Orsi. Michele was a gifted asset whom Cesari addressed as Master but, more importantly, put up Michele's work for sale under his own name, subject to a fair cut.

Within months of joining Cesari's workshop, increasing sales of his work allowed Michele to spend evenings at taverns, repaying Lorenzo's past generosity and, with Mario, Prosperino, Spada and a widening circle of friends, including established painters Orazio Gentileschi and Anibale Carracci, late nights turned into carousing, gambling, rowdy disputes and sometimes brawling. Avoiding police night patrols, they staggered drunken to the tenement as the sky turned pearly grey.

Rising still woozy one morning, Michele's joints ached, and he sweated profusely and trembled. By afternoon, Cesari noticed Michele was unwell, touched his forehead with the back of his hand. "You're burning up. Go home, Michele. If it's contagious, I don't want everybody infected." He gave Michele a small bag of coin. "See a physician."

He barely made it to the apartment, hauled himself up the flights of stairs, legs trembling, and, although his temperature was high, he shivered and shouted, "Spada… Lorenzo!"

Drenched in sweat, Michele moaned. Someone wiped his face, arms and chest with a cool cloth. He slowly returned to the world rather than an inescapable cave of nightmares. His entire body ached, head splitting and arms heavy. "You are back with us, my son, but you must rest." A monk in a patched brown habit and white apron touched Michele's forehead with the palm of his hand. "The fever's broken at last."

"Where am I?"

"The Conzolatione hospice."

"How?"

"Your friend… Lorenzo and another…"

Once his eyes focussed, he glanced around a long dormitory, his cot furthest from the door. A near life-size, tortured crucifix in the old style hung on the end wall beside him. He vaguely remembered being half-carried, half-dragged along dark narrow passages. Michele stared at the kindly face of the brother but pictures, dreams and remembrances blotted out the old monk's features.

To avoid Fabrizio's insistent pestering, he left the Sforza castle and took a shortcut. A grinning man with close copped hair he vaguely recognised leered at him, dragged him by the hair into a black narrow alley, smacked his head, then threw him against the building. He threw a punch but this man was no overweight half-uncle but stronger, more agile and hit him hard in the face. He slumped against the wall. The man caught him by the neck, turned him around and jammed his left arm high up his back, causing so much pain he thought his arm was dislocated. The seams of his breeches cracked and split as they were torn down… then excruciating pain… blood on the back of his thighs but worse were the names the man grunted and, when Michele gasped with pain, he hissed, "Bardassa… you're enjoying this…" The sergeant took his time but when he strained, becoming frantic, gasping as he stabbed harder, spittle sprayed on the back of his neck… zia… scopate facile… He flinched when the monk stroked his forehead.

Master Simone noticed blood on his shirt and sent for his brother Battista at the seminary, but Michele couldn't speak for shame. His brother was the last person he wished to see but Battista was unusually gentle and finally coaxed him to say what happened but when he said he recognised the man was the sergeant of the watch and what he had done, Battista let go of his hand, knocked over his chair and, as he rose, smacked Michele's face.

"How dare you slander a decent man! Our families have respected one another for generations; he is an officer of the law, a family man, one of the statue-bearers of Our Lady at her festival." He slapped Michele again. "Liar. Don't excuse your sin by blaming an innocent man. Dear God, you allowed yourself… can you not see the jaws of hell gaping to swallow you? Get on your knees." Further blows around the head. "Beg forgiveness of Our Saviour… say a confession."

"But it's true, Battista." He glanced up but only so far as the silver crucifix tucked into Battista's sash. His ears rang from another violent blow to the head. "Confess your lies or I swear I will report you to the archbishop and have you excommunicated." As his voice rose, it cracked, piping like a boy and the incongruity stunned Michele. His usual response would have been to lash out with fists but Battista's insistent piety rendered Michele impotent.

Battista was a fervent follower of Archbishop Borromeo's near Savonarola mission which carried great weight at the seminary and beyond. In a veritable bonfire of the vanities, the archbishop issued ever more stringent moral edicts not only for clerics and religious but also the laity, enforced by his private household army – famiglia armata, the sergeant being one of their number. For the Merisi-Aratori to have given a son to Holy Church was not only to continue the legacy of uncle Father Ludovico Merisi but added further distinction to the family. By his spiritual fervour, Battista usurped his older sibling and effectively headed the family by the sheer force of a second son invested with the power of a future priest. Battista landed a further heavy blow. "Confess your lies."

When Michele made a false confession, Battista gripped his hands. "Go on, say I am an abomination in the eyes of God, a degenerate creature, and pray God will eventually grant grace to forgive and renew me… say it. Say it!"

"I am degenerate…" It was his brother's final triumph.

Tears poured down his face as he mouthed again, "I am degenerate."

He was startled when the old man leaned down to hear his whispered confession and gently squeezed his hand. "My dear son, how could you be degenerate? You are a child of God and Our Lord Gesù died for your salvation. What torments you?"

"Could God ever forgive me, brother?"

"Of course, he does… and always will if you're sincere." The old man blessed Michele with the sign of the cross on his forehead, then told him to drink a thin brown earthy liquid. "Verbascum Mullein, good for the throat and chest."

"I know of it, Father."

He lightly tapped Michele's cheek, then said he should rest, turned and went to the next cot where the patient lay unconscious. Michele noticed the patched habit, one hip higher than the other, his apron hitched up, the strings tangled with his rosary beads. How different from the priests in their soft linen soutanes, fine cottas edged with lace and chasubles woven with silk and gold thread. The monk reminded him of Father Neri; his cassock patched and frayed at the collar and sleeves. Michele turned to face the wall, the nailed feet in his peripheral vision, the plaster cracked, chipped and there was a dark greasy line at the height of the cots the length of the wall. The memory of the sergeant in the alley returned unbidden. When finished, the sergeant shoved him against the alley wall, his grimace lit by a sliver of moonlight, and, as he drew up his breeches and tied the drawstring, he spat, "That'll teach you to take the piss out of me when you're bragging with your loudmouth pals… and that Sforza boy."

Michele rolled onto his back and watched the old monk leave by the far door, limping and bearing the agony of his wasted hip joint as if it were a blessing.

Michele's apprenticeship ended when he was seventeen, short by comparison with most but Master Simone said he had taught him everything he knew about painting and encouraged him to go to Venice. It was said Simone was a pupil of Titian. He didn't say so himself but never contradicted the assumption and signed at least one of his paintings – allievo di Tiziano. Being fond of Simone, he pretended to see elements of Titian in his work which in truth he never could; his figures seemed too mannered. He promised to visit Venice, but it was a while before he made the journey. Simone had plenty of work in Milan and generously farmed out small jobs until Michele saved enough to go to Venice, hopefully with enough funds and time to establish himself. He bought a mule and told his mother and sister he would soon be leaving and delayed his journey when his mother fell ill. She said it was nothing serious and encouraged him to go, so he set off early next day.

Somehow Battista got wind of his plans and arrived unannounced. His greeting was hardly out of his mouth before he steered Michele to the door and muttered the evils of Venice and if he must go: "Keep yourself pure, Michele, in body and spirit, and remember Venice is renowned for the mortal sin of sodomy."

"Don't go on about that again."

"You committed a mortal sin, Michele; don't ever forget that, and you slandered a good man. If I were not your loving brother, I would have dragged you to the magistrate but because I didn't, I share some portion of your guilt." He noted Battista had chosen the sin of omission. Knowing Battista well, he would never confess any sin other than the most trivial; anything more serious might jeopardise future preferment. Ambition, arrogance and pride were his brother's unconfessed sins.

He packed the mule, one pannier for clothes and the other filled with drawings, painting tools and materials and set off towards the rising sun. The road out of town was clear and so quiet he wondered if it was a holy day but the peace was broken by the sound of his name drawled in a mocking see-saw, *Mich...e*le! He turned to see the sergeant striding after him. *Mich...ele!* He dug his heels in the mule's sides to make it trot but his tormentor easily caught up and snatched the reins. "I hear you're leaving us, Michele... Good! You were a poor fuck, so good riddance. I heard your brother didn't believe you." He laughed, puckered his lips and blew a kiss. "*Bardassa.*" He let go of the reins and slapped the mule's rump. Since the awful night, he had only caught sight of the sergeant a handful of times, usually at the Duomo during the high festivals where he was given precedence, always first at the altar rail, mouth gaping, tongue out to receive a fragment of the host. It was obvious Battista had spoken to him, almost certainly to apologise on the family's behalf. It was the kind of pious, mad thing he would do to slither into the sergeant's good graces. How like their calculating half-uncles.

The floating city was splendid and more beautiful than anything he had seen before and strangely oriental or what he imagined oriental might be. Although the palaces beside the canals were on show, it was a secretive place, a masked society even when not en fete. He found the lodging house at the address Simone gave him, nowhere near the palaces on the Grand Canal but exposed brickwork where plaster had fallen from the walls and ceilings, damp and cold.

It was there Michele met Sicilian Lorenzo, who, like himself, was trying to make a living from painting. If he stayed a decade, it would be impossible to see every painting in Venice, such quality and fluency made his work appear old-fashioned and stiff; consequently, when anyone asked to see his work, even though Lorenzo encouraged him to, he claimed not to have brought any. The work of Tintoretto and Veronese overawed him, not to mention Titian, and Giorgione, especially in his use of colour and texture. He recognised his efforts were poor by comparison. It would take years to acquire such versatility and ease of representation, so he simply scribbled notes to record the Venetian use of colour by Titian and Giorgione and another he had never previously heard of called Sebastiano del Piombo. He only saw one painting by Sebastiano on the organ shutters in the church of Saint Bartholomew near the Rialto bridge. Each figure was placed before a dark vaulted arch with columns either side. Saint Sebastian on the right, rendered a near naked youth bathed in light but Michele's attention was mostly drawn to the figure of Saint Bartholomew who appeared to emerge from dark shadows.

He expected his savings to last several months but the city was far more expensive than anticipated, made worse because he accepted his meagre efforts would not attract employment. Not only that, the shock of the encounter with the gloating sergeant as he left Milan cast a dark, deepening shadow. He could not shake off the shame that contorted into seething rage as he lay abed, fantasizing vendetta and waking Lorenzo when he occasionally shouted in the night. In time, he began plotting revenge. Through Lorenzo, he put the word that he wished to buy a sword and a man approached him in a tavern as arranged.

The night, Michele left; Lorenzo gave him an address in Rome where he said they might meet again. He stole a boat, the sword wrapped in canvas, and rowed to the mainland. He returned to the stables where he had sold the mule, took another and ambled towards Milan in easy stages, travelling by night so no one would recall seeing him and sleeping in fields and barns by day.

Approaching Milan, he let the mule loose in a field and walked the last few miles, entering the city at dusk armed with sword and dagger. He searched the back alleys for his prey, but there was no sight of him. He dare not go near his house, the building where he was stationed or local taverns and was cautious not to be seen by apprentices and acquaintances. He hid during the day in an old barn near the edge of the city where he secreted his saddle bags and only ventured out a shadow at night.

Each evening, he scouted alleys, streets and piazzas where it was likely the sergeant might appear strutting and carousing. It was necessary to catch him alone but he had no luck until the fifth night when by chance, he caught sight of a familiar cocky but unsteady swagger. Michele knew it was him even before seeing the familiar surly profile. It was near Santa Maria della Grazie where he began following him until he entered a narrow passage. It was too great a risk to follow him into the blackness, so he ran to the parallel street, arriving at the crossing ahead of his quarry. It was a few minutes before the sergeant reached the crossroad, humming and strutting to where Michele waited, armed with knife and sword. Slightly breathless, he paused a second to exhale, his heart thumping fast. Before the sergeant knew what happened, he rushed forward and stabbed. He aimed for the heart but hit the collarbone. There was a hiss as he withdrew the knife. The sergeant coughed and stumbled and, as he went down, Michele stabbed his gut with the sword and felt the blade hit the back of the pelvis. He grabbed the sergeant by the hair so there would be no doubt who killed him.

"Who's a whore now, bastard!" He stared at the pale face, mouth gaping, blood frothing as he struggled to form words. Michele spat in his face. "I'm the last thing you'll see before you die." He let go his hair, the body slumped and the head hit the ground with a heavy crack. In his over excited state, he paced up and down hissing. "I got you… bastard! I got you." He was frantic, pacing up and down with rising anger that the sergeant had died too quickly. He stood gasping, robbed of the revenge he craved, these few moments of death no match for the half hour of agony and humiliation he suffered. He sobbed with rage, dropped to his knees and fumbled at the sergeant's breeches to grasp the still-hot wrinkled balls, dropped his sword, swapped the knife to his right hand to sever and shove them in the sergeant's mouth, so everyone would know it was vendetta for a sexual crime but footfall rang in the alley behind him. He picked up his sword and cloak and fled.

He camped in a derelict cattle shed several nights, regretting he had not castrated the sergeant so his death would be put down to a disturbed robbery rather than a settled score. Having established his Venetian alibi against the murder, he made his way to the high road and cadged a ride on a wagon and made his way to Simone's workshop but the moment the master caught sight of him, he rushed over and pushed him into the storeroom. "My God, Michele, you must be mad to show your face here. Everyone knows… he almost died. Everyone's looking for you; there's a price on your head."

The sun would soon be up, so Simone made him stay the day hidden in the store room. After breakfast, he gave Michele a letter. He tore it open, noticed the date was weeks past and barely scanned the familiar tight handwriting then tore it into small pieces.

"Bad news?"

"My mother died."

Simone's wife, Angelica, emerged from shadows and stroked his face. She was always kind, indulged his occasional blasts of temper, made sure he changed his clothes and sometimes cut his hair. "Your poor mamma, Michele… I will pray for her… and for you."

After nightfall, Simone led him to the road leading south, gave him money, a mule, some painting materials and a sack of food. "Get as far away as you can… Rome or Naples, change your name but stay away and don't write; it's too risky. I know what the sergeant did, Michele. I can't condone revenge but won't be your judge either. I leave you to God's mercy. May He grant you forgiveness, solace and a safe and prosperous journey. But from now on, Michele, live a good life and remember your dear mother."

Michele stared at the nailed, bleeding feet. *My journey wasn't very prosperous; I had to sell the mule to buy food.* He gritted his teeth. *I should have cut the bastard's throat in the alley.* Unable to let go of his rage, he raised his eyes to the sagging head of the crucified looming above him. *Have I committed a lesser sin because the bastard survived or forever condemned because I still wish him dead?* The old monk limped between cots, muttered encouragement, cradled heads as his patients supped medicines he prepared, cupped their hands in his as he uttered prayers for their recovery, consolation or preparation for those beyond healing. He tenderly nursed Michele back to a semblance of health, and when he returned to the tenement, he caught sight of his reflection in a looking glass. His skin was yellow, damp with sweat and his temperature still high. Cesari sent wishes for his recovery and understood he needed time to fully recover. During the day, apart from the calls and chatter of neighbours and children's piping voices echoing in the courtyard, the apartment was peaceful.

After a couple of days of fitfully sleeping, he propped up the mirror, draped a sheet over his right shoulder and under the left arm and began a self-portrait as a street urchin. He under-painted in burnt umber and blended the lighter, yellowish flesh tones in ochre, adding small amounts of white for highlights into which he mixed a little white chalk dust to suggest glistening sweat. It was an accurate likeness despoiled by sickness, swollen, jaundiced eyes and blanched lips. He only worked when alone and hid the canvas behind other unfinished work when he heard the lads arrive in the courtyard noisily laughing and joking. Lorenzo brought black and white grapes and peaches which Michele used as props and cropped the lower body by painting a low table between the viewer and the figure. The black grapes and two peaches were placed close to the edge of the table and, as an afterthought, he tied a brownish-wine-coloured fabric in a bow with the loose end on the table to integrate the figure with the foreground. He held the white grapes in his left hand, becoming the right in the reflection.

The picture was almost finished before Michele allowed others to see it. Lorenzo was enthusiastic as ever and suggested he call the painting Bacchus and add a coronet of vine leaves. In desperate need of money, Michele presented the Bacchus to Cesari who was amused by the blatant transformation of a street boy to Bacchus. By chance an art dealer, Signor Valentino, happened to visit the workshop to see if there was something new for sale. He loved the Bacchus on sight and said he had a client in mind: His Excellency the Cardinal del Monte. Cesari said he had already considered such a proposal. The two vied to claim the closest association with His Excellency.

Chapter 6
Cardinal del Monte 1594

Michele was immediately drawn to His Eminence, a handsome man in his early forties who looked years younger. His dark hair was cropped short and he wore a fashionable trim goatee, his eyes sparkled lively and welcoming and emanated an aura of stillness. His black soutane was beautifully tailored with scarlet piping and sash with an old wooden cross rather than gold encrusted with gems. Despite the quality of his soutane, Michele noticed his clothes were rather worn. When presented, Michele doffed his cap, genuflected and kissed the cardinal's episcopal ring.

"Welcome, Master Michelangelo." He stroked the wooden cross with his left hand and smiled. "Master Cesari and Signor Valentino speak highly of your talent." He gestured to several of Michele's paintings displayed in the salon. "I'm particularly taken with what might be called... *Sick Little Bacchus*. An interesting conceit, recreating yourself in a state of sickness." He tilted his head. "But, my son, I see you have recently been unwell."

"Sweating sickness, Eminence."

"I think you're not fully recovered. We must arrange proper convalescence. Would it be inconvenient to move into my household, my home? My physician will tend and help you recover strength."

"I'm grateful, Eminence, but I must work. I have paintings and Master Cesari..."

"Master Cesari, would it create difficulties if Michelangelo were to move into the Palazzo Madama? I understand there must be certain matters... but, surely, we could come to an arrangement. As for your work, Master Michelangelo... Michele? Have no concerns about continuing your vocation; our mansion has many rooms." He smiled. "The upper storey receives plenty of light, and I'm sure you will find one or two rooms to your liking. You may find other artists up there too, musicians and poets, I'm informed all sorts come and go by the back stair. We are a happy family."

The Palazzo Madama was a grand building in the Piazza Navona, previously home to Medici popes and Catherine de' Medici, the mother of three French kings. Del Monte was Papal legate to the French church in Rome, his Bourbon ancestry made him a natural choice. Michele chose three adjoining rooms facing north for steady light. He set up the largest room for a workshop with a view of the church of San Luigi dei Francesi beyond the rooftops. His meagre possessions hardly filled a corner of the bedchamber. The room between workshop and bedroom was used to store props borrowed from Cesari and others and to ventilate the smell of spirit and oil between the rooms either side. The cardinal's factotum welcomed Michele and suggested he take furniture from storerooms in the attic. He was given a tour of the upper floor to meet some of the cardinal's household attendants, pages musicians and retainers. Once it was agreed the rooms he would have, the factotum touched his arm. "On a delicate matter, master, His Eminence noticed your clothes are rather worn and wondered if you might see his tailor, at His Excellency's expense."

"I won't wear livery…"

"Oh no, that's not His Eminence's intention."

Small groups of musicians and singers took turns to entertain His Eminence and guests, Michele included, which prompted him to begin a painting of a boy playing a lute. Mario from the tenement modelled and one of the musicians loaned a lute and books of sheet music he said were among the cardinal's favourites. It was more than two weeks before he next saw the cardinal when he was invited to his private salon. "There you are, Michele. I see your health is much restored, and you look well in your new clothes. I notice you chose black."

"I'm of gentle birth, Eminence; my family are landowners and enjoy the protection of the Colonna."

"No issue, my dear. I recognise you are from a good family. Indeed, the Lady Costanza, her cardinal brother Ascanio, and I are well acquainted. You have an aristocratic eye, observing and interpreting the way a poet sees the world with grace and humanity. Many modern painters paint what they think a patron wishes, but you paint things as they are, so we come to see the world through your eyes and thereafter, change the way the world is perceived. It is the fundamental difference between craft and artistry."

"I'm flattered, Eminence."

"No flattery between us, Michele. My regard is genuine and, in time, I hope we will consider one another friends. No more ceremony but to the point, may I see what you're painting?"

"I have a painting in progress, Eminence, and with your permission, I'll bring it down."

"Why don't I come to your studio?"

Michele persuaded Lorenzo to grow a goatee and crop his wavy locks of which he was immensely proud and dressed him in a brown monk's habit. The old monk at the Conzolatione hospice arranged the loan of a habit but it was so worn it was worth nothing.

"Keep it, Michele, with our blessing."

When he left, Michele slipped a handful of coins into a collection box opposite a statue of Our Lady. Lorenzo baulked when he was told to put on the habit. "It's dirty."

"It is not. Smell… It's worn but freshly washed."

Lorenzo sniffed the habit, reluctantly undressed and Michele slipped the robe over his head, tied a cord around his waist and arranged the pose, lying full length propped up on a pile of cushions. "It might be fresh washed but itches."

Michele drew a diagonal from the top right corner to bottom left corner of the prepared canvas; nine by twelve palmi and drew Lorenzo with a fine umber line just below the diagonal with only his exposed left foot above the line. It took three days to block in the reclining figure in monochrome, raw umber, burnt Sienna and yellow ochre. For the face and hands, he substituted burnt umber as a base for warmer flesh tones. The head was given special attention and the likeness was completed in a few days. He noticed Lorenzo, once bearded, bore a striking resemblance to the cardinal and looked hardly younger. The left hand was cupped, and the right touched his chest where the robe was torn revealing the lance-wound to Christ's breast. From the outset, he decided there would be no floating crucifix in the traditional manner but golden light alone would represent the divine presence. Mario posed for a nude angel to support the saint and rather than a landscape background he brushed three yellow-orange near-horizontal lines to suggest the afterglow of a setting sun reflected in a quietly rippling stream.

The painting was a gift of thanks for the cardinal's kindness and generosity; Saint Francis of Assisi being the cardinal's namesake. He aimed to present the picture on the fourth of October, the saint's feast day. When dry, the painting was covered and hidden in the corner of the storeroom, and only then began work on the cardinal's first formal commission. The subject was a concert of youths to reflect his passion for music.

He invited Michele to dine tête-à-tête several times and, as they conversed, they were serenaded by a small band of musicians who discreetly played and sang in the anteroom. He noticed the musicians were pale and sang with French accents. The most beautiful of voice and looks sang with a slight lisp and faraway look in his eyes and fine-tuned his lute as he sang. The boy's voices were high falsetto but none were castrati. When Michele asked them to model for the painting, they refused. "D'you think we're bardassas?"

Mario, the dependable Minniti, posed for three of the boys. For the most important central figure, Michele modelled the likeness on the singer with the lisp, altering Mario's features accordingly. The painted singer coolly stared beyond the viewer; his chest exposed with exaggerated high arched eyebrows... like a cheap bardassa. Michele grinned when he draped a crimson satin fabric over Mario's right shoulder to exaggerate the contrast with his pale skin and painted his fingers longer than they really were. The second figure was seen from the back with even paler skin and reading the score. On the left, he added a younger version of Mario with wings and a sheaf of arrows to suggest Cupid and in the background, a self-portrait, a sick little Bacchus, a ruffian at the concert. Michele invited Cesari and friends, painters Orazio Gentileschi, Prospero Orsi and Annibale Carracci to see the painting.

Orazio was intrigued by the solidity, volume, light and *reality* of the figures. "You say there are flaws but they don't offend my eye, and, in any case, we all disguise our weaknesses."

Cesari liked the violin and lute painted in strict perspective. "Plotted through a strung grid I imagine."

It was noticeable Annibale barely spoke. The party was in full flow when Spada appeared in the doorway. "Michele, what's this?" He held the Saint Francis painting upside down.

"That's not for public... not for here..."

Orazio turned the painting right side up and leaned it against the wall. "Saint Francis... I've not seen such a living figure before, as solid as a Michelangelo but somehow... he has a soul."

Cesari agreed. "It's a new way of painting... should I say, a new way *of seeing*. I don't like the boy so much."

Prospero squinted. "Yes, his head's a bit small. The model for Francis is good... obviously the cardinal." He stepped closer. "You've got him to the life."

Annibale agreed. "It's certainly del Monte… younger maybe."

"I painted it as a gift for the cardinal's name day. He's been particularly good to me since my illness."

Orazio laughed. "Bravo! We have a duty to keep good patrons sweet, but will he take kindly to be caught with a nude boy?"

"What d'you mean?"

Spada smirked. "Everybody's heard the rumours."

"The cardinal's a decent man and anyone who says otherwise—"

"I'm only repeating…" Spada raised his hand. "It's only what I heard; it's said he likes the boys…"

Michele caught him by his shirt collar and threw him against a chair that collapsed under his weight. Cesari and Annibale held Michele back. "Don't ever say such things about the cardinal, here or elsewhere. D'you hear me, Spada? I'll break your neck if you say anything like that again."

Helped up by Mario, Spada grinned. "Raw nerve, Michele?"

Michele lunged at him again but Cesari and Annibale intervened and Orazio steered Spada out of the room.

By the time he returned, Michele was calm. "He's gone, forget him."

Annibale put his arm around his shoulder. "Spada's trouble I grant, but he may have a point. I see you intend the figure to represent a sort of spiritual consolation but maybe you should add wings to make it clear it's an angel."

"Angels! Angels, in this day and age! Why are we expected to paint such nonsense, whoever saw an angel? Gesù! Truth to nature's the only fit subject for me."

"I agree, but, if priests want angels, angels they'll have. It's our stock-in-trade."

"Michelangelo never painted angels, certainly not with wings."

Orazio cut in. "I don't know about Michelangelo but I agree with Annibale; make the boy an angel."

Michele stared at the painting for a long time. "I'll think about it… now let's eat and drink and forget painting for a while."

A little drama was arranged, so Michele happened to be in the corridor when His Eminence entered the salon to be surprised on encountering the *Concert of Musicians*. In early September, the gilt-framed painting was displayed in His Eminence's grand salon. The cardinal shared his delight and introduced Michele to invited guests.

When supper was served, guests were serenated by the Spanish castrato Pietro Montoya, on whom Michele had based several versions of a Lute Player. Del Monte also arranged boy singers from the Sistine Chapel choir, arranging music at St Peter's being one of his duties at the Vatican. They sang Monteverdi's third book of madrigals for five voices, and the painting dominated conversation for an hour.

A certain princess adored the subtle contours of the figures, the fine design and pale flesh. "Surely, Master Michelangelo, these are aristocratic youth pretending to be rustics, and I see they sing with grace, and in the modern style; tongue low just behind the teeth…"

A particularly florid Marchese suggested the central figure must be Apollo because of his divine face… and such pale flesh.

His companion agreed. "The dark figure in the background must be Marsays."

The other nodded. "I must speak to Francesco; I must have something by this fellow… from Milan I believe, with Colonna connections."

"I believe so but, speaking of Colonna, I heard the second son, Fabrizio…"

Hearing Fabrizio's name, Michele strained to hear the conversation but was engaged by a guest who asked him to describe the underlying meaning of the painting. "Is the darker fellow, Pan, to represent rustic nature?"

The cardinal invited Michele to attend him next day. "What a triumph, my dear; congratulations, I hope my page delivered…?"

"Thank you, Eminence, you are too generous, I never expected…"

"Tut-tut… Let's not talk of commerce and no false modesty, you are moving into higher circles and there are much greater prizes to be had. Tip the Colonna card a little."

"Eminence, are you suggesting I should deceive?"

He tapped Michele's wrist. "To mention the Colonna as patrons of your family is no deception. I believe you were playmate with Costanza's boys. What others read into that is their business." He laughed.

Despite his exquisitely tailored soutane and opulent surroundings, for a moment, he seemed boyish and Michele felt affection and protective towards him and at that moment thought the cardinal read his mind.

"Michele, very few know me as you do, I hope we are friends." He smiled. "Call me Francesco when we're alone."

"I think you're always alone, Francesco."

"A little higher on the left, too far, yes… yes." The chaplain clasped his hands together. "It is wonderful how the image of the saint expresses such ecstasy, bathed in light cast by Our Lord's presence. I have seen other versions with the crucifix and little golden lines from the hands and feet of Christ to the hands and feet of Saint Francis but this is—"

"I apologise for interrupting, Father, but what time will His Eminence be here tomorrow?"

"He says Mass at seven, then…"

The door behind them closed with a light click and Michele turned to find the cardinal had entered. "Michele, my dear." Francesco embraced Michele, nodded to the chaplain who bowed and retired. "I realise this is a different surprise from the one you intended. Let me see this remarkable painting. How marvellous." He held Michele's hand as he scrutinised the painting. "Yes. I am moved by the beauty of the beloved Francis as he swoons in ecstasy from the agony of wounds of love."

"But why spoil the surprise, Francesco. It is a gift…"

"And an exquisite angel, such tenderness, indifferent to Francesco's pain but wondering at the special grace Our Lord bestows." He turned from the painting. "What a gift, Michele, and how generous."

"It's thanks for all your kindnesses, the only thing I have to offer."

"The widow's mite. Bless you, Caro, but I cannot accept such a gift, however generously offered and with such love."

For a moment, Michele hesitated. In any other circumstance, he might have flown into blind rage… but this was Francesco and his face betrayed regret. Eventually, he stammered. "But… why, Eminence?"

"Because, my dear, we live in an imperfect world, riven by unkindness and cruelty and every action, every minute detail judged according to conventions and, sadly, prejudice too. How often base suspicions and accusations besmirch innocence. Come, sit with me." They drew up chairs and sat side by side against the wall opposite the painting. Francesco kept a tight hold of Michele's hand. "How perfectly the picture sits in this room, the figures loom out of the darkness. It is no longer a painting but rather the very event played out before our eyes. I only wish I could keep it."

"I don't understand why you can't."

"My house has many rooms." He smiled. "Nothing happens in my home that I don't hear about; perhaps, I should say my house has many ears. I hear there was a jolly party but for your assistant, is his nickname *Spada*?" Michele nodded. "From what I hear, young Spada was quite right to say that rumours spread. Chatter spreads becoming slander, which, like wafting smoke, is difficult to dispel."

He smiled. "However, libel is not. Libel is recorded, written down, it is fact." He rose, crossed to the painting and stood several minutes with his hands clasped behind his back, staring in silence at the picture. Eventually he turned. "And this painting, Michele, is fact, as readable and as potent as the record of a real event… although the face is not precisely me, it is a younger version of me and without doubt… me. The saint faints in ecstasy, it becomes me, raised up by a near naked youth. If I accept a painting, let's say a Bacchus, a naked Baptist or to be completely ridiculous, a youth… bitten by a snake… my friends will say what learning and cultivated refined sensibility and even a little risqué." He looked back at the painting. "This beautiful image is so truthful… too truthful, and likely to set off rumour or confirm rumours I'm aware already circulate. Saint Francis consoled by an angel and Francesco del Monte consoled by a youth. You see my point?"

Michele stared at the floor. "I meant no offence, Eminence."

"No offence, my dear. I am truly overwhelmed by your generosity. It pains me to let the painting go but with your agreement, I would like to send it as a gift to my boyhood friend, Octavius Costa. He is of noble Genoese family of papal bankers, and it occurs to me we ought to promote your work further afield. Rome, after all, is a hothouse of slander and dangerously insular."

Several days later, Michele met the chaplain on the stairs. "When does it leave?"

"Soon, but you must apply yourself to a fresh commission. His Eminence suggests Bacchus, perhaps a little slanderous but not libellous… he said you would understand, but, Michele, I hope you understand why I had to speak to His Eminence… his reputation."

Michele shrugged, and, when the chaplain had gone, he picked up the purse and spilled the contents on the table. "Sweet Gesu, a hundred scudi." It was the most he had received for a painting.

Chapter 7

Among Strangers 1598

Paulo only accompanied me because he knew I was determined to leave, the kid brother he never had, and assumed duty to protect me. After only a few hours from Bergamo, he said we should return, but I was insistent and although increasingly reluctant, he stayed with me. No doubt after the first arduous five days when we reached Bologna, I'm sure he imagined I would agree to turn back. Truly, I was anxious at first but, as a snake sheds its skin, and days passed I was even more excited. It was another six days until we eventually heard the great bell booming in the Arno valley below us and first caught sight of Florence, dominated by the red domed Duomo. We were overawed by the towering city, but, whereas I was thrilled, Paulo was apprehensive as I shouldered my way along bustling streets and alleys, urging him to keep up. Entering a wide piazza dominated by a towered building that seemed to lean over us, I ran towards a familiar white giant that stood before the palazzo. I pointed and laughed. "David, and he does have a tiny prick."

These days, I laugh remembering how Paulo abandoned me in Florence to spend the night and our money on a young prostitute. I was furious he left me to find my way back to the small room we shared with apprentices. Next morning, I demanded all the money we had left and went on alone, leaving him penniless. I took the road south and, an hour or so from Florence, a cart rumbled by, driven by a man and woman with several children sitting among sacks. The woman spoke to the man and the cart drew up. She smiled and asked where I was going and, when I said Rome, she gestured I should climb aboard. The children stared at me for the first mile or so but soon lost interest. The girl smiled occasionally but looked away when I returned her smile. When the woman asked why I was alone, I invented a story about travelling with my older brother who died in Florence, and I had to go on alone to join a seminary in Rome.

"I'm sorry about your brother. How did he die?"

"He vomited in his sleep and choked. He'd been drinking." She stroked my arm. "We weren't close. He was my step-brother."

"But it's dangerous to travel alone… how old are you?"

I ignored her question. "It's as far back to Milan as it is to go on to Rome."

She smiled. "I suppose so. We're going as far as Poggibonsi." From the sacks of provisions, I presumed they had a farm or homestead.

At Poggibonsi, the mother, Doria, would not let her husband leave until she arranged for a friar on his way to Rome to take me under his wing. I guessed kindly faced Brother Thaddeus was not yet twenty. We set off, and it was not long before a small carriage pulled up to offer the friar and me a ride and, within a few hours, we arrived at Sienna. We ate at a small tavern and, when I offered the few coins I had, Thaddeus covered my hand and nodded to the owner who bowed and left, returning with a bag of provisions. "Bless you," was all Thaddeus said as we stood to leave. "I'm going on via Citavecchia along the coast. It's been many years since I've seen the sea."

"I've never seen the sea."

When asked why I was travelling alone to Rome, I decided to be truthful, admitting I had run away from home with an older friend. "But why are you alone now?"

"My friend spent most of the money we had on… a street girl."

"You should have returned home to make amends with your family."

I spoke about my father and half-brother's brutality to me and my mother but was careful not to mention Father Gennaro. "I'm going to Rome because I want to become an assistant to an artist from Caravaggio… near Milan. My pa's a painter and I hope Master Merisi will take me on. Have you heard of him?"

Thaddeus shook his head.

By nightfall next day, we were in sight of the sea and kept going until we reached a beach that arced towards the lights of a small town Thaddeus said was Porto Ercole. We set up camp for the night, collected rocks to make a firepit, twigs and dried branches found under bushes near the beach to make a fire and shared provisions. The evening was cool and the breeze from the sea further chilled the air. Both of us were soon drowsy, wrapped our woollen cloaks around us and the gentle slap of waves lulled us to sleep. I suddenly woke. The sky above was black with a million glinting stars, and I was cold and my teeth chattered. On waking, the heave and slap of the ripples of waves was the first thing I heard. I sat up and drew my cloak around me, looked up and saw Thaddeus praying, facing the sea. I stood and shuffled to the shoreline where my feet sank in damp sand. I called his name, but he didn't respond for several minutes until eventually he crossed himself, turned and smiled. We slept further nights on beaches at Citavecchia and Santa Marinalla.

We entered Rome from the west to the sound of bells near and far. The buildings dwarfed what I knew from Bergamo, Caravaggio and even Milan which I once visited. Only Florence compared with the noise and bustle of people's calls over the rumble of carts, heavy wagons and clatter of coaches, clangs from metalworks and sawing and hammering. Within the din, the country sounds of bleating and mooing of sheep and cattle on the way to slaughter, their droppings curdled aromas of cooking. I covered my mouth and nose as we passed the leather workers ponds; the stink caught the back of the throat and made me nauseous. Thaddeus led me into the city past towering tenements and churches, new and ancient. We shared our last meal at a small tavern.

"What will you do, Cecco? How will you find your master from Caravaggio? Rome is a big place." I shrugged. Thaddeus took me to a small oratory where a monk gave him the kiss of peace. He asked for a quill and scrap of paper. "This young fellow, Francesco... Boneri... Cecco is looking for a painter called..."

"Michelangelo, Michele Merisi from Caravaggio. Have you heard of him, Father?"

The monk paused a moment. "I don't recognise the name."

Thadeus urged, "Who are the best-known painters here? One of them might know of him."

He pouted. "The Carracci, maybe Gentileschi and Cesari, yes Giuseppe Cesari for sure; his work is everywhere and I hear many artists work for him. Shall I write their names down... can you read?"

"Of course, but not long words... or Latin."

"There's Cesari, as I said, and Baglione; he's a member of the academy. If this Merisi fellow is any good, the academy will know of him... maybe he's a member."

Before we parted, Thaddeus handed me a purse. He wouldn't hear of me turning it down, and I knew he would replace what he gave me in a day or so from offerings of alms.

He smiled. "I collect money to distribute to those in need, as you are Cecco. Now find your Michele and my blessings." He made the sign of the cross on my forehead, kissed my cheek and we parted.

A full purse was temptation to thieves, so I went to an osteria and sat in a secluded corner where I ordered sardines and salad and surreptitiously counted the contents on the bench beside me. I was surprised there was more money than I had when I robbed Pa. Looking around to be sure I was not observed, I separated a few coins which I put back in the purse, and the rest in a pouch I untied from my belt and slipped into my breechcloth, tightened the strings and felt the cool metal against my balls. When I finished the meal, I ordered another cup of wine and, when served, saw a young man enter the room. He had olive skin and his hair was shiny blue-black, thick and hung in rat's tails. He looked around the osteria and saw me in the shadows, hesitated a moment, then walked directly to me. "Buy me a drink... please." Without invitation, he sat opposite and, seeing I was alarmed, went on, "I'm not causing trouble." His hands shook, reminding me of Pa when he was desperate for a drink. I waved to the pot boy and pointed to my cup.

Moments later, the innkeeper came over. "Is he bothering you?"

"No."

"You know what he is..."

I frowned. "He's not bothering me... and I don't know what you mean."

"You're too young to understand, I suppose, but he..." He prodded the young man's chest. "He's what's called bardassa." I shrugged. The innkeeper leaned over me. "Men pay to fuck him."

"Oh."

"Oh indeed." It took a few moments to make sense of what I heard.

The thin young man's hands trembled. "Are you hungry?" He nodded. "Please give him something to eat and some wine."

"On your head, son."

When the innkeeper was out of hearing, I asked, "Is it true what he said... bardassa?" I almost whispered the word.

He nodded. "I was pretty just a few years ago. Easy money then, just shut your eyes and let them go at it... but you don't know what I'm talking about." He smiled. "But when everybody's had you five times, there are plenty of pretty boys arriving every day to take your place in the Eternal City." He tapped the table. "Ignore me... I'm a ghost." I could see he had been handsome, fine features, aquiline nose, sharp jawline, dark eyes and wavy hair, but gaunt, dark circles around his eyes, the skin of his cheeks drawn tight over the sinews and bones beneath had aged him.

"What's your name?"

"Giovanni… Giovan Battista. My family name was lost, years ago, but everyone knows, or knew Giovan Battista… at least once."

I was about to feel for the paper with list of artists when two young men appeared and slapped Giovan on the back. "Here you are and who's your friend?" They sat down. "I'm Marco, and this is Luca."

Giovan hissed, "Piss off."

"That's not very friendly; we just want to meet your friend… he's pretty…"

Giovan slapped Marco's face and turned over his stool as he rose. "I said fuck off."

The innkeeper rushed over. "Out now… all of you." I picked up my sack and stood. "Not you, you can stay." He shoved the others towards the door.

I touched the innkeeper's arm. "Let him stay; he didn't do any harm. I ordered food for him."

"He's no good for you, son, take your money." He pushed Giovan and the others into the street. "Don't come back." Turning to me, he said, "How old are you?"

"Fourteen."

"Liar, you're no more than ten."

"All right, I'm… thirteen." It would be the truth in time.

"And you're on your own; d'you have anywhere to stay?"

"I'm trying to find my brother Michele… Merisi. We're from Caravaggio."

"Never heard of it."

"Our mother died a month ago… he doesn't know… about Mamma, and I don't know how to find him."

I noticed a young waiter carry the plate of sardines meant for Giovan but seeing the empty table he pirouetted and made his way back to the kitchen. I heard the innkeeper say, "You've nowhere to stay."

I shared the waiter Giulio's bed, and, as guessed, he was the innkeeper's son. My chores were to wash kitchen pots, pans, trenchers and utensils, clear and clean tables, slop leftovers into a pig bin, sweep and wash the floors. Any spare time I spent searching for Michele Merisi. The first night I fell asleep exhausted but was woken by violent shaking. I assumed there was an earth tremor but turned to see my bed fellow energetically palming his cock. Once he was relieved, the room fell quiet again. The same performance was repeated early next morning and every night. I watched but Giulio was not the least embarrassed.

After one impressive session, I asked, "Do you confess to the priests?"

"None of their fucking business… they're at it themselves anyway." Giulio grinned. "There's a lass with big titties and a lovely arse. I'd love to fuck her but she's a cock-teaser. What do you like?"

My face tingled, and I blushed. "Oh that—"

Giulio laughed and waved his cock. "You'll grow out of it." He was carefree and didn't mind me blatantly staring when he was naked, having adopted me as a kid brother. "How's it going looking for your Michele?"

"Not good. I lost my list of painters so I've gone from church to church to try to get the fathers to tell me who painted such and such a picture but they're not helpful. One told me I should speak to Gentileschi… Orazio. Have you heard of him?"

"I don't look at paintings. I only go to church when Dad makes me and then I only look at the girls." He grinned. "Did you find this… Orazio? Did he help?"

"He has a big family workshop. He thought I was looking for work and left it to one of his assistants to tell me to go away. I tried to ask about Michele but nobody cared to listen. I don't think my brother's doing very well."

"Don't lose heart. Rome's a big place but it's only a matter of time before you find him."

I presumed Michele was also down on his luck, so I started trawling the taverns but soon learned that was risky. Many presumed I was bardassa and tried to pick me up. Some were insistent and, several times, I had to scarper from the tavern, although the streets, especially the alleys in some districts were just as perilous.

At one tavern, a dark figure approached me. "I know you… you were kind to me."

It took a moment for me to recognise Giovanni Battista. I had not seen him since he was thrown out of the tavern several weeks past. His breath reeked of sour wine and his once expensive clothes were even more stained and threadbare. "Giovan!"

His gaze was barely focussed but eventually said, "You offered me a meal. I never thanked you." He lurched towards me and tried to kiss my cheek but I recoiled. He froze and turned to leave but I caught his sleeve.

"I'm sorry. Men keep trying to pick me up."

He turned to regard me for a moment. "I know what that's like." His teeth were stained but regular and I saw that perhaps just a couple of years past, his smile would have dazzled.

I held on to his sleeve. "Stay… let's talk."

His smile faded. "I've played the mare too long to be your stallion. For Christ's sake, Cecco, half an hour ago I sucked off an old man for a cup of cheap wine." I had no idea what he meant as he walked away but I followed a few paces behind, not sure if he wanted me to leave him alone or follow.

A man caught me by the arm. "You're pretty. I hear you're friends with my boys Marco and Luka."

"They're not friends."

"You could get to know them better."

Giovan punched the man, grabbed me by the jerkin and dragged me along the street, turned a corner and pushed me into another tavern where he leaned against the doorframe and kept watch a few moments to be sure we were not followed. His lurching, stumbling gait had given him momentum and it was unlikely the pimp would recover quickly enough to follow us. We went to a table in the shadows.

The owner came over and bellowed, "Out! You're not caging drinks in my gaff."

"I have money." I put down more than enough to pay for a flagon of wine. "Two glasses, please."

She hesitated a moment, then laughed… Her big breasts wobbled, likely to overflow her bodice. "Glasses… Marchese." She curtsied. "Plain pottery cups or nothing… imagine the cost of replacing smashed glass by these drunk bastards." Giovan smiled when she left with her parting shot, "No tricks, understand?"

He nodded. She kept a good house, not one of those who made a little on the side from pimps. Once served, Giovan let me pour wine at my pace. Eventually he said, "What do you want to talk about?"

"Why did you come to talk to me?"

"How do I know?" He lifted his cup. "I needed a drink I suppose."

"I think it was more than that. Before Marco and the other… joined us, you tried to say something to me. I think it was important."

Giovan sat back and put down the cup. "I don't remember." He shut his eyes. "Maybe… maybe, what I thought at the time was the same as I saw just now. You're alone, Cecco, and the vultures will tear you to pieces. Gesù. How old are you?"

"I'll soon be thirteen."

"You're very precocious."

"What's that mean?"

"You have an old head on your shoulders more than I ever had." He moved his hand to his cup but let it lie rather than raise it. There was a long silence before he went on, "I was you about four years ago. Four years, and now I daren't look in a mirror. I looked good then, fifteen and fresh meat. It was easy money, rich priests, magnates, marcheses and a couple of cardinals." He chuckled. "I thought I was better than the rest, better looking, cleverer, and I had a job which meant I didn't depend on the money and enjoyed the expensive gifts. I was never like amateurs and the desperate, making just a few denarii and pinching the odd ring or coins to make enough to survive."

"What was your job?"

He laughed. "Junior secretary to a notary."

"You tried to warn me."

He pouted. "I've seen too many country lads and pretty boys who've run away from home. Everyone wants them while they're fresh, it's easy money and name your price. But in a month or two, three at the most, they're replaced by fresh meat, no longer centre of attention and it's the new boys who can name their price. Some try to hang on to their looks, change their hair, wear garish clothes and makeup… you saw Marco and Luka. Others are known for special… talents, but they can never compete with the young, fresh and innocent. Yes, that's what I would have warned you about. I knew you were special. You offered me food and drink without hesitation… didn't judge me and it's my turn to return the favour."

"What favour?"

"With your looks and age, you could make a lot of quick money." He fell silent and stared at the window. "I thought it would last forever, but I had no purpose in life, aimless and eventually… nobody wanted my spoiled goods." He took a small sip of wine, regarded me and tilted his head to one side. "Tell me your story, Cecco, my friend… and your purpose. Maybe I can help you. After all, I know the underbelly of Rome very well."

I was surprised by his sudden change of mood from melancholia to enthusiasm. I briefly outlined events from leaving home with Paulo, thanks to Father Gennaro's attentions, then going on alone to Rome to find my brother Michele.

As I spoke, Giovan interrupted from time to time, not for explanation but simply to draw conclusions. "You mentioned the priest, but the friar… did he fuck you too?"

"No. No, he was kind."

Giovan stretched his hand to top up his cup, but I drew the flagon slightly out of his reach. "Yes, drink's my downfall more than sex. In time, wine was necessary to perform with the older, fatter, uglier and poorer. I drank to oblivion to forget what I had to do and what I had been. The notary eventually threw me out became I became shabby, forgetful and… ugly… Ha, Apollo to Tithonus in a couple of years. How's that for a wasted education?"

"Who are Apollo and Titsanus?"

"It doesn't matter, Cecco, just let me help you find this painter."

There were just a few topers in the tavern by the time I swept the floors and put candles on tables in preparation for supper, so I asked Giulio if I could go for a few hours. He nodded, and I ran to meet Giovan who remembered a painter who was an occasional client.

He didn't know his family name but remembered he once mentioned the painter Giuseppe Cesari. "He's our best chance to find your brother."

On the way to Cesari's workshop, he asked me what my brother looked like and laughed when I admitted I had never met or seen him. We entered one of the side streets off the Piazza San Luigi and found Cesari's workshop. Above the door: *Maestro Giovanni Cesari, Cavaliere d'Arpino – Pittore*. Inside it was stifling hot with the overwhelming smell of oil, canvas and wood. Near the door the wall was hung with an assortment of paintings, the largest was about life size of a boy offering a basket of fruit. It was the best by a mile, presumably from the hand of the master, Cesari.

A young assistant appeared form the back room. "What d'you want?"

"My young friend and I would like to speak with Master Cesari."

"Cavaliere d'Arpino you mean, about what?"

"It's a private matter."

"He's not here."

"Perhaps you could help. How long have you worked here?"

"About three years."

"Ah, so you must know Michele—"

I took over. "Michelangelo… Michele Merisi from Caravaggio. Is he here?"

He laughed. "Michele! He's much too grand to work here these days. He has his own workshop."

"So, he's doing well."

"If winning the contract for the best commission in Rome is any measure, I'd say he is."

"Where's his workshop?"

"Just around the corner in the Piazza Navona. Michele's one of del Monte's boys at the Palazzo Madama."

"Who's del Monte?"

"His Eminence Cardinal del Monte."

Leaving Cesari's workshop, Giovan and I passed the French style church of San Luigi and into the Piazza Navona with the Palazzo Madama on the right. The guards would not listen and didn't believe I was Michele Merisi's younger brother and certainly not my concocted story that now our parents were dead I was left alone. They laughed when I asked if they would to pass a message to Master Michele. They would not even confirm he lived there. For several days, Giovan and I stalked the piazza but there was no sign of the man described by the apprentice at Cesari's workshop: dark, longish wavy hair, neat beard and moustache trimmed close and medium height; he always wears black and goes armed. Giovan and I returned to the piazza most days to look out for Michele and persuaded Giulio to give me additional shifts to make extra money, not only kitchen boy and cleaner, I also waited on tables when hands were short. Well into my second month in Rome, I was despondent and, despite being over tired, lay awake most of the night barely aware of Giulio's performances.

As the sun rose one morning, I lay daydreaming and devised a fresh plan. If Michele was becoming famous and obviously inaccessible, I decided to approach Cesari for work as an assistant. At least if I worked for Cesari, he might help me contact Michele but, to be taken seriously, I needed to show aptitude. Next day, I trawled Giovan's haunts and found him sitting in an alley 'round the corner from the Osteria dell Moro. I assumed he was drunk but, when I shook him, he quickly stood and kissed my cheek. There was no smell of wine on his breath nor urine on his clothes, and he wore a doublet in better repair than the one he customarily wore. Without preamble,

I asked if he knew where I could buy materials, paper, charcoal, bistre and white chalk. "The best bet would be Cesari's workshop."

"I'd rather not… I've decided to approach Cesari for work."

"In that case, give me a list, and I'll find what you need, probably on the Corso and the obvious place to buy paper is the Via dei Chiavari." From the paucity of available paper and drawing materials, my father grudgingly allowed me to use, I knew artists' materials were expensive. I used to draw on the backs of Pa's preparatory drawings or erase previous work with damp bread or scrape away darker ink with a sharp blade. I offered a handful of coins to Giovan who took half and memorised the list.

The following days I made a dozen drawings of Giulio by candlelight as he lay sleeping, sometimes covered by a blanket, other times sprawled naked, commandeering most of the bed. It was the first time I drew a nude figure, the most difficult subject I attempted and faithfully recorded every detail, first lightly outlined in charcoal with shaded areas in orange-brown chalk and highlights stroked in with chalk. Working all day and drawing most of the night by candlelight was exhausting, and my sight became blurred but considered the dozen drawings were good enough to show Cesari what I could do. I spent money saved from wages to have a new jerkin made and bought a canvas satchel to hold drawings, extra sheets of paper and wrapped charcoal and chalk in a scrap of linen. I rehearsed my introduction to *Signor Cavaliere d'Arpino…* and practiced doffing my cap.

Signor Cavaliere… Maestro Cavaliere, I am the brother… I am from Caravaggio… Signor Cavaliere, I am Francesco Boneri, from Milan. I was trained by my father… Maestro, you are the best painter in Rome. I have brought drawings to show what I can do… Signor Cavaliere, I hope you might… Signor Cavaliere…

To keep anxiety at bay, the day I planned to present myself at Cesari's workshop, I spent the morning sweeping, clearing tables and washing pots and dishes and, in the late afternoon, put on the new jerkin and reached under the bed for the satchel, swept with my arm but felt nothing. I knelt down to look under the bed but the satchel was gone. My instant response was panic but gradually let my shoulders drop and breathed deeply. There must be a sensible answer which, indeed, there was, preceded by a roar and thunder as heavy footfall stomped up the stairs.

"Where's that bastard?" Before I turned to face the door, it banged against the wall. Carlo charged in and grabbed me by the collar and violently shook me. "Dirty… little… bastard." Each word accompanied by a vicious slap across my face.

Giulio appeared behind his father and pulled him away. "What are you doing… What's he done?" Carlo tossed my crumpled drawings on the bed.

"What are you doing with my drawings—"

Carlo hit me again and swivelled around to face his son. "And what have you been up to with this little shit? Fucking him apparently. I warned you to sleep with one eye open but you had to have him for a cheap shag."

Giulio laughed. "Don't be an ass, Pa." He picked up the drawings. "They're good. You can see I was asleep, so what's the harm?"

"What's the fucking harm… Don't you see… if this gets out…"

"How could it?"

"Well… the maid found them for starters and you know how gossip spreads, before you know everybody'll think you're a sodomite."

Carlo let me go, and I carefully gathered the drawings together, trying to smooth away the creases. "That girl had no right to steal my satchel, she's a thief, and I should call the sbirri to have her arrested."

Carlo raised his hand to hit me but Giulio pushed him away, sat beside me and put his arm around my shoulders. "Let's not be hasty. Why did you make the drawings when I was asleep… in a way you stole something from me. You didn't give me a choice… D'you understand?" By now, I sobbed. "It's all right, Cecco. Nobody's calling the sbirri, just tell me why you drew me."

"I'm sorry… I found where Master Michele lives, but he won't—he doesn't know I exist. I'm not really his brother. I decided to try to get work as an assistant to Master Cesari, but I need to show him what I'm capable of." I began to wail. "I can't afford a model."

He picked up the drawings. "How did you learn to draw like this?"

I wiped my eyes with my thumb. "My father's a painter. He gave me lessons. I had to draw fruit and vegetables and portraits, a few landscapes… Artists draw the nude, to sharpen your wits because the nude is the hardest thing to draw."

Giulio laughed. "I look pretty hard here."

Carlo grunted. "It's not funny." He snatched some of the drawings from Giulio and made me offer up the sheaf of others. He glanced at them a moment, then left thundering down the stairs.

I felt guilty after what Giulio said, "I'm sorry, I didn't mean…"

I gasped. "What's your pa doing with my drawings?" I ran out the room and down the stairs, but Carlo was nowhere in the main rooms, so I rushed to the kitchen where I saw my drawings the moment they were dropped into the fire. They curled, darkened and burst into flames, shrinking and withering to ash. I shouted, "What are you… don't!" I picked up a large, long handle pan and hit Carlo as hard as I could. Giulio caught me from behind and wrenched the pan from me before I could strike again. Carlo howled, turned and punched me so hard in the face I went down, losing consciousness.

Giulio loomed over me. "Cecco."

I came around to the sound of weeping and lay on a couple of tables pushed together, my jaw throbbed, and my head hurt having hit the ground hard. I turned my head to see it was the maid who found the satchel was crying, her tears begged for mercy but recalling the drawings as they burst into flames, I spat at her. "*Fica!*" She ran out of the room with her apron held to her eyes.

I heard Carlo shout, "As soon as he's on his feet, I want him out."

"Pa, it's pissing down; he meant no harm."

"The bastard hit me from behind."

"You burned his drawings and knocked him out, a twelve-year-old, for God's sake."

"Old enough to hang. He's getting off light."

At the door, Giulio handed me my sack, satchel and old jerkin from the bedroom. I took off my new jerkin, put on the old and folded the new one into the satchel. A heavy thunderstorm had finally broken the heat wave. Giulio rubbed my back as I held the sack over my head and clutched the satchel to my chest in the hope my new jerkin wouldn't be ruined. In the street, the rain was torrential but, thankfully, the oily sack fibres gave some protection as I ran towards another tavern further along the street, splashing through deep puddles soaking my shoes. On entering, I noticed the bardassas Marco and Luca with a man I vaguely recognised and guessed was their pimp. He corralled them in the far corner and bent his head towards them and whispered. They gestured to invite me to join them but, remembering Giovan's cautions, I waved and turned to the door. The rain still poured, and I was hesitant to get even wetter.

Someone caught me by the shoulder. "Cecco, come, join us…"

Chapter 8

Bardassa 1596

"There are boys you could have for a few coins. Boys don't bring their problems home, which is half their charm." Spada laughed. His braying grated but worse was the mix of lust and disgust. *Spada*, by name and by nature. "If you're bothered about your reputation as the big man, there are boys who are perfect girls. The best are in the Uffizi arcades in Florence." He smirked. "Those with teeth are good but the ones without…" He sniggered. "My point is, there's a pretty boy lives off the Corso… not any cheap bardassa… actually quite expensive but then, all good things come at a price."

"You would know about that but why would I visit a bardassa?"

"Because you work too hard… work, eat, sleep, and work again. You never stop, Michele; you're not a monk, and you're becoming tiresome. I'll see you again. I'm meeting Onorio; remember Onorio… the architect." He scribbled something on the corner of one of Michele's sepia studies. "It's probably not his real name, but who cares? You have money now, Michele; for God's sake, enjoy it."

That the cardinal rejected the painting still stung, but he agreed with the chaplain, the cardinal's reputation was paramount and he would not repay kindness with churlish resentment. He had the lads prepare materials for the *Bacchus* but recalled Francesco's throwaway suggestion about a youth bitten by a snake so two canvasses were stretched, one nine by ten palmi, the other seven by six and set them side by side. The *Bacchus* was as yet un-visioned, but he scratched a curious zigzag design on the smaller canvas which clarified the composition since the gesture described the action of someone recoiling from a bite. The subject buzzed and distilled into a poem, little more than doggerel but like the painting, not yet resolved.

A boy bitten by a snake
Would his life be usurped?
Not alive nor dead,

Rereading the poem, he grimaced, utter shite and screwed up the paper.

At the market, he saw a street urchin slide his hand hidden under his ragged cloak to steal a peach, but the old serving woman cracked a thin stick over his wrist. "*Zingaro sporco!*" The woman's son rushed to grab the youth but, as he scarpered, he barged into Michele, who caught and shook him. For a moment, he thought to let him slip away since not so long ago he was the boy stealing fruit. Instead, he gave the fruiterer a handful of small change. "I'll sort him out for you." He gave the boy a light tap on the head and dragged him to the corner of the street. "Are you hungry?"

"What's it to you?"

"I'll give you a meal and some money if you model for me."

"I've heard that before…"

"I'm serious, I'm a painter."

"I know what you're after."

Michele smacked him again. "Don't cheek me. I'll give you this much." He opened his hand. "Model for me for a week, six days, Sunday off and six good meals… yes or no?"

The boy's eyes lit up and he nodded. Michele dressed him in a clean white shirt, pulled it off his shoulder and stood him behind a tall table strewn with fruit and a glass bowl of roses placed to the right. Michele modelled the gesture he saw the boy make when the old woman hit him with the stick which the lad copied and Michele made several quick studies, then drew the pose in a day, blocked in with reddish-brown ochre and the deepest tones in raw umber.

By the third day, he had painted the head making the boy frown and gasp. Lighter tones were applied over the mid tones with little need for exaggerated modelling. Next day, he tucked a white rose behind the boy's right ear, the whorls of the petals echoed the curls of his bushy hair and spent half a day painting the hand with middle finger bent down in the inverted gesture of the horns. The boy's fingernails were caked with grime which were carefully rendered. The far hand was painted monochrome, little more than underpaint with only the index finger highlighted in pale yellow ochre. The shaded side of the shirt was painted deep pink over a dark umber base. He spent much time and effort painting the folds of the shirt and once the lad was paid and gone, several days were spent regarding the near finished picture. The *Z* form of the composition gave movement lacking in the picture of the musicians, and although brother to the boy with the basket of fruit, the handling was more fluent. The addition of cherries, grapes, quince and a glass vase with a pink rose on the table almost finished the painting but although the model said he could find him a snake, none materialised during the week and now he was gone.

"You paid him how much?" Spada tapped Michel's arm with the back of his wrist. "Pazzo! You could have had the boy I told you about for half that, and he'd model for you for nothing into the bargain."

Michele shrugged. "He was a good model and he was broke… Remember being broke, Spada?"

Arriving at a much smarter tenement than the one he shared not so long ago, he asked an old woman leaving the building for Dario. She tutted, pointed up the stairs and showed three fingers. It was a heavy door painted black which gave a dull thud when knocked. It was several minutes before the door opened a crack. "Who is it?"

"Spada gave me your address."

"Who is this, Spada?"

"Spada… Lionello… His name is Spada…"

"Ah, Lion… Ill Conte. Yes, come, come." The door opened to a large reception room, the creature, an Egyptian mummy, neither male nor female, faggoty queen or scrawny old prostitute was dressed in layers of gaudy coloured fabrics. His hand gestures were fluid and every movement slow and calculated. "My name is Draško and Dario will be ready soon. Shall I take your hat, Marchese?"

"No." He took off his small black cap, folded and tucked it in his doublet. "How long will he be?"

"Patience, Marchese, please take a seat. Dario must prepare."

"How many… visitors—how many each day?"

"Only one, Marchese… the Divine is, of course… exclusive."

"How much…?"

"My dear Marchese." He tapped Michele's arm. "How could you raise such a matter…" He hurried to the door at the end of the corridor, listened a moment and pattered back. "I don't think he heard… please don't mention coin in the Divine's hearing. Come, Duce, sit by me." He led Michele to a settle in front of the shuttered window. He smiled, revealing missing upper and lower front teeth, waggled his tongue between the gap and he slipped his hand up Michele's thigh. "Shall I arouse you, in preparation?"

Michele pushed his hand away. "I don't think…" He had doubts about Spada lauding this unseen divinity and began to imagine a not too fragrant snaggle-toothed boy with bad breath.

"May I offer you refreshment while we wait on the Divine… wine, sweetmeats perhaps or wine?"

"Yes, wine." The creature went slowly across the room to an open door, bowing slightly before vanishing into the void. A few moments later, he reappeared with a beaten brass tray bearing a flagon of wine, two smoky Venetian glasses and a dish of delicacies and fruit. Draško set the tray on a low table and poured wine, offered a glass to Michele and slowly sipped the other; his eyes never left Michele's face. "Sweetmeats, Principe?"

He shook his head. At the same moment, he saw a small panel in the wall opposite slide open and was observed from the dark. A bell tinkled.

"Ah, Principe, Dario will receive you now." Presumably, he had been favourably regarded.

Draško led him to the door and slipped his hand between his legs. "Very nice, Marchese, you will give as much pleasure as you will have." He gently tapped then opened the door. "A handsome prince to see you, darling." Michele was gently pushed into the room lit by candles on tall tripods. The air was heavy with the aroma of Frankincense and the room was richly decorated.

As his eyes adjusted to the dim light, he saw brocade and silk cushions scattered around, and at the centre of the jewel box reclined a near-naked, hairless, pale-skinned youth reclining on a bed dressed with violet sheets. The youth's hair was tied back with a purple silk scarf, his head tilted as he regarded Michele, eyes half closed with an expression between allure and disdain. His eyes were dark, the lids outlined with kohl and noticing Michele hesitation, gestured to a large flagon of wine to top up his glass, then laid back against the cushioned divan. He stretched, threw aside the sheet that covered his nakedness, then drew up and opened his legs revealing a crease, which under other circumstance would be indecent, even crude but, after all, it was the contract between them. Michele slowly stripped, observed through half-closed eyes and when he slid beside and stroked him, his pale flesh was silk smooth, polished with almond oil, his hair scented with rose water and his supple languid body provoked hunger. In truth, Dario was the first boy Michele harnessed and saddled so when he roared, his howl reverberated around the jewel box. He shuddered, consumed by cold flames, bitter vinegar, and finally purged of all shame.

In the days and weeks that followed, his concentration was shot; however hard he tried to resist, most days ended at Dario's door. Painting, reading, carousing or even the occasional impromptu music party at the palazzo could not distract from overwhelming passion... more than passion—obsession which Dario fuelled by occasional words, smiles and rare reciprocated caresses that suggested he offered more than mere transaction. In Dario, he recognised a fellow artist by the way he appeared to yield his entire being but, in fact, gave very little, absolute involvement in the moment yet utter detachment. His allure was intoxicating and Michele was seduced by his cool acquiescence with no further expectation than the exchange of perspiration and money. Many days and nights were spent with Dario that creatively rendered Michele a eunuch, unable to start the commissioned Bacchus or continue work on the boy with a snake.

Most mornings, he rose early as ever, the canvas for the Bacchus on the strainer prepared but reproachful and blank as Dario's gaze. Determined to defy Dario's magnetic attraction, he sat before the half-finished painting of the boy bitten by a snake, the bitten finger frustratingly unfinished but unwilling to paint a snake from imagination. He needed a specific snake, aspis, horned or ursine, but a grass snake would do. He stared at the painting a long time, then jumped up to pace the room, his movements increasingly erratic and enraged, unable to add a single brush mark. He swore and slang the loaded brush across the floor, spattering paint up the wall. He stormed out of the palace, marching blindly across the piazza, ending up in a bar in an alley off the Corso. He ordered a flagon of Fiano and drank until he was unable to resist making his way to Dario.

After a tortuous month, Michele decided to make the Bacchus the means to break the circle of inactivity to fight fire with fire by attempting to capture the first moment he met Dario. As soon as he entered the jewel box, he asked Dario if he would pose for a painting. After a moment's thought, Dario merely shrugged and said he would think about the offer. Michele assumed he was politely refusing and soon lay beside him, the suggestion evaporated as they slowly entwined like vipers.

It was Dario who raised the matter at his next visit, stipulating he would not come to the workshop. "I stay here. I won't leave here." Without doubt, he discussed the matter with Draško, seeking his permission, which seemed likely, given the outrageous amount of money he demanded. Once agreed,

Michele set up a divan in the reception room where there was daylight. "What is this painting?"

"Bacchus. The god of wine and…"

"Greek god… I won't pose naked."

Michele nodded, bemused by sudden modesty but, after all, his stock in trade was a different commodity, sex rather than nudity. Perhaps, the image of his alluring body freely available for the gaze of untold numbers might diminish his market value. For sure, Draško was likely to hold such a view. He dressed Dario in a fine ivory cotton sheet draped over his left shoulder in the style of a Roman toga. Dario instinctively posed; his head inclined as he proffered a glass of wine as instructed.

The sessions went well and, although occasionally overwhelmed by flushes of desire, he managed to find the necessary calm by applying a repetitive mechanical method to recreate the forms of the anatomy, muscle, bone, concave and convex forms, mixing subtle colours to recreate the pallor of flesh. He worked in front of the shuttered window so the light fell from behind, causing shadows to collect at dark edges in more or less icon-style as he did when he made the angel from cracks in the ceiling of his bedroom in Caravaggio. But rather than an icon of Christ, the god-man was translated into pagan form. Coolly observed, Dario was surprisingly well muscled, which became a subtle reference to Michelangelo's male impersonators but when the face was almost finished, he recognised the portrait of Dario was too handsome. He had a fine nose, sharp jaw and high cheekbones, only his almond eyes were softer, feminine in startling contrast with his otherwise manly features. The contradiction, he recognised, was the source of his obsession.

In just a few weeks, he had painted the body and in three whole daylong sessions the drapery, which had to be painted rapidly because the pattern of folds changed each day. Dario's chest was near centre of the painting where the glow of perspiration was almost as white as the fine cotton fabric in contrast to the sunburned hand holding a dense black crepe bow across his torso. The tanned forearms meant Draško must occasionally permit Dario to leave the apartment. Long sessions, daybreak to dusk were tiring and occasional uncontrollable lust left both exhausted.

Each night, Michele fell into bed and woke late, fully dressed and shod. His first thoughts were of the painting which he saw in detail in his mind's eye. Although the body of Bacchus was finished, the portrait of Dario was unresolved, his reddish-black hair was loosely touched in and the hand holding the bowl of wine by contrast was delicately rendered. He made a mental note to borrow some of Francesco's Venetian glass, remembering a fine carafe and drinking bowl. The position of the figure now raised a problem that being almost at the centre of the painting the figure appeared to slide towards the bottom of the picture. He fretted several days until waking to the solution after a long dream-crowded sleep. In his half-conscious stupor, he knew how to resolve the form and nature of the painting, it was a profane icon and therefore required an altar with offerings to the god: perspective lines of the table created a triangle, leading the eye upwards to counterbalance the weight of the torso bearing down. The table, an altar, was dressed with carefully placed offerings, naturally, wine and grapes with vine leaves.

He counted the bells to ten, perhaps the latest he had lain abed in years but finally got up, stripped naked and wiped himself with a damp cloth rinsed in a basin. Lorenzo had left bread, ham and cheese on a platter. It occurred he should hire Lorenzo; even though his work was middling, he was a good assistant and owed him something if only to save him from Cesari's ill temper. He sniffed his shirt, unchanged most of the week, the underarms reeked of acid sweat and breeches of dried urine. The fine clothes Francesco had tailored for him were dolefully worn, spotted with splashes and dabs of paint, seams split and multiple snags and tears. Lorenzo complained, he wore clothes until they fell apart. He decided to visit Francesco's tailor to order a new wardrobe. Now that he had money he ought to dress the part. He drew on clean underwear, a shirt and the least soiled of his breeches and jerkin and before tossing clothes worn the day before into the corner, felt the moleskin purse sewn into the lining. There was only a single scudo and a few denarii; one scudo less than expected and, having spent the past few days with Dario, it was obvious where the money had gone.

Michele arrived with Mario by wagon at Dario's tenement. He led Mario to the apartment and rapped on the door. "Principe, you are even more eager than usual, and not alone."

He shoved open the door, covered the painting with a cloth as Mario dismantled the easel and packed paints and brushes.

Dario appeared in the corridor. "Why are you taking the painting away, darling?"

"I'll add details at my workshop. I'm sure you'll be glad when the smell of paint is gone."

Dario's eyes followed Mario as he carried the covered painting out of the apartment. "I will miss seeing it." He crossed the room, his nude body barely covered by a richly embroidered gown, his flesh so pale he glowed in the golden morning sunlight.

He stood before Michele a moment. "I think you're leaving for ever."

When Mario took the last of the materials from the apartment, Michele tossed him coins to pay the wagoner and told him to take the painting back to the palazzo. As he left, Mario gave a bemused grin, Michele's frequent absence now explained. He winked but Michele scowled and jerked his head towards the door. He turned to Dario. "That's right; I won't be back and you know why." Dario sat on the divan and allowed the robe to fall away but what in the jewel box was alluring seemed clumsily and crude by daylight. "Cover up, Dario; you make yourself cheap."

There was a scream and a blow to Michele's head. "Don't speak to the Divine this way… You are a bad man."

Michele drew a dagger to more screaming from Draško's gap-tooth gape. "Divine, my darling, I will not let this man kill us." He uttered unintelligible guttering and spat. Dario glanced up at Michele and seemed genuinely confused.

"Where is my money, Dario?"

"I know nothing of money."

He grabbed Draško's skinny arm, but he bit Michele's hand. Michele slapped him and shouted, "Where's my money?"

"You paid fair price for a perfect boy, beautiful and he sat weeks for you to paint."

"I don't pay models more than I earn… Do I have to search the place?" Without waiting for a reply, he began opening drawers, searching cupboards, slashing mattresses and overturning furniture, searched vases and clothing. It was pointless; there was no money, probably in a Frescobaldi bank by now. He was breathless with rage. "Why have you done this to me?"

Dario remained silent but slyly glanced sideways at Draško who brazenly gloated as he stared up at him. "Goodbye… Conte!"

He caught Draško and pressed the dagger against his throat; his mockery turned to wide-eyed terror. He glanced at Dario. "Shall I cut his throat… my final gift? He's a cheap thieving pimp. I know you're not bad. I'll dump his corpse in the river; no one will ever know. Say the word…"

Dario gently drew Draško from Michele's grip and stood in front of the creature and shook his head. Michele caught Draško again and nicked his ear, severing the lobe. Both Dario and Draško gasped. "You will never tell anybody I was ever here, you understand?"

Dario pressed the sleeve of his gown to staunch the bleeding. "We say nothing."

"If I hear the faintest rumour, I'll tell the sbirri… the police… you know what that means."

"I say nothing… Draško will say nothing."

Mario had set up the painting by the time he returned to the palazzo and continued smirking until Michele snapped. "Stop it! Not a word about this to anyone, especially… you understand."

Mario crossed his heart and, although smiling, swore silence in the name of the Virgin. Michele barged past him to look at the picture. Even half-finished, he was satisfied; the anatomy, skin texture and drapery were the best he had done but the face was too masculine for the rarefied tastes of Francesco and his circle who favoured androgyny.

In the following days, the foreground fell easily into place, a low table with a large bowl of fruit with grapes, apples, peaches, lemon and pomegranate spilling its seeds. The vine leaves wilted and the fruit turned pock-marked and bruised, suggesting the passage of time as Dario's perfect body and faultless skin in not so many years would inevitably age and spoil.

A palace servant accompanied Michele to the glass store where he chose a rare purple-brown tinted Venetian glass carafe with an undulating pie-crust rim and a large shallow drinking bowl. He placed the carafe to the left of the table and Mario held the glass bowl for hours as Michele painted the smoky near-transparent glass that merely obstructed light at the edges. Michele poured the carafe to three quarters with dark arterial blood red-purple wine and the drinking bowl almost to the rim, painted in thin layers of glaze and concentric ellipses in the glass to depict ripples or perhaps, Dario's heartbeat. He took a short pause to stand almost an hour, scrutinising every detail, especially the still life. The real fruit now gave off a sickly-sweet smell, the peaches dusted with grey powdery mould and grapes crinkled and desiccating.

He was pleased to have caught flares and reflected light in the carafe but glancing at the real carafe noticed movement in the reflected light. He gently rocked side to side and recognised his reflection. It took barely four brush marks to add a tiny, blurred self-portrait, which few would notice. But it was Dario's beautiful face that remained out of key, a portrait of a real person, a youth with a limped gaze at odds with the cynical conceit of the painting.

The answer was Mario's features, ruddy cheeks and boyish looks, his chin fuller with a slight cleft and his lips set in a typically ambiguous half smile. He carefully and reluctantly wiped away Dario's face and, with little underpainting, substituted Mario's features and added dark exaggerated arched courtesan-style eyebrows and replaced Dario's ruddy-black hair with Mario's darker hair, painted with sharp edges to suggest a wig. He had been intrigued by a woodblock print of a courtesan from Japan, a gift Francesco said was from a Portuguese cardinal. As an afterthought, the outline was too severe; remembering Lorenzo's suggestion for *Sick Little Bacchus*, he fashioned a coronet of vine leaves, predominantly green turning gold but, in the time it took to paint the arrangement, one of the leaves turned intense red.

Leaving the Bacchus to dry, Michele turned to the unfinished youth bitten by a snake which he intended to sell to replace the money stolen by Draško. He asked about for anyone who had a snake but with no success until a young page knocked on the studio door.

"Master Michelangelo, I heard you're looking for a snake." The boy held a small canvas bag tied with cord.

"You have a snake?"

"Not exactly, signor." The boy shook the bag until a small black lizard about a palm in length eventually dropped onto the table. It froze and the page cupped his hands around it to prevent escape. "I found it on the wall by the back entrance. It was chilly this morning, which made it sleepy so it didn't run away. I thought I'd keep it but someone said you were looking for a snake." He looked up at Michele. "But I suppose snakes don't have legs though. I'm sorry I wasted your time, master."

"You obviously slept through Bible lessons, young man."

"I did not, signor. I hope to be an altar boy at San Luigi and maybe one day at St Peter's."

"Don't you remember the Bible says God cursed the snake for tempting Eve and took away its legs so it had to crawl on its belly."

"So, snakes were lizards when God made the animals."

"Until they were cursed." Michele scooped up the lizard and dropped it back in the bag and offered the page some coins. "Master Guido, you have changed the meaning of my painting."

The boy counted the coins, smiled and slipped them in his purse. "Thank you, master."

"Thank *you*, young man."

"I've heard a lot about your pictures, master. May I see them?" *Bacchus* remained covered but Michele let him see the unfinished youth now to be bitten by a lizard. He was visibly jolted at first sight. "Ho, signor, I've never seen a picture like that before, even His Eminence's pictures. Did you make the one of the musicians?"

"What did you think of that one?"

"It is good indeed, signor, but the boy's hand is all wrong."

Michele laughed. "Yes, I forgot to correct it... You won't tell anyone, will you?"

"No, sir, but it's still a good picture."

Michele offered him more coins but the boy solemnly offered the money back. "I can't take this for telling the truth, signor."

"A little extra for the lizard."

"Can I have the lizard back when you've painted it? I would like to keep it for a pet." Michele nodded, then watched the boy scurry away and stood staring at the blank workshop door and wiped his eyes.

Michele laid four shallow strips of wood on the table in a rectangle, put the lizard inside and gently pressed a small piece of clear glass so the creature's legs were slightly splayed. The lizard was painted from directly above, working rapidly, so it would not be trapped too long. Within hours, he blocked its near black silhouette with suggestions of scales in barely lighter tones. The creature almost blended into the background, so, at first glance, it was difficult to see why the boy was startled. After cleaning his brushes, he uncovered Bacchus, set a chair ten paces back and scanned the painting by the inch.

In general, he was pleased but something was missing on the lower right side. The compositional triangle pointing to the face seemed incomplete on that side. Even with Mario's face replacing Dario's portrait, the painting retained the allure of the first moment Michele saw him, and, however humiliating the final hour, the scores of hours in his company were among the most luxurious and alluring of his life and perhaps the first time he fully engaged in manly passion. It had been exhilarating to surrender with complete abandon with a compliant young man cocooned from the world in a sealed jewel box. At their first meeting, he was startled by the beauty of the reclining near nude youth, and, when he slowly unbuttoned his doublet, his little black hat fell to the floor. He picked it up and dropped it on a cushion.

By sunset, Michele had painted his folded hat on the table at an angle to complete the right side of the triangle pointing to Bacchus' face. It was hardly necessary to view the picture more than a few moments to know it was finished, whole and in detail. He glanced at the boy now to be bitten by a lizard and saw the same unity. Covering both pictures, he put on doublet and cap and went to find Mario and Lorenzo to celebrate. Next morning, Michele was upset to find the lizard's rigid corpse under the glass. When Mario and Lorenzo arrived, he mentioned the dead lizard. They were amused he was upset. "The page wanted it for a pet."

"He'll survive, unlike the lizard…"

The cardinal entered the studio unannounced. He wore a riding habit and Michele genuflected in surprise, Lorenzo and Mario likewise. He embraced Michele and offered his hand to the lads. They dipped to kiss his ring. "Bless you both. I wonder if I might speak to Master Michele alone." When they left, he continued, "Forgive my intrusion, but I am desperate to see the new painting. I heard it's finished." He fiddled with his crucifix. "May I see?" Michele removed the cloth with a flourish and the cardinal stepped back in astonishment. "Heavens, you surprise with each new painting. I am… it's exquisite… the detail, glowing flesh. Was the young man… did he just leave us and was he not the angel in the… earlier picture?"

"Master Mario posed for much of the picture."

Francesco continued to take in the painting. "Yes… ah-ha, lovely." He laughed. "I see the man reflected in the wine flagon and the little black hat you've worn in our presence. If I am not mistaken, this painting is confessional."

"All my sins are mortal, Reverend Father."

"Don't brag, my dear." Francesco tapped him with his riding crop. "I see another covered painting, would you mind?"

"I think it's finished and wonder if you will remember how you inspired it?"

"Another Bacchus?" He stood close to the painting. "What's that under his hand… ah, a lizard. Did I suggest that…?"

"In a manner of speaking."

"You love to tease. You see me as a lizard?"

"No, of course not, but I hope you remember what you said at the time of the Saint Francis… painting."

He stroked Michele's arm. "I remember making various suggestions but, now I recall, didn't I say a snake?" He turned to examine the picture even closer. "The handling is quite different from the Bacchus, but I suppose it was important the subject is more animated where the other is more… restrained, in every sense, and how intriguing is this boy bitten by a snake, or lizard, a modern interpretation of the sting of original sin. I'm delighted with the Bacchus, Michele. I intend to invite some illustrious guests in order to enjoy a little bragging of my own." He made to leave, then turned. "The Bacchus. I'll have it for my dear friend, His Grace the Grand Duke of Tuscany. When his brother died, he gave up the cloth in order to marry to make heirs. I succeeded him as cardinal.... He shares our sense of humour."

The two paintings were hung together in the cardinal's grand salon, with the *Lute Player* and *Saint Francis in Ecstacy* before its departure to Genoa. In the following months, many of the cardinal's noble friends bought or commissioned works, often versions of earlier paintings.

The *Saint Francis* was covered with fine cloth, embroidered with the cardinal's coat of arms and carefully placed on a wagon draped with rich fabric similarly emblazoned. Francesco blessed the cart, drivers and four liveried guards as the cavalcade ostentatiously left the courtyard. The gifted Saint Francisco was witnessed beginning its journey to Don Ottavio in Genoa and was widely reported.

Chapter 9

A Haven 1597

"There you are, Michele." The cardinal wore lay-clothes, black quilted doublet laced and with decorative mother-of-pearl buttons, russet brown cloak and wide brim hat with a pearl letter B broach that attached a plume of white feathers.

"You asked me to attend, Your Excellency."

"You brought a cloak. Excellent, walk with me."

"Where are we going?" A page handed the cardinal kid gloves and a walking cane and he and other servants bowed as Michele followed him to the street. "You're not taking your coach or a bodyguard."

"We're not going far." He caught Michele's arm. "You're my bodyguard." Although incognito, the cardinal radiated a magnetic authority that passers-by of all rank instinctively saluted or bowed. They strode along half a dozen streets, eventually arriving at a large house near the Via Veneto. He handed Michele the key and they entered. "Welcome to my private casino." In the sparsely furnished and modestly decorated grand house, Francesco led Michele to a room with shelves of books, scientific and measuring instruments and dried plant samples. "My cabinet, my inner sanctum, my haven. Only my closest friends know of it and only a few have been invited. Vincenzo Giustiniani and one or two others and now, Caro, you are one of our little family to share my secret sanctuary."

Michele ran his fingers over the books, squinted through a magnifying glass at several specimens and drawings by Francesco. "These are beautiful, Francesco, so precise."

"Stop… stop, Michele; they're poor things by comparison with miracles you perform and that is one of the reasons I brought you here. It is the acuity and brilliance of your observation that attracted my attention to those first few paintings Master Cesari brought to me. I and others of my acquaintance are interested, among other matters, in certain diseases in plants, and it was the accuracy and detail in the way you depicted pitted fruit and vines that clearly identify specific maladies."

"I paint only what I see."

"Ah, but see" – he pushed a sheaf of his drawings towards Michele – "see how I capture the surface but you not only see but render with accuracy, how shall I say, by some means I don't understand, what you paint becomes that which you see. When I look at your work, it is as though I have never before seen whatever you have painted. You cast light into the darkness, into the very soul of nature in whatever you observe. You see... you see *for* me, for us all. It's in your nature, in the nature of artists, or should I say, of certain artists. Perhaps what you see is re-created by your doing... I believe the way true artists see is the origin of natural science."

A deep silence hung between them as Michele considered the cardinal's observations. "But, Francesco, you see into men's souls. You see in me what I cannot."

The cardinal walked around the table and picked up a music manuscript. "I read the notes, Michele, but you play... you sing them."

"I've never heard you melancholic."

"Bless you, but I promise it's not melancholia. It was grace that brought you to me and I have the privilege to serve your genius. Don't laugh. I saw your potential from the first picture Master Cesari showed me, and I will do everything in my power to serve your God-given talent." He picked up a glass prism and held it in a shaft of light. "Look, Michele, the first utterance of the Logos... *let there be light...* see how light divides into a rainbow as the first light divided into all matter."

Michele and Mario dragged a hand cart loaded with plaster, waxed sheets and painting materials, ladders and long planks. Mario covered the tables, cupboards and floor with the sheets and rigged up ladders with planks laid across the width of the room at waist height. They spent several days chipping off old plaster and making good, then Michele left Mario to lay on the arriccio rough plaster layer on the shallow concave ceiling. The cardinal asked Michele to portray the elements personified by the ancient gods, Jupiter for air, Pluto earth and Neptune water.

When the painting was first discussed, Michele mentioned the ceiling was concave; Francesco smiled. "My own Sistine ceiling."

The design had Jupiter supported by an eagle on one side and on the other Neptune with a sea horse and Pluto with three-headed Cerberus. In the middle, a huge globe of the sky with constellations and succession of zodiac symbols. It was the first time since his apprenticeship Michele had drawn a full-size cartoon but never for a complete ceiling fresco. Mario cut the cartoon into sections, one for each day's work and pinpricked outlines in preparation for transfer of each section to the ceiling by dabbing a gauze pouch of powdered charcoal to make dotted outlines in the wet plaster.

Mario was showered with plaster. "Michele! What in God's name are you doing? That's a whole day's work."

"Two days… where are the sections for the Pluto… you didn't throw them away?"

"No, they're with the others, but what was wrong with what you'd done?"

"I hate fresco. I don't mind working fast but loathe working from drawings rather than directly from the figure."

"It looked good to me."

"Not good enough. Clean up here and plaster the corner section and when you've laid-on the intonaco, bring us some food." Mario mixed whiting and marble dust and, when thoroughly combined, added the mixture to lime water comprising quicklime and water in proportions one to three. "There you are, master."

Michele dipped his finger in the mixture and rubbed it between index and thumb to ensure it was smooth and free of lumps. "It'll do."

"Sweet Gesù, Michele, you'll break your neck."

Michele stood naked astride a looking glass, precariously balanced on planks bridging the ladders. "It's the only way to paint myself from underneath."

"You'll crack the mirror; the planks are moving even as you try to stand still." The mirror bounced as Michele jumped down but didn't crack. "What d'you think?"

"What do I think? Well, you can see right up your arsehole and the eye of your prick. What will the cardinal say about that? I can see us having to chip this bit off again." Michele laughed. "You're very coy." He shook his hips, slapping his cock thigh to thigh.

Mario bowed deeply. The cardinal's exquisite clothes and large feathered hat made him seem younger, almost boyish. He turned to look at Mario. "Michele… this is…?"

"Mario… Eminence. Mario Minniti."

"Ah, the young man in my Bacchus picture. Bless you." He gripped Mario's chin. "A good likeness, Michele. Now let us see." He took off his wide brimmed hat, handed it to Mario, looked up and slowly scanned the ceiling. "Magnificent… I adore it. Our secret companion to the Sistine ceiling."

Michele slyly glanced sideways at Mario. "Eminence, do the nudes offend? My assistant here is anxious that pubic hair might be too much… and his privates too."

The cardinal glanced up at the Jupiter, then across at Neptune with dangling penis and testes and smiled. "Mario, my son, nudity represents divinity and purity, nothing shameful and no part of the body God gives into our care can ever be considered indecent, only the ill-educated or ignorant blush."

Michele nodded to Mario who genuflected and left. When alone, the cardinal touched Michele's arm. "It is more than I expected. Your Jupiter is a reply to Michelangelo's Almighty creating the planets, and your ceiling has unified perspective rather than the Sistine scheme of varying viewpoints. What a pity so few will see it in my lifetime in my secret place. I trust your discretion, and your assistant, Mario… is he discreet?"

"He is, but what does he have to tell?"

"This place… and contents." He took down a book from the shelf: *SIDERIUS NUNCIUS. G. GALILEI.* "In itself, this book is not dangerous but based on the author's calculations, what he deduces would not please the Curia."

"What could displease the Curia in… *messages from the stars*?"

"That Jupiter has moons."

"Why's that significant?"

"In itself, it is merely interesting, unless that observation leads to speculation and other conclusions."

"Such as?"

"If Jupiter has moons as the earth has a moon, what follows, as in heaven, so on earth. If Jupiter has moons, perhaps earth is merely a planet like any other?"

"Does that matter?"

"Again, of itself it doesn't, unless that leads to speculation that instead of the sun, moon and stars rotating around a fixed earth, rather the moon, planets, stars and even the earth, rotate around the sun."

"Surely everyone knows this; why else would Columbus sail west to reach the east?"

"Indeed, but Columbus never drew attention to the proposition that the earth is spherical but now in our present times of uncertainty and questioning, Holy Mother Church cannot suffer further challenges to her authority."

"Challenges…? I thought the issue was the nature of bread and wine." He absentmindedly aligned the prism with the magnifying glass and tilted the telescope, then looked up shyly.

"Another gift from Galileo." He arranged his drawings in order and laid the neat pile alongside the telescope.

"*That the earth be not moved…* Of course, Copernicus said something similar decades earlier and was more or less accepted by the church without murmur. Indeed, Pope Gregory adjusted the calendar on the strength of his calculations. But that was before the schism Protestants read scriptures in the vernacular and objected to Copernicus' theories on the grounds they were not biblical: *the world also shall be stable, that it be not moved.* This meant Holy Church could not be outflanked in biblical authority by those she considered heretics, hence the Council of Trent and… Inquisition."

"It has written nothing that the Curia objects to, don't forget, we are speaking in the abstract and in strictest confidence."

"I swear on my eyes…"

"No need to swear; it is true I see no conflict between Copernicus and Galileo and Holy Scripture; indeed, I believe natural science, art and Holy Church together lead us to a deeper understanding and communion with God's miraculous creation." Before returning to the Palazzo Madama, Francesco looked up again at the ceiling. As he gazed at the painting, turning his head to concentrate on details that caught his attention, he eventually leaned towards Michele. "The colour is extraordinarily rich for fresco."

"It is, but then it's painted in oils. Fresco's too pale, colour washed out with no body and too little time to blend."

"What about the state of Leonardo's Lat Supper. Isn't that oil on plaster?"

"It is, but this chamber is nowhere near a steamy kitchen… So, it will last. At least five hundred years…"

Chapter 10
Contarelli Chapel 1599

The chapel was little more than a shallow niche and the church fathers were determined it should be finally completed after several decades of neglect. Cesari's workshop decorated the ceiling and surrounds in fresco, leaving blank spaces for the altarpiece and wall panels. The decoration of the chapel was commissioned as a memorial by the family of the late Cardinal Mathieu Cointrel, known in Italian as Matteo Contarelli. The pope agreed to transfer the legacy to the governing body of St Peters to oversee expenditure and expedite completion.

The commission was for three paintings on the life of the patron's namesake to show Christ calling the tax collector to be a disciple, the saint's martyrdom and an altarpiece. Measuring the dimensions of the chapel, the two side paintings had to be square and the altarpiece narrower. Michele noted that even at midday, the church was dim, which suited his developing style with figures looming out of the dark. Checking the marks made on the measuring stick he told Mario: the two big pictures will be about thirty palmi by the same and the painting over the altar a little shorter in height and two-thirds the width of the other two pictures.

When business was concluded, the father superior spoke a short prayer for the success of Master Michelangelo and that his work would glorify God. Kindly, by nature, nevertheless Michele suspected the father superior was unhappy the commission had not gone to a more renowned painter. It was obvious that del Monte, plenipotentiary to the French Church, had pulled strings and called in favours on Michele's behalf with his close friend the Abbate Giacomo Crescenzi, who had been delegated to commission the decoration of the chapel.

As Michele walked the short distance to the Palazzo Madama, the euphoria of the task was tainted by sudden anxiety about the prospect of painting such big pictures with large groups of figures. The largest group he had painted before were the musicians for Francesco, the cardsharps were half-length but the scale of the Contarelli demanded life size figures and his subjects to date were not particularly dramatic, any drama conveyed by a glance or subtle gesture, *Boy Bitten by a Lizard* the sole exception.

As if to parry the challenge, rather than enter the palazzo, he quickly went on to the joiner to order strainers, stretchers and frames for the three paintings and to the sail makers to buy canvas. The martyrdom held the greatest dread so was the first Michele chose to confront as though stalking prey. The cardinal's secretary had a brother, a military officer who arranged for three mercenaries to pose as Matthew's killers.

Although they had fine physiques, they were indolent, and, when he tried to manoeuvre them, grasping their shoulders and waists, twisting and turning into the necessary poses, they flinched, became skittish and joked that that kind of thing would cost more. They moved constantly, shifting their weight, chattering and constantly scratching their balls and, each day, arrived later and swayed and trembled, hungover from drinking sessions the night before. By the end of the first week, Michele paid Mario and Lorenzo to stand in for the figures already begun but they were nowhere near as muscular as the soldiers. Each day, the mercenaries returned more boisterous than before, mocking the cushy surroundings and complaining they had to stand so long.

By Friday of the second week, Michele had enough and told them he didn't need them any more. At that, they became threatening, having enjoyed generous payments and helped themselves to some of the props, including an expensive officer's helmet with feathers, a couple of swords and Venetian glass used in the Bacchus painting. As soon as they left the studio, Michele ran down the main staircase to tell the chaplain to fetch officers of the watch to catch the thieves. Thankfully, the stolen articles were surrendered without resistance but one of the Venetian glasses was cracked and weapons were confiscated, including the sword Michele bought in Venice.

He painted nothing the next few days, just stared at what he had painted so far. The figures were too close to the bottom of the painting, so architectural details were painted high above the main action to raise the eyes and disguise the fundamental compositional error. Michele became morose and tried to ignore the flaw but, about six weeks after starting the martyrdom, the cardinal asked if he might view progress. Francesco always respected Michele's need to work undisturbed and usually saw only finished work but the Contarelli commission was won based on his connoisseurship. At first sight, Francesco barely hid his shock. There was a yawning gap in the middle of the painting between the figures, which were too small and over-elaborate architectural details positioned far too high above. "It's bad, isn't it?"

"I wouldn't say that, Michele. I don't know your working methods but, as an amateur critic, there appear to be several unresolved… matters."

"I'm not sure I can manage large scale subjects."

"Be calm, my dear." The cardinal turned to Lorenzo and smiled, who returned his smile until realising he wanted to speak privately to Michele.

When alone, he continued, "Michele, you have great innate talent but not this. You're trying to emulate Raphael or Titian. Your paintings never depict action but rather they reflect upon action." After a few silent moments, he gripped Michele's shoulder. "You must find the core of the subject. What did Matthew's ministry mean and how was that fulfilled by his martyrdom?"

Michele sat in silence a moment and recalled his first thoughts. *Illumination. Matthew's calling is the moment his life turns from darkness to light.* He shut his eyes a moment and, when he opened them, he found Francesco quietly regarding him. He nodded and smiled. "I have to start again but no one must ever see this, and I need better, more dependable models; mercenaries… don't know how to pose."

Francesco glanced at the sepia studies pinned to the wall. "There is the energy you need to bring to the paintings, the searching light, but why hire mercenaries?"

"They have the right bodies, killers with toned muscles and know how to handle weapons."

"Why not hire a single model for an executioner? Choose the man with the best physique and pay him well to pose alone so he can't play the fool. Never allow yourself to be outnumbered is, I believe, a reliable military strategy."

Rather than having Mario or Lorenzo over-paint the wreck of the martyrdom, Michele sent them away and did the job alone, laying on several thin layers of darkened raw umber with the nagging concern the canvas might retain the scars of the aborted attempt beneath. He was proud of the usual immaculate finish of his paintings with just the right amount of paint conveyed to the canvas surface. But by painting out the first attempt, there remained the dreadful prospect in future years of pentimento images appearing through the later layers of paint.

Preparing the new surface took over a week to dry and, each evening as the light faded, he left the palazzo to eat. He scoffed food and downed a jug of wine that darkened rather than lightened his mood. He avoided Onorio and Annibale and even Lorenzo's unswerving devotion was likely to irritate. Only Mario had the sense to simply listen without offering encouragement or suggestions. Having so spectacularly failed with his first efforts, it would be a disaster if word got out; mockery would be merciless and commissions likely to dry up overnight. If he couldn't pull off the commission, the Contarelli chapel would finish his career.

He examined the surface of the new prepared canvas at various points each morning and although touch dry it required perhaps a few weeks before beginning the second version. He spent days staring at the dark blank square, apprehensive that a new interpretation was still unresolved. After a month of anxious indecision, he gradually switched his attention to ideas explored through small sepia studies for the painting of the Calling of Matthew. The layout of the chapel meant logically the painting of the Calling would be on the left wall and the Martyrdom opposite but the martyrdom would be first seen on entering the church from the west end. He considered reversing positions but on reflection decided to stay with the paintings in the natural left to right sequence with the light source for both paintings originating from the altar wall. That decision concentrated Michele's thoughts about the Calling. If the true light fell from the altar, then the figure of Christ should enter from the right side so that light was not merely the agency of illumination, but Matthew was enlightened by Christ's presence and his calling.

The Calling was now clear in his mind as he loaded a long-handled brush with a mixture of raw umber and a black he marked the point where the top of Jesus' head would be on the canvas, then a line indicating where his feet would stand and using a straight edge drew a long line to indicate the angle of the light from an open door which precisely pointed to where Matthew must be positioned.

Pausing before the canvas a few moments, he put on his doublet and went in search of Jesus. He persuaded a waiter from an osteria in the Via de Fusari near the Piazza Maggiore to model for the Christ. His name was Giacomo and had a somewhat priestly bearing, tall, handsome, slim with a fine head, aquiline nose, good beard and hair. Michele worked obsessively on Giacomo's head, beautiful, exposed neck and raised right arm with the hand pointing along the line of the shaft of sunlight. It took ten days and the

Christ figure was almost finished, painted mostly in shadow except for his illuminated pointing hand. The first time Giacomo pointed his languorous hand, Michele was instantly reminded of… He put down his brush to search a pile of studies in the storeroom, rifled through drawings of details of the Sistine ceiling made not long after his arrival in Rome. Among studies of the *Creation of Adam,* he *was* surprised it was not God's hand he remembered but the hand of Adam.

He examined the study through the mirror to see it in reverse and by making only slight adjustments to the hand in the painting, recreated the gesture from the fresco. Christ, the second Adam… the Divine Christ… Christ the Man. When he mentioned he was looking for models for Matthew and his companions, Giacomo suggested several characters he knew from the osteria and on the nod introduced Michele to three drinking companions: Ottavio, a large, bearded man; Ernesto, a clerk who wore spectacles; and the third was a younger man called Gith, with sunburned pale skin, evasive about his background but his hesitant, mostly argot Italian was spoken with a thick English accent. Giacomo said he heard he deserted from an English merchantman at Genoa. Michele merely shrugged, set up a table in the studio and arranged the models in a group with Gith closest, counting money at the far left, Ernesto putting down a coin between Ottavio and Gith, but when Ernesto removed his glasses, Michele told him to keep them on.

"Did people wear spectacles in the time of Our Lord?"

"No, Ernesto, we are here and now."

The group was outlined in raw umber and the figures were blocked in within a week, and Mario was posed with his arm leaning on Ottavio's shoulder. They were dressed in present dress in contrast to Jesus' traditional garment. Each model was called individually as Michele worked on details. In less than five weeks, the left side was near finished.

It was the state the cardinal first saw the Calling. "I painted out the other… It was insufferable." The cardinal pulled up a chair, gestured to Michele to sit beside him and nodded to his page who served pastry tarts and sweet wine. The cardinal selected a peach tart and gave it to him, and then a glass of wine. When the page had gone, he lifted his glass. "To you, Michele." He swept pastry crumbs from his cassock, then looked up at the painting, slightly squinted as he contemplated the canvas a long time, then stood and crossed to the picture to examine it in detail. He pointed to Mario. "Your assistant when you painted the fresco in my cabinet… and wasn't he my Bacchus? Ah… and who is this pretty young man counting money?"

"I'm told his name is Gith, apparently a deserter from an English merchantman."

The cardinal smiled. "A heretic."

"I never asked."

The cardinal laughed and examined the portrait of the young Englishman. "Gith the Englishman, what does he think and believe? That bread becomes flesh and wine blood, or are they simply symbols or metaphors. Does he believe the former or the latter, should he be blessed or burned? I hear Elizabeth of England is dying… apparently terrified."

"Of Hellfire?" Michele grinned.

The cardinal mused. "Hellfire… what nonsense. Simple conscience because she killed her cousin. Politically necessary in her precarious position. Even princes can only play the cards they're dealt. The Scottish queen was an alley-cat but since she was of the true faith, she died absolved, a martyr, never mind her husband murdered by her lover. But Elizabeth is consumed by guilt. Poor woman. The Curia was too blind to see how subtle she is and Spain was petulant. His Holiness Sixtus V held her in great esteem and recognised she's not a Protestant at heart. If she is head of her church, so what? Why isolate her with constant threats to dethrone her? Idiocy! We could have kept her in the fold; she has said she never wished to see into men's souls, how more plain could she be? I hear she loves good music, including composers of the true faith, which absolves her of almost everything in my book." His eyes twinkled. "In confidence, of course…" He took a step back and nodded to the painting. "I like the figure of Our Lord – wonderfully commanding, approachable and immensely attractive. I wonder why he's alone, shouldn't there be disciples, Peter and James and John perhaps?"

"That would be too symmetrical, four and four, why don't I add just Simon Peter?"

"Peter. Yes, keeper of the keys… Peter to stand between the viewer and Our Lord as Holy Church mediates between the faithful and Heaven. I believe the fathers of San Luigi would appreciate the reference and diplomatic nicety of the association with the Vatican." He stared at the canvas, tapping his lip. "Yes… yes." He stepped back to stand beside Michele. "The shaft of light, the first element of creation, that great burst of light in the void. Our Lord's gesture embodies the act of creation by the Logos." He leaned to inspect the hand, then returned to his chair. "What about the space in the middle?"

"I thought to add a figure leaning towards Christ, seen from the back."

The cardinal stood a while longer, staring at the painting, then sipped the last of his glass and kissed Michele's cheek. "Wonderful. The best you've done and different from anything before, more unified. Let's hope the Martyrdom is soon resolved. I look forward to the finished work."

Michele painted St Peter between Christ and the viewer, obscuring all but Christ's head and arm, his dark green coat contrasted with Christ's red sleeve and his beige cloak glowed yellow in the warm golden light. Peter's pointing gesture echoed that of Jesus' but whereas Christ's gesture was emphatic, Peter's was hesitant. To bridge the two groups, Michele added a window with an open shutter to break the flat wall above Peter's head and spanned the space to the mid-line of the painting. The window frame formed a cross, the panes covered with oil cloth and the open shutter cast a shadow parallel to the line of the shaft of sunlight that illuminated the dark recesses of Matthew's former life, cleansed by his acceptance of the offer of grace and a prefiguration of Christ's cleansing the temple. The painting was of a piece and, as it neared completion, days were spent scanning every minute detail. A nagging doubt remained over the void in the painting and the equal total of six figures… four and two.

Whatever dreads and anxieties Michele had about the martyrdom, he was certain the Calling was a success and boosted his confidence as he prepared to restart the martyrdom. He widened the search to labourers and men who worked on the wharves, recalling the half-naked young man standing in the mud the day he arrived in Rome. The sixteen or seventeen-year-old would now be twenty-four or five and having matured in body and spirit would have made the perfect executioner.

After several days searching the docks and wharves, Michele suddenly saw his executioner working on a barge. He was younger than the youngest mercenary and better looking stripped to the waist, his hair tied back with a strip of cloth to prevent sweat running into his eyes. He worked rhythmically, lifting and tossing sacks from the barge onto the pier, which gave him a torso fit for the Sistine ceiling. Michele approached and introduced himself as Master Michelangelo da Caravaggio. "I'm commissioned to paint pictures for the church of San Luigi and I would like you to model for me."

"Never heard of you." The young man winked at his mates and grinned. "That's a new one. Why not just say you want to suck my cock?" He grinned and raised his arm as the lads whistled and joked.

Michele smiled. "If you like… but, seriously, I truly am looking for a model to paint."

"You want me in the altogether?"

"Almost… you would play an executioner."

"What would it pay?"

"Whatever you earn in three days, I'll pay you each day."

"Gesù, Marco!"

"Hey mister, I'll model starkers if you like and I'd let you suck me off as well."

"Sorry, lads, it has to be… Marco? But I don't have time to haggle." Michele turned and walked briskly away but barely reached the cool shade of the warehouse when he heard footfall.

Having found his executioner, he stood in front of the new prepared canvas in the fading evening light and used the long straight edge to draw lines corner to corner, then measured the distance from the bottom edge of the canvas to the level of Christ's feet in the Calling and drew a horizontal line. He measured Christ's height from feet to shoulder and drew a second short horizontal line on the blank canvas. The painting had taken shape in his mind during the painting of the Calling. The composition would have four areas of action centred on the executioner and the fallen dying Matthew. He made exploratory sepia studies having learned from the Calling how to arrange clusters of figures to suggest a larger group but, whereas the composition of the Calling was calm, the diagonals would be a more dynamic geometry for the Martyrdom. Overawed by his surroundings and shy, Marco gasped when Michele told him to strip. "You mean completely—"

"Not paying you this much for you to play the shy boy. I want to see you flex muscles and stand for hours as I paint. Get undressed and stand like this…"

When nude, Marco's embarrassment provoked an impressive erection. "Sorry, master."

"Just get into the pose and keep still."

Michele had Lorenzo lie on the floor, his right arm raised, told Marco to step over Lorenzo's legs, grip his wrist and hold the stance rehearsed earlier. Marco gripped Michele's favourite sword in his right hand. Beginning with

Marco's now softening penis fixed almost on the crossing of the diagonals, Michele rapidly drew the pose, carefully measuring distances so the forward foot on the established bottom line corresponding to Christ's feet in the Calling and the upper line to Christ's shoulder, indicating where the top of the executioner's lowered head should be to ensure the figures in both paintings were the same scale. Lorenzo fell into the ideal pose, slightly foreshortened and the only instruction from Michele was to open his hand in Marco's grip.

Next day, Michele tied a loincloth around Marco's waist and asked him to tie back his hair the way he did when working on the barge. He dressed Lorenzo in a borrowed habit, black chasuble with a crimson cross over a white alb tied with a rope at the waist. Michele spent several weeks painting the central pair, leaving just the proportions of Lorenzo's head to be replaced by an appropriate model of the right age. The surrounding areas were darkened, and Michele sketched a group of figures modelled by Lorenzo, Mario and others.

The painting emerged during the next few months, including an altar and steps with a curious deep step to suggest a baptismal font to accommodate Matthew's lower arm. Although nothing near the scale of disaster of the first version, he recognised anomalies in the Martyrdom caused by the number of figures on the left side of the painting. A figure modelled by Lorenzo with arms raised in shock stumbled and drove the executioner's assistant towards the left corner of the painting, whose braced arms visually restrained the toppling figure above and those behind him. Other figures rushed from the scene, including a portrait of Mario wearing his favourite feathered hat and a self-portrait glancing back as witness to the murder, with an expression of sympathy. It was a struggle to resolve the complex interplay of light and dark but, even though satisfied with the near complete left side, it was increasingly urgent to resolve how the weight of figures on the left might be counterbalanced on the right.

About the time the Martyrdom was restarted, the temperature rose alarmingly and the atmosphere was oppressively humid. Michele sweated and stripped to his breeches to paint but, with the uncertainty about the resolution of the right side of the painting and the sweltering heat, he dismissed everyone until the unbearable weather turned cooler. For two days, he lay on the bed with the windows open and shutters closed. He tried to read by candlelight but his eyes drooped and closed every few minutes.

The next morning the sky was dark as thunderclouds massed, the humidity was almost worse than the heat and his head ached until, in the early afternoon, the storm broke. The continual crack and rumble of thunder and lightning flashes lit the room with spectral light. By early evening, the rain was so heavy San Luigi was barely visible; the wind battered the shutters and the temperature dropped by the minute until the air was refreshingly chilly. He was hungry; he quickly dressed and ran down to the piazza, threw his cloak over his head and swiftly made his way to a favourite tavern. A young lad stood in the doorway, apprehensive about stepping into the pouring rain. He smiled a roguish grin as Michele entered. He hesitated… but the lad was much too young. In any case, he noticed a familiar bardassa; they nodded to signal they might meet later.

Chapter 11
Man in Black 1599

Dark clouds encroached from the west of the city building, grey-purple mountains all day until the blessed downpour began late afternoon. Giulio rubbed my shoulder and wished me luck when I covered my head with my canvas bag and ran along the street towards the nearest tavern. In just a few minutes, my clothes were soaked, breeches stuck to my thighs and, when I ducked into the tavern, I shook the bag, adding to wet pools on the uneven stone floor. I raked my wet hair with my fingers and wiped my face with the back of my sleeve. I immediately noticed the bardassas Marco and Luca with a man I guessed was their pimp. They nodded and gestured inviting me to join them, but I shook my head and turned to the door.

The rain still poured and there was no sign of it letting up. Someone caught me by the shoulder. "Cecco, come, join us…"

I smiled at the pimp and said I was leaving but he grabbed me by the hair and dragged me towards Marcus and Luka. I struggled; the seams of my jacket cracked but the man hit me hard in the face. My legs buckled from the second blow that day. I went down but the pimp suddenly fell on top of me. A man in black stood over us. I was pushed aside as the pimp struggled to rise and stabbed with a knife but the dark man drew his sword; it flashed like lightening and the flat of the blade cracked on the pimp's head. No blood was drawn but the man was dazed. The dark man lifted me up and led me to the door, and, when we stepped into the alley, he threw his cloak over our heads.

"Won't he follow us?"

"He won't risk a fight with a swordsman." He pulled the cloak down to rest his arm on my shoulder. "D'you want to come home with me?"

I grinned. "I thought you'd never ask."

The man in black led me up the stairs to a long corridor with a door at the end where the smell of paint was overwhelming. "You're a painter."

The man quickly crossed the room to cover a large painting with a sheet before I had time to see the subject. He asked, "What's your name?"

"Francesco."

"No last name I assume." I hesitated. He pouted. "I know what it's like trying to out-run your past."

"My family name's Boneri... Francesco Boneri."

"Cecco!" He grinned. "I'm Michele... Merisi." It was a bolt of lightning. I struggled not to give away my surprise and felt the floor fall away beneath me. Despite two months searching, it was he who found me, rather than me him... as if it was somehow ordained we should meet. He was speaking. "You're shivering."

He fetched blankets and tossed a red one that draped over a high back chair beside me. I had no clear idea what Michelangelo Merisi from Caravaggio might look like, but he stripped naked before me, medium height, lithe, sallow skin, black head and body hair, a thick black bush around his cock – dark hooded eyes, full lips, neat moustache and beard. I had not imagined how he might look, perhaps expecting him to be like me, a paler Lombard. "Take off your wet clothes." I was self-conscious and mildly aroused as I stripped, aware of the early onset of my own manly hair. I occasionally glanced at him as he dried his hair on a cloth. Standing naked and shivering, I was relieved when he wrapped the red blanket 'round my shoulders.

He was draped in a deep brown blanket and rubbed my shoulders to warm me. "Since you robbed me of my supper, are you hungry?"

I nodded. We padded barefoot into the next room. He opened a cupboard where there were pieces of dry cheese, half a spicy sausage on a trencher with olives, half a loaf of day old bread and olive oil. We helped ourselves and ate standing and gulped cups of neat wine. He led me into the third room where there was a large bed and a couple of chairs. I expected to be dragged down onto the bed, but he took a chair, sat and nodded to the other. We ate in silence.

He sucked his oily fingers. "Your accent's Lombard... like mine."

"I'm from near Milan."

"Where exactly?"

"A small town you wouldn't have heard of... Bergamo... It's not far from Milan." Of course, he'd know Bergamo, but I played dumb. "You've heard of it?"

"I should, I'm from Caravaggio." He crumbled cheese onto a large piece of bread, dribbled olive oil and bit like a wolf. He chewed a long time, then swallowed and took a deep swig of wine. "So…" He belched. "You ran away from Bergamo…"

I took my time before saying, "I had to get away."

He chewed another mouthful of bread and sausage and, after swallowing, nodded. "What did you do?"

"It's nothing I did…"

He sat in silence, giving me time to race through my past to select what to say and what to omit. "My pa beat my ma. He was brutal, not just with his fists… every way. He had a son by his first woman, a half-brother. Ha, no brother to me… he was worse. He hated me and Mamma and picked on us. I can't remember any time he didn't smack or punch me for no reason. When Ma told him to stop, he beat her. She was always bruised by what passed for a husband… a father. It got so bad Ma said I should leave otherwise…" I couldn't speak for a while. "I couldn't leave her, but she said I must or both of us would be killed." I was in a daze reliving events, remembering Pa laying into Ma with his belt and me reeling, falling to the ground from a blow to the head. I didn't mention Father Gennaro.

Michele's chair creaked, and I was back in the room with the big bed beside us. I could speak no further, stood, my body trembled and my mouth silently gaped. Michele simply watched, staring with concentrated intensity. I wiped my slimy nose on the blanket and my eyes on the back of my wrist. Michele handed me a rag which I took to a chest covered in black leather in the corner and poured water into the bowl from a jug and bathed my face, using the rag to dry.

"You must be tired." I nodded. He put his wine goblet on the floor and went to the bed and slumped down. I stood, hesitant. He turned, patted the bed beside him and drew the blanket tighter around himself to signify I was safe. Still unsure, I sat on the bed and rolled into a cocoon beside Michele who, from the sound of his breathing, was already asleep. I lay awake hearing the quarter hour bells ring and the rain subside with the sound of water dripping from the eaves. It was difficult to make sense that only hours ago I was certain Michele Merisi would remain a phantom but had met him and lay beside him in a cardinal's palace. I woke feeling Michele's arms around me and lay with eyes wide until I realised he was simply comforting me. I gradually relaxed and became tearful. Apart from Mamma, no one else had protected me and held me safe.

The priest held me by the collar of my jerkin and dragged me along the corridor. By chance, the cardinal appeared in conversation with a man in livery. He glanced up, handed papers to his attendant and gestured the priest to bring me to him. I expected the worst but the cardinal smiled. "Now, chaplain, who is this?"

"I caught him stealing, Eminence."

"I wasn't stealing… I wasn't… Signor."

"You are addressing His Eminence."

The cardinal smiled again. "That's what they call me. But what do we call you, my son?"

"Francesco, Eminence. Francesco Boneri."

The cardinal laughed. "I'm Francesco too. Perhaps you might now let him go, Father. I don't think he'll run away… will you… Cecco?"

"No… Eminence."

"Now we know your name but who are you and why are you in my house?"

"I'm staying with Master Michele Merisi, the painter, I'm his…"

"A new assistant… That explains why you are here and who you are. I expect you got lost in this sometimes confusing house."

"No, Eminence, I came looking for—"

"Now we have the truth."

"Let him speak, Father. What were you looking for, Cecco?"

"I heard Your Eminence has some of Master Michele's paintings. He never lets me see what he's working on. He gets angry if I ask to see them."

The cardinal gave a wry smile. "It's Master Michele's biggest commission to date, and he is not so confident… but he will resolve the matter. I have faith in his talent but little hope he will learn a modicum of humility and patience. Now, let us find a painting by Master Michele."

He caught my hand and turned to the chaplain. "Will you join us, Father?" The cardinal led the way to the floor below where the rooms were grander with tall round arched windows with views of the piazza below. We entered a large salon where in pride of place was a painting of a boy in a white robe, offering wine to the viewer across a table strewn with fruit and a wine decanter on the left side. The boy seemed familiar; his head crowned with vine leaves. I gazed in amazement. "Michele painted this?"

"He did indeed."

"And you own it."

"I do but not for long. I had Master Michele paint it for a dear friend."

I felt the cardinal watch me as I stared at the painting. "Tell me what you see, Cecco."

I went closer. "It's Mario... the boy, and he's at a party, passing a bowl of wine to somebody – to me..." I laughed and clasped my hands. The cardinal was delighted by my reaction to my first sight of a finished painting by Michele. "It must be a festival because he's wearing vines in his hair and the leaves are yellowing... so it must be well after harvest time but before Advent, maybe Michaelmas." I stepped closer and squinted. "The fruit isn't very fresh either, seen better days and ha! I see somebody in the wine flagon, Eminence. Somebody just arrived and Mario's passing the wine to him." I turned to the cardinal. "Did I tell it right, Eminence?"

"Perfectly, Cecco, I couldn't describe it better but what if I were to tell you there is another meaning in the painting?"

"Is there, signor... Eminence?"

The cardinal came to stand beside me. "Let's say Mario is play acting. He's pretending to be the god Bacchus. No doubt you've heard of the Romans and their pagan gods?" He glanced sideways to see me nod. "To the Romans, Bacchus was the god of wine and wine makes people... tipsy, so they say, and do wild things." He saw my reaction, touched his cross and murmured a brief prayer, then opened his eyes. "Where was I?"

The chaplain prompted, "Bacchus, Eminence, the god of wine and riotousness."

"Thank you."

He spoke directly to me. "But Bacchus was not a real god, not like the one true God of Abraham, Isaac and Mary and Joseph, so Mario is pretending to be a pretend god, and you are correct, Cecco; it is a party we are seeing but why do you think the fruit is over-ripe and the vine withered?"

"Maybe it's a party for poor people."

"Ha, yes...and why not? Pitted fruit is all they can afford but that is a reminder that we will all age and wither and die. We die because we are mortal and only through the sacrifice of Our Saviour do we have the hope of eternal life." The cardinal stood in silence beside me as we continued looking at the painting.

"Eminence, who is the man reflected in the flagon?"

"The man in black might stand for all men; after all, we are all invited to the feast."

He turned to the chaplain. "Speaking of feast..." The chaplain nodded.

The cardinal touched my shoulder. "Have you eaten?"

"No, Father... Eminence..."

He smiled. "*Father* is acceptable to me, Cecco. I value my priestly vocation more than the status I have been called to." He led me and the chaplain along the corridor and into a smaller room with a table set with a platter of Bream and salad.

"I should go, Eminence, to leave you to your dinner, if somebody would show me the way back to Michele's workshop."

"Join us, Cecco, I doubt you've eaten properly today."

"Michele feeds me…"

"Father, send someone to invite Master Michele to join us, if he can spare the time." He recognised I was anxious about dining with a cardinal, unsure of proper table manners, and I glanced at my dirty fingernails.

"Come, Cecco." He went to a table where there was a jug and bowl with small neatly folded towels alongside. "Would you wash my hands?"

I lifted the jug and poured water over the cardinal's hands who washed them with soap scented with herbs and oil. I poured more water to rinse and held a towel, reminded of the altar boys in the church at Bergamo. I was surprised when the cardinal lifted the jug and poured water over my hands, handed me soap and a towel after rinsing. I took the towel and quickly dried my hands and nodded. The cardinal touched my cheek and blessed me. Being alone with him made me uneasy, expecting him to slip his hand between my legs any moment as Father Gennaro had done. I snuck a glance at the cardinal. He was handsome, I guessed barely forty with dark almost black hair cut short, neat moustache and French style little beard. His soutane was fine linen but the red piping was worn, elbows shiny and the cuffs frayed here and there. The cardinal noticed he was being appraised and smiled. The chaplain arrived with Michele, and I relaxed.

Chapter 12

Martyrdom 1600

Since the heat interrupted work, it was necessary to build momentum so he began work on the altarpiece. Matthew and the Angel was the subject, and it began well. The model for Matthew was the same as the Martyrdom and sat cross-legged on a scissors chair; the boy model leant across him, guiding the saint's hand as he wrote his gospel. The painting was complete in just over seven weeks. As agreed, Michele arranged the framing and installation above the altar covered by a curtain in preparation for its formal unveiling.

Satisfied with the finished altarpiece, he returned again to the Martyrdom. He began painting an altar boy screaming as he fled the scene to the right, with the incident in the osteria in mind. Cecco, by now, had stayed several weeks and taken under Mario and Lorenzo's wings. To earn his keep, he modelled the flight from the pimp in the painting. However, work was interrupted by Francesco's page who delivered an invitation to attend the cardinal. Following the page down the stair, the moment he entered the room, the atmosphere was far from welcoming. After kissing Francesco's hand, Michele noticed Abbate Crescenzi, trustee of the Contarelli Legacy, and two other brothers from San Luigi. He had only met the Abbate once. Francesco stood a little apart from the Abbate and Michele was unsure about the proper form so simply bowed to the Abbate and nodded to the fathers. Beyond them, he recognised the fabric that covered the altarpiece when it was delivered to San Luigi.

Francesco broke the silence. "Master Michele, the fathers at San Luigi have raised concerns about the altarpiece, the angel seeming instructive rather than inspirational and Matthew appears rather… dishevelled."

"With your permission, Eminence."

The Abbate stepped back to uncover the painting. "Master Michele, what a wonderful painting you have made and under other circumstances would grace any private chapel. However, our congregation of simple pilgrims would not understand the image you have created. I think they would be surprised, even shocked by the idea of dirty feet hanging over the altar in the face of the celebrant."

Another spoke, "The picture is indecorous and likely to upset simple congregants and frankly indecorous is not strong enough... It is vulgar."

Michele began to speak. "But Masters Peterzano and Giovan Ambrogio both painted similar poses in Milan—"

The cardinal interrupted, "I would not go so far, Fathers, to describe the painting as indecorous. I do not believe the painting strays far from Cardinal Gabriel Paleotti's *Catechism for Painters* in the matter of decorum; indeed, it is a wonderful embodiment of the teachings of the Archbishop Cardinal Borromeo in Milan, and especially the recently late father Filippo Neri who expressed the dignity of the meanest in our pastoral cares. Would you not agree, Abbate? We might further discuss Oratorian Cesare Baronio's thesis that the Matthew Gospel was written in Hebrew, the language of the people at the time of Our Lord... but rather than debate the matter, I suggest I hold the painting in trust until Master Michele paints another version taking your views into consideration."

"But wouldn't another artist... perhaps Master Cesari, after all, he painted the decoration of the chapel?"

"Master Michele has the commission and it would be an insult to both Master Michele and, without conceit, to myself since he is my protégé. What do you say, Father?"

The outspoken brother stepped forward but the Abbate continued, "Of course, Eminence, you offer a fair solution." The cardinal offered his hand to each and exchanged the kiss of peace with the Abbate. The cardinal's secretary and head page accompanied the brothers out of the room.

"Sweet Gesù, Francesco, why didn't you allow me to speak?"

The cardinal held him by the shoulders. "If you spoke in anger, you would have lost the altarpiece and perhaps the other two pictures. You have almost completed the Calling and brilliantly retrieved the Martyrdom and now you will turn a new altarpiece into a further triumph."

"They hate the reality of Matthew being just a man, they want a wooden saint... It's hypocrisy."

"Now, now! No need to slander our Christian fathers. You criticise Michelangelo for being too theatrical, make the angel inspirational and Matthew contemplative, hearing the angel who inhabits a different realm." He smiled. "Sit... sit with me, Michele, just a moment." As they sat, the cardinal closed his eyes and his lips slightly twitched as he prayed in silence.

Michele's anger and tension abated. "You're right, of course, as always."

The cardinal opened his eyes and smiled. "Bourbon blood." He laughed. "I considered how the picture being taken down might be interpreted across Rome so, when the fathers first approached with their objections, I spoke to my dear friend Marchese Giustiniani. I invited him to see the painting privately last night. He is delighted to pay the same as the fathers at San Luigi offered. I will arrange an introduction. The Marchese is a collector on a grand scale."

Francesco's prayers were not in vain as the new altarpiece fell effortlessly into shape, and Michele was excited that, although the painting followed an older iconic tradition, it was reconfigured in a modern dynamic form. Matthew was painted in a red martyr's cloak over a golden yellow robe, kneeling on a stool, writing his gospel at a desk, turning to glance upwards as a boy angel swooped down to inspire and count theological points on his fingers. The angel hovered above encircled by a swirling white fabric womb that placed him between the realms of heaven and earth, his words heard in Matthew's mind rather than seen. To emphasise Matthew's earthbound state, one leg of the stool on which he knelt hung over the edge of the picture, to create unease, even anxiety that the saint might tumble into the chapel. The canvas was taller than the earlier version to give continuity with the larger pictures. The painting was done quickly and was more fluent and engaging and Michele grudgingly admitted it was better than the earlier manifestation.

The cardinal invited the fathers to view the finished altarpiece with Giustiniani and a certain Marchese Mattei in attendance and with Francesco's permission, Michele arranged for Mario, Lorenzo and Cecco to attend. He even bought new clothes for himself and for Cecco. This time the atmosphere was vastly different, murmured conversations, smiles and occasional laughter.

The cardinal raised his hand and spoke, "Abbate, Fathers, Marchese Giustiniani, Marchese Mattei, Master Michelangelo and company, I have no doubt that all here wish to congratulate Master Michele on a remarkable painting, surely the crowning glory of the Contarelli chapel and a worthy companion to the Calling and the Martyrdom which I vouch, will be a sensation once installed."

Cecco, as the altar boy, running, screaming and glancing back wide-eyed at the dying saint added motion in contrast to the still, contemplative centre of the Martyrdom and went some way to counterbalance the weighty crowd on the left side. He spent a great deal of time on the boy's face, catching the fleeting frown and the almost audible scream in the echoing void. Nevertheless, even the addition of the screaming Cecco was not enough to balance the heavy left side and once again, work slowed as Michele hesitated.

Working direct in large scale presented unforeseen issues requiring greater ingenuity to resolve how to balance the composition of the Martyrdom and the question of the void in the Calling… to leave or to add an extra figures? Answers often came in dreams or by chance; unbidden thoughts and remembered events, like Cecco screaming as he struggled to free himself from the pimp in the tavern. Contemplating how to resolve the Martyrdom, he concentrated on the fine blood trails on Matthew's alb. The first stab would have been delivered as the saint stood at the altar so the blood ran along the line of the folds, but the second as he fell, the blood ran across the folds.

Working on the subtle thin lines of blood, the altar beyond hovered in his peripheral vision and, as details of the saint's robes were completed, the upper part of the painting above the fallen saint was suddenly revealed. He made Cecco reprise his angelic role, stripped naked and arranged on a table in a pose, leaning down with a stick in his hand to represent a martyr's palm offered to the dying saint below. He painted clouds to separate the angel from the earthly world rather than reprise swirling fabric. The addition of the angel also went some way to counterbalance the weight of the figures on the left and stabilise the painting, but there still remained an empty bottom right corner.

After almost six months, Spada returned and resumed bullying. "What's going on, Michele?" He pointed to the paintings. "Mario… Mario here, Mario there and there and who's this, this and this? All very pretty I notice… especially Jesus, and this one in the loincloth…"

"Stop this."

"Why aren't I in any of these paintings when that bardassa, what's his name… Cecco… he's everywhere."

Cecco sat up in the cot in the corner of the studio and looked fearful. Michele shouted, "You're not in the paintings, Lionello, because you weren't here. You said you'd be away a month but turn up half a year later like a bad dream. I only paint what I see, I don't work from memory."

"Bastard! You know I had a good commission, but we're not all the great Michele Merisi."

Spada demanded Michele repaint the head of the screaming boy fleeing the Martyrdom to expunge Cecco and substitute his portrait but Michele refused. Cecco's image was appropriate because his screaming, tearful face was his first memory of him at the tavern and was touched by how fearful Cecco had been as he sat exposed and vulnerable in the cot as Spada ranted. Spada flounced out without physically attacking Cecco, but the threat was real and Michele was braced to defend the boy at any cost.

The completed Calling included a back view of Spada gazing up at Christ and dressed in new costly clothes to outdo Mario; black and white doublet and white hose, a hat with red and white feathers and armed with an expensive sword, a pun on his family name; assuming it really was his name. Once finished, he regretted Spada filled the void which in truth was painted under duress. The void heightened the drama and contrast between the sacred presence of Christ and the activities of the tax gatherers. The cardinal had said as much and when Michele said the model was Lionello Spada, he merely murmured, "I see."

The two paintings were displayed in the cardinal's salon, angled to face one another. Seeing them from a greater distance than the confines of the workshop, Michele felt the Martyrdom was less successful than the Calling. The left side was a little confusing at first sight, the clouds added to support the angel a little conventional and the late addition of two nude boys at the bottom right side was a compositional necessity to add further weight and numbers to the right to balance the intense activity on the left. The boys were only half figures, over which Michele agonised for weeks. He tried to find space to paint a bench or ledge but there was no room. The cardinal cautioned that the closest boy's naked buttocks might cause offense so painted a dull green fabric to suggest a cloak which partially obscured the buttocks for the sake of modesty with the unintended benefit that a fold in the fabric echoed the line of the executioner's arm. The nudes were a direct challenge to Michelangelo's ignudi, the difference being Michele's youths joined the viewer in contemplation of the martyrdom whereas Michelangelo's slaves were theatrical participants, conscious they were observed in the business of attaching garlands of oak to the cornices. Michele's boys drew the viewer into the scene from the threshold of the painting.

When finally displayed in the church, the paintings created a sensation throughout Rome. A ceremony of blessing was arranged and Francesco officiated. Within days, Michele received a commission to paint a pair of paintings, the *Crucifixion of St Peter* and *Conversion of St Paul* for the Carasi Chapel in Santa Maria del Popolo. The cardinal also informed him he had received an approach from another high-ranking source but was not prepared to say from whom until a firm proposal was agreed and urged Michele to capitalise on the Contarelli success and start the paintings for the Carasi as soon as possible. He suggested Michele see the Michelangelo frescos and sent a message to the Vatican to arrange a viewing. Michele was delighted to meet Father Giacomo again but despite his enthusiasm, he found both frescos uninspiring. There was no relationship between the figures, the action was stilted and the steep landscapes were suffocatingly airless. However, he made several quick studies, more out of respect for Francesco and Giacomo than any enthusiasm. *When will I rid myself of this troublesome sculptor…*

Chapter 13

The Jesuit

For several days, Michele noticed Francesco was particularly light-hearted, even playful and often hummed to himself but when he raised the matter, the cardinal became coy, pouted and pressed his finger to his puckered lips. "A secret."

Work was well underway for the Cerasi but he gradually switched his attention to a commission from Cardinal Maffeo Barberini for a sacrifice of Isaac. The subject pricked the memory of Cecco pinned down by the pimp in the tavern, the flight from a murder, a silent scream, the imprint of a hand over the mouth. He stared blankly at the wall until the echo of a muffled call for help was interrupted by knocking.

It had been a long day, and, as he wiped his hands on a rag, he scanned the second version of the Conversion of Saint Paul, but, before he could concentrate on the day's work, the knocking was insistent. "Yes, what is it?"

One of Francesco's pages gently pushed the door open and, without entering, said, "His Eminence invites you to attend him."

"Francesco, what's so urgent?"

"Michele, I have a pleasant surprise for you."

"What is it?"

"All in good time but, when I present you with my gift, you must keep matters between us formal… but not too much ceremony."

Michele smiled, anticipating an introduction and possible commission from some prince of state or church. The cardinal nodded to the page who threw open the doors to the antechamber. The dark silhouette of a priest hesitated a moment before entering the salon, bowed to the cardinal and turned to Michele. "It's good to see you again after all this time, brother."

Michele stood rigid, staring at the priest and after a long silence turned to the cardinal. "Excellency, who is this man?"

"Michele, I am delighted to reunite you with your dear brother."

"It's me, Michele, Battista. it's been a while but, surely, neither of us have changed that much."

"I'm sorry, Father, but I don't have a brother."

"Michele, this is your brother, saving your presence, Father Battista. I know you have a brother; my agent made enquiries to be certain the man is who he says he is…"

The priest touched his breast and gave an unctuous bow.

"Your informants are mistaken, Excellency."

"But one of your former colleagues at Master Cesari's studio said you mentioned a brother."

"A mistake, Eminence. Whoever said such a thing confused me with someone else, so my apologies to the reverent gentleman, but I have no living brother. Sadly, he has wasted his time and his search for that poor lost soul must continue." He dreaded Francesco might mention Costanza Colonna; if he did, his denial would be impossible to maintain.

"With Your Excellency's permission, Michele, you have a history of bending the truth, but don't insult His Eminence by lying in his presence and compounding your sin with Peter's denial."

"A pretty speech, Father, but a waste of breath. It's impossible to invent what I never had."

"Please, Michele, be reunited with your kin; let there be concord here, whatever past histories."

"Francesco, you are kind to have taken such pains and I thank you but I swear…"

"Don't, Michele! Don't make a sacred oath unless it is the absolute truth." The cardinal touched Michele's lips with his finger. "Your soul, Michele – your precious soul." Visibly upset, the cardinal bowed. "I leave you together in the hope the matter may be amicably resolved." The page bowed as the cardinal left, then glanced back anxiously as he closed the heavy doors. Battista rushed towards him and smacked his face but Michele immediately retaliated with a punch that felled the priest, drew his sword and grabbed Battista's raised, defending hand.

"You would dare strike a sanctified priest. Will you attack me the way you did the sergeant? Of course you're my brother. Even older and bearded, presuming to wear the black of a gentleman, I'd recognise that evil nature anywhere."

"Bitter as ever, Battista, and stuck in a backwater parish... with me, a member of the household of a cardinal and all Roman nobility want my work."

"I've seen your disgusting paintings, the glorification of sodomy and that's what you are – a sodomite, and you accused the sergeant of your own vile practices."

"Surely, you don't still believe that dirty pederast—that bastard? No decent man, never mind a priest, would take the word of a stranger over his brother, or do you owe him favours... or maybe let you watch him bugger altar-boys in return for absolution."

Battista howled. "Filth, you're corrupt to the core. Let me up... let me up."

Michele wrenched his wrist to keep him down. "I've learned a great deal about fighting since the days we played with the Colonna boys, when you pretended to be such a good boy in front of the Lady Costanza. I see your game but you'll get no preferment from my cardinal."

"I can imagine the preferment he gives you... *travestito*!"

Michele brought the flat of the sword down hard on his head. "Francesco is the kindest soul in Rome, and I won't allow you to try to blind him with your fake piety."

"You're as evil as an English heretic."

"English heretic!" He laughed. "How many English heretics do you know... How many English do you know?" He laughed. "It's all the same, fretting about the meaning of a piece of bread or sip of wine but to finish this, you will tell Francesco you are mistaken, then fuck off."

"If I don't?"

"I'll admit you're my brother and why I am horrified by your presence because when I was a boy you and the sergeant debauched me. I swear I'll say this by the blood of Christ and the Holy Virgin."

Battista stared wide eyed. "You would jeopardise your immortal soul."

"Ha, my soul! I've nothing to lose... but you do, Battista. That you fetched up here demonstrates how desperately ambitious you are, but a scandal would put paid to that. Rome loves scandal, rumours spread fast, whether it's the truth or not... the more outrageous the lie, the more it's wished to be true and licked up and taken for proven fact." He pulled Battista to his feet, gently brushed imaginary flecks from his cassock and tapped his cheek. "I'm the most famous painter in Rome. You'll get no preferment on my back, so go home, Battista; be a big fish in a small pool, go bully schoolboys."

Without knocking, Michele entered the cardinal's private chamber.

"Eminence, Father Battista is leaving."

Francesco glanced up from his desk and Battista knelt to kiss his hand. "Excellency, I came with good intentions to reunite a brother with his family. My only wish was to arrange an advantageous marriage so he might have a normal family life and happy future. I am only sorry to have imposed upon Your Excellency's good graces and hope you understand my concern."

"Your concern does you credit, Father Battista. I hoped matters would end differently. Brotherly love is a sacred bond but, sadly, not here… not today."

As Battista stood, Michele caught his arm. "I would love to have had a brother like you. Such concern for a sibling's wellbeing. I hope you find what you're looking for." Battista merely glared back as the page ushered him from the cardinal's presence.

The cardinal slumped back in his chair. "I meant it for the best, Michele."

Michele sat on the desk. "I know you did, Francesco, and I appreciate your efforts, now and in the past."

He leant forward and kissed the cardinal's cheek. "What do you think the priest is up to, if he really is a priest?"

The cardinal eyed Michele a moment. "Apparently, he's been in Rome several years, studying moral theology at the Jesuit College before taking up a post as subdeacon… in Bergamo from memory. Near Caravaggio, I believe."

"If he's been in Rome for years, why not present himself sooner, why now if he really were my brother? Perhaps he saw the Contarelli paintings and heard I came from Lombardy?"

"Why would he take the risk you would accept him as your brother?"

Michele shrugged. "Perhaps he lost a brother… and needs to find another – a replacement." After a long silence between them, he changed the subject. "You're sprouting grey hairs, Francesco."

"Don't mock me, rascal."

"It suits you; it gives you greater gravitas. You've been the boy-cardinal long enough, Francesco."

"I'm old as the hills, my dear."

"You're young at heart and always will be and too gentle for your own good. Look at the way you indulge me."

"Since you raise the matter… and one I should have raised a while ago, Michele. You rely on my protection too much. Naturally, I'm always concerned for your welfare, as the little disaster today has shown…"

"I appreciate your kindness and good intentions—"

"Let me finish! It's come to my attention you, let's say, have become somewhat boisterous in public. You are the undoubted premier painter in Rome and should guard your status and reputation."

"I become so absorbed in my work, it demands such concentration… the standard is so high and each commission more prestigious than the last, thanks to your good offices. I have to ensure high quality work… I'm sure you understand, Eminence."

The cardinal didn't look up. "You need occasional recreation. I understand but perhaps sometimes you go too far, encouraged, no doubt by certain friends. The name Spada comes to me from various sources. What is he to you? Is he a good fellow, a good influence?"

"Lionello and I were close…"

"No details, I don't want a confession, but is he truly a good friend? Does he enrich your life or does he feed on you for his own advantage?"

Michele moved a chair to sit beside the cardinal. "He had great power over me in the past."

"Is it blackmail? Does he hold something over you? My agent informed me he knew a great deal about you and your… the Father Battista."

"What have you heard?"

"Don't be defensive… we all have matters we hope will never be seen in the light of day. I'm urging you to be cautious for your reputation. Is this influence—" Francesco noticed his page was still in attendance. "Gianni, my son, see when dinner will be served." Once the page was out of earshot, he continued, "Is it a physical attraction… is he one of the boys in the paintings?"

"He modelled for a figure in the *Calling of Matthew*, the one with the sword but a few others in the early days at the doss-house… He comes and goes but I would never let him stay. He stole from me when I was ill, but he's out of my life now." Neither spoke and the atmosphere was tense.

Eventually the cardinal sighed. "I'm reminded Vincenzo's invited. Do you have anything he might like? I suggest a St Luke, perhaps a painting within a painting, a companion for the St Matthew he took off your hands."

"For next to nothing, it was a bargain."

"Unfair, Michele; he saved your embarrassment and when Giustiniani buys anyone's work, at any price, it is good for their reputation."

"Yes, he did, and I'm grateful to him and to you too. I bet you put the idea in his mind."

Francesco glanced out the window to hide his smile. "I might have suggested something but Vincenzo's his own man… He—"

"Do I hear my name taken in vain?" Giustiniani kissed the cardinal's hand.

"Don't mock, Vincenzo. I'm rather fragile today; no need for formality."

"Precedence matters, a prince of the church over a mere Marchese."

"So where do I fall, Vincenzo?"

"Prince of painters I suppose, Michele; your namesake was called divine in his lifetime and they say the Emperor Charles picked up old Titian's brush. Perhaps I should kiss your hand too but friendship above all."

Over supper, Giustiniani discussed investments but the cardinal became uneasy when he mentioned financial ventures in which they were mutually involved, conscious of the half dozen servants waiting on them, flapping ears and no doubt, flapping tongues. "Perhaps this is for later, Vincenzo."

He glanced at the cardinal, then around the room. "Yes, yes, of course. Tell me, Michele, do you have anything for me?" He laughed. "I already have an altarpiece, but what about a secular allegory?"

Francesco pouted. "I suggested a St Luke to partner the St Matthew for your chapel."

"A wonderful idea but even better, a San Francesco, perhaps a version of the one painted by Michele… Where is it by the way?"

Francesco simply said, "Genoa."

"I would love to have seen it again."

Selections of fruit sorbets were served and the trio retired to a private salon. The cardinal dismissed the servants for the night. Giustiniani spoke barely above a whisper. "I couldn't help overhearing mention of a disturbance earlier, something about a long-lost brother."

"My fault I'm afraid, a terrible mistake. A priest from Milan approached me, claiming to be Michele's brother. It seemed plausible; I had my chaplain look into it, but the matter was complicated by a misunderstanding. A colleague of Michele's remembered another assistant had a brother, a priest from Milan, and my chaplain assumed that referred to Michele."

"I think I understand… so, Michele, he was not your brother."

"No."

"Then I assume he must have known he was in error when he saw you?"

"He believed he recognised Michele and seemed adamant they were brothers. I'm sorry for him."

"He thought his search was over, but, sadly, he's not my brother."

"I heard you were rather angry when he persisted."

"I wasn't entirely sure I was the object of his visit. He was particularly unctuous towards Francesco. I think he was seeking preferment. Had he presented himself honestly and directly, it might have been a different story... but then he is a Jesuit."

"But how presenting himself as your brother would that help him gain preferment knowing he wasn't... That's a little complicated, wouldn't you say?"

"It was obviously a carefully laid plan. Hearing of my little fame in Rome and being from near Milan I suggest he spoke to people who knew me, including my so-called friend from Cesari's workshop, who wrongly believed I had a brother and saw an opportunity to approach Francesco."

"Surely such a gamble was risky."

"Actually, I *did* have a younger brother called Giovan Pietro. This priest was from Lombardy and may have known I had a younger sibling... but what he didn't know was Pietro died in childhood after I left for Rome. Maybe he knew about the rift with my family and gambled I hadn't heard of Pietro's death. If so, might I not have presented him to Francesco as worthy of preferment and an imposter would have got a foot in the door."

Giustiniani nodded. "Yes, I think I see and I suppose one can't be too careful."

Michele glanced at the cardinal who sat back in his chair, head tilted, regarding him as though for the first time, sceptical, not taken in for a moment by lie compounded on lie but didn't ask the obvious question: *If the priest hoped to pass himself off as the younger brother, Giovan Pietro, why did he present himself as Giovan Battista?* Michele knew his argument was threadbare and Francesco's silence proved he did too and was aware he had been played; Michele had made a fool of him and at that moment he almost burst into tears, recognising everything between Francesco and he had changed forever...

"It is admirable how you protected Francesco's best interests."

Vincenzo was blithely unaware of Michele's bitter regret and Francesco's sadness. Michele was cut to the quick when Francesco simply said, "I count myself blessed knowing Michele." Francesco remained the consummate host, urbane, generous as ever and complementary to both guests, but *guest* is how Michele now felt rather than a beloved friend and family member. The room condensed to a glass globe as though seen from a great height.

He responded when appropriate but his mind was elsewhere: *Battista did this*. As ever, he had bested him and done him harm. Although Battista's ambition was checked, nevertheless he had swamped Michele's boat. Knowing Francesco well, he was not sunk; his cardinal would never abandon him but their intimacy was certainly finished. *Why would Francesco not reproach or confront me? I'd prefer his anger to his unwavering loyalty and unspoken forgiveness.* True, he was no longer dependent on Francesco's influence or financial support, even though it was certain it would always be offered but Michele could no longer accept it. He was heartbroken and miserable.

Francesco was the only loving father he had known since the sudden loss of his papa and a loving brother he had never known in Battista... a brother who used what was left of family money to pay ninety-six scudi to Master Simone not for any benefit for Michele but rather to be rid of him. Francesco never raised the matter again, remained as constant as ever, but Michele could no longer bear the thought that light had penetrated the depth of his soul. Shame was the cause of his retreat and fury towards Battista that the deep scar inflicted upon his younger self by the sergeant had been torn open by his unwelcome reappearance.

The cardinal's love and support never wavered, but Michele's reaction to Battista and his denial caused great embarrassment, knowing Francesco had taken such pains to bring siblings together, only to have his kindness and generosity thrown in his face. Since their meeting, Francesco's calm generosity of spirit was an example he ached to follow in the mould of Father Filippo Neri. Occasional hooliganism was indulged by the cardinal so long as previous sins and crimes remained unknown. Battista was in possession of intimate details of Michele's past life which he hoped he had shed during the arduous pilgrimage to Rome a decade ago. His violent response to his nemesis raised smoke that indicated a smouldering secret that might easily be fanned into a bonfire likely to consume his career.

Another matter bound to come to light soon to further embarrass Francesco concerned Frederico Zuccari, president of the Accademia di San Luca, who briefly visited the Contarelli Chapel with a colleague Giovanni Baglione. At San Luigi, Zuccari sneered at Michele's paintings and, to Baglione's delight, turned his back on them. When relayed to Michele, he laughed, savouring the fact that if they so hated his work, it betrayed their petty envy.

That would have been the end of the matter, but Michele heard a young member of the accademia, a certain Girolamo Sampa, a sycophant of both Zuccari and Baglione, gloated and repeated Zuccari's slurs. Sampa had an eye on advancement at the academy but Michele was not prepared to allow the insult to go unpunished. He scoured the neighbourhood near the accademia several nights until he found Sampa and, when alone in a dark alley, gave him a severe beating. During the attack, Michele unsheathed his sword and Sampa wrapped his cloak around his arm, so the thickness of the fabric rather than flesh received the slash. His intention was his usual practice to hit Sampa with the flat of the blade but the fight became scrappy. Lights appeared at the entrance to the alley and Sampa shouted for help. At risk of being outnumbered, Michele swiftly left but not before he was recognised.

Although the case was brought to court, the matter was taken no further, and Michele was satisfied. He had answered Zuccari with a violent response and sent a clear message to Baglione and the accademia. However, the incident was forever recorded: *19th November 1600 AD arrested for assault: Michelangelo Merisi da Caravaggio, a painter living in the house of the Most Illustrious and Reverend Cardinal del Monte assaulted student Girolamo Sampa with a stick and sword...*

Francesco undoubtably heard of the attack and other violent acts leading to brief stays in the Tor di Nona prison and frequent arrests for carrying weapons. Nevertheless, Francesco remained loyal and arranged Michele's early release each time without hesitation, compounding Michele's shame.

Chapter 14

Angels and Boys

Seeing Michele was about to start work, I quickly pulled on my breeches and jerkin and tidied the cot. I was about to leave when Michele asked, "Where are you going?"

"You're working." Since meeting the night of the storm, I usually shared Michele's bed but occasionally slept in the middle room if he was restless, which was often, until Spada… Lionello Spada, appeared and told me to sleep on the cot in the workroom. Each day, I left the palazzo to explore the highways, byways, churches, taverns, workshops and wharves. Michele gave me a few denarii and occasionally a soldi or two if I had modelled. I hesitated at the door.

"Stay." I was surprised by the invitation and more so when I was allowed to see all the paintings in the workshop. I wondered if Michele knew the cardinal had shown me the Bacchus. Mario lifted the sheet covering the painting on which Michele was working. When the image was revealed, I gasped, not simply in awe of the scale but also the sensation of looking into an adjacent room where the figures were as real as those in the world this side of the canvas.

Michele asked, "What d'you think?"

I stared at the canvas but couldn't find words to describe what I was seeing or what I thought. "It's like the cardinal's picture… but realer."

Michele laughed and nudged Mario. "*Realer*."

"I meant…"

Michele slipped his arm over my shoulder and drew me close. "I know what you mean; you can stay while I work if you like."

I nodded, then looked back at the painting and this time noticed it was suspended by a spider's web of strings to a frame. "What's that?"

Michele glanced at the painting. "The strainer…The canvas has to be stretched in all directions before it is prepared and ready to paint on, otherwise it will sag or ripple. When I'm finished, Mario and Lorenzo will nail it to a frame and, when gilt-framed, it will look as neat as Francesco…

the cardinal's picture." He paused a moment. "The painting shows Gesù calling Matthew the tax collector to be his disciple. See, the light from behind Christ falls on Matthew and his fellows caught in the act calculating how much of the taxes they can rake off for themselves."

Mario told me later he had never heard Michele take pains to explain his paintings. "He certainly likes you."

Michele usually slept fully dressed, indeed rarely changed his clothes and fell exhausted into bed whether he had worked for hours with barely a break or spent half the night crawling from tavern to osteria, becoming louder and drunker by the hour. He only went carousing between paintings to dispel the tension of acute concentration necessary to create the finished image.

The morning dawned. Yesterday, Michele worked from first light until almost midnight, and I was exhausted, having modelled the first time, by my calculation, over fourteen hours. The altarpiece for the chapel in San Luigi was well advanced when Michele got me to pose for the angel perched on a high table, swathed in swirling white linen tacked to a makeshift frame, counting off points of theology on my fingers to Matthew who turned towards me, pausing as he composed his gospel. The saint was dressed in a red-orange robe kneeling on a stool at a narrow table, poised to hear inspiration from the angel swooping from above.

Mario said Michele didn't like painting angels; he thought it was ridiculous but was persuaded by the cardinal who said the writer of the Matthew gospel was represented by one of the four creatures surrounding God's throne in the Book of Revelation. Matthew was represented by the form of a human, depicted as an angel in the painting. He said the other three creatures were the lion of Mark, eagle of Saint John and the calf of Luke. I particularly liked the altarpiece, not just because I was the angel but it was the first time I modelled for him. I posed almost a week until he turned his concentration to the billowing drapery separating me, the angel in the heavenly realm, from Matthew in this world. I also modelled for two figures in the Martyrdom painting, another naked angel leaning down from above the altar to offer Matthew his martyr's palm.

Posing was painful; my ribs and hip bruised after a week of straining to hold the twisting pose, lying for days on my left side on a table. There had been rest times and meals at midday and early evening but leaning almost to the floor from the table caused cramps and my entire left side still ached by morning. I examined my side which was bruised and remembered Mario saying there would be further days and probably more until Michele was satisfied. The other figure I modelled for the Martyrdom was a screaming altar boy fleeing the scene, looking back in horror. I was pleased to be part of such important paintings but, when Spada returned, he made my life miserable, called me a bardassa and tried to make Michele send me packing, but Michele wouldn't hear of it.

Michele lay awake staring at the ceiling. "I'm bruised, look." He turned to see where I pointed to my left side which carried most of the weight of my body.

"I see."

"I can't go on; it's too painful."

"Mario will arrange more cushions, and they'll strap the wings on you today." He seemed distracted but I risked mentioning I heard the first version of altarpiece had been turned down. I was surprised when he stopped, turning his hand in arcs and, without looking at me, simply said, "The Fathers said the painting was indecorous and the saint looked gormless." He grinned. "They were upset because the angel was guiding Matthew's hand as though he was an imbecile. The cardinal saved the day and one of his grand friends bought the picture."

That confirmed what Mario and Lorenzo told me but omitted the ripe language. He was probably more confident now that the other paintings had progressed so well. Many years later, it occurred to me that Michele and the cardinal were like paired carriage horses; the cardinal's influence helped Michele win the Contarelli commission, putting His Eminence's reputation as a connoisseur on the line. It was a leap of faith since Michele had not painted such large pictures before and, if he failed, the cardinal would have been embarrassed and Michele's career would have suffered serious setback. I often overheard him say such-and-such a painter would surely be ashamed to show such-and-such a painting in public. It explained why he worked so hard with such intensity and anxiety and, when a painting reached near completion, he spent hours examining the painting, searching for the slightest flaw to ensure he was never embarrassed. Once the paintings for the Contarelli Chapel were installed, Michele relaxed and was more rested after sleep, unbroken by pacing the workshop, candle in hand, fretting over a detail in the painting. From our first meeting, he appeared confident but now it was less a pose. He was increasingly preoccupied with the next commission of a pair of paintings for the Cerasi Chapel in Santa Maria del

Popolo and, as he began, his mood became tetchy as tension mounted and, again, he became increasingly withdrawn and rarely spoke.

I watched Mario and Lorenzo at work with great attention to learn how they stretched canvases. My pa always worked on pine wood and, although preparation was similar, it was necessary to apply many more layers of gesso to make an ivory smooth surface. On the other hand, canvas was prepared with glue, then gesso and a dark base coat that preserved the weave of the canvas. I not only committed everything to memory but made notes with little drawings to show the way they pierced the canvas about a palm width from the edges with thick strings, drawing the string over the strainer frame, then looping the string through the next hole in the canvas and over the strainer again, repeated at a leisurely pace, stretching the canvas from opposite sides until not only creases were pulled out but the canvas sounded like a drum when tapped. They eased the tension very slightly before wetting the canvas and applying gum Arabic. Lorenzo said the canvas would shrink overnight as the gum dried and, after another coat, they applied several layers of gesso. The glue and gesso filled the holes in the warp and weft of the canvas and, after a couple of days, allowing the surface to thoroughly dry, they applied the first of three base coats of burnt umber. The process took almost three weeks to allow each layer to thoroughly dry before Michele began working on the paintings. In the meantime, Marchese Vincento Giustiniani's liveried servants collected the rejected altarpiece which had been covered, stored out of sight in the middle store room and I noticed Michele left the workshop hours before it was collected.

I stood tiptoe to try to see over the head and shoulders of the crowd of dignitaries, aristocrats and clerics pressing towards the chapel. The Contarelli was the fifth chapel from the west doors, on the left near the sanctuary between the Chapel of the Blessed Virgin and the Chapel of the Blessed Sacrament in the church of San Luigi dei Francesi. Lorenzo, Mario and Filippo Triesegni lifted me up but, even so, it was impossible to see Michele's paintings from where we stood halfway along the nave. The crowd pushed back to make passage for the fathers of San Luigi who processed from the vestry towards the chapel. The fathers led the Contarelli family sponsors, Papal delegate and, finally, Cardinal del Monte, who held Michele's hand high as he arrived at the chapel to begin the ceremony. *In Nomine…*

We crossed ourselves and said amens but, thereafter, although we heard the voices of the cardinal, the senior father at San Luigi and other grandees speak, we could not make out what was said except for brief silences between speeches and amens that followed prayers of dedication. I saw the cardinal sprinkle the paintings with rosemary dipped in holy water. The ceremony was brief, barely twenty minutes and closed with applause for Michele who left with the cardinal and sponsors. The lads and I left the church since it was obvious it would be hours before the crowd dispersed and decided to return later to see the paintings with a clearer view of them in situ. As candles were extinguished, the darkening church smelled of new wood, paint and incense. We saw the Lady Costanza Sforza-Colonna and other high-ranking dignitaries talking to Michele as they left the church.

"He's not really one of us any longer." It was a strange comment but Mario continued, "He lives somewhere between us and the aristocrats and high priests, not one of us but not one of them either."

The church slowly emptied, and we stood aside until we were able to make our way along the aisle to the chapel which appeared to open like a book as we approached. The chapel was lit by a score or more flickering candles that animated the figures as they loomed out of the walls with even more presence than in daylight. There was little time for us to take in the magnificence of the finished paintings before we were shooed out of the church by two of the fathers who took us for ruffians bent on stealing alms or, more likely, valuable candles.

Outside the church, we met Spada. "Ho, Mario, Lorenzo, Filippo… and the bardassa! So, Michele's shagging him now; how his standards have fallen."

"I'm no bardassa and at least I'm not a lowlife pimp like you."

The lads pulled me back, expecting a violent reaction from Spada, but he merely laughed, tapped my cheek. "It's well past bedtime for this child." He turned and went to the church as the priests were closing the doors. We could not hear what was said until Spada raised his voice. "I'm Michele Caravaggio's friend and companion and have come to see the paintings." The doors were slammed in his face. Spada stood rigid a few moments before running, kicked the door and shouted, "Fucking bastards, sons of whores, boy fuckers…" and further ranting insults until the door suddenly opened and a father stepped out and hit Spada over the head with a stick.

Spada was taken aback, clutched his head and rushed screaming at the priest who caught him again across the face with the stick, grabbed him by the scruff of his neck, turned him around and kicked his arse. "Now piss off." When Spada hit the ground, the lads and I whooped, laughed and clapped. The priest tucked the stick under his arm, ignored our applause and calmly walked back into the church and the Piazza San Luigi rang with the sound of the door slammed and bolted.

Cardinal Nephew Scipione Borghese gave Michele the opportunity to lay the ghost of his namesake Michelangelo for once and all. The pope's nephew, recently elevated to cardinal, was anxious to have a painting by Michele, of whom he had heard good reports and, naturally, Francesco made the introduction. Borghese wanted a St John the Baptist, in the traditional form of a boy with a lamb.

Before starting the painting, Michele took me to the Sistine Chapel in the Vatican. He pointed. "There, the one leaning back terrified. That's the pose I want... See how the legs are spread, then the body twists with the near arm moving away from the viewer? Remember it."

In the workshop, Michele set up a low plinth with cushions covered with a red cloak, a sheepskin, a linen sheet and pulled and prodded me into the pose, leaning much further back than the Sistine ignudo with my right arm supported by a rope tied to my wrist, the other end nailed to the wall. He arranged the shutters so the light fell at a steep angle.

The painting was done at a steady, rhythmic pace with no revision or second thoughts. The most difficult task for me was to keep my head looking over my shoulder at Michele. I held the pose for hours with few breaks and felt the tension and aches in my hips, occasionally causing cramps or spasms but there was no sympathy. He roared at me to stop constantly twitching but later admitted my moving revealed subtle anatomical details of shoulder blade, ribs and exposed hip bone and ripples under the skin, easily recorded as they occurred and admitted my constantly changing facial expressions kept the pose animated and fresh. Michele made further studies of a ram at the holding pens, its head and fleece harmonised with the golden glow of my painted flesh. The ram's head closely dovetailed into the space between my head and raised arm and like the *Boy Bitten by a Lizard*, the geometry of the young Baptist was a dynamic Z form, with a background of dark foliage and the branch of a tree barely visible in the shadows. Apart from the Baptist and the ram, the only other detail was a Verbascum Mullein plant, which flowered around the time of the feast of St John on the twenty-fourth of June. The dominant pattern of colour was gold, white with a deep rich vermillion red cloak and contrasting textures of flesh, fleece, pelt, woollen and cotton fabrics. I was only allowed to see the painting when it was finished. "You made me look like a kid... My cock's bigger than that."

A second version was commissioned by Prince Doria Pamphilj. I groaned. "I don't have to sit again?"

"No, I'm having the painting returned to be traced."

Apparently, the Papal Nephew was flattered it would be copied, presumably adding to the value of the original. I had never seen tracing paper made before. Lorenzo used the thinnest paper and polished oil over the surface so that, when dry and pressed against the painting, outlines of forms and shapes were faintly visible through the now translucent paper. Michele traced the outlines with thin charcoal, occasionally lifting the paper where edges were indistinct. Once the tracing was complete, it was turned over and rubbed with chalk, then reversed again and laid on the canvas prepared with a dark umber base. A blunt metal stylus scored the charcoal outlines onto the base. When the paper was removed, the ghostly image appeared comprising broken and unbroken white lines, often reduced to a series of dots, which Michele linked applying black outlines, rubbing away the chalk ahead of the bristles. It was a good day's work and I was intrigued to see the finished painting beside the same image reduced to skeletal outlines and, thankfully, Michele working from the original painting meant, apart from occasional sessions, I had little modelling to do.

A further interpretation of the Baptist with the ram was commissioned with the stipulation: *in your usual manner but more discreet...* Michele said I needed time to recover from the aches and cramps and thought to ask Mario to model, but he was increasingly preoccupied courting the young woman he was preparing to marry. I was startled the evening Michele returned with a boy in tow. Another of the flotsam and jetsam feeding the city's underbelly with the same tale as any country lad come to find fame or fortune or escape their past. His name was Gianni, or so he said, a farm boy with a strong Furlan dialect, recently arrived from near Udine in the Veneto from a scattering of homesteads not worthy of a name. Michele said the youth, I guessed he was about nineteen, had nowhere to stay and offered a meal and bed for the night. He slept in a small cot where Mario or Lorenzo slept if they were too tired or tipsy to go home. Michele tossed Gianni a blanket and went to bed in the next room. I followed him but slept in the chair. Gianni's milky white torso was in stark contrast with his ruddy face and arms, the stigmata of honest labour.

As the painting progressed, Michele stripped away anything superfluous, the background brown monochrome with a reed cross and begging bowl and wrapped a white sheet around Gianni's waist, which, drawn tight against his groin, led the eye up the inner thigh, which slyly drew attention to the teasing eroticism of the pose. Of course, Gianni, was available, and I saw Michele relished ravishing him with his eyes the way the cardinal's chaste sensibilities were perhaps heightened by paintings, music and poetry. The swirling folds of the red cloak, the colour of desire as much as martyrdom, contrasted the stillness of the figure. The painting was less a religious image but rather the spiritual elevation of an ordinary youth, his head tilted downwards with a sideward glance as though contemplating something beyond the painting.

As I half-expected, the painting was rejected but Michele was not unduly displeased and it remained with him for several months. Without doubt, the version of Saint John modelled by Gianni, apart from the two versions I modelled, was among the best and most mature to date where incongruities of style, covert eroticism and the spirituality were seamlessly drawn together in perfect unity. Michele found other waifs to model versions of youthful Baptists. I cannot deny I was jealous, particularly of Gianni, because I could tell Michele liked him but, recalling Spada's fits of jealous tantrums, I kept my feelings to myself. After all, they came and went but it was me who carried his sword when we went for supper or met the usual crowd and held his cloak when he was in a scrap.

When the copy of the Baptist was finally finished, I stared intently, astonished by the way the light raked my body from high on the left, highlighting the shoulder, hip, legs and the ram's head, casting the torso to the groin in shadow. I could not say which of the two versions I preferred, even side by side, there was little difference between them. Once dry, Michele sent messages to the Papal Nephew and Prince Doria Pamphilj, informing them their paintings were finished.

Chapter 15

Supper at Emmaus 1601

And it came to pass, as he sat at meat with them, he took bread, and blessed it, and brake it, and gave it to them. And their eyes were opened, and they knew him; and he vanished out of their sight... Luke 24:31

Since his arrival in Rome less than a decade earlier, Michele was confident that not since the unveiling of Michelangelo's Sistine frescos had there been such a fuss over a suite of paintings. The Contarelli paintings were feted and depreciated in equal measure, dividing broadly on generational lines, but what Michele found most satisfying was hearing his name mentioned in every church, palace, tavern and street corner and, especially the temple of rumours, the Piazza Navona. Undoubtably, he was now the most famous painter in Rome but, determined not to be known as the second Michelangelo, he decided, like Leonardo, to adopt the town of his childhood, insisting friends, supporters and allies call him *Caravaggio*. Adversity had propelled him from a minor painter to greatness, equal to not only Leonardo but also Michelangelo and Titian.

A friend of Francesco, the Marchese Ciriaco Mattei, commissioned a Supper at Emmaus for his private chapel on the strength of the Contarelli paintings. The Marchese was a member of a powerful family of three fraternal households, living in adjoining residences similar to an ancient Roman Insula surrounding the Piazza Mattei. The triple palace was home to Cardinal Girolamo Mattei, younger brother of Marchese Ciriaco and the youngest of the brothers by a decade was Asdrubale. The three brothers were immensely wealthy by inheritance, increased by advantageous marriages and astute investments.

Introduction to the Mattei created an opportunity for Michele to leave Francesco's household on the pretext that there was more space in the Mattei palace. The commission for the Supper coincided with another from the cardinal brother Girolamo Mattei, who wanted an altarpiece on the subject of the death of the Virgin for the church of Santa Maria della Scala. However, Michele did not mention to Francesco he was leaving until the *Supper at*

Emmaus was well underway and from shame had avoided the cardinal for several months. He knew he would greatly miss Francesco's subtle mind, theological acumen, kindness, fraternal and avuncular loyalty for whom, for a season, he tried to be the best he could.

Finally, Michele begged an audience with Francesco to discuss the theological importance and meaning of the Supper, the biblical early post-crucifixion reappearance of Christ. Francesco became eloquent as he addressed the theology of Jesus, cloaked in anonymity, hearing the grief of the disciples as they walked from Jerusalem, offering hope, and finally breaking bread in a characteristic manner that led to his recognition as the resurrected Christ. The meal re-enacted the Last Supper and confirmed the Mass as the central rite of Holy Church. In addition, the subject was a powerful statement of Catholic Counter Reformation doctrine, specifically the miraculous transubstantiation of the host when consecrated bread and wine miraculously become flesh and blood of the risen Christ.

Francesco went on to stress a direct correlation between the ubiquitous presence of the body of Gesù and the bread and wine of the Mass. He asked Michele to hand him a Testament. "Not that. I mean the old Latin Bible and carefully read and translated the gospel texts. In St Luke, we read: *And it came to pass, as he sat at meat with them, he took bread, and blessed it, and brake it, and gave it to them. And their eyes were opened, and they knew him; and he vanished out of their sight."* He gave Michele time to contemplate the text, then continued, "There is also an oblique reference to the blessed presence in the gospel of Matthew: *For where two or three are gathered together in my name, there am I in the midst of them.* So, my dear, the Emmaus encounter refers to Our Lord's earthly ministry and in our present time, indeed… all time."

The cardinal sat at the desk on which Michele perched when he denied his brother and there was a catch in his voice when he responded, "You gave me meat, drink and took me in when I was a stranger…"

Francesco gently squeezed Michele's hand. They avoided eye contact. Michele coughed and quickly continued, "Who are the disciples mentioned in the text? Cleopas and Simon. Is that Peter, Simon Peter?"

"It's not clear."

They talked until the sun set and, when the cardinal bade him goodnight, Michele hesitated, then said goodbye and hurried away. He spent the evening alone at an osteria where he barely touched supper. The following days and nights were spent raking the inns and taverns for models, having decided Gesù in the Emmaus painting should have the same presence as Michelangelo's Sistine Chapel Christ and the disciples would be rough labourers. He found Simon Peter at a bar near the Tiber. The man, Eufrasio, was in his late forties, a tanner who stank to high heaven but matched the character he had in mind and conformed to the traditional type with thinning hair, high forehead, slightly hooked sunburned Roman nose and greying beard. Cleopas appeared in the form of Ermanno, an unkempt teacher with a ragged beard. He said he knew of the painter Caravaggio and offered to sit for meals and the chance to watch Michele paint.

The Christ figure was elusive and, after searching almost a month, he considered asking the model for Gesù in the *Calling of Matthew*, but he was nowhere to be found. The matter was unexpectedly resolved when Cecco and he were drinking at a bar in Trestevere. Michele casually glanced around but still no one matched the model in his mind but, cutting through the din, he heard a thick resonant Neapolitan voice behind him speak with quiet command. "Waiter… more wine." Without turning and from the tone of his confident but gentle voice, he was sure he was his model.

Michele tapped Cecco's hand who sat opposite and jerked his head. "What d'you think?"

Cecco glanced over Michele's shoulder, stared a moment, then grinned and nodded. Michele slowly turned and looked at the solid frame, thick neck and full clean-shaven face… Handsome but maybe a little too fond of pasta.

"Who're you lookin' at?"

"I'm looking at the face of Christ Our Lord." Neapolitan crossed himself.

His name was Calimero. He agreed to model and was anxious to get started. Mario and Lorenzo had prepared a canvas with a dark base coat in tempera. Michele used two measuring sticks converging from a horizontal to be the front edge of the table, the triangle of equal lengths was to meet at the apex where Christ's head would be. The equilateral triangle created a stable, calm centre, containing Calimero's sheer size and easy authority. When shown the pose, he instinctively raised his right hand to shoulder-level in blessing and, without lifting his elbow from the table, hallowed the bread with his lower left hand. Michele moved the lower hand until it resembled that of Christ in the Sistine Last Judgement. Once Calimero assumed the role of Christ, his other models began to act their parts. The two disciples sat on Savonarola chairs from the attic and Michele rehearsed the story, that Christ should remain in pose and Cleopas and Simon focus on him. The silence of the room was heightened by the slight creak of the scissor chairs, Michele slapped the measuring stick on the table with a cannon crack. Calimero slightly twitched but Eufrasio was startled, threw out his arms and Ermanno on the left griped the arms of his chair as he struggled to rise…

"Hold that… hold and remember."

He quickly brushed the outlines on the canvas in raw umber until the models became too fidgety to continue. Progress on the Emmaus was put off by the looming deadline to complete the Cerasi commission. He rejected the first versions, having followed too closely the Michelangelo frescos in the Pauline Chapel. The commission specified the pair be executed on wood, unsympathetic to his evolving style which needed the resistance of canvas rather than the smooth surface in near icon technique of thin layers of pigment. Worse was the figure of Christ, barely supported by an angel appearing to crash to the ground. Fortunately, it was agreed the final painting and its companion, Conversion of Saint Paul, could be done on canvas, which allowed him to work rapidly and, with ideas and preparations for the Emmaus commission coming together, the Cerasi paintings required only final details to complete.

Michele ordered a dais for the Emmaus painting to raise the set and characters to match the height the painting would be seen above the Mattei chapel altar from the position of a kneeling celebrant. The wall in the workshop was illuminated from the upper left from the highest open shutter, all the lower closed so the wall was raked by light. The set was arranged, a table draped in a borrowed Holbein rug covered with a white tablecloth. Michele directed Mario to place items on the table, a still life with small bread rolls, a jug with a glazed vine motif, a carafe of pure water, a high polished small pot which reflected light from the tablecloth and in the middle a roast chicken. Michele gestured left or right, closer or back as Mario moved each object until Michele was satisfied. He then placed a basket of fruit close to the edge of the table, inching it closer until a third of the basket precariously overhung the table and, by chance, cast a shadow in the shape of a fish.

Hearing of the construction of a dais, the cardinal's curiosity was pricked. He sent his page with an invitation for Michele to join him for supper. Michele expected the meeting might be tense. When they first met, their initial friendship rapidly transformed from patron and protégé into a many layered accretion of lover and beloved and more than friendship, espousal.

Early days in the cardinal's household, Michele expected physical favours would be required in return for the cardinal's unstinting labours on his behalf. Francesco was a handsome man whom Michele found attractive but matters were resolved one evening as they talked into the early hours and Francesco suggested they should retire. He gave Michele his usual kiss on both cheeks but Michele caught Francesco's face in his hands, kissed his cheek and then his mouth. The kiss lasted seconds until Francesco stepped back. "Bless you, Caro, but, as much as I would dearly love… I made a vow of celibacy."

Michele grinned. "Don't all priests?"

Francesco smiled, then gently took Michele's hands. "But, for me, that vow is absolute. I am member of a louche circle where priests, bishops, and, I dare say, popes break vows of chastity, but I am blessed with the grace of celibacy. I cannot judge those who struggle with such temptation and fall short of Christ's example since I fall short in many other ways."

He glanced at the *Concert of Musicians*… "Beautiful things not the least among them." But in the months since the unwelcome appearance and rejection of his brother and the cardinal's care and generosity bringing them together, Michele felt exposed by the light that penetrated the gloom in his recent paintings. That he had remained at the Palazzo Madama indicated his loathing to leave behind what he considered a new life, having shed the past and memories of dark alleys.

On his arrival at the salon, they embraced and were hardly seated before Francesco asked, "I imagine the Cerasi is finished?"

"Ah, the Cerasi." He laughed. "A priest at Santa Maria del Popolo asked why I put the horse in the middle of the painting and Saint Paul on the ground. Does the horse represent God?"

"Your reply?"

"No, but he stands in the light of God."

"Bravo! Francesco tapped his knife on the rim of his wine glass. But I'm impatient to hear about the Emmaus."

"It's going well. It is still above if you ever wish… I value your insight and miss…"

"I am always here, Michele." They sat in silence a moment.

To break the slight atmosphere, Michele continued, "I copied Christ's gestures from the Sistine Last Judgement, as he blesses the food and wine and hallows the table, which, as you said, represents the altar in remembrance of Abraham's offering of Isaac."

He spoke so fast it became a gabble, the words spilled and tumbled. "The white tablecloth is Jesus' shroud and the table represents the slab on which he was laid in the tomb. I dressed Christ in a red robe with an ivory cloak wrapped around him to indicate he is both sacrifice and High Priest. The bread and wine represent the Mass, of course, and the true presence. *He that eateth my flesh, and drinketh by blood, dwelleth in me and I in him.*" By now, Michele was breathless and close to tears, rushing to let Francesco know how much he valued his learning and support and regretted his betrayal. He knew it was the end of the dearest friendship he ever had and dare not look up at the cardinal who would see his eyes were red and spilled tears. It would be wrong to appeal to Francesco's limitless pity and to let him see how remorseful he felt.

After a long crackling silence, Francesco cleared his throat. "Wonderful. You listened and contemplated, and more. When may I see the finished painting?"

"Allow me a few more weeks."

"Deferred pleasure."

Between lengthy periods staring at the painting, he paced the room, flicking attention between the painting and the still life… He mumbled the significance as though reciting his catechism, clear water, bread and wine, elements of the Eucharist, vine tendril pattern in blue on the white glazed jug with a carafe of clear water beyond. A glass of diluted wine every altar boy knew was the blood and water sprayed from Christ's final wound from the spear thrust. Among the fruit in the basket teetering on the edge of the table, grapes, further reference to wine and to Christ himself in the St John gospel: *I am the true vine, and my father is the husbandman.* Michele had pinned Biblical references on the wall from a Bible in Italian, loaned by Francesco. He frequently studied them, then returned to stand before the unfinished painting. The two disciples, Cleopas on the left, seen three-quarters from the back, and, on the right, Simon Peter called by Christ to be a fisher of men, his identity suggested by the cockleshell badge on his greasy leather jerkin. A bright white cloth twisted and wrapped around his waist represented the towel Christ wrapped around his waist when he washed the disciples' feet at the Last Supper. It was a gesture of humility and obedience and anticipated Peter's future priestly role as Bishop of Rome, his arms flung wide in a pre-figuration of his own later crucifixion. Eufrasio, as Peter was similar to the man described in the gospels, explosive, given to dramatising but endearingly human. Cleopas, realised by Ermanno, a quiet man who instinctively gripped the arm of the chair and, although in three-quarter back, his surprise was realised in his raised eyebrows and dropped jaw. Michele had torn the dark olive-green coat over the right elbow to reveal the white shirt beneath to indicate poverty and like Peter's hand appeared to project out of the painting.

Del Monte contemplated the *Emmaus* with great attention, certain it was the last painting Michele would complete under his roof. Michele glanced alternately at the cardinal and the painting but it was difficult to gauge his thinking. He stepped forward to examine details several times, with great attention and read the biblical texts Michele had selected and pinned to the wall. He took down several of the sepia studies. Noticing his page's interest, he handed them to him. "Guido, what do you think?"

"Me, Eminence?"

"You, Guido, yes."

"I like the disciples but I don't recognise Our Lord; it doesn't look like him."

"What does Our Lord look like?"

"He's slim and handsome and has lovely eyes."

"You have seen Our Lord, Guido?"

"Yes, in the churches, Excellency. Master Michele's Gesù in San Luigi is more like him."

"Now, Master Michele, have you seen Our Lord?"

"Indeed, I have, Eminence, in the street, in the taverns and the markets in the joiner's yard, the stables and the barges on the Tiber, the beggar at the door, the kind old woman in the fish market and, very occasionally, the rare, good priest."

The cardinal laughed. "And the occasionally ill-tempered artist."

Michele offered the page a coin.

"Thank you, master, but could I have one of the drawings instead?"

"Why not. Take your pick and keep the coin."

Guido chose one of the sepia studies, nodded and genuflected to the cardinal and left.

"He's a good boy. I wish at least I had once been as innocent."

"Don't be so hard on yourself, Caro."

"You haven't said what you think of the painting, Francesco."

"Let's sit." Michele put the two scissor chairs close together. "You notice I hesitate. My first reaction, as always, is astonishment. It is a tour de force, as you well know. Your technique is even more improved from the

Contarelli paintings and your interpretation of the subject is original and engaging."

"But…"

He touched Michele's arm. "Don't be concerned, this is not the same as the San Luigi altarpiece. In fact, I would say this is the painting in which you address deep truths about faith, perhaps your first truly religious painting. By that I mean you have put much thought into symbolism but subtly disguised rather than trumpeted about. You focussed on the subject without distractions, the rather alluring executioner and pretty boys… but my point is that, in this painting, Christ has come to minister to sinners, not the high and mighty, like me and my kind."

"You're a good man, Francesco… a simple pastor to those in your care, a true servant, not a master."

"Stop, stop, Michele; spare my blushes."

"It's true… you treat your page as if he were your child, and I've never been treated so well, not by kin, clerics or masters… my mother Lucia excepted and the Lady Costanza."

The cardinal stood and gently held Michele's shoulders. "We are here to discuss the painting and, when you invited my opinion, you said you thought there is something incomplete about the picture. From studying the painting closely, I humbly suggest there are two things you might consider. When we spoke, you said that despite the disciples' gestures, the painting remained static, and I agree. The triangle at the centre of the painting contains the theology of the Holy Trinity, the Incarnation, and the sacrament of the Mass, the ubiquitous presence of the body of Christ… I'm no painter and do not understand the mysterious processes which brings a work of art into being and am of little help, except for what you said just moments ago when you mentioned the pastoral duty of service." He slipped his hand into his cassock pocket and withdrew a small book of the gospels, flicked pages and began to translate: "From the gospel of John, we read: *He rose from supper, laid aside his garments, took a towel and girded himself… poured water and washed the disciples' feet, wiped them with the towel with which he was girded.* You have referred to that passage with the cloth around Peter's waist but before I go on… if I trace the lines of the triangle, all but Christ's right hand raised in blessing, falls inside the equilateral triangle. How aware are you of that?"

Michele shrugged. "Why is it significant?"

"Nominate the Holy Trinity."

"Father, Son and Holy Spirit."

The cardinal raised the gospel. "Within the Trinity, how does St John describe Our Lord?"

"The Word."

"Yes, *Logos*. The Word made flesh and it was the Logos who *spoke* the creation and who also entered the world for our salvation. Christ, therefore, is one with the Trinity but also one with creation... not to rule but to serve."

"I don't follow."

"Let me put it this way: the perfection of the Holy Trinity was changed by the creation. Each stage of creation was uttered – let there be light, matter, dry land, vegetation, animals and, ultimately, mankind. The perfection of creation being that man is no slave but has free will, the tragedy being that free will begat the worm of self will." Francesco noticed Michele frown. "I'm sorry, my dear, I'm one of those useless theologians but what I mean is that to emulate the creative force of the Word, perhaps you should shatter the perfection of the static triangle by introducing something else, perhaps an unbalanced triangle."

Michele nodded. "Yes, there needs to be another figure..."

At his palace, Marchese Mattei rose to address the assembled company. "Honoured guests, we are all acquainted with the work of Master Michelangelo Merisi, creator of this remarkable painting, which is more than I had hoped." After light applause, Marchese Mattei invited Francesco to speak and bless the painting.

"Dear friends, I believe this altarpiece will be recognised among the most important paintings of this new century and, indeed, for all time. Marchese, Excellency, ladies, gentlemen and guests please be seated."

Francesco stood to the side of the altar and, when all were settled, clasped his hands together. "In my humble view and sincere belief, this *Supper at Emmaus* establishes a standard few will ever come close."

He referred to his prepared script. "In the painting, Master Caravaggio has found solid, original interpretations of traditional symbols and in his fidelity to and empathy with the human dignity of his models has expressed from the apparent mundane, something moving and deeply spiritual. Master Caravaggio wilfully refuses to conform to certain, may I say, tired mannerisms, conventions and petty restrictions but remains faithful to the teachings of Holy Mother Church." He turned to gesture to the painting. "We see an image of Our Lord which many may find puzzling, even disquieting. He does not resemble traditional images of Christ; he is clean shaven and has a powerful physique. Was he not a carpenter for most of his earthly life and did he not suffer unparalleled pain as he bore for us the sins of the world? Our Lord was no weakling, and His disciples are not dressed in Roman togas. One is a poor fisherman with a pilgrim cockle shell, his leather apron greasy from gutting fish… and the other a labourer, see the tear in Cleopas' sleeve. The painting, of course, restates the institution of the Holy Sacrament at the Last Supper, re-enacted at Emmaus.

"Master Caravaggio understands that paintings are composed of symbols which even the poor and un-tutored may easily read but, since literacy is becoming more widespread, he is free to deepen the meaning within those common symbols. The objects on what becomes an altar, includes the elements of the Mass, bread and wine and the little pot on the right suggests the bitter herbs of the Exodus. The basket of fruit rehearses the doctrine of the church, note the cast shadow in the form of a fish, the Ichthus being the earliest Christian symbol of faith. The fall and original sin are indicated by the pitted apple, the fall of Adam now saved by the grace of Christ the untainted first fruit of the Resurrection. Other symbols include a lemon, the bitterness of our earthly lives and figs remind us we must always be in season for Our Lord's return and the hope of glory. Then the pomegranate, symbol of Holy Church, the many within one faith but conscious of division – the skin is split and the basket hangs over the precipice that schism threatens. The table and the figure of Christ, the True Presence, the manifestation of the sacrament of bread and wine are contained within a perfect triangle which of course represents the Holy Trinity."

He glanced up at his audience. "We now consider the serving man, who does not merely fill a space but represents those who have not heard the call to faith and does not yet recognise what is revealed to the disciples. The servant casts a dark halo behind Our Lord… Might we presume he was among those in the crowd who called for His crucifixion? Note also that Christ's right hand raised in blessing is close to the servant and breaks out of the confines of the triangle of the Trinity, which indicates our incarnate Redeemer offers salvation to all from within and without time and space."

After a long pause, he continued, "The scriptural description of the supper at Emmaus refers to *meat* and the chicken is just so but also represents sacrifice – life given to sustain life. In that sense, the chicken represents the crucifixion." He smiled as he paused. "The hen's egg's a symbol of the cycle of renewal and because the legs of the chicken are intact there is further reference to the Old Testament prophecy that, though the Messiah would suffer agonising death, *a bone of his body would not be broken*. Beyond that, the painting poses a challenge to the fourth person at the table… to you, my dear friends, and me. The painting is a charge on faith and belief; Our Lord's hands are positioned so there are no visible marks of the nails which poses the question: Do you, pilgrim, with Simon and Cleopas, recognise the risen Lord or do you share the blind ignorance of the serving man? *Blessed are they who have not seen yet believe.* This painting is about revelation, of God in Man and God Sacrificed, who spared Abraham the ultimate sacrifice but for our sakes did not spare his own Blessed Son."

Chapter 16

Amor Vincit Omnia 1602

Del Monte arranged a supper party to celebrate the success of the *Supper at Emmaus*, inviting Costanza Colonna, Vincenzo and his brother Cardinal Benedetto Giustiniani and Michele, serenaded by musicians and choristers from the Sistine Chapel. After supper, the party retired to the salon and, during convivial conversation and laughter, Francesco touched the Marchese's arm. "No commission for our dear Michele tonight, Vincenzo."

"How could I be so forgetful, Francesco? My sincere apologies, Michele. But what shall we commission? Ideas, my lady, Francesco… Brother?"

Cardinal Benedetto smiled. "We were speaking of Virgil's Eclogues earlier and whatever Vincenzo maintains, I hold to my view that eclogue, in the Greek, is a choice or balance… as in a conclave to elect a pope."

"Brother upset Francesco there."

Francesco laughed. "No teasing, Vincenzo; you've flogged that horse to death. My chances of election were as good as non-existent, especially against Borghese… but to the point Benedetto, however good your Greek, I am not convinced. I suggest contemporary usage applies and suggests a simple pastoral literary form. What do you say, Costanza?"

"I take your side Francesco; sometimes a flower is just a flower. Michele?"

"With my lady's forbearance and exclusion from all this crap, by Christ's blood, just damn well tell me what I should paint."

Costanza laughed. "Michele!"

Benedetto snorted a spray of wine over the table and repeatedly coughed.

Vincenzo patted his back. "What bovine table manners, Brother. Very pastoral, perhaps Francesco's right."

Francesco slapped the table with the palm of his hand. "There we have it, madam and gentlemen, while we Pharisees philosophise, the Carpenter addresses the job in hand. If you can't decide Vincenzo, may I suggest *Amor Vincit Omnia*… let all yield to love."

The Lady Costanza tapped her knife on her glass. "Well said, Francesco. Love Conquers All it is, Michele."

Giustiniani rubbed his brother's back. "If you survive this fit, Brother, perhaps you might commission a companion, let's say… Sacred and Profane Love."

Benedetto mopped his soutane and said in a hoarse voice, "Certainly, worth consideration."

Cecco would have preferred to stay at the Palazzo Madama where he felt at home, but Michele was keen to start the Giustiniani commission. Mario and Lorenzo already prepared the canvases at the Palazzo Mattei for the Cupid and the *Death of the Virgin*. Michele dragged his bed against the wall and assembled a variety of objects which he placed on and around the bed. He borrowed a lute, viola and sheet music from the musicians at the Palazzo Madama and Onorio Longhi loaned a set square. Giustiniani had servants deliver old pieces of armour from his attic and a coronet he had no idea was there. Michele sent Cecco to beg a set of wings from Orazio Gentileschi who was reluctant because *that bastard Merisi held on to a valuable rug I previously lent him.*

Michele laughed. "It's Francesco's rug."

"My leg keeps going to sleep and my shoulder aches holding up these sticks." Michele ignored complaints and completed the figure in three weeks but altered the pose when he saw Cecco scratch his backside. He wore the wings, eagle or vulture feathers stuck onto a wire frame and Michele curled one of the feathers forward to stroke Cecco's upper thigh to enhance the illusion the wings were real. "The feathers stink. I reckon I'll catch fleas."

"You don't need worry; fleas would die from your stinking sweat." Cupid was depicted rising from bed, surrounded by attributes conquered by erotic love, each object observed and drawn through a grid strung on a frame. Cecco was positioned on the front corner of the bed, folds and creases carefully arranged. Michele turned and twisted Cecco into the pose he wanted and showed him how he wanted him to hold the arrows. "Now open your legs… wider."

Vincenzo Giustiniani invited Cardinal del Monte, the Lady Costanza, his brother Benedetto and a wide circle of friends to view the finished Cupid at the Giustiniani Palace. Once the party was assembled, Vincenzo took

Costanza's hand and led guests to his private salon where the painting was covered by a green cloth. Vincenzo welcomed guests and hoped they would enjoy the first view of the latest painting by their dear friend Master Caravaggio.

"Michele has painted an extraordinary painting of Cupid who recklessly fires his arrows without regard for station or propriety, occupation or empire and rules all of us. I present *Amor Vincit Omnia...*"

Cecco drew aside the cloth and stood for a moment beside his painted image, then moved away as the company stepped forward. Vincenzo roared with delight and raised his glass. "To Master Caravaggio and Amor." Everyone toasted the painting. Cardinal Benedetto quickly turned away, clearly uncomfortable and fiddled with his crucifix. "Perhaps my lady might prefer to withdraw?"

"Why, Benedetto?" The Lady Colonna laughed. "I'm no washerwoman without learning and well able to understand and appreciate the allusions."

Vincenzo grabbed Michele around the neck and laughed. "All laid waste by Cupid... Wonderful, and so much for a mundane pastoral."

Benedetto did not respond as Vincenzo continued, "I will keep it behind an arras."

"Probably wise, Brother."

"No, Benedetto, not shame nor pretend modesty but simple theatrics. This is my prize painting to be kept in reserve for visitors, to savour, amuse and perhaps to shock. It is the companion piece to Francesco's Bacchus, but where his Bacchus is an invitation, this is veritably post-coital." He laughed. "And I notice the dirty little bugger's wiping his arse on the sheet..."

"Basta Cenzo!" Benedetto stepped forward and kissed Francesco. "Excuse me, Eminence, I have an appointment. Madam, Vincenzo. Master Caravaggio, good evening."

"Must you leave, Benedetto? I hoped you would dine with us."

Benedetto was at the door but did not wait for a page to open it. "Thank you, Brother, but I must..."

Out of the corner of his mouth, Vincenzo stage-whispered, "Benedetto was always the serious one. I suppose he was more fussed over than me."

"I'm surprised he was so upset."

"Don't concern yourself, Francesco; he knew what he was about to see. He sent Baglioni, the fellow from the accademia. I kept the painting covered but heard my servants let him steal a peep."

Chapter 17

Being Cupid and Isaac

Michele pushed me onto the bed, caught me by the throat, razor in hand, leaned back and pressed the cold steel against my belly.

I shouted, "No!" He ignored me and began shaving my pubic hair. "Be careful, I don't want to end up a eunuch. Cazzo, that blade's blunt and, Gesù, I'm sore." Michele spat on my belly and continued scraping but, when he started shaving my balls, the blade tugged and stung. "Ahwoo, stop!"

He was irritated, then slipped down the bed and spat again and licked the spittle over my balls and quickly finished the job, tugging my cock out of the way by the foreskin. He stared down at me and, for a moment, I expected him to caress me. He grinned and the sounds of the palace and the street faded to utter silence. My chest rose and fell but his grin faded and his face became stony. He stepped away from the bed and went to the workshop. I stared at the empty doorway until my erection shrivelled, then rose and crossed to the large mirror leaning against the wall. I was startled by my doubly naked self.

To lighten the atmosphere, I called, "I look like a plucked chicken." I heard him laugh. His voice was hoarse. The sheet was littered with spidery curls of hair which I swept rolling and tumbling onto the floor.

Cupid was a difficult pose. I sat on the edge of the bed, my right foot on the floor, the other tucked behind with my legs splayed wide. In my right hand, I held a sheaf of sticks to represent arrows, and I wore a moth-eaten pair of wings borrowed from Orazio Gentileschi which had a cloying, sickly smell. Michele was pleased with the pose and only slightly changed it when I turned to scratch my bum. Michele later told Giustiniani that Cupid was wiping his arse on the sheet, which amused His Excellency.

"A wet fart." He laughed and repeated many times among his louche friends. Although it was a long pose, I knew Michele enjoyed the painting, liberated from theology, decorum and taste. Well, before it was finished, I recognised the painting was the brother to the cardinal's Bacchus, with me playing Eros, as Mario had played Bacchus. In the finished painting, I am surrounded by symbols of arts and industry, a coronet, armour, musical instruments and an architect's set square, all trampled underfoot. The portrait, of my body as much as my face, was painted with obvious affection, he caught my grin and the sheen of my skin and, although now older, he exaggerated my pointy foreskin to look like a boy's.

The last day Michele worked on the painting, I watched him refine details of the creases and folds of the sheet but he suddenly painted an elaborate crease below the tip of my foreskin, to form the head of an enormous erect penis rising between my legs. When finished, he laughed, caught my head and kissed my forehead. I was elated by the unexpected show of affection, but he gently let me go and left the workshop. I recognised there was always reticence on his part from the day we met. Even though I usually slept in the same bed, he never took advantage.

The Cupid was never publicly displayed but its reputation was known across Rome and further afield. Giustiniani held a grand reception, inviting the cream of society to the unveiling and had me dressed as a page. He presented the painting *Amor Vincit Omnia…* nodded to me, and I drew back the green curtain. There were gasps, applause and laughter. I quickly moved out of the way, thankful I was spared the embarrassment of being recognised as the model. Before I left the salon, the Marchese smiled. "Pity my little joke misfired. The model revealing the painting, but never mind." He squeezed a whole scudo in my hand. "Well done, young man."

Marchese Mattei commissioned an *Arrest of Christ in Gethsemane* painting, about the same dimensions as the *Supper at Emmaus*, probably intended to be a companion piece. Once completed, strangely there was no response from any of the Mattei. The mood in the workshop became subdued with the unmentionable dread that another painting might be rejected until Mattei servants came to deliver payment and collect the picture. Michele was away, so Mario held the money but, when he returned several hours later, Michele swore and cursed, barging into the table, sending plates and pots skittering and shattering on the ground. Mario and I instinctively froze.

"That cock-sucking Giustiniani cardinal!" He slammed down a pot of paint that spattered the walls, his shoes and hose, and I stepped closer to the paintings to prevent damage. Mario and I knew to stay silent until the furious storm passed. "The bastard…" It took time before Michele stopped pacing, ranting and began arranging the remaining pots of paint in a regular pattern. "Did you add oil to these, Cecco?"

Mario intervened, "Yes, he did, Michele. Don't take out whatever's happened on him."

He drew up a stool and sat, wiping the splashes from his hose with a rag dipped in spirit. The gentle rhythm of stroking calmed his temper and eventually he looked up. "Benedetto Giustiniani presented Baglione with a gold chain in reward for that shitty painting of *Divine Love*. Ha! That was insult enough but a gold chain… *Divine Love*, my arse. You've seen it?"

Mario and I hesitated to confirm we had. "Yes…"

"Well, he's made a second version and the bollocks painted me as a boy-fucking devil and that bastard Benedetto Giustiniani gave him a gold chain."

"Does it matter? Everybody knows Baglione's paintings are shite."

"He tried to copy my way of working to attack me, so why did Benedetto ask Baglione when his brother wanted him to commission a companion to the Cupid from me?"

No one responded, not wishing to invite further ire. "He did it to spite his brother; it's the only reason… Pharaoh was wrong; he should have ordered the deaths of every *second* son. "

Of course Michele also meant his own younger brother, and it was a tragedy Michele didn't trust Cardinal del Monte. At the time, I didn't know the move to the Mattei palace was a consequence of Michele's guilt and inability to accept the cardinal's love freely offered. From then on, he began to act like an adolescent engaged in increasing hooliganism and self-destruction that was to drive him inevitably to disaster. He should have known the cardinal, that skilful diplomat who knew men's souls, would soon have seen through the brother's shallow piety and probably advanced his career elsewhere, perhaps Genoa or Florence, anywhere he had connections. After all, he gave Michele's paintings to beloved friends, not simply tokens of affection but to spread Michele's fame beyond Rome.

Michele decided to leave the Mattei residence and, as the lads and I began packing, an unexpected commission was received from Cardinal Maffeo Barberini. It was unclear if Francesco had worked on his behalf but it was Barberini's major-domo who came to discuss details for a private altarpiece of Abraham about to sacrifice his son Isaac to include the ram caught in the thicket. "How long would such a painting take?"

"I suppose there must be an angel; that's three figures. How much is His Eminence willing pay?"

"The same as you got for the *Taking of Christ*."

"You know how much Marchese Mattei paid?"

"No… but there were more figures in the *Taking of Christ* and, as you say, an Isaac requires just three."

"And a ram."

"Yes, a ram too."

"Rams are hard to paint."

"I imagine they are… but not for someone with your talent." Michele was in no position to haggle too much because Barberini was a coming cardinal, who knew, even papabile? He hesitated a moment before suggesting a figure three-quarters higher than for the Taking and, with a handshake, the deal was sealed.

"I will arrange the contract and remit a quarter as guarantee. Thank you, Signor Merisi."

"*Caravaggio,* signor. I am known as Caravaggio."

Michele hired a cordwainer called Ignacio to model Abraham, and I was Isaac. The arrangement was simple. I lay across a table with Ignacio behind, forcing me – Isaac – onto the altar, his thumb pressed into my cheek. The knife poised in Ignacio's right hand the moment before slitting my – Isaac's – throat. The blade was terrifying; I needed no prompt to pose, gasping in a silent scream. Michele indicated where an angel would appear, barely entering the picture from the left to restrain Abraham's arm and worked quickly, desperate to finish the painting as soon as possible.

He took me to the holding pens near the slaughterhouse to make studies of sheep and chose a curious gentle ram unaware of its impending fate. He asked Mario to block in the angel and arranged a curly-headed model to sit several days. The result was stiff and flat; Michele said he would adjust and refine Mario's effort later.

When modelling, I frequently called out to Ignacio, "You're hurting me." I noticed Ignacio grimaced and gritted his teeth as though he enjoyed restraining me and several times Michele told him to ease off which he did but pressure soon intensified. I flinched from time to time, an involuntary spasm from being tightly restrained. At every rest break, I worked my jaw and felt the imprint of Ignacio's thumb below the cheek bone, the ache only slowly faded. The main figures, Ignacio and I, were finished in under a month.

The last day we posed, Michele spent most of the time flicking his eyes between us and the painting, barely adding a mark. Finally, he wiped the brush on a rag and merely said, "Finished."

Ignacio stood, arched his back and the muscles cracked. When I tried to rise, he pressed me down, caught me by the loins and began rocking his hips back and forth. I struggled to push him away but the hip movements became more insistent and I could tell he was excited. He held me down just a few seconds but long enough that I began to struggle. Mario laughed but Michele froze, glanced at my screaming features in the painting, then back at Ignacio who played up to Mario and by now even Lorenzo shared the joke but, as I struggled to get up, Michele erupted, "Stop that!"

"It's a joke, just a joke."

Michele rushed at Ignacio and knocked him to the floor. "Get out!" I drew a blanket around me. Michele stood in the middle of the room, trembling with rage.

The room was silent as Ignacio quickly changed into his own clothes, then stood, slightly stooped. "My money…"

"I paid you enough already… Fuck off and don't come back." Ignacio didn't move, so Michele grabbed him by the collar and rushed him to the door. I drew the blanket tight around me and stared at the painting of the boy pinned down by the older man. The picture seemed to say more than a simple Bible story. In the distance was a town or a memory of a town. It was the only time I saw Michele paint an outdoor scene.

One occasion when Michele worked on the painting, I said, "It's Caravaggio!"

"You recognise it."

I nodded. "It's not the real Caravaggio. I was only there a couple of times with my pa but it feels like Caravaggio."

Michele stood in a trance. "I doubt I'll ever see Caravaggio again." In a whisper, he said he remembered his mamma Lucia leaning against a doorway, head tilted, one foot crossed over the other, holding a basket of vegetables and smiling. "She reminded me of the Madonna in the Sanctuario dell Fontana…"

I frowned not knowing what he meant. "It's a statue; the people of Caravaggio built a shrine over the place where a peasant girl had a vision of the Virgin." He caught his breath.

I sensed speaking about Caravaggio reminded him of his mamma and realised fear of arrest prevented him from visiting her grave. I didn't understand why he included Caravaggio in the Abraham and Isaac painting or why he painted the town in daylight. All Michele's paintings I'd seen were staged indoors, impenetrable voids, almost suffocating backgrounds but the painted town was more a dream, even a yearning for Caravaggio of stone and mortar. In the years since he arrived in Rome, he said he rarely thought about his family, having come to consider the Palazzo Madama his home. Certainly, the only home since the last days spent with his mother and sister at the real but distant Caravaggio after his papa, uncle and grandfather died of the plague. His lost youngest brother Pietro and his mamma Lucia he said seemed like ghosts.

Having taken me into his confidence about his memories of his mother, I wondered if he would ever tell me why he fled Milan and whether the rumour he almost killed a police officer was true but he never spoke about the matter to me nor, apparently, to Lorenzo or Mario. The same was true of the brother he vehemently denied. It was Lorenzo who told me about the Jesuit priest who presented himself to the cardinal saying he was Michele's brother Battista. Lorenzo said the Jesuit was a cold judgemental Pharisee but the cardinal was as kind and forgiving as his saintly namesake from Assisi but, having violently paid back Battista in his own coin, Michele cast himself adrift from the cardinal. I could tell Michele was ashamed, longing to return to the haven of the cardinal's goodness but was shackled to Battista by hatred and denial… Peter's sin. Ripples continued to rankle and Michele clearly blamed Battista for his self-imposed exile from the cardinal's hearth and home and reports and gossip would not have gone unknown by the devout Mattei family.

Although Michele said the painting was finished, he never added a brushstroke to the angel Mario had sketched in. Either he forgot or didn't care to paint another angel. The angel, I supposed, personified the small voice in the mind that was the boy's reprieve. Of course there had to be an angel; otherwise, Abraham's change of mind would be in defiance of an unreasonable, insane demand. The face of Isaac was among the best he had done, more or less a straight portrait of me. The portrait of Ignacio as Abraham was also a close likeness but made to look older, his beard elongated and greyer. Michele caught Isaac's expression of terror and Abraham distracted by the enormity of his resolve to cut his son's throat. I watched him make studies of the ram at the holding pens near the slaughterhouse. The ram appeared a willing substitute for Isaac, a link to Christ's willing sacrifice. The ram in the pen was a gentle creature that chose itself by lifting Michele's hand with an upthrust of its bony head. I saw the ram as the substitute for Isaac subtly expressed by the underside arc of the ram's horn, which echoed the arc of the profile of Isaac's head. In the *Supper at Emmaus*, there were similar geometries and aware that even in the brief time since the Supper painting, correspondences and geometries seemed to occur without premeditation as the upward curve of the dagger blade echoed the broken tree branch with the view of Caravaggio beyond. Was it possible Michele was aware of what he was doing or was his hand guided by an unknown force, perhaps envisioned during restless dreams in the night when he tossed and turned, a dagger-shape broken tree branch pointing back to Caravaggio, his past and hence the violence and fury towards Ignacio?

Lorenzo and I prepared colours and Michele often worked the powder in the mortice before adding walnut oil. Whether it was a means to heighten his concentration or simply habit to ensure the final consistency was the very smoothest, who knew? During a break, Lorenzo arrived as food was prepared. Mario and I made pasta with sardines and a large bowl of salad leaves, finocchio, cucumber, bread and olives. The lads and I sat at a small table but Michele paced the studio, eating salad, bread and olives with his fingers.

"You have paint on your hands, Michele."

He glanced at his hand with a large leaf of lettuce halfway to his mouth, his fingers smeared with lead white. He shrugged and mumbled as he ate. "My food always tastes metallic, that and olive oil."

All but Lorenzo laughed. "It can't be good for you."

Michele licked his fingers. "If I die... I die." The general mood lightened and conversation turned to gossip; such-and-such a pimp had marked his girl, so-and-so was said to have been given such-and-such a commission and shared opinions about what strings had been pulled and by whom. Nevertheless, having witnessed Michele's bafflingly uncontrolled fury towards Ignacio, everyone carefully avoided mentioning him and no one dare raise the name Baglione who had just completed a Resurrection of Christ for the Church of the Gesù.

When it became public knowledge the commission was also in the gift of Cardinal Benedetto Giustiniani, Michele was incandescent. Lorenzo stood in front of the near complete *Abraham and Isaac* to prevent him from slashing the picture as he rushed towards it. Mario grabbed Michele from behind and even though thrown to the side, the sound of the table going over, the smash of glass and paint pots was enough to distract Michele from what appeared to be his intention to attack the painting. Then I didn't understand why he directed his rage at his own paintings. It seemed an act of self-punishment as though he felt deep down his work was not good enough whatever the adulation he could not bring himself to believe. Perhaps it was the reason he was scathing of other painter's work. He stood with his arm raised, gripping his favourite dagger and gasping. Eventually he lowered his arm, dropped the knife, his shoulders slumped, chest heaved and stood breathless before Abraham and, in impotent rage, howled, *"Baglione, fucking Baglione... Baglione!"*

I once asked Lorenzo why he thought Michele flew into such towering rages. "Surely he knows Baglione is not half the painter he is?"

It was a while before Lorenzo responded, "When I met Michele in Venice, I sensed something haunted him." He hesitated. "I believe something happened to Michele when he was young."

"One of the Sforza boys?"

"I don't know about the Sforzas..."

"It was common knowledge he used to play with the Sforza lads when the Lady Costanza visited Michele's mother."

Lorenzo pouted. After a moment, he asked, "Do you know anything about the rumour that Michele seriously wounded a law officer in Milan?"

"There was gossip but I was young. I never knew if it was just chatter, you know small towns..."

"I'm sure there was something behind the rumour."

"What do you think might have happened?"

Lorenzo poured two cups of wine and handed one to me. "If it's true, one thing I'm certain – Michele never lashes out without provocation or reason. He has a keen sense of justice... but often bides his time so any retaliation might seem unprovoked. I guess whatever the truth. It happened after he left Venice. I remember he was very withdrawn; he spoke little except to moan he would never be as good as Titian or Giorgione and, in the last days before leaving, he asked me to arrange for him to buy an illegal sword."

I smiled. "The first of many."

Our conversation lasted into the night, and I felt a little lightheaded, having drank several cups of wine. I was surprised when Lorenzo said I seemed unhappy. He looked me in the eyes and slowly coaxed me to tell him how Michele shaved me for the Cupid. "Apart from modelling and chores around the workshop, he doesn't really want me. I thought we were close but he's become suddenly distant with me."

"Maybe shaving you he saw you as a boy."

"I'm no child; I'm fifteen."

"But he remembers you when you were… twelve?" It was a while before Lorenzo continued, "I said when we were in Venice, I sensed something haunted him. Something serious enough to provoke a violent retaliation. Let's think… an officer of the watch, an older man and a boy."

I recalled Father Gennaro but avoided mentioning him. "Michele would never allow…"

"It wasn't a matter of allow… the man was older and physically strong, and, if Michele was still an apprentice, he couldn't have been more than fifteen or sixteen."

"My age."

Chapter 18

Fillide

When Michele lived at the Palazzo Madama, the cardinal instructed servants to ensure Michele was served regular meals which were usually barely touched and models usually wolfed down the food. In the Mattei household, Michele rarely ate during the day and steadily drank diluted wine as he painted, which had no effect on his concentration but, by nightfall, he was exhausted and took Cecco and whoever was in the workroom for supper. He had to get out of the workshop which was hot and humid and the smell of oil was overbearing. Compared with the atmosphere in the workshop under the roof of the Mattei palace, the air in the street was relatively fresh. His shirt reeked of oil.

In the early years it took to establish himself, he lived a near monkish life, working all hours on a continuous succession of commissions. He counted the number of paintings completed between his arrival in Rome to the most recent, including the *Taking of Christ in Gethsemane*, the various Baptist paintings and Abraham and Isaac; the total was forty-four. Up to now, he worked hard and intensively but, since the shock of Battista's appearance and the fracture with Francesco, Michele became reckless and extravagantly boisterous as he took increasing amounts of wine. In addition to the lads, he caroused with Orazio Gentileschi, Filippo Triesegni and, sometimes, Spada if he was in Rome, but, particularly, Onorio Longhi whom he followed into deeper waters. In their cups, they encouraged one another in increasingly outrageous behaviour, stoning windows and brawls occasionally resulting in injuries. What passed for honour after several flagons of wine was the spark that ignited petty rivalries, slights and feuds.

Baglione's *Resurrection* was eventually installed at the Gesù, becoming a provocation for further lawlessness. Orazio, Onorio, Michele and friends attended the unveiling. Their muttering and laughter were frowned on by the congregation and the Fathers asked them to leave the church.

As they shuffled to the door, Michele called out, "The bastard tried to copy me." They retired to a tavern where ridicule increased in proportion to their consumption of undiluted wine. Michele climbed on the table, belching and swaying and began to compose doggerel:

He deserves to be known as John Cunt... who finds fault with someone who would be his master for a hundred years...

He stamped on the table as he versified until Filippo Triesegni grabbed his ankle. "Hold... hold, Michele, let me write this down." He took out his notebook and a scrap of sharpened lead. "Start again..."

He doubtless deserves to be called John the cunt,
Who undertakes to find fault with another
Who would be his master a hundred years...

Onorio re-filled everyone's cup. "Go on, Michele..."

My words... with my words I refer to painting,
Since this man claims to be... no, claims to be called a painter
Though he never could rank with me... with that man...

Orazio joined Michele on the table to add a verse.

You who presume to find fault
With other men's paintings, but yet know your own
Are still nailed up in your house
Because you are ashamed to show them in public...

In the small hours, the innkeeper threw them out and, after another hour of laughter and loud gabbing that echoed off the walls of the alleys, locals shouted – *Vaffanculo*. They replied with shouts and curses until they were doused by a pot of piss. With foul insults and repeatedly kicking the door with shouts of "Come out, you dirty bastards", they eventually staggered off, barely holding one another upright.

Michele hoped the painting on the strainer would be finished in time to be in place for Holy Week the following year. *The Entombment* was commissioned for the Chiesa Nuova and Michele worked on the stone slab supporting the group of figures: St John the favourite disciple and Joseph of Arimathea carried the dead weight of Christ's corpse with the Virgin and two other women mourners behind. His concentration was interrupted by the recollection of Baglione's *Resurrection* and the stab of envy that he missed what would have been the perfect companion for this present painting. However much he tried to push the matter aside his irritation would not abate, repeatedly erupting in bursts of rage. He stretched, stood back from the painting and poured sour wine from the flagon left uncovered the night before. The painting was a worthy successor to both the Contarelli paintings and the Emmaus.

It had the unity of a sculptural group and combined the drama with greater subtlety and integration of theology, *Ave Verum Corpus*: the true body, the Mass literally incorporated in the body to be laid on the altar of a rough-hewn slab of stone. Mary Magdalene in the background, her arms raised, was perhaps a little overdramatic… He smiled. Fillide modelled for both Marys. He laughed aloud at the memory of her standing with hands on hips and screeching like a fishwife: *two for the price of one, you bugger, Michele… you do try it on.*

It was Onorio who introduced Michele to Fillide Melandroni. "She's a tart but what a woman." He grinned. "Like a piece of velvet, ha!"

She may have started on the streets, possibly one of Tomassoni's girls, but, by the time Michele met her, she moved in higher circles, not a beauty exactly, pretty and rather boyish with roguish seductive eyes, her gaze well-rehearsed. She reminded him of Cecco, and it was perhaps her boyish looks that first attracted him when they were introduced… *Was it in '97?* The first night he spent with her, her features waxed and waned from girl to boy, and she insisted he stay… no quick knee-tremblers for Fillide. In the morning, they talked. She said she'd heard of Master Caravaggio and saw several of his paintings in the churches she attended. She loved the *Conversion of Saint Paul* in Santa Maria del Popolo. He thought she may have seen his paintings at Giustiniani's; she was certainly his type and his caste was the object of her ambition. She got Michele to talk, invariably taciturn and hesitant, Francesco being the only one he opened his heart about his work, but, as a successful entertainer of men, she knew how to draw him out and how to listen. At first, he made monosyllabic comments and answers to her enquiries but, in her silences, a trickle became a torrent, talking about his paintings – those completed and ideas as yet unrealised. He raged he lost the commissioned to paint the *Resurrection*, certain he would make a better job of it than Baglione. She seemed genuinely interested but, as a consummate professional, she kept the client's attention on himself rather than her nipples or muff. He noticed how liberally she used olive oil… pig bladders probably chafed. She smiled. "Go on…"

"Would you model for me, Fillide?"

She gently slapped his arm. "I'll have you know, young man, I'm not a cheap tart... How dare you proposition me to be one of your slutty models?"

"I'll pay proper models' rates."

"I should hope so..."

"Will you?"

"Perhaps... but I hope I don't end up as a boy in your paintings."

He drew away from her and sat up. "I only paint what customers want."

She slipped her arms around him, but he shrugged her off. "Don't be upset, Michele; I'm only teasing."

"I have to go... especially if I didn't perform to your required standard."

"Don't be like this, Michele, come back. I know all sorts of men and what they like... and what they think they like. You came with Onorio and stayed because you didn't want to lose face, *bella figura*. I know you're no virgin but I know the lay of the land. I've known too many men and I can tell the ones who fuck their women but make love to their boys..."

In haste to leave, he slipped on his doublet before the shirt, slumped otherwise naked on the edge of the bed, groping for the rest of his clothes tangled on the floor with those of Fillide. She shrieked, "Michele, you look ridiculous..." She crossed her hands over her breasts and was helpless. "Your bony arse... it's shiny white." She was reduced to fits of laughter. He slipped off the doublet and lay down beside her again.

She wiped her eyes and, although there were occasional giggles, she gradually calmed and began gently stroking his hair. "Friends?" He nodded. "I like you, Michele. Any time you want company or to talk... or anything else... don't be a stranger and, yes, I'll model for you, and we'll show how alluring a female saint can be."

Indeed, for about a year and a half, Fillide modelled for saints and sinners, a fine St Catherine and, at his behest, even slightly frowned when she played Judith hacking off Holofernes' head as though butchering a pig.

"Michele, enough, I'll get frown lines and that's not good for business."

He didn't see her for a while, thanks, he imagined, to her pimp, if she still had a pimp. In time, he heard she was living in the lap of luxury with her client, a count whom, no doubt, she wrapped around her little finger. He wished she were still around. She would have made light of Baglione's daub for Benedetto Giustiniani and a copy in which he depicted Michele as a devil caught in flagrante with a naked Cupid. Baglione's attempt to emulate his style was pedestrian but nevertheless hit his target... in Francesco's terms:

"Libel". Baglione made public what many assumed in private, that Michele was a sodomite but what rubbed salt in the wound was his helplessness to retaliate. His fragile *bella figura* façade, even with Fillide's collusion, was torn away by her disappearance, leaving him exposed to the transparently obvious accusation in Baglione's painting. Spada, Onorio and others wouldn't care less if he coupled with goats but his wider reputation and lucrative church market was too valuable to put in jeopardy.

Mario answered a loud banging on the door to two men. "Are you Master Michelangelo Merisi?"

"Who wants to know?"

"You are summoned to court." The stranger doffed his hat and, with a half-hearted bow, pressed a document into his hand.

"What's this?"

"A charge of libel."

"Libel… who?"

"Master Giovanni Baglione makes the charge."

When Mario handed him the paper, Michele laughed. "Baglione, what does he have to bellyache about?"

An hour later, Orazio Gentileschi came to say he had also been summoned along with Onorio and Filippo. "Someone copied and printed the poem… it's posted everywhere."

"Who'd be so stupid?"

"Filippo wrote it down at the time."

"He couldn't afford to print it. Where would he get the money, unless… Onorio?"

They went to speak to Onorio and, crossing the Piazza Navona, saw scores of the printed poem posted on every wall.

Orazio tore down several. "Sweet Gesù, how many copies are there?"

Officers of the watch in the square marched up to them. The sergeant caught Michele by the arm. "Signor Merisi… Signor Longhi, you are both under arrest on a charge of libel."

"We've already been served summonses. Why this… why now?"

"My orders, gentlemen, are to arrest you both on sight."

Chapter 19

Baglione

He swaggered into court, dressed in his finery and wearing the gold chain presented by Cardinal Giustiniani. When called to give evidence, he played to the gallery like a cheap actress; he claimed Orazio and Michele had libelled him because they were jealous. That caused raucous laughter from friends and supporters.

Baglione had to raise his voice to be heard above the ridicule and barracking. "They are jealous… jealous, jealous because I won the commission for the *Resurrection* for the Gesù."

As the din subsided, he whined interminably about the hurt and the damage to his reputation, interrupted by mocking *Ahs* and *Oos*. Michele grinned at Orazio but both they and co-defendants were surprised when a witness for Baglione was called since none of his supporters were at the tavern that night.

Orazio murmured, "Who knew Baglione had friends?"

The witness, Tommaso Salini, claimed he was a painter and acquired copies of the verse from Filippo Triesegni which he had passed to Baglione *as a friend would do*. He relished the attention, repeated he was a painter and went on at length to explain his acquaintanceship with Filippo, claiming that not only Baglione's picture had been attacked but also himself, *because I am Gianni Baglione's companion at the academy*. He listed painters whom he claimed distributed the verses, including Mario Minniti who was helped by the bardassa, Giovanni Battista, *who is known to be frequented by both Michele Caravaggio and Onorio Longhi…* He went on to say that Filippo told him the authors were Michele, Orazio Gentileschi and Onorio Longhi. He also suggested Michele knew Filippo had copies and told him not to let them fall into the hands of Baglione.

Onorio called out, "Hearsay… hearsay, this is not evidence." Onorio and Michele were called in turn to answer the charge that they both knew the bardassa Giovanni Battista, which was irrelevant except to draw attention to Baglione's pictorial libel in his caricature of Michele as a satanic pederast.

Michele simply said he had never known the whore and, when the same allegation was put to Onorio, he blustered he was married with a large family; it was an insult to his honour and manhood to imply he would even consider visiting bardassas. When called to testify, Filippo admitted he had been evasive when Salini tried to guess who the authors were and went on to say they had agreed that, if Salini would teach him how to paint cast shadows, he would tell him who had composed the verses.

When asked if he told Salini, Filippo pouted. "He never taught me how to paint cast shadows… so I never told him."

Michele laughed aloud, even though Filippo had unwittingly revealed he knew who the authors were. Curiously, the court did not pursue the matter further.

The case dragged on for days and, eventually, on 13th September, Michele was called again. After formalities were repeated, he was asked which painters he knew. He reeled off a list, including Cesari, Orazio, Annibale Carracci and also Baglione, adding that nearly all those on the list were good friends but not all were good painters. When asked to explain, he said a good painter knows how to paint well and *to imitate well natural subjects*. Then he was asked to list painters he regarded as friends and those he regarded good painters. Michele was careful to distance himself from Orazio Gentileschi, saying they had not spoken for a couple of years. "But I don't know any painter who would praise Gianni Baglione as a good painter."

At that, Baglione stood to harangue Michele. "Bastards! Why would I have better commissions than you if I am not a good painter?"

The judge told him to sit and remain silent.

"Signor, am I not allowed to defend myself?"

"We have heard your evidence, Signor Baglione; please be seated."

The judge nodded to the notary. "Continue."

When asked if Michele had seen many of Baglione's works, he answered, "I have seen nearly all his works, namely the Great Chapel in Madonna dell' Orto, a picture in St John Lateran, and lately *Christ's Resurrection* in the Gesù."

"And what do you think of Master Baglione's *Resurrection*?"

Without hesitation, Michele replied, "I don't like this painting because it's clumsy. I regard it as the worst he has ever done and, of all the painters I have spoken to, none like it, except perhaps one, who is always with Baglione and whom they call his guardian angel."

He grinned and turned to Cesari, Orazio and the rest. "When the painting was unveiled, this guardian angel was standing by, praising it; by *he,* I mean Tommaso Salini, who's known as Mao." Michele glanced around the court, shrugged and continued, "Mao daubs a little I understand, but I have never seen any works by him."

There was a ripple of laughter and even the judge smiled. After further questions about friends and acquaintances, he was asked if he was in the habit of writing poetry. He laughed. "No, signor, I don't amuse myself composing verses... either in Italian or Latin. I have never heard of the existence of rhymes or prose works against Baglione."

When dismissed, Michele bowed to the court with obvious disdain and, as he passed Baglione, he doffed his little black cap, fingers gesturing the horns on the blind side of the court.

Orazio Gentileschi was recalled and, when asked the same opening question as Michele, his voice boomed to disguise his nervousness, repeating most of the same list of leading painters in Rome and also included Baglione. "These belong to the first class." Without pause, he quickly went on to suggest that friendly rivalry between painters was common, could be earthy and gave the example of Baglione's *Sacred and Profane Love* put up to rival Michele's *Amor Vincit Omnia*. Michele closed his eyes. Orazio tried to retrieve the matter, saying Michele's painting for Marchese Giustiniani was preferred by the majority even though Marchese Giustiniani's brother, Cardinal Benedetto, presented Baglione with a gold chain. Having realised that referring to the comparison between the rival paintings, he confirmed Michele had motive to attack Baglione, Orazio repeated there was always general rivalry among painters, including rivalry between himself and Baglione and Michele. He ended saying despite rivalry with Michele, he recently lent him props, thereby contradicting Michele's claim they hadn't spoken in years.

On parole from the Tor di Nona, thanks to the intervention of the French ambassador, almost certainly at the behest of Francesco del Monte, Michele's mood echoed the permanent half-light of the prison. His brief sentence created ever greater support and regard among younger painters, but his release left him in a state of misery. He was now twice bested not only by Baglione's depiction of him with a nude boy and now he had won the libel case.

At heart, Baglione was aware of his mediocrity, which was his motivation and determination to destroy Michele's reputation, jeopardise future commissions and his premier status in Rome, which left Michele with a dilemma: to complain about Baglione's painting was likely to draw further attention to the allusion of sodomy but, powerless to challenge him directly, left him exposed. Francesco had gently but firmly rejected the *St Francis and the Angel. Slander is difficult to prove, Caro, but libel is not. Libel is recorded; it is tangible...*

During and after the Baglione hearings, friends kept their distance, a sign of how isolated he had become. Even though it was obvious Onorio had contributed to the verses and probably paid for the printing, he saved his own skin by playing the simpleton when called to witness a second time. He had a large family to maintain, so Michele bore no hard feelings when Onorio escaped imprisonment by leaving Rome. Filippo, Mario and Lorenzo were ever loyal but, at the conclusion of the case, the result was almost irrelevant since Michele undoubtedly slandered Baglione but the conviction put Michele's relationship with del Monte further beyond hope since his depiction of Michele as a sodomite might rebound on the cardinal. The conviction for libel made worse the initial rupture with Francesco caused by Battista's attempt to shoulder his way into His Eminence's good graces. It was widely known Michele treated his brother like Cain and his denial and lack of remorse was probably considered an insult to Francesco. Other than Francesco, Fillide was the only confidante he trusted, but she was out of the picture, thanks to her new status. For Fillide, modelling for Michele was more financially advantageous than any pimp was likely to allow her to keep. The money from Michele and other wealthy clients was her means of escape and the route she had obviously taken. He missed her earthy good humour, unquestioning friendship, above all her fierce loyalty and, in the early days, occasional enthusiastic couplings. Now that Fillide was gone he felt less inclined to drink until senseless but Onorio and others continually coaxed him from the workshop.

At the Tavern of the Blackamoor one evening, they shared several flagons of full-bodied wine and ordered artichokes. When they were served, the waiter said half were served in butter, the other half in olive oil. Michele grunted. "Which are in butter and which in oil?"

The waiter shrugged. "I don't know…" He picked up a spear which flaccidly sagged and shoved it under Michele's nose. "Sniff and sort it out yourself."

Michele lurched up, knocked over the bench, ditching Cecco on the floor, and threw the plate in the waiter's face. "You son of a whore, you're not talking to some peasant…"

Blood poured down the waiter's face from a gash below his eye and stained his shirt. He mopped his face with his apron and ran out of the tavern. Michele spent the night in goal, his friends, as ever, left him to face the charge alone. Only Cecco stayed but, when he argued, the sbirri told him to shut up. "Whatever you say, we know you're lying. We're not stupid. The sword isn't yours, so bugger off before we arrest you too."

In the following months, Michele was charged with further offenses, throwing stones, damaging property, repeatedly going armed and wounding. One occasion, he was stopped in the Alley of the Buffalo by an officer of the watch who asked if he had a licence to carry a weapon. He produced the paper, which was accepted to be in order. The officer saluted. "Goodnight, signor."

Michele snatched the licence from officer and spat, "Up your arse."

"I don't want to hear that kind of language."

"Up your arse, I said."

He was arrested and, again, spent the night in the cells.

Chapter 20

Loreto and Entombment

Painting drew him into a world of action and reaction, expressed through colour, revealed by light where tensions and stresses bound the mechanical application of paint that took on an existence by some strange alchemy, a transubstantiation – paint becoming flesh and blood, fabrics, metal, stone and darkness and light…

During the lost hours he worked, unrelated thoughts intruded, and he muttered, "I know… I know! I know I waste the same energy on a pinprick as the more serious onslaught from Baglione." He closed his eyes in the hopes the chatter in his head would cease. After several moments of breathing deeply, his attention drifted to the memory of the self-portrait he included in the *Arrest of Christ* painting, somewhat rejuvenated, less care worn than the reality of the stranger in the looking glass but he had not flattered himself. It was an honest depiction of a rather plain man; no one would give a second glance yet no one before him had painted such a head… seen and painted without artifice.

It had been a decade since he slunk into Rome, with flawed technique, during which time increasing command of his work had taken him well beyond early expectations and outstripped even his own ambition. His subjects came to fruition with increasing novel interpretations, executed with powerful mastery of technique: The Contarelli, Cerasi, Emmaus and above all the Cupid… were sensations in turn and early flaws and weaknesses were resolved or at least elegantly disguised to create the illusion of perfection. Technically, the *Arrest of Christ* was a backward glance to the Emmaus but the latest commissions for an *Entombment* and *Madonna of Loreto* would be of a different order. It was certain and, without doubt, as though pre-ordained.

He had seen and was obsessed by a woman he wanted for the Loreto painting. Her name was Maddalena Antognetti – Lena. She was on the game and one of Ranuccio Tomassoni's girls, more beautiful than Fillide but lacked her vivacity and ambition, her clients much further down the social ladder. He never confided in her as he had Fillide. Nevertheless, Lena's natural beauty was undimmed by her profession and her air of stillness necessary to ply her trade was alluring to clients and perfect for the image of a slightly remote Madonna.

Unfortunately, a notary, Mariano Pasqualone de Accumulo pestered Lena for more favours than she was prepared to sell. She leaned downwards, posed against the doorframe, one foot crossed over the other and, as Michele worked, she mentioned Pasqualone's insistence was annoying. When he didn't respond, she assumed Michele concentrated so hard she was not heard but he tracked down Pasqualone to warn him to leave her alone but he continued to threaten Lena, saying he would see off *her pimp*. Michele decided to finish the matter. Catching him unawares one night, he thrashed Pasqualone, hitting him with the flat of his sword. Bruises were worse than the head wound, which, although superficial, bled profusely.

Realising his attack would likely be considered unprovoked and Pasqualone would identify him, Michele had no alternative but to get out of Rome. He chose Loreto, the landing place of the Holy House miraculously translated from Nazareth. He spent time working on ideas for both the Madonna and the *Entombment* but, to start the paintings, it was necessary to return to face inevitable charges. He surrendered to the court; his defence was to admit a grudge and gambled that, as a notary, Pasqualone would not wish his involvement with a prostitute revealed. Surprisingly, Pasqualone raised the true cause in court: *over Michelangelo's girl*. That suggested Michele might be considered a pimp, so he quickly admitted his guilt and ended his confession with an apology: *I am sorry for what I did and wish it could be undone. I beg his forgiveness and peace and, if Mariano had a sword in his hand, I would regard him as a worthy adversary.* Pasqualone felt justified, accepted the apology and payment and the matter was resolved, freeing Michele to return to work.

Both the *Madonna of Loreto* and *Entombment* paintings raised profound considerations of death, salvation, the hope of resurrection and pilgrims' consolation at the feet of the Madonna and Child. On completion of the *Arrest of Christ* for Marchese Mattei, Michele concentrated all his attention on the new commissions, the vision clear, the composition and form of the *Entombment* in particular came into focus. The lowering of the body of Christ onto the slab raised matters he wished he could have discussed with Francesco but loathed to presume on his time and generous nature but there was no one else whose judgement he trusted to share his deepest thoughts.

He struggled to imagine what Francesco might say about the ending that death represents – *Ave Verum Corpus*. Hail true body crucified, dead and buried with only faith that He would rise again. Closing his eyes, he copied Francesco's slow, considered gesture, touching his forehead, chest and shoulders to signify the five wounds. Without Francesco, Michele was mute and action, painting or brawling, his only voice.

The form of the *Entombment* revealed itself to Michele when he visited the Fathers of the Oratorio at Chiesa Nuova who wanted the subject of the lowering of Christ's body into the tomb, rather than a pieta, thankfully avoiding comparison with his namesake. As they spoke, Michele's attention was arrested by the altar, how Christ was sacrificed and laid on a slab of rock… Isaac without reprieve. That fired his imagination rather than the dry philosophising of the fathers. It was a spiritual companion to the *Abraham and Isaac* and not just a theological exercise but a rite, a drama, as the missal is moved three times on the altar during the Mass re-enacting the trial and condemnation of Christ and the eating of flesh and blood. A great slab of crudely cut rock would be an altar to support a tableau of figures at the celebrant's eyeline with Joseph of Arimathea looking down to engage the onlooker in the action. *See how heavy this lifeless corpse truly is.*

Giacomo – the waiter from the Osteria in the Via de Fusari, who modelled Christ in the *Calling of Matthew* – agreed to model again and was not shy posing naked. He lay on a shallow dais with his legs supported over the back of a chair. His body was the most beautiful Michele ever saw, pale and without blemish. As he painted Giacomo, it occurred he shared the same name with Michele's attentive priest at the Sistine Chapel.

Other models came and went as needed. Lorenzo modelled for the favourite disciple Saint John, his fingers pressed between two ribs in Giacomo's side, translated in paint as the wound, anticipating the incredulity of St Thomas. An older matron agreed to pose for the Virgin but would not accept a fee, the honour of representing the Holy Mother was enough reward. "My grandchildren and their grandchildren will forever have a memory of me."

It was obvious Fillide had gone for good, so he found a young woman who vaguely resembled her and favoured similar clothes. He paid her to pose for both Marys, as though they were sisters with no attempt to distinguish one from the other, one close to the body, her head shaded, looking down, and the other raised her red eyes and hands to heaven… *Why?* The model who posed for the first Matthew altarpiece was hired to represent Joseph of Arimathea holding Christ's legs; the weight of Giacomo's legs pushed

Joseph's left elbow towards the viewer echoing Cleopas' torn sleeve in the *Supper at Emmaus*. He spent long days painting the body of Christ, with the pallor of death, mouth open in his last gasp of breath, lips turning purple. The near arm sagged to rest on the rock, the natural fall of the fingers suggested legs stepping down as though to the underworld, the significance recognised only later. Below the hand, he painted Mullein leaves, the plant dedicated to John the Baptist, among the first, with Adam and Eve, to be released by Christ from the prison of death.

When Michele began the *Madonna of Loreto*, he heard Annibale Carracci was commissioned by Cardinal Madruzzo to paint the same subject for Sant' Onofrio. They had not met since they worked on paintings for the Cerasi Chapel, which, without doubt, marked the stark difference between their work and now distant, strained friendship. He anticipated a restrained interpretation of the Loreto story, adhering to Cardinal Paleotti's discourse, demanding strict adherence to doctrinal matters and decorum, but Annibale's *Translation of the Holy House* was a ludicrous concoction, depicting a Madonna squatting with the Child on the roof of a flying house supported by angels. Michele laughed aloud. A priest called, "Silence in the Lord's House."

Chapter 21

Death of the Virgin

I anticipated Michele's position at the Mattei household was untenable when the wounding of Pietro de Fossaccia became public knowledge. Michele threw a dish in his face in retaliation for the insult of waving flaccid artichoke spears under his nose and touching the food. That not one of the Mattei brothers attended the unveiling and dedication of either the *Entombment* or the *Madonna of Loreto* clearly suggested disapproval of his crumbling reputation. To pre-empt matters, Michele gave notice by letter he was leaving and received a brief but polite response delivered by the major-domo.

It took several days to cart Michele's and my possessions to the new address, a small house on the Vicolo dei Santa Cecilia in Biaggio. The house was rented from a woman called Prudentia Bruni for forty scudi a year which was reasonable and offered enough rooms and space to live and work. I had few possessions and Michele little more but he hired a wagon to move furniture items and packed chests. Lorenzo and I carried the paintings, including the overdue and barely started *Madonna of the Rosary*, commissioned by Luigi Carafa-Colonna on behalf of the Duke of Modena. It was the largest and heaviest and, with other smaller paintings, it took several journeys to complete the move. Michele used the two rooms of the upper storey with high ceilings as workshop and store. The two large paintings in progress were set up in the workshop with a large expensive mirror and a round convex mirror leant against the wall. The other smaller room was used to store materials and a large two poster bed and side tables. The rest of the furniture was arranged on the ground floor, a kitchen dresser of white poplar wood, a small chest covered with black leather, a folding bed, a red painted table, chairs, stools and another chest containing bowls, glassware and utensils, cutlery, books and items of clothing.

The day was over by the time the wagon left, so chests were left unpacked, a pair of brass candlesticks were found, and I lit candles. Before retiring, Michele knocked nails in the wall to hang up his swords within easy reach of the bed. He also unsheathed a dagger and slipped it under the mattress, close at hand. Michele slumped on the large bed, Lorenzo and I sat on a rolled-up mattress and shared bread dipped in oil and balsamic vinegar, olives and a flagon of wine. We were exhausted, and the sun had hardly set before we were asleep.

Michele first heard mention of Ranuccio Tomassoni from Fillide. It was assumed Ranuccio was her pimp. Michele told me he wasn't sure; surely, he would never let such an alluring woman out of his clutches. Furthermore, her looks and ability to charm whatever she wanted from any man meant, by the time Michele knew her, she had acquired many high-born clients who would offer any amount of protection, indicating she was and, always had been, her own woman and would never tolerate control by any man, especially the likes of the Tomassoni. It was the reason Michele persuaded her to model for the biblical Judith, coolly severing the head of the Assyrian general Holofernes. He gleaned from Fillide the Tomassoni clan had interests in many ventures, some barely this side of the law and many well beyond. Their interests included protection, blackmail and running girls. Ranuccio, the darling second son, was increasingly a big man in the streets of Rome, his status enhanced by his older brother, Captain Giovan Francesco, a former pontifical guard.

Michele met Ranuccio by chance at a tavern frequented by painters, pimps, whores and bardassas not long after he finished his portrait of the recently elevated Calimero Borghese to Pope Paul V. Michele observed Ranuccio, a handsome bit of rough, the type he liked from time to time with the swagger of a young buck with big balls, broad shoulders, narrow waist and hips.

Ranuccio caught him staring. "Who d'you think you're looking at?"

"You! If I hadn't already painted Jesus, I would have chosen you."

He left his companions and approached Michele, flagon of wine in one hand and drinking cup in the other. "You're a painter?"

"I am."

He gestured around the room, slopping wine on the floor. "Painters are ten a penny here. What have you painted?"

"Many pictures."

"What subjects?"

"Such and such."

"Where are they?"

"Here and there."

Ranuccio banged the jar on the table so hard it was surprising it didn't shatter; the bloody wine slopped and spattered his clothes. He lunged at Michele but, in a single movement, Michele drew the dagger tucked inside his belt and brought the blade up under Ranuccio's chin. The tavern fell silent. He pressed the point of the knife to barely puncture the skin, smiled and shook Ranuccio's right hand with his left. "Michelangelo Merisi da Caravaggio, painter to the Pope and His Excellency the Reverent Father Cardinal del Monte and, since you ask, my pictures hang in the Church of San Luigi, San Agostino and in the collections of Marchese Giustiniani, Marchese Mattei and a few others whose names I've forgotten… at your service, signor."

Ranuccio laughed, pushed the blade aside and wiped a droplet of blood from near his Adam's apple. "I've heard of you." He winked. "I saw your paintings in San Luigi. Yes, everybody loves your pictures. Have a drink with me, Master Michelangelo."

"Caravaggio… I prefer to be known as Caravaggio."

"Where's Caravaggio?"

They became friends of sorts. Ranuccio enjoyed the kudos, knowing the most famous painter in Rome, and Michele was attracted by Ranuccio's dangerous reputation, good looks and swagger but aware association with the Tomassoni was a double-edged blade. Spada and Onorio could be wild when drinking but the Tomassoni, Ranuccio and his brother Giovan Francesco were known to be particularly dangerous. Michele sensed Ranuccio saw him as a means to widen shady family business interests to acquire a veneer of respectability.

In Michele's circle, only Onorio was as loud and aggressive as the Tomassoni crowd, and he frequently fell in with them. Ranuccio was impressed Onorio was architect of the church of San Carlo al Corso and, like Michele, dangled potential access to higher social and wealthy circles. Where Onorio bragged about his patrons, Michele regretted ever mentioning his and was alarmed when Ranuccio and friends banged on his door one evening that led to a night of riotous carousing. Next morning, Michele was hungover and trembled. Thereafter, he kept the shutters closed after sunset and, however insistent the banging, never answered the door, which made Ranuccio's sudden appearance in his house one evening particularly alarming. Without thinking, Mario had opened the door, letting him in or more likely Ranuccio simply barged him aside. "I expected grand rooms… You're famous, why live in squalor… no offense."

"Welcome, Ranuccio, to my humble squalor."

"I heard you lodged in Cardinal del Monte's household."

"That was some time ago."

"You were crazy to leave the cardinal's house. I hear he was a good patron, many useful connections."

"I needed bigger workspace and this suits me well enough."

"Ah, I see your latest picture… a Madonna. With St Anne and Our Lord as a toddler… Ha, they're crushing a snake. I understand, Gesù and the Madonna destroy the snake in the garden of Eden." He stared at the painting several minutes in silence. "D'you think it's true?"

"What's true?"

"Good always triumphs."

"I only paint what I'm told."

"I don't believe that for a second. I heard some of your pictures were turned down because they weren't fit for what the priests want the gullible to believe."

Michele was intrigued Ranuccio was well informed. "Only one painting, the second version was accepted… very well received actually."

Ranuccio laughed. "Rumour breeds as it travels." He turned to look again at the painting, then drew aside the drapes covering the *Entombment* and the *Madonna of Loreto*. He stepped back. "Cazzo! I've never seen such real." He went slowly between paintings, eventually returning to the unfinished *Madonna of the Serpent*. "Who's the model for Our Lady?"

"I don't recall her name. I use many models, most prefer anonymity… and the money."

Ranuccio smiled. "I think I know her. Didn't she model with the baby in the other Madonna picture?" He continued staring at the picture, then casually said, "You knew Fillide, I believe."

"Yes, she modelled for a St Catherine and Judith. She was a good girl, a street girl in the early days, but she's done well for herself. I haven't seen her in a long time. I would have preferred her to model for this Madonna, the one with the snake."

"You really like her. She was a good model. A good girl…" Ranuccio grinned. "But I hear Lena's your girl these days."

"She modelled for the Madonna of Loreto, although…"

He stared unsmiling. "So you do know her. I heard you had a ruck with somebody over her."

"He claimed to be her fiancée but she said he was pestering her. She asked me to warn him off."

"I see. You were protecting her. Were you her protector, Michele? Is the boy yours?"

"What boy?"

"The boy – that boy in the painting."

"No, no! He was a year old when Lena first modelled for me. The painting is a vision of the Madonna and Child. I needed a woman who had a year-old boy."

After a brief pause, Ranuccio relaxed and smiled. "Fathered by someone else."

"Obviously."

"Father… unknown." He grinned. "Like Jesus…"

The *Death of the Virgin* was commissioned for the church of Santa Maria della Scala in Trestevere by Laerzio Cherubini somehow connected to the papal court, but Michele was working on final details of the *Madonna of the Serpent* for the Society of the Palafrenieri, the Vatican Horse Guards. The subject was formally titled *Madonna and Child with St Anne* but the inclusion of the snake was Michele's idea. The Palafrenieri intended the painting for their chapel in St Peter's. The captain and others who came to view the finished painting were delighted and keen to see it installed and final arrangements were agreed for collection and delivery to the Basilica. That his painting would be seen forever near Michelangelo's Pieta made him light headed.

The *Death of the Virgin* was his largest painting to date and the prospect of another crowded composition resurrected anxieties that haunted him since the struggle to complete the Contarelli paintings. Since working on the Saint Matthew pictures he had acquired a large cast of models, so once the strainer was delivered and the canvas stretched and prepared, he set up a bed in the workshop so he could work day and night. He arranged models to explore poses for the apostles. Lena would model the Virgin and Michele thought she might know other girls for the Marys. The height of the canvas, just one palm width short of the ceiling, meant the composition would necessarily be divided horizontally with the bed, heads of the disciples and architectural details marking three major divisions. Placing a melon on the bed in the position where the head of Our Lady would rest established the focus for the painting with four dominant figures around the bed. Three of the apostles bowed their heads, falling like notes in a musical scale, leading the eye to the

Virgin's face; the closest apostle to the Virgin held his head in his hands as he wept. A younger man, presumably the favourite Saint John, knelt second from the left and also covered his eyes, expressing the most obvious distress, echoing his balding counterpart, Saint Peter. The Saints John and Peter were in line with a figure standing back behind the head of the Virgin, his head supported by his hand which created a counter angle to the falling arc, leading the eye to the head of the Virgin. Michele was desperate to begin work on the Virgin, sending Lorenzo to ask if Lena would come soon, but he returned saying she was not at her lodgings. Michele put out the word he urgently needed Lena to model for him but without response. Usually, she would turn up within a day or so but almost a week passed until he could wait no longer, went to her lodgings and banged on the door. An old woman answered, saying she had not been seen for days. "Her boy's here so she should be home soon enough. She sometimes stays with a friend."

"Tell her, Master Caravaggio the painter wants her to come to him the moment she returns."

"Oh, we know of you, master. Sound's urgent, signor." The old madam cackled. "If you're discomforted, we have other girls; they'll scratch your itch."

"Are you sure you don't know where she is?"

One of the girls leaned over the old woman's shoulder. "You must know she's Tomassoni's favourite."

"Quiet girl."

"Ranuccio. Is that where she is?"

The old woman retreated, shoving the younger girl behind her and slammed the door in his face with the sound of shot bolts. However long he banged and kicked the door, there was no response.

The sergeant of the papal horse guards and four men arrived with a cart to take the *Madonna of the Serpent* to St Peter's for the unveiling the following Sunday 26th July. The lads started to cover the painting, but Michele insisted it was driven to the basilica uncovered as Michelangelo's David had been drawn through the streets of Florence and instructed the soldiers to fix a notice to the cart and call out to passers-by:

Madonna of the Serpent by Master Michele da Caravaggio on its way to be installed at St Peter's Basilica.

When the wagon was out of sight, he had Lorenzo pose on the bed in place of Lena. After shouting at Lorenzo to stop laughing, he managed to dress him in the robe he arranged for the Madonna. It was a woollen red dress, similar to the colour of the garment worn by the Christ in the *Supper at Emmaus*, but Lena was taller than Lorenzo, so Michele raised the skirts to reveal the expensive silk lining and his bare feet. Lorenzo shrieked in falsetto, "O, Signor Michele, I am not that kind of girl."

Cecco laughed and clapped. "Shut up. It's not the first time you've worn a dress and you've had more than your skirts raised in the past."

He sketched the position of the head, three quarter facing the viewer, one hand resting on the stomach, the other arm towards the viewer to show off his ability in foreshortening. The ankles and feet were exposed. "Lie still, Renzo and Cecco, stop chattering like monkeys or get out."

Standing back to apprise the painting, it was clear the arc fell *too fast* from the head of the first standing figure on the left to the bald head of Saint Peter near the Virgin. His heart sank; he had to repaint the Peter figure further to the right to make sense of the composition. The paint was wet enough to wipe out the figure but, when he sent Cecco to fetch a cloth, they heard rumbling in the street. He opened the shutters to find dark clouds hastening on the night, but it was obvious someone was drumming on the door downstairs.

"Hurry, Lorenzo, get dressed. It might be Lena."

Lorenzo removed the dress and quickly put on breeches and shirt and padded barefoot down the stairs. Michele covered the painting, the drumming abruptly stopped and there were excited voices. He was halfway down the stairs where he met Onorio, Spada and another coming up.

"Michele, stop working. We're going to a party."

"I've too much work…"

"You always have too much to do. You've not been out with us once in over two months."

"Because every time I go with you, I end up in the Tor di Nona."

"It'll be fun."

"You may have fun, but I'm the one always arrested."

"Only because you fancy the officer of the watch—" He slapped Spada's face, leaving red finger marks. "It's a joke, Michele." Spada threw back his head and stared down his nose, a reminder he still believed he controlled Michele through ashes of lust.

He smoothed Michele's shirt. "Change your doublet. This one's covered in paint; it's a rag and cost a fortune."

"Where are we going?"

"It's a surprise."

He was anxious when they arrived at the Tomassoni house, but there was a remote hope he might see Lena. The house was en fete, torches lit up the front door decked in mock-splendour wreaths of oleander and the sound of music. Most of the Tomassoni were dressed in garish costumes barely this side of sumptuary laws. The feast table was ostentatiously laden with roast chickens, piglet, duck and pheasant, lines of carafes filled to the brims with wine and arrangements of fresh fruit and flowers. Ranuccio stood beside his wife. She was beautiful and, from her engorged breasts and residual bloated stomach, had recently given birth. The Tomassoni matriarch stood on the other side of her son, decked with expensive jewellery which heightened the contrast with her craggy face and wrinkled, spotted hands but what was bizarrely incongruous was Lena standing between the matriarch and the older brother Giovan Francesco. It was a curious tableau.

Ranuccio approached. "Everyone, welcome my friend – the most famous painter Signor Michelangelo Merisi da Caravaggio – and his company… and the celebrated architect Signor Onorio Longhi."

To a ripple of applause, Ranuccio steered Michele to the table where he poured glasses of wine, then toasted, "To Caravaggio and companions."

Cecco, Mario, Lorenzo and Spada nodded and Michele was introduced to the matriarch whose fixed smile and vacant eyes signified nothing. Ranuccio's wife smiled as Michele's lips hovered over her hand.

Ranuccio spoke to Michele in a whisper when they reached Lena. "I believe you two have a previous association."

Lena laughed and winked but, when Michele started to say, "I've been—" She slightly shook her head and glanced sideways at Ranuccio.

Onorio joined them. "I've not yet been introduced to the most beautiful woman in the room." He bowed to Lena and kissed her hand, unaware or uncaring he had insulted the host's wife.

Lena giggled and leant towards him. "You were Michele's Madonna; I recognise that wonderful face." As though he had not met her before, he nudged Michele. "No wonder you kept her under wraps, she's exquisite." Hearing music, Onorio led Lena to join the dance.

Ranuccio's expression was thunderous. "Excuse me, I…" He went to stand beside his mother who slightly raised herself on tiptoe, jigged to the rhythm of the music and stared vacantly ahead, her hands crossed tightly, gripping an ivory fan.

After a long silence, Ranuccio's wife turned to him. "I have seen your paintings, Master Michelangelo."

"Michele."

She giggled. "Michele, as I say, I've seen your paintings at St Luigi, and I am impressed, more than impressed actually; they are beautiful."

"Thank you, a sincere compliment since truth is beauty."

"Very philosophical. But seriously you see the world as it is, good and bad, saints and sinners, and you tell the truth as you see it. Others paint pretty pictures, honeyed saints, decorous sinners and fat putti with pink arses."

He grinned. "You're gracious, but what do you know about pretty paintings or arses for that matter?"

She laughed aloud, grabbed his arm and leant towards him. "I know the truth when I see it, especially a good arse. Why shouldn't we women appreciate the same things as our so-called betters?" Before he could respond, she said, "You know Lena."

He hesitated. Perhaps Ranuccio had told her to fish.

"She modelled for me… yes."

"Don't be concerned. I know she's Ranuccio's girl." She shrugged. "I bear the kids, but he gets rid of his dirty water with her." She laughed and tugged his arm. "I hope I shock you, Michele."

"I don't think anything you say could shock me, lady, but forgive me, I was never told your name."

"Lavinia."

As they bantered, Michele glanced up to catch Ranuccio glaring. He forced a smiled but continued to stare until distracted by a roar from the company which circled the dancers. Even though the tune was not a Volta, Onorio lifted Lena up with his hands between her legs. Lena shrieked hysterically, her cheeks red and hair damp with sweat. The musicians increased the tempo as Onorio swirled her around until they almost fell into the crowd. Everyone laughed and clapped until Ranuccio grabbed Lena by the wrist and dragged her out of the room. Michele strode towards the door, but Lorenzo wheeled him away. Mario laughed. "The cat's out of the bag now."

Spada brayed, "Nothing the whole world didn't know already."

Michele tried to shrug off Lorenzo's grip. "We have to do something; he's probably beating her senseless."

Spada stood in front of Michele and gripped his shoulders. "There's nothing we can do; in any case, she's just a street whore." He wrenched free of Spada's hold and was about to follow Lena when he noticed Onorio cross to stand near Ranuccio's wife and lean towards her. They whispered to one another. She barely nodded, turned away and left the room. The Tomassoni matriarch was left standing alone, still gripping her fan. Onorio glanced around to ensure he was not observed, then paused a few minutes and slipped away, following Lavinia. Michele scanned the company; no one else had noticed what passed between them and recognised Onorio's attention to Lena was a charade to keep Ranuccio off the scent.

In the morning, he heard movement in the studio. He lay fully dressed and hungover, having drunk at least a flagon of wine in a tavern on the way home, propped up by Lorenzo and Cecco who were also worse for wear. Lorenzo had stayed the night and Mario must have arrived early to prepare the workshop for the day's work. Cecco lay fully clothed and snoring beside him. His head ached when he got up and staggered, feeling sick. He went carefully down the stairs, feeling dizzy, and called to Mario, "Don't move anything; just clean the brushes and open the shutters. The smell of paint makes me…"

"On top of wine no doubt."

"I'm starving."

Mario opened the small food cupboard which, apart from mouldy bread, was empty. Michele picked up coins scattered across the floor by the bed and handed them to Mario. "Be quick."

When Mario opened the door, Michele heard, "Is Master Caravaggio at home?"

Michele went to the door surprised by the arrival of the captain of the horse guards. The captain saluted. "Good day. I'll come straight to the point… I'm sorry to say the cardinals insisted the painting removed from St Peter's. They're unhappy, cackling something about lack of decorum. I suppose they mean the tits and the boy's cock, as though they hadn't seen plenty of both."

Michele glanced over the captain's shoulder to see men lift from the wagon what was obviously the painting covered with a grey cloth.

"I know this is a blow, Michele, and, thank God, the painting wasn't damaged. Some of the priests were pretty violent, slapping the picture like a whore's arse. But the news isn't all bad. The Cardinal Nephew, Scipione Borghese, offered to buy it from the Society so nobody's out of pocket. His Eminence's men will arrange collection and transport. Again, Master Caravaggio, I am deeply sorry to be the bearer of unwelcome news." He handed Michele a sealed note, saluted, mounted his horse and the painting was carried into the house. As the cavalcade moved off, Michele opened the letter. It was a note of comments made by several priests and functionaries at the Vatican. He briefly scanned the paper: *In this painting, there is but vulgarity, sacrilege, impiousness and disgust. One* would *say it is a work made by a painter that can paint well, but of a dark spirit and who has been a long time far from God, from His adoration and from any good thought…*

Michele knew that particular comment expressed sentiments towards his work held by many in the Curia. He screwed up the paper, slammed the door, his knees buckled and he vomited. Cecco helped him to the bed, lay beside him and gently stroked his back.

"Michele!" Someone shook his shoulder. "Michele, are you awake?" He turned over to see a double blurry silhouette of young man and a tall woman.

"It's me, Michele…"

"Lena."

She and the young man beside her came into focus… Cecco. Lena leaned down and kissed his brow. "I'm sorry to hear about the painting."

He sat up. She handed him a cup of wine, which he sipped, and looked up at her. She smiled but her face was swollen and bruised.

"Ranuccio?"

She nodded and pressed her hand on his chest to prevent him from rising. "Don't be angry, Michele; he's not worth your precious time." She sat on the bed and looked up at the painting. "Is that where I would be dead?"

He nodded. Her lip trembled. "It's a pity I can't model for her. I would have liked that. I played her in life in the last painting with my boy as her son." There were tears in her eyes. "I can't model for you any more, Michele."

"He can't stop you."

"Yes, he can. If that's what he wants and, God help me, he's what I want, and I can't help myself."

"You love him." She began to cry and nodded. "Is the boy his?"

She tucked her hair behind her ear. "I couldn't say for sure but hope he is."

He stroked her hand. "Couldn't you come when he's not around?"

"I'm scared, Michele. I'm even frightened he'll find out I was here. You don't know what he's capable of; I have to go." She went towards the stairs but hesitated. "I hope you find another Mother of God and may She bless you." She draped a scarf to cover her face before going silently down the stairs. He heard the latch click as she slipped out the door.

With her leaving, Michele fixated on searching for a model for the Virgin to shield his disappointment. Lena was his ideal and scouring the streets, taverns and brothels for her replacement was increasingly frustrating as the Virgin slipped beyond his reach, becoming ever more remote by the day. The woman he needed must resemble Lena, so fixed was her image of the Virgin in his mind. She had been his *Madonna of Loreto*, already becoming widely known as the *Madonna of the Pilgrims*. She attracted so much love and adoration he wanted the same for the Death. As the painting progressed without the central figure, he considered approaching Orazio Gentileschi to see if his girl would model for him, with a chaperone if he wished. Artemisia was about sixteen, not much older than Cecco and mature for her age, but she was homely rather than beautiful and doubted Orazio would allow her to model. Apparently, she was painting commissions and a valuable source of family income.

Banging was incessant. "Caravaggio. Hello, Michele. Halloo, we know you're at home."

Mario was apprehensive and stood by the door. "What shall we do?" Cecco drew Michele's sword from its scabbard and handed it to him.

"Christ, every time someone bangs on my door, it brings Devil's work."

Michele pushed Mario gently towards the door, handed him a dagger. "When I nod, open but stay behind the door."

At the signal, Mario quietly slid the bolt aside and yanked open the door. Michele rushed into the street, sword and dagger in hand to find four revellers in carnival masks. They laughed and raised their hands in mock surrender. "Careful, Master Caravaggio, you'll scratch yourself."

"What do you want?" One doffed his hat and, from his light reddish-brown hair, Michele recognised he was Ranuccio's younger brother, Mario. "We've brought a gift from an admirer."

The four lifted a heavy sack, stepped over the threshold and dropped it with a dull thud. "Enjoy your gift, Master Caravaggio." They left, bowing and laughing.

Mario slammed the door and shot the bolt. They stared at the musty sack, the canvas heavier than painters' flax, sodden, muddy and stinking of the wharves. It was tied with thick cord. The sacking was oily; Michele gestured to Mario to pass him the sharp knife but rather than hand it over, Mario stooped, sawed the cord, pulled open the canvas, leapt back and shouted, "*Gesù!*"

A woman's head lolled to one side, eyes open, teeth exposed by the slightly parted taut purple lips. Her hair was wet and her greenish pale face was damp. Michele knelt, gingerly turned the face towards him and, even though swollen, he saw what he already knew. He stroked her hair, then stood, crossed to the table and poured three glasses of wine to the brim. His hands trembled as he offered one to Mario, the other to Cecco. "Drink, you're in shock."

Cecco spoke first. "Who would do this?"

"Ranuccio. It was Ranuccio."

Michele gulped wine. "He wants me to paint her as the dead Virgin."

"He's mad. You can't, Michele… You shouldn't paint a murdered woman as the Holy Mother."

Cecco crossed himself. "Call the watch, Michele, tell them it was…"

"Who would believe me? What proof is there? A dead woman in my house, you know what they would say and with my record." He drew his forefinger across his throat.

"Wouldn't it be better to tell the watch before Ranuccio tips them off?"

"He won't tell anyone."

"You don't know that. It's a warning of what's in store for you. I'll go to the Palazzo Madam or the Colonna palace…"

"No, Cecco."

He took another gulp of wine. "I don't want the cardinal or the Colonna involved. Maybe you're right about Ranuccio, but I'm certain he won't do anything until I've painted her. It's what he wants; he slit her throat and drowned her in jealousy and fury but now he's consumed with remorse. He wants her immortalised in the painting."

"But why?"

"Because he loves her… He wouldn't share her so he killed her so no one else could have her."

"But she's one of his working girls. How could he be in love with her?"

"If other men had her, he knew she didn't care but if he thought she cared for someone…"

"He's crazy."

"Mario, listen… listen! Help me put the red robe on her and lay her on the bed and then you must go."

"I won't leave you and Cecco here alone."

Michele stared at him. No longer young Mario. Now he was a married man. "Think of Carlita."

After several minutes when Mario stared him out, Michele eventually released a long sigh. "If you must. We're safe until the painting's finished." They struggled to carry the sodden weight of the corpse upstairs. It was heavy and sagged and, reaching the workshop, they gently let the bundle down on the floor. "Now, go home and take Cecco with you."

"I'm not leaving you here alone."

Cecco was equally adamant. "I'm not going either."

Michele stared from one to the other then muttered, "Stack a chair on the high table and a stool on top and put up four lighted candles… and close the blind." He stripped Lena naked and dressed her in the red robe. It was only when she was out of the sack that they saw how her body, face, chest and arms were badly bruised. She must have put up a fight before Ranuccio killed her. They arranged the body to match the pose worked out with Lorenzo as her substitute and Michele immediately began correcting the rough sketch of the face, mixing and applying true colour and tone.

Mario and Cecco mixed colour to his instructions. "Base yellow ochre, add a little burnt umber and a tiny amount of azurite, I'll adjust and put in the white…" The grey pallor of Lena's face was turning greenish by the time the sun rose after working through the night. Mario went to reassure Carla he was well with the half-truth that Michele had found the perfect model and they were working hard to finish the painting.

They continued through the next day and into the following night without pause. Cecco prepared pasta with basil and olives which they ate as they worked. Eventually, Mario had to light fresh candles but, an hour after sunset, Michele's sight was blurred and all three were exhausted. Mario slept on the cot downstairs, but Michele stayed in the workshop and slept in a chair with Cecco on the bed. He felt safer sleeping close to Lena's corpse rather than let her out of sight to haunt his dreams. Mario slipped out at first light to buy bread, cheese, cured ham, fresh fruit and wine. Michele started work as soon as he woke and completed the portrait, hands and feet around midday. Apart from a break for food, the Madonna was finished by nightfall.

He sipped wine as they regarded the picture. Lena's body had swollen alarmingly, recreated in the painting, her bloated belly not only a ghastly memorial for her orphaned child but also the Virgin who bore Christ. The folds in the dress were different from when Lorenzo posed which Michele adjusted as the painting progressed but, by nightfall, Lena had become the Virgin. He tapped Mario on the arm to wake him. "We must get her out of here."

They stripped her of the red robe and dressed her in the grey dress the dirty river water had dried in stiff creases. Her body was even more swollen, lips and fingers beginning to turn black as they wrapped her in the sack but, before closing it, Michele put a small wooden rosary around her neck, tidied her hair as best he could before hiding her face for good and tying the cord. They lugged Lena down the stairs and reverently laid her by the door until the street was quiet.

Hearing bells toll two, Cecco went out to be sure the street was empty and, when he gestured all clear, Michele hoisted the sack over his shoulder. Cecco scouted ahead and Mario hung back as they avoided the Corso and took back streets and alleys on the way to the river. Michele dreaded bumping into the watch and listened for the familiar rhythmic footfall and faint clank of breastplates and buckles. They repeatedly ducked back in alleys when they saw lights or heard voices.

They froze when they heard a gang of boasting bravos. Cecco waved his arm for Michele to stay back and watched the lads make a line to piss against the wall. Once relieved, they slowly moved away, their laughs and loud bragging echoed off the walls until they dispersed at the next corner. Cecco waited a few moments, then signalled Michele to follow. Their luck held and were relieved when they reached an alley that ended at the riverbank near the Ponte Sisto. Michele let down the sack in the shadow of the last building opposite the shiny leaden river. He slipped down to squat on the ground, breathing heavily and exhausted, not simply carrying the dead weight but also the anxiety they might be caught.

He was not sure if he really intended to put her back in the river; it seemed sacrilegious but if not there, where? Leaning against the wall, he said the body would be soonest found if it were left where it was. The lads nodded, perhaps relieved and desperate to leave.

Michele told Mario to go home. "Don't let anyone see you." He nodded and disappeared into the black alley. Michele and Cecco walked quickly, taking a wide circuitous route to get as far from the corpse as possible. Michele held his sword against his hip, checking every alley before turning each corner. They avoided main streets where palaces had guarded entrances or illuminated by torchlight. There were many detours as they made their way from the river. It was more than an hour before they arrived back at the house. Michele ached from the weight of carrying the body and his leather doublet was damp, stained and stank of the mouldy wet sacking. He stripped and, after kicking the doublet into the corner, Cecco washed him with a soapy cloth. He closed his eyes and tried to relax into the rhythmic wiping of his neck, shoulders back and chest and Cecco helped him to the bed where he rolled onto his side and, within minutes, lightly snored.

Michele assumed Lena's body would surely be found early next day but there were neither reports nor gossip. In the evening, he said he would go to see if her body still lay where they left her but Cecco said it would be crazy to return in case the body was watched. After half-hearted protestations, he finally agreed. In the next three, four, five days there was not the slightest rumour, no doubt she was presumed to be another unknown prostitute killed by a randy client who had his way but lacked the money to pay her modest rate. Michele was appalled the murder of women was so common it was barely worthy of report or comment.

The painting progressed rapidly. He moved the Saint Peter figure further right to complete the arc of heads ending with the Holy Mother's face. He intended to paint a weeping Mary Magdalene in the foreground but it was days before he found a replacement who was thinner facially than Fillide but favoured similar clothes and wore a dusty pink-orange bodice over a chemise and fashionably uncovered hairstyle. She posed leaning forward, head in hands to echo the gesture of the male figure on the far side of the bed. Once the weeping Mary was finished, he addressed the void in the top third of the painting and decided to paint the roof beams of the ceiling at the house and, recalling Francesco's state bed with drapes and hangings, told Cecco to fetch the red cloth used in half a dozen St Johns and nailed it to the rafters draped in a great swag leading the eye into the painting. He meticulously recreated every fold and crease in three tones and, by the end of the week, was satisfied the painting was finished and sent Cecco with a message to Cardinal Mattei to inform him and the fathers of Santa Maria della Scala that the painting was ready.

Chapter 22

Lena

It was sweltering and the child continued to whinge, so Lena stripped him and sat him on her lap. Michele watched as she soothed the boy. When the child was calm enough to continue, Michele said she should leave him naked if he's happier. She put his clothes on the stool, then walked him across the room, his feet on hers and the boy laughed. Michele swiftly altered the figure of the boy, wiping away the clothes and painting the now nude Christ child. Naturally, the boy could only hold the pose for short periods but Michele was unusually patient, and I noticed he was able to work from memory between rest and play periods. In all, he needed his models only three days once the boy was painted and the mother's face and upper body was done.

It was the same when he arranged for an older woman to pose for Saint Anne. He made her considerably older, her face, neck and chest darker and worn in contrast to the milky flesh of the Madonna. He painted her as she was, a peasant woman, but standing with her head inclined, hands lightly clasped, she had a monumental dignity of someone who'd lived a hard life, used and abused yet probably retained a core of simple unquestioning faith having made ten thousand confessions and said a million rosaries. Her dress and two cloaks swathed around her tired body.

One morning I drew off the cloth, and, as I glanced at the old woman, I saw it was my mother… the tilt of her head, clasped hands and her outdoor cloak swathed around her against a cold, cruel world… Not Mamma as I remembered her like the protecting *Madonna of Loreto*, but *with* her dislocated jaw, the way I imagined she was likely to become. I rushed from the workshop before I was convulsed by sobs and wandered aimlessly along alleys and streets until exhausted and slumped on the rim of a dribbling fountain in the corner of a tiny square.

In the following days, I watched Michele lovingly paint the older woman, unaware of my grief and certainty I would never see Mamma again. Finally, he painted a writhing snake, its head crushed under the Madonna's foot, the child's foot on hers. I recognised the child represented the second

Adam, his mother the second Eve, the child's extended arms anticipated his crucifixion, the whole painting foreshadowing a pieta. I thought the so-called *Madonna of the Serpent* was among the best I had seen Michele do, not simply because he had unknowingly painted a memorial for my mamma, whether she were alive or not… but also because, like the Madonna of Loreto and the *Entombment*, it spoke directly, especially to those who shared hard bitten lives. I knew Michele slipped away to the Palazzo Madama several times, presumably to discuss ideas with the cardinal, but it was the way he so quickly saw a novel form for the painting when Lena stripped the child to cool him and seeing the boy's sheer joy, freed from restricting clothing and the game of walking on his mother's feet. Consequently, I felt the shock as keenly as Michele when the painting was rejected, as Mamma was defeated by life and abused. It didn't matter the Cardinal Nephew snapped it up; its rightful place was Saint Peter's.

The *Death of the Virgin* for Santa Maria della Scala was Michele's next and largest commission. He wanted Lena to model for the dead Madonna, but she was Ranuccio Tomassoni's girl and Michele had fallen into Ranuccio's orbit. Indeed, he may have indulged Michele's interest in Lena at first to cement a form of friendship, but I assumed he became concerned Michele might profit from Lena's street business. Ranuccio's suspicion may have heightened when Michele was prosecuted for attacking the notary… Pasqualini who pestered Lena and in open court claimed Lena was *Michelangelo's girl*. After the riotous Tomassoni party, Lena disappeared for several weeks. Michele repeatedly sent me to Lena's place, asking her to model for the Virgin but there was never a response. Even when Michele finally went himself, there was no luck. She eventually turned up at our house, hooded and her face covered. I saw bruises on her face and she was terrified she might be followed but needed to tell Michele to his face she could not model for the Virgin. We never saw her alive again. Michele believed Ranuccio killed her in a fit of jealous rage and dumped her body in the Tiber. Overcome by remorse, he had her body fished out of the river and left her corpse at our door.

I remember the younger Tomassoni boy saying, "Here's a gift from an admirer; enjoy the present, Master Caravaggio."

When Lena's body was uncovered, I stood in shock and disbelief. It was the first time I'd seen a dead body, much less a murdered woman, a naked woman at that, with hair between the legs and cold, pale greenish flesh, her throat slashed. Mario yelped when he opened the sack, and I felt sick. We stood around her corpse, not knowing what to do and was horrified when Michele said he was going to paint her as the Virgin as he would have done if she had come to model for him alive. He said Ranuccio sent the body for him to immortalise her. Mario said we should call the sbirri but neither of us could change Michele's mind and the longer the body was in the house, the more dangerous for us all. I thought the Tomassoni would tip off the sbirri and expected them at the door any moment but Michele was certain that so long as he painted her, we were safe and was confident Ranuccio would do nothing until she became the dead Virgin.

At the time I didn't understand why Ranuccio killed her even when Michele explained it was because he loved her but wouldn't share her and came to believe she had feelings for Michele which made him mad with jealousy. From the moment I first saw Ranuccio, I realised he was in awe of Michele and at first not particularly concerned that they shared Lena, even excited by making love to Michele at one remove but the thought she might prefer Michele cast him outside the triangle. I thought Michele was mad to allow the body to stay in the house for even a moment but he was stubborn. Mario and I reluctantly helped dress her in the red garment and, when her body was arranged on the bed, he insisted we both leave but we refused and spent the next day and a half in states of acute anxiety and dread until Michele finished painting the corpse. We were exhausted, having slept only a few hours, and Michele hugged me tight as we tried to sleep on the cot in the workshop.

He whispered, "I daren't sleep out of sight of the corpse because otherwise she might haunt us."

After nearly thirty hours, Lena's body became bloated, her feet and hands blackening and the house was filled with the sickly, earthy smell of death and we needed to get her out of the house. We wrapped her in the sacking again and decided to leave the house after nightfall, dreading the risk of running into the night watch. We each gulped large cups of wine and, when we left the house, I scouted ahead, Michele carried Lena over his shoulder and Mario kept lookout behind. From the direction he indicated, I assumed he intended to put her back in the river. Fortunately, there were not many people abroad in the early hours. The greatest risk of discovery was when we needed to cross a main street. I called Michele forward, waited until there was no one in sight, then we ran across to the next dark alleyway. When we eventually arrived at the river, Michele paced up and down because he couldn't bear to simply dump her in the murky water. I squatted in the dark, shivering on the verge of panic, the longer we were there, the more likely were we to be caught.

Michele suddenly said, "We have to leave her here. She'll be found in a matter of hours." He insisted Mario now go home and, once he slipped away, hugged me. "Are you all right?" I could tell he was as fearful, away from the relative safety of the house, as I was. A chilly breeze from the metallic river ruffled my hair, and I shuddered. Michele draped his cloak around me and we hurried back to the house with his arm over my shoulder.

Returning to the Vicolo, Michele slumped into a chair. I lay on the cot and stared into the dark with the odour of death lingering in the room. In the following days, there was no rumour or gossip about the discovery of a murdered woman and, by the end of the week, Michele assumed she must have been quickly buried in a communal pit. I found it impossible to stave off images of Lena... her barely visible sightless eyes and worse, the stab of guilt and horror that dogs might find her before the authorities and I was sure Michele felt the same. He fretted not knowing what happened to Lena's body and was the reason he worked so hard and fast to finish the painting, at least to put her to rest in the picture... her memorial. It was several weeks before the painting was finished. For some reason, he traced several figures and repainting them further to the right. I didn't understand why until I noticed him pivot his arm at the elbow in an arc that ended at the Virgin's head. It was clear he had found a better composition. Finally, he hired a young woman he painted leaning forward, head in hands to echo the gesture of one of the male figures on the far side of the bed. I supposed the weeping woman was Mary Magdalene, unaware at the time Lena's full name was Maddalena.

I thought the painting was finished and the longer it remained in the workshop the more anxious I was and, when he said it wasn't finished, I snapped, "You made your confession... now let the painting go."

He simply continued to sit before the canvas for hours; my anxiety turned to panic. Eventually, he told me to fetch the red cloth from the chest and nailed it to the rafters draped in a great swag and painted so accurately it appeared to hang from a beam as if in front of the picture on the left side and swept back into the room on the right. The beam marked the surface of the canvas, the dangling end of the fabric seemed to hang in this world, like the hand of Peter and Cleophas' elbow jutting out of the Emmaus painting. Finally, he sent the painting to the framer and I delivered a message to the fathers at Santa Maria della Scala that the painting would soon be delivered by the framer. About a week later, a message arrived, asking Michele to urgently attend the church. He thought the framer might have damaged the painting on the way to the church. We hurried to Santa Maria. The painting was not in place in the church but covered by a cloth in the refectory.

When the painting was uncovered, Michele nodded. "Yes, I didn't finish the end of the bed supporting the Virgin's feet… and the legs of the disciple on the far side of the bed don't match the upper part of the figure when I repainted them closer to the Virgin."

I had not noticed the mistakes either and Michele said I should fetch materials and brushes to make corrections but, before I reached the door, the head priest said the church could not accept the painting because it was a disgrace and disrespectful to the Holy Mother.

Other fathers chimed in and Michele became angry and, when I heard someone mention Michelangelo's Pieta, he snapped, drew his knife and would have slashed the painting if the brothers hadn't held him back. They wrenched the knife out of his hand as he struggled and howled like a dog and punched and kicked to free himself. I dashed to him and stroked his face and tried to calm him but he continued to struggle. He stared me in the face as though he didn't know me. I couldn't help weeping and the father superior gently lifted me up and knelt down in my place. It was a long time before Michele, still held down, no longer struggled.

The head priest gestured for everyone to leave but, as they filed away, I hid behind a lectern to stay nearby. The priest spoke in a low murmur, saying he understood it was a terrible blow and surprisingly said it was a wonderful painting. That caught Michele's attention. The priest sat and, when Michele eventually joined him on the bench, the priest pointed, saying the way the light fell across the painting was God's interpretation of a Master Caravaggio. The priest spoke softly, so I was unable to catch much of what he said.

I vaguely heard Michele mention Lena at which the priest sharply raised his voice. "Are you telling me you painted a dead woman?" When Michele nodded, the priest asked how she died and Michele said she had been murdered.

"You killed her?"

"No, of course not!" He sat in silence a moment, then muttered something about the Tomassoni and the workshop.

The priest paced up and down, coming to an abrupt standstill before Michele. "You colluded with the murderer."

Michele leapt up and shouted, "Can't you see? The Lena I painted for the Loreto had to be the same for the death of the Virgin…" It was then I understood why Michele insisted Lena had to be the dead Madonna. "If she was the *Madonna of the Pilgrims*, why shouldn't her death, however awful, become the body of the Holy Mother who also suffered."

The priest was now toe to toe with Michele and angry, saying he abandoned her body in an alley, leaving her to be buried in unhallowed ground with no last rites. He was even more enraged when Michele said he'd told him everything under the protection of the confessional… "We're alone and you have a duty to absolve me."

The priest roared, "*Not so!*" He stood rigid, eventually covering his face in his hands. Michele sat down and stared at the painting. The priest turned away, walked around the room, counting the beads of his rosary. It was a long time before he returned to sit beside Michele and spoke in a faint voice and at great length, but I was too far away to hear. The father emphasised points with his fingers. Michele nodded and occasionally inclined his head as he responded.

Then I heard the priest say, "You understand? No vendetta."

Michele nodded.

The priest told Michele to kneel, then made the sign of the cross. *Ego te absolvo.* Left alone, Michele sat before the painting a long time. Maybe he thought he should let the father believe he had said the rosary a few times although I was sure he wouldn't. He often joked, *All my sins are mortal.* Eventually, he stood and made his way to the door. I stepped out of the shadows and, as we left the church, he slipped his arm over my shoulder. "Did you hear all that?"

I nodded. "Some."

I woke to an empty house. I imagined Michele had been arrested or had drunk himself unconscious and abandoned by so-called friends. Anxious for his safety, I folded cheese in a roll of prosciutto to eat as I went in search, starting with the local taverns and goals. It was early afternoon when I found him slumbering in the corner of a bar halfway across the city. I woke him, and we barely spoke. He leant on my shoulder as I guided him to the Vicolo to find the landlady had locked us out and nailed a note to the door: *The painter Caravaggio owes his landlady, Prudenzia Bruni, twelve weeks' rent.* Michele swore and kicked the door.

Even though I was frustrated by the craziness and drinking, I kept silent. I understood how melancholy and humiliated he was by the rejection of the *Death of the Virgin*. At that moment, there seemed no fight left in him. He leant against the wall a few moments, then told me to stay by the house until he returned. I sat on the ground, hugged my knees and, from the chimes of the bells, waited over two hours before he reappeared. Without a word, he gestured to me to follow and we walked in silence to a house opposite the Colonna palace. A servant answered the door and we were greeted by a gentleman, Andrea Rufetti, a Colonna agent, a lawyer I think.

I came to know Rufetti well. He greatly admired Michele's paintings. He was welcoming and gave up half the house, including three bedrooms, two living rooms, a workshop and a serving man and woman to clean and provide meals if needed. I mumbled I wouldn't give up half my home under any circumstances, but Michele said it was a Colonna house and Rufetti was probably instructed to take us in. I was more concerned about how we were going to get our possessions back, especially Michele's paintings. All we had were the clothes on our backs.

Next morning, Michele arranged a wagon, but the waggoner was shocked when Michele split the blinds with an axe and, despite complaining, I was heaved up and shoved through the window. Michele shouted to me to hurry, but I couldn't find a key. Suddenly, the door was shattered, and I barely escaped a blow from the axe. Michele shouldered the door and rushed in, axe in hand. "Gesù, I could have been killed."

Michele ignored me and rushed up the stairs. Lorenzo and I brought out the dresser, tables and bed and Michele brought the rolled-up *Madonna of the Rosary* cut from the strainer and returned to fetch the large first version for the Cerasi painting of the *Conversion of Saint Paul*, then the big mirror, the convex mirror, blankets and costumes. Once his paintings and materials were carefully stowed, Michele was impatient to leave. I checked the house to make sure we had taken everything of ours. The waggoner complained he would be arrested for abetting theft if the sbirri turned up and was even more alarmed when the landlady and her daughter appeared, screaming and shouting. He whipped the horse, Michele and Lorenzo sat next to the waggoner and I had to run to climb on the cart. As we gathered speed, Prudenza hoiked up her skirts to show her threadbare muff, then turned to expose her bare arse and farted. She ran after us until she had to lean over to catch her breath, her podgy hands on her knees and screamed in impotent rage, threw a handful of horse shit that fell well short of the cart. Michele laughed aloud and directed the driver to Rufetti's house.

Rufetti's servant woke me early and urged me to quickly follow him to Andrea's quarters where Michele lay on a small bed with a doctor in attendance. Michele was drenched in blood from a wound to his throat and ear. He claimed it was an accident. The physician had cleaned and sewn the wound in his neck, salved with honey and bound. A Colonna lawyer attended, who said the criminal court must be advised of Michele's whereabouts because the wounds suggested a fight or ambush. Michele was adamant there had been no fight; it was just a fall. The lawyer didn't believe a word and reminded Michele of the penalties for duelling, commented on his reputation for brawling and questioned if he had a licence to carry arms.

"I do, from His Eminence Cardinal del Monte."

The following morning, a clerk of the criminal court arrived with another Colonna lawyer as well as the master of the Colonna household. The clerk asked Michele to confirm he was Michelangelo Merisi, but Michele said he preferred to be known as Caravaggio the painter. The notary seemed irritated when he scribbled the change on the paper, then asked Michele to describe the events and how he came to be wounded. Michele muttered he had fallen and cut himself on his sword but couldn't remember where because he lost consciousness. The clerk was not convinced the wounds were the result of a fall and asked if there were witnesses. Michele simply said no one else was around. Noticing Lorenzo and me, the notary asked, "Were these gentlemen witnesses?"

When Michele said we were not, he asked who we were, and he shrugged and gestured in our direction. "My assistants Francesco Boneri and Lorenzo Carlo who are here for concern for my wellbeing."

Andrea said Michele had arrived at his house before noon the day before in the state the clerk could see and since there were no witnesses there was nothing more to add. The clerk asked Andrea to confirm he was in the employ of His Excellency Duke Marzio Colonna but the master of the household intervened, "That is irrelevant to your investigation." Once the clerk had quickly written his report and read it aloud, the Colonna lawyer requested a copy for His Excellency the Duke.

Assuming the matter was concluded, everyone stood but the clerk stood over Michele. "Be advised, Master Caravaggio, you are forbidden to leave this house under a penalty of a five hundred scudi fine. Is that understood by all here?" Michele spent the night in Rufetti's quarters and Lorenzo and I went for supper.

Lorenzo was in high spirits, relieved Michele was recovering but I was angry. "Of course it was a fight. He knew who attacked him. Will he ever learn?"

"D'you think it was the Tomassoni?"

"I doubt they'd let Michele off so light. Ranuccio loved Lena and blames Michele for her death."

"But Ranuccio killed her."

"He's devoured by jealousy and blames Michele. He's not in his right mind and I think he'll come after him sooner or later and he won't be left with a few superficial wounds."

"Dear God, I hope you're wrong, Cecco."

Chapter 23

Ranuccio 1606

There were always patrons in the market; Giustiniani for one, the Mattei, the Barberini and, since his uncle became Pope, the Papal Nephew Scipione Borghese but another rejected painting was depressing and cause of further frustration. Although patronage by the illustrious was good for reputation and flattery was always useful, he preferred his paintings to hang in churches to be seen by ordinary people rather than just rich and powerful aristocrats and cardinals. Was he not Father Filippo Neri's painterly spiritual son? The poor and pilgrims never object to dirty feet and love seeing their lives of struggle, pain, poverty and shabby clothes reflected in the pictures. Those priests who presumed to determine what the poor and untutored may or may not be permitted to see stood in the way of the simple faith of the people. Of course, the *Supper at Emmaus* had been the most complex examination of theology, liturgy and dogma reserved for the private devotion and contemplation of the Mattei but in the *Madonna of Loreto, Entombment, Madonna of the Serpent* and *Death of the Virgin,* dogma and theology was absorbed by the images and spoke directly to the everyday experience and devotion of all who saw them. His paintings were of the people's Gesù and their Madonna but, sadly, *Our Lady of the Serpent* and the *Death of the Virgin* were destined for private chapels, no longer the churches and people for whom they were painted.

Since they delivered Lena to his door, there was neither sight nor sound of the Tomassoni or their bully boys. Although Cecco and the lads remained apprehensive and fearful, Michele was not. His token confession was no more than simply telling the priest the bare facts of Lena's murder and her elevation as the dead Madonna. He was not sure why he told the priest, except his delirious state of rage at another rejection was somewhat sated by throwing the horror of Lena's death in the priest's face in revenge for his practiced seminarian words of justification for removing the painting. "Ha!" That the common congregation of the faithful would be upset indeed! The real cause was the snivelling sensibilities of the priests.

Nevertheless, despite his lack of fear, the Tomassoni remained a very real threat but rather than panic or flee, in the passing curiously tranquil days, he concentrated on painting a further San Francesco. An image of the kneeling saint contemplating a skull with a wooden cross teetering on a rock in the foreground. Colour was subdued, his robe grey-brown, the features no longer those of the cardinal, longer hair and un-trimmed beard with the pale stone-grey skull that focused the saint's attention on the precarious, transitory path of life. After two weeks or so, it seemed the blow may have passed, that Ranuccio was preoccupied with regret, guilt and remorse until such hopes were undeceived by violent thundering on the door announcing the Devil's arrival.

Cecco leapt up and opened the shutters a crack. "It's the Tomassoni, the brother Mario and bullyboys. Ignore them, Michele."

"I can't hide forever." He wiped the brush on a rag, slipped a dagger up his sleeve but Cecco rattled down the stairs ahead of him. "I'll open the door." He unsheathed Michele's sword from the scabbard hanging on the hook on the blind side of the door. Michele slipped the knife from his sleeve and tucked it in Cecco's belt behind his back and nodded.

When Cecco opened the door, Michele imagined the Tomassoni barging in and knifing him to death but, instead, he heard, "Message for Master Michele from Ranuccio… You're invited to a party at the Tomassoni house tomorrow evening. Do you accept?"

"Yes."

The atmosphere was riotous, swilling drink, chanting filthy songs with half a dozen whores in various states of undress. Michele realised he had been wrong to accept the invitation and told Cecco they were leaving but were intercepted by Ranuccio's boyos. "He wants to see you in here." He was asked to surrender his sword and was pushed into a small chamber. Cecco was kept outside.

"Michele, come in."

"Seems I had no choice."

"Always suspicious, Michele, always defensive… the cause of all your trouble. You over-react to the slightest matter, which is why you're easy to play, but I'm impressed you have the balls to accept my invitation." Michele felt the reassuring pressure of the dagger, tucked out of sight in his belt under his doublet.

Ranuccio struggled to appear relaxed but was feverish, his fingers flexed and he spoke quickly, "We haven't seen you in weeks, working on the painting of the dead Virgin, I suppose? You work so hard, Michele, perhaps too hard. Did you hear Lena drowned?"

"I heard."

"Tragic. A shock for everyone and worse, she imperilled her immortal soul cutting her throat and falling into the Tiber." He crossed himself. "May she rest in peace." For a moment, he lost his usual swagger, his shoulders drooped and he covered his eyes with his hand. He was silent and, when he spoke, his voice was hoarse and tremulous. "Is the painting finished?"

"It is."

"Where is it?"

"You've not heard it was rejected by the priests."

Ranuccio uncovered his reddened eyes. "Rejected!"

"The fathers at Santa Maria said it was wrong to depict Our Lady like some filthy whore from the slums."

Ranuccio banged his fist on the table. "Who has it now?"

"I heard Gonzaga of Mantua is interested in it."

"So, she'll never be seen. I'll never see her again."

Head down, he leaned over the table, his weight supported on his fists. "I thought you were fucking her, Michele… but I was taken in. You played me for a fool, you and Longhi."

"Onorio?"

"I thought he was covering for you by flirting with her to put me off the scent, but now I know how it was." Through gritted teeth, he snarled. "Do you only sleep with boys, Michele? I heard about the Baglione trial and Cecco or is that your cover for fucking married women?" Michele smelt the sour wine on his breath. "Is it yours?"

"My what? What's mine? I don't understand."

"Don't lie. I saw you together, giggling and pawing each other."

"Who?"

He shouted, "Don't pretend you don't know what I'm talking about."

"I don't…"

Michele backed towards the door and slipped his hand behind his back to grasp the handle of the knife. "You killed her because you thought she had my kid… but I told you."

"Not Lena, you whore-mongering pederast. I'm talking about Lavinia."

Michele laughed. "Your wife?"

"Don't deny it. I never slept with her for months because I was with Lena. I saw you mauling each other at the party. Who else could have got on the nest?"

"I never met her before that night, and she'd already given birth." Ranuccio's rage ebbed and ran to self-pity.

Michele's temple throbbed, and he felt light-headed with fury. *Onorio! Onorio, you bastard… not content with five kids you have to get another on Ranuccio's wife, and now he knows he killed the wrong woman. He'll never believe anything I say.* All he could do was to finish the matter and damn the consequences.

He was surprisingly calm when he spoke, "I'm sorry, Ranuccio, sorry you killed the woman you loved."

"Y-you pathetic son of a whore."

Ranuccio lunged but Michele drew the dagger and, again, got it under his chin. He backed towards the door and, as he opened it, Ranuccio called out loud enough for everyone to hear, "Michele Caravaggio, you dishonoured me and, by God, I'll kill you. I swear by the Holy Virgin, you will be dead by tomorrow night. I'll see you on the Campo Marzio tomorrow by the old mausoleum. I don't care if it's Sunday, I'll see you at three unless you're a coward as well as a boyfucker."

Michele almost stumbled over Cecco, who gripped his arm and whispered, "The Pope banned duels; this can't happen."

Michele shouted, "I accuse Ranuccio Tomassoni of stealing ten ducats by trickery, so I challenge him to a game of tennis to decide whose right."

The last Sunday in May, Michele with supporters Paulo Aldato, a guard at the Castel Sant Angelo, Onorio Longhi and Petronio Toppa, an old soldier drinking companion, made their way to the Campo Marzio, between the twin ghosts of the mausoleum of Augustus and the unfinished new Borghese palace. Onorio carried a roll of canvas, concealing Michele's sword and Petronio had racquets and balls as though they were on the way to a game of tennis. They arrived at the pallacorda as church bells tolled three. Ten minutes later, Ranuccio arrived with his brother Giovan Francesco and Lavinia's brothers Ignazio and Frederico Giugoli to support the fiction that Michele was the father of her child.

As they approached, Michele called, "Late, Ranuccio… afraid?"

The younger Giugoli brother gave the horns. "You're the one who should be shitting yourself; we'll use your head for a ball when Ranuccio's done with you."

Ranuccio drew his sword and rushed at Michele who drew and parried the slash. Ranuccio laughed, enjoying catching Michele off guard. They circled one another, both making occasional lunges, easily parried. What was expected to be a vicious fight seemed half-hearted as though simply to have turned up was enough.

The younger Giugoli continually goaded Ranuccio. "Come on, brother, kill the shit; look at him, limp-wristed queer."

Ranuccio dropped his guard to shout, "Shut up!" At that moment, Michele's thrust tore Ranuccio's sleeve, leaving a thin wet bloodstain. He almost apologised but Ranuccio retaliated with a stab to his face, nicking his cheek. The burning sensation roused him to retaliate until half-hearted lunges turned into a messy scrap as both drew daggers.

After a quarter of an hour, both were tiring; any cut or scratch was accidental until Ranuccio stabbed Michele in the neck. There was plenty of blood but it seeped rather than jetted like a fountain, indicating no major blood vessel had been cut. For the first time, it seemed Ranuccio might take the opportunity to kill Michele rather than arrive at some bloody stand-off, honours even; a draw.

Gianni Tomassoni voiced Michele's fear: "You have him… Finish him, Ranuccio."

Both protagonists were galvanised; the fight turned furious and deadly, attacks aimed at heads, hearts and throats. Both received and gave deep gashes and, as Michele reeled away hurt, Ranuccio dash forward to deliver what must be a fatal stab aimed for his heart. Michele wheeled around to parry but stumbled and stabbed wildly with the blade and was thrown back by contact with Ranuccio's charging weight as his sword penetrated Ranuccio's groin exiting at the crease of his buttock. Ranuccio screamed, fell sideways and Michele felt the blade sever ligaments and the great artery. Blood sprayed a foot and a half in an arc from the wound and more when the blade was withdrawn, pulsing and soaking the dry earth.

Paulo shouted, "Get Michele away" and to Giovanni Tomassoni: "Help your brother."

He tore Ranuccio's shirt and jammed it into the gushing wound. "Hold this tight; press hard."

The older Giugoli brother took over, pressing the wound but Ignazio stood rigid, mouth gaped as he gasped. Michele held his neck to staunch the bleeding and bent down to murmur in Ranuccio's ear, "You killed Lena and now you've killed yourself. I didn't do this; it was the hand of God… It wasn't me who cuckolded you. It was Onorio Longhi, so take that to hell with you."

Giovan Tomassoni may have heard, drew his sword and slashed Michele's head. Petronio rushed forward to drive Giovan away, but Giovan turned on him and stabbed him several times. Onorio and Paulo intervened to separate them and called on the Tomassoni to get Ranuccio to a hospice. "Go now before the sbirri get wind of this."

Paulo struggled to help Michele to stand and Onorio said he should be taken to the Conzolatione to have his wounds dressed and find help. "I'll see you later." Paulo collected Michele's weapons, wiped the blood from the blade, then wrapped the sword and dagger in canvas and draped Michele's cloak around his shoulders high enough to hide the neck wound. Suddenly, Cecco appeared, having followed and watched from a distance. He rushed to help when he saw Michele was wounded and took charge. Cecco and Paulo supported Michele who weakened with every step, his shirt soaked in blood. Cecco said they should take Michele to the Consolazione, but Michele insisted he would only go to Andrea Rufetti's house. "But that's crazy; it's the first place the sbirri will look."

Michele muttered, "I need to get my things… get away from Rome… Paulo, take Petronio to the Conzolatione. He's in a bad way. Cecco will help me get to Rufetti's." Paulo hesitated, obviously unhappy leaving Cecco and Michele alone but, taking the weapons with him, he left to tend Petronio. Michele leaned heavily on Cecco as they staggered away from the pallacorda.

Chapter 24

Emmaus 1607

Michele told me to stay away from the fight, but I followed anyway and watched from some fifty paces but, even from that distance, heard Ranuccio yelp when he was hit, slipped and fell with a jet of dark blood arcing from his groin. Michele staggered too and I ran to help as fighting broke out among the two parties. When I was a few steps away, Michele almost fell into my arms, seriously wounded, his face a red mask and shirt spattered and blotted with blood.

Someone shouted, "Get him away."

Michele pressed the collar of his shirt hard against the cut in his neck to staunch the wound. It was slow going but being a hot Sunday and, thanks to the riposo for more than an hour, there were few people abroad but they still avoided main streets where possible. Twice, Michele had to lean against a wall and, within a few streets of the Colonna palace, we entered a small square where Michele almost fainted. I helped him to sit on the rim of a small fountain and scooped handfuls of cool water to his parched lips and mopped the wound to his head from which blood trickled down to his wrist and dribbled like pink starfish into the water. Not daring to linger too long and risk attention, I helped Michele stand and limp on.

As he slumped against a wall in the dark of an alley, I thought we wouldn't make it to Rufetti's house but Michele slid up the wall and insisted we go on. As he leaned on my shoulder, I said we should go to the Conzolatione but he insisted we go to Rufetti's house. We took back alleys to avoid the risk of running into the sbirri. It was arduous and slow going. I held him round the waist and he leaned heavily against me and slipped several times, barely conscious from blood loss. We only just made it to Rufetti's house when Michele collapsed, barely conscious, as I banged on the door, looking over my shoulder, dreading we might have been followed by either the Tomassoni or seen by the sbirri. Andrea's servant opened the door.

I barged in calling, "Andrea... Andrea!"

He ran down the stairs. I pointed to the open door. He quickly took charge and helped me and the servant lift Michele into the house and lay him on a low couch. He told me to go to the palace but, seeing I was covered in blood, went himself. It seemed an age before he returned with a doctor and four liveried Colonna guards. The doctor bound Michele's wounds, draped him with a blanket, then the guards carried him to the palace.

I fretted and helplessly rushed from Andrea to the doctor and anyone who might answer me. "Will he live? How bad are his injuries?"

Andrea tried to calm me, saying Michele's wounds were serious but, according to the doctor, not life threatening... unless... I knew he meant unless infection set in. Andrea coaxed me to wash and provided fresh clothes. He instructed a servant to burn Michele's and my bloodied clothes and told me to consider what I should say if the sbirri asked me questions. "Duelling is a capital crime, Cecco; he could be executed... be careful what you say; perhaps it was just a fight over some trivial matter?"

Throughout the night and next day, Michele slipped in and out of consciousness, sometimes sleeping deeply, other times agitated and shouting. All I could do to divert my attention from my worst fears was to wipe his forehead with a cool damp cloth and whisper, "Michele, it's me... Cecco." There were comings and goings in and around the palace. Papal officers arrived but, although they surely suspected Michele was sheltered in the Colonna household, they made no attempt to enter. I lost track of time and Andrea coaxed me to eat. I wasn't hungry but, eventually, when the crisis passed, I took some bread and broth.

While he was unconscious, Michele's wounds were stitched, salved and dressed and over many hours he lapsed in and out of sleep. I was exhausted and slept fitfully until Andrea woke me to say Michele and I were to be taken from Rome for safety, but I was not informed where. On the third morning before dawn, Michele was carried to a coach, blinds drawn and the Colonna badge hidden under a blue velvet drop. I climbed in and sat beside Michele. He leaned against me, his head on my shoulder and sucked breath through his teeth when the coach rocked as it moved off. We took a circuitous route and eventually I recognised we were going towards the rising sun. An hour or so on the road, we were met by a smaller older carriage and a wagon filled with our possessions collected from Rufetti's. The journey onwards was uncomfortable, the carriage less well sprung, stuffy and smelt of old leather, the roads increasingly rutted and Michele was in pain, pressed his hand to his bandaged throat, saying the jolts of the carriage pulled the stitches. He occasionally slumbered, murmuring and woke with a shout. He stared wide eyed. "Where are we... where are we going... do you know?"

"Away from Papal jurisdiction is all I was told. D'you remember what happened?"

"The fight..." He fell silent. "It was messy. I killed Ranuccio. He *is* dead, isn't he? Were you there?"

"At a distance."

"I don't recall... how?" He touched the bandage.

"Giovan Tomassoni turned on you when Ranuccio went down and may have killed Petronio who saved your life. Onorio and Paulo managed to disarm Giovan; he was a raving lunatic. Ranuccio was unconscious, dying... maybe dead already."

"The sbirri must know it was me."

"Andrea said the Tomassoni claim you ambushed them and Ranuccio was unarmed. With all the howling and weeping, the sbirri didn't take them seriously. I think the Colonna were tipped off by the sbirri who must have guessed where you were. They could have arrested you but from bits I overheard, Cardinal Borghese warned the Colonna to get you away. I don't know if his uncle authorised your arrest... unless... maybe the Pope intended Scipione to tip off the Colonna. He's bound by his own law to have you arrested but would he really want you to swing?"

He glanced at me. "I vaguely remember... you got me to Andrea's house. How long was I out?"

"A day and more... Your wound was infected. We weren't sure you'd survive."

"What about my things, paints, brushes, the canvas for...?"

"Everything's in the wagon; all your things, paintings, tools, brushes and paints are safe."

"I suppose it could have been worse. Thank God I left the St John pictures and others at the Palazzo Madama or with the Mattei."

After a while, I said, "I wonder if the *Death of the Virgin* was delivered to Mantua?"

Michele pouted. "Ranuccio wouldn't touch it but with him dead, the family would destroy it for sure; they wouldn't understand what it meant to him."

We arrived after dark at a huddled hill town dominated by a large basilica and fortress. Rather than the fortress, the carriage went on to a large farmhouse about two miles from the town in the foothills near Palestrina. The coach driver said the Colonna fortress was too obvious a hiding place. I asked where we were and it was whispered: *Zagarolo*.

We stayed out of sight in the carriage with blinds down while the driver and waggoner went to the house. A few minutes later, the driver returned and Michele stepped down and slowly walked to the house leaning on my shoulder. Entering the cool airy hall with small windows high up, a large, blackened fireplace dominated one wall with a great spit and perfectly piled pyramid of split logs in a niche to the side. On a long refectory table was an opened missive with the Colonna seal. The older of two men greeted Michele with a deep bow. "Welcome, Master Caravaggio, and your guest. My brother and I will do everything to make you comfortable."

Michele sat heavily. "Your names?"

"Excuse me, master, I'm Fabio, my brother… Stefano."

"I presume you're Colonna tenants."

Fabio tilted his head. "We're discreet, master."

"No more *Master*… I'm Michele and this is my dear friend Francesco – Cecco. Who else is here?"

"My brother and I live alone. My wife died two years ago… We were not blessed with children, although Stefano was our baby I suppose." The younger rolled his eyes and elbowed the elder. "We make a reasonable living, sheep on the uplands a few beef cattle in the lower grassland, goats, chickens and rabbits in the pens. An old couple come each morning to take care of the house. Emilio tries to keep the buildings in reasonably good repair and his wife Lucia cleans and cooks. Fabio said he had been instructed to prepare three rooms, one for use as a workshop with steady north light. It's a rambling old place, so we put you at the far end with north facing windows. Do you feel well enough to see your rooms?"

"In a little while. I'm sure arrangements are fine." When rested, Michele slowly walked along the corridor, leaning on me and any ledge or item of furniture for support. The three rooms were spacious and materials, easels, stretchers and paints were in the furthest, largest room.

After almost a week, a message was delivered by a Borghese agent, a commission for a penitent Magdalene for a client, probably Scipione himself. That his agents knew Michele's whereabouts meant he was party to Colonna arrangements and surely Borghese had colluded in our escape and likely the Pope also knew of Michele's whereabouts. A pretty cousin of the brothers modelled for the Magdalene with the old lady Lucia acting as chaperone. Michele asked the Borghese agent to return with a brocade dress for his model and paid him generously for his trouble. It was ten days before he returned with a fine dress.

During an afternoon working on the Magdalene, Michele let Stefano watch him paint. It was something he rarely allowed, even I didn't see him painting for weeks when we first met. As he painted, he asked Stefano simple questions: how much fleece was expected, how much milk the goats produced and how many eggs for sale once their needs were met? Stefano was flattered by the attention of the famous Roman artist, who turned paint into his living cousin and the blessed Magdalene came to life, casting off the vanities of her former life. He said he had never travelled further than Palestrina and, when asked when he was next likely to go, he answered, "Week on Thursday."

M to Sr. Mario Minniti,

I have heard nothing since I arrived here. I am starved of news and not knowing what's going on drives me mad. Have you or L heard anything? What is the news – and how is His Eminence? Even he hasn't written. I am well in health, my wounds mending – slowly. C is with me and my work goes well. The person who delivers this will bring your reply.

M

There was a further long delay before the courier returned to Palestrina and several more days before Stefano collected a reply.

L to M,

I recognised your handwriting so opened your letter to M – Carla and he left to go home – you know where. I should warn you T hired people. I plan to leave Rome now that M is gone so it is lucky you wrote – this place could be watched. I told the courier to be careful when he leaves. I think you know where I come from, write to me there. There's little time so I wish you well in health and spirit. May Our Lady look after you and C and I pray we meet again.

L

Lorenzo's letter was disappointingly brief but no surprise in the circumstances. The Tomassoni wouldn't hesitate to take revenge on his friends, so it was a relief to hear Mario and Carla had gone to Syracuse.

Thankfully, Lorenzo must already be safely on his way, if not already in Messina. There was no mention of the cardinal or whether the Colonna or Borghese had made any representation on Michele's behalf to the Curia, although contact with either would have been difficult. He passed Lorenzo's note to me to read, then burned it. After the finished penitent Magdalene was dispatched and advice of credit received, the enormity of his position began to sink in. The Tomassoni had contacts and low cunning. He became increasingly anxious, fearful to leave the house in case they were tracked down. The twilight between black velvet sleep and the light of day was haunted by recurring torments and most nights Michele woke soaked in sweat and Cecco shook him several times. "You were shouting."

He sat an hour stroking Michele's head. Isolation and the unknown were twin torments, both mentioned increasingly vivid and bizarre dreams and remorse and loss drained Michele's habitual energy for work. In any case, commissions arranged before Ranuccio's death were almost certainly void and rejection of the *Madonna of the Serpent* and *Death of the Virgin* might have further weakened his standing. How self-satisfied Baglione must be, his revenge complete and Orazio, Annibale and even Spada privately pleased their greatest rival was out of the way.

As they lay in the dark one night, he murmured, "So, this is death… the world carries on without pause."

One evening, old Lucia served thick lamb stew with farrow beans and Stefano said, "It's no wonder you're so nervous. You must feel like a lamb in a pen before slaughter."

Fabio glanced up, wide-eyed. "Brother!"

"Oh, I didn't mean—" Michele smiled to reassure him he took no offense.

Next morning, Michele woke early. "Cecco, d'you remember the commission for Marchese Patrizi? He wanted a second version of the *Supper at Emmaus*. At the time, I was preoccupied with the Loreto Madonna and *Entombment* so let the commission slip. Patrizi may have forgotten or might no longer want anything by me but it's something… at least I would think about other things than… running away from Rome, home and friends with just the clothes on our backs like refugees. Think, Cecco, our welcome at Zagarolo, Fabio, Stefano… it's the Emmaus story."

In the following days, he sat alone, contemplating the subject, remembering conversations with the cardinal as they unravelled the layers of meaning; theological, liturgical and human but now only relevant to a distant, rarefied audience. Isolation, uncertainty and anxiety changed everything, and now he saw the subject afresh. From memory, the first Emmaus was twelve by eighteen palmi, so the new version should be the same. "We have no strainer that size and it's too great a risk to order one from Rome." No painter in Rome ordered canvas, strainers or frames anonymously or without bragging.

He asked the brothers if they knew of a dependable local quality joiner and Fabio acted as go-between, explaining with the aid of Michele's diagrams how a strainer should be constructed, rigid enough to stretch and hold canvas taut, with holes for the strings and a separate frame with cross pieces and interlocking corners onto which the finished painting would be nailed. Within a week, the strainer and frame were delivered ready, assembled, and Michele was pleased with the quality of work, especially the precise corners. Fabio and Stefano helped string and stretch the canvas onto the strainer and watched as Cecco applied the preparatory layers of glue, gesso and several layers of umber darkened with a little black. In the days waiting for the base layer to dry, Michele shared his thoughts about the levels of meaning and how they were interpreted by symbols and references to doctrine, theology and philosophy but what would those signs and symbols mean to the uninitiated to Fabio, Stefano, Emilio and Lucia?

Cecco was delighted by his returned enthusiasm being drawn into his thoughts in conversations and he smiled. "Why don't you ask them?" Over supper, he wondered if anyone remembered the Emmaus story. They shrugged and smiled. After a while, Fabio spoke, "I think Gesù appeared to some disciples after the resurrection but it was only when he blessed the meal, the disciples recognised him."

Stefano sat back. "Why wouldn't his disciples recognise him if they knew him before?"

Michele paused before responding, "Yes, that seems odd if they lived with him for... three years. Do you remember any more of the story?"

"Only that they walked from Jerusalem."

"Do you have a Bible?"

"We do, but it's an old Bible, and we can't read Latin."

Fabio fetched the book from a shallow cupboard in the corner, crossed himself, kissed the book and gave it to Michele. "Our parents inherited it from a cousin who was a priest. Can you read the Latin, Michele?"

"A little, and it's possible to get the gist by looking for similar Italian words." He took the book. "I think the Emmaus story is here in Luke."

Thereafter appeared in another form... they walked to the country should Christ... not have suffered... He was walking with the disciples away from Jerusalem. He read silently then: *And he would go further, stay with us, it is evening... he went to stay with them.* This is the important part: *As he sat and ate with them, he broke bread and blessed it and gave it to them... their eyes were opened, they knew him and he vanished from sight...*

Stefano pouted. "I still don't understand why they didn't recognise him sooner."

"Who's the hand with the beard and reddish-brown hair?"

"I'm not sure who you mean."

"Him in the yard... by the barn."

Lucia flapped her arm. "Oh, that's only Bernardo."

Emilio laughed. "Lucia thinks she's a bit above the farm hands." She tapped Emilio's arm. "I beg your pardon. Don't heed him, signor."

"Do you think he would sit for me... model for a character in my painting?"

"He's very shy, spends months up in the hills."

"He's a shepherd?"

"The best we have. Who would he play... if he agrees?"

"Jesus."

"You mean Our Lord Jesus?"

Michele smiled. "Yes."

"You mean you want Bernardo to play the part of Our Lord?"

"Why not?"

"Well... he's just a shepherd."

"The best you have you say."

"But what would he know about playing Our Lord and Saviour? He's not exactly a saint."

When supper was served, Emilio and Lucia hardly said a word and, whereas they often joined in conversation once the table was cleared, they left soon after platters, dishes and pots were washed and put away.

"They were quiet this evening."

"They're upset by something I said. I asked about the hand with the long reddish-brown hair and beard."

"Bernardo. Has he said or done something?"

"No, nothing wrong, I asked Lucia who he was and if they thought he would model for Christ in the painting."

Stefano laughed. "Bernardo… You mean *the* Jesus… Gesu Christ?"

Michele grinned. "By your accounts, he's your best shepherd."

"What's that got to do with him playing Jesus?"

"Apparently, he's a good shepherd."

The workshop shutters closed, the Holbein rug draped over a table and I covered the rug with a crisp white tablecloth. Michele said the still life on the table would be reduced because it occurred to him the stranger's presence had not been catered for and so he chose only a bowl of asparagus spears, two small bread rolls, a jug, an empty metal platter placed near the front edge of the table but this time only the rim projected over the edge.

Michele said, "Visual tricks in the past are no longer necessary to titillate the tastes of the high ups, and I'm determined to paint for a different audience: the simple folk of our immediate circle, those involved in the re-enactment, a poem to the simple faith of the humble, the honest poor, those Father Filippo Neri spoke to and the accidental family we're now blessed with."

Fabio asked Bernardo if he would model for the great artist from Rome.

"If he's such a great artist, what's he doing in Zagarolo of all places?"

"He's been ill and needed to recover here near the mountains, away from malaria in Rome."

Bernardo pouted. "What does he pay?"

"He's offered each of us two weeks' pay for one week modelling."

"Who's *each of us*?"

"All of us, Stefano, Emilio, Lucia and me."

"What about the goat boy and her who looks after the chickens and…?"

"There are only five figures in the painting; it's not a Nativity."

"You'd need the ox and the mule for that."

"Will you do it?"

"Well, let's think. Who am I supposed to be anyway?"

"Jesus."

"What, *our* Jesus?"

"Yes."

"Seriously… me! Wait till I tell—"

"Bernardo, no. You can't mention this to anyone. It's a secret, a gift for a famous person in Palestrina so if the word got out—"

He grinned. "Palestrina, eh? I bet I know who that Lordy is."

"I said a secret—and a strict secret."

Bernardo winked. "I heard nowt and I'll say nowt on my mother's life."

"You're a grand man, Bernardo. So you agree?"

"I suppose so."

Stefano sat at the front left corner as Cleopas and Fabio as Simon Peter on the right, his hands gripping the corner of the table and staring towards Bernardo playing Christ who sat on the far side of the table. Stefano wore his winter coat and Michele draped a russet cloak over his left shoulder. Fabio wore a brown jacket open at the neck with a white undershirt and ivory cloak worn by Christ in the earlier Emmaus draped over his left arm. Bernardo wore his dark grey winter coat he wrapped around himself on cold nights on the high hills. His neck and chest were visible. Bernardo's blue-grey coat suggested the colour scheme, the entire painting in warm evening light, dark- and mid-browns, orange and gold with Christ isolated in dark blue-grey. The geometry of the composition was less rigid than the first Emmaus with Christ in a more traditional position to the left of centre. His head was at the apex of a shallow triangle that leaned to the left almost defining the angle of the raking light that illuminated the scene from that side. A second shallow triangle leant to the right, its apex at Fabio' ear modelling Simon Peter. To the right of Christ, Emilio's head formed the apex of both triangles. With positions resolved, Michele asked Bernardo to sit behind the table and told him to bless the food. He raised his right hand at head height, with two fingers and thumb stiffly held in the Trinitarian blessing.

"What's that, Bernardo… what are you doing?"

"Blessing, you said… what else? That's how the priest does it."

"It looks as though you're play-acting."

"What else should I do? You said I should bless…"

"I didn't mean the way priests do it."

"Well, what are you asking me to do then?"

"Listen, Bernardo, forget what I said. Sit with your hands in your lap… now lean forward and, with your right hand, imagine you are stroking a child… a lamb."

Bernardo sat back, shrugged his shoulders and muttered under his breath. He sat a moment, then leaned forward, put his left hand on the table and gingerly raised his cupped right hand, his lips slightly pursed.

"That's perfect, don't move." In an hour, Michele drew the main forms of the head, measured the distances to the hands and drew their outlines and shadows in near black. Before allowing Bernardo to take a rest, he marked positions of his arms on the tablecloth with charcoal and in turn marked the positions of Stefano and Fabio. Emilio was the next figure. He simply stood with his hands gripping his belt, a characteristic stance Michele noticed him adopt many times. Lucia wondered aloud when she was likely to be needed. He rehearsed several approaches with me how to tell her he'd changed his mind about the fifth figure but he just smiled. "When I'm ready, Lucia… I can't rush the painting."

She was placated for the moment and he asked Bernardo to sit the next few days to work on the Christ. Concentrating on the head, he pitched the middle tones slightly orange brown and, as the features developed, noticed Bernardo was not truly present. Models usually betrayed a sense of knowing, aware they were observed but Bernardo was distracted, a slight frown and what he recognised to be his habitually pursed lips. Once the thicker, lighter tones went on, the forehead was divided by a subtle half tone which appeared to catch a slight frown and once the outer and inner orbital highlights and those on the bridge and tip of the nose and the neck were gently applied, the head was finished.

Next day, he painted the hands and blocked in the dark, near black base coat for his clothing and spent hours mixing lighter blue-grey in preparation for the middle and light tones of the folds. When satisfied with the colour palette, he had Cecco mix larger amounts. There was precious little blue azurite available but, since he only used it as a tinting agent in this case to make grey cooler, there should be enough. At the end of the day, he contemplated the finished face of Christ which conveyed something deeper, not merely sadness but of someone troubled.

During supper, Michele said, "Stefano, you wondered why the disciples didn't recognise Our Lord until he blessed and broke bread. I believe I have an answer." He dipped bread in olive oil and, after chewing a moment, said, "He'd changed."

"What d'you mean?"

"He was not in disguise but changed… by brutality and humiliation. He suffered the horror of passing through what for us is the end."

Fabio thought a moment, then said, "But he rose from the dead… the resurrection…"

"But he couldn't forget what he suffered at our hands."

"But didn't he forgive us? *Father, forgive, they don't know what they be doing.*"

Michele leaned on the table, his head in his hands. "It's true. He forgives us the scars we inflict but, although he forgives, the wounds are permanent, and he was scarred by what he suffered." He found it difficult to continue without his voice trembling. Cecco rubbed his back.

After a moment, Michele murmured, "The resurrection was not simply return to life but a life changed by abandonment, beating, humiliation and an agonising death on the cross."

In the shadow of his sheltering hands, tears ran down his face and his mouth gaped. "Everything stripped away, no certainty, utter despair when even God turned His face away. The prophecy of what was to happen was no longer dressed in poetic language but lived through pitiless brutality, flesh cut by canes and whips and pierced by nails hammered through flesh, nerves and tendons, hands and feet twisted in agony and trembling and spasms as blood was lost by the pint. Agony and isolation felt and known and suffered so that the resurrection was not triumphant but the haunting of a perfect life fulfilled."

Stefano's curly hair was in contrast to Christ's lank hair, simply parted down the middle, Fabio's sunburned face was creased, the tendons of his neck exposed by the tension of sudden twisting and turning in recognition. Emilio's furrowed brow was highlighted and ribs of thinning hair lovingly recreated. The scene was as sacramental as the first version but with all the theology and layers of dogma wiped away. It was indeed the re-enactment of the Mass but not the grand Masses of St Peter's or the great Roman churches, but the first Mass at Emmaus, a simple gathering together of two or three with the promise of the ubiquitous presence, more real than the expectation of a miracle of bread becoming flesh. When Lucia saw the painting, she simply said, "It's finished."

Michele regretted he had left her out but even she could see there was no place for her; nevertheless, he said, "But it's not finished until I paint you, Lucia, and the pattern of the rug has to be done."

"You don't have to bother, master, I'm just a vain old woman."

He insisted she pose with a joint of roast beef on a platter, her skin paler and forehead and neck even more creased than Emilio's. He was touched how the couple were almost interchangeable, brother and sister rather than man and wife. He told Cecco that including Lucia fucked up the composition but this painting cannot be perfect… I understood what Michele meant, how her addition drew the eye too far to the right… the first version was a perfect composition in detail and unity, this second – flawed – was more truthful to the spirit of the story. Indeed, the Christ is smaller in scale than the other figures. Had Emilio and Lucia not been included, the natural perspective of the disciples in the foreground with Christ further back was acceptable but the servants were the same scale as the disciples in the foreground so Emilio loomed over Jesus, almost dominating him as a man might a boy. Under other circumstances, Michele would have repainted Emilio and Lucia or even painted them out but the diminished Christ was the reality of the painting. Christ was not the master but truly servant with human cruelty and suffering eternally inscribed in his flesh.

In the following weeks, Michele spoke about making a break for Venice, hiring a wagon and carriage from Palestrina to escape the seductive confinement at Zagarolo. Fourteen years ago, he said he knew his work was old-fashioned but now, with the exception of Titian and Giorgione, all other Venetian painters seemed mannered by comparison with his mature work. He was certain he would find patrons on the strength of his known success with the possibility the Colonna and Scipione Borghese might help, although their influence in the Papal States and Spanish territories might not be as great in Venice since the alliance between the Venetians with the Turks caused a rift with the Papacy and Spain and there was further friction between the Venetians and the Papacy over the insistence that Venetian clergy were immune from secular prosecution. But before pursuing the idea further, he received a letter delivered by courier from Rome who awaited a reply. Michele recognised the handwriting and was elated as he broke the un-stamped wax.

My dear, you cannot imagine how distressed I was hearing you were injured but relieved you were spirited away. Despite rumours, I have faith and believe the incident, as my agents report, was truly an accident. Your whereabouts remained a mystery and all the birds who knew anything have flown, until a certain agent of your protectors, Sr R, gave me some details, but I begged him not to tell me where you might be – which I pray is a safe haven. I hear you are much recovered and that darling boy C remained loyal when matters were grave. I send my blessing. Be assured you are constantly in my prayers and hope there will be swift resolution and that you may soon be permitted to return. I understand SB he has raised your situation at the highest level.

God Bless you my dear son and friend…

F

Destroy this letter for both our safety.

He was overjoyed to hear the cardinal still had his wellbeing at heart and was not entirely forgotten. Under Francesco's post script he drew a line under which he replied:

I return your letter for safety, read with immense joy to hear you do not hold me in contempt. I assure you the incident was not intended and, if I could have time back, I would prefer to be called a coward than accept the challenge. There is not enough space to convey everything I feel but know the depth of gratitude to you, your generosity and kindness. I hope a commission for a second Emmaus painting from Marchese P is still wanted, and I have also painted a David and Goliath for HH, via SB, which I hope will support my cause in that quarter.

God Bless you, and do not forget me.

M

Chapter 25

Amanti

Far from the din of Rome, brawling, carousing, lawlessness and interrupted work, Zagarolo was a haven of calm and at the centre was Cecco. Amid the anxiety and uncertainty, there was unexpected solace and joy when Cecco became more than a foundling, invaluable assistant, a model and closer than a companion and friend. No longer the madcap jester whooping, cavorting and carrying Michele's weapons, the instruments of Michele's status and, by association, Cecco's. Still amusing and always able to raise Michele's spirits, he had imperceptibly matured, no longer a boy and more than a youth, not only in body but in responsibility and dependability. More than that, he was loyal, he stayed and took control, always there, day and night, in the workshop, conscientious, attentive and anticipating Michele's every need, freeing him to concentrate solely on painting.

In the weeks since the fight with Ranuccio, the burning slash of a blade, grind of metal on bone and spray of gore were momentarily relived from the fog of half-memory. Recovering his health at Zagarolo, he lay several mornings in bed when Cecco changed bandages, cleaned and tidied the room and made Michele comfortable. He watched him rise naked, no longer the pudgy Cupid or youthful Baptist but now lithe and manly. His hair was a black as ever, longer and shiny and had grown a thin moustache over his upper lip, not much more than a shadow, and neatly trimmed pointed beard. He watched over several days, fascinated, as Cecco quietly moved around the bedchamber and workroom, putting things in order, sniffing and gathering clothes to be washed, cleaning and shaping brushes standing them bristles up in a pot, adding drops of walnut oil to prepared paint and ground distilled crystals of urea to powder for a rich yellow or Verdigris scraped from a copper tube. He separated egg yolk for addition to mixed colours to add body and lustre. Never hurried, he completed every task by the end of the day.

He always knew Cecco was devoted, but he was uncertain whether his feelings were reciprocated or ran deeper than affection and loyalty, but, since the night the pimp dragged him by the hair, kicking and yelping, Michele had been determined to protect and take care of him. Despite difference in their ages, they were alike in many ways but, whereas he never mastered his humours and temper, Cecco was now calmer, self-confident and, in the past weeks, he realised feelings ran deeper than he imagined. There were weeks of longing until the evening Cecco rubbed his back as he wept at the supper table speaking of Christ's suffering. He had recognised Michele's fragility, led him to bed and gently hugged him. It was a union of love made flesh and lust sanctified by love the first time the two merged into in a single tangle-limbed body.

Michele decided to paint a David and Goliath for the Pope. Cecco modelled, his moustache and beard shaved and his shirt stripped off his shoulder with Michele's favourite sword held in his right hand and a sack of grain in the other. Cecco naturally tilted his head and stared at the sack and Michele painted his torso in the same technique as the body of Christ in the *Entombment*, with dry light tones over grey underpaint to suggest skin over ribs and muscle. The David was painted in days and Michele modelled for the head of Goliath. Cecco held the large mirror upright as Michele mouthed a silent scream. *David with the Head of Goliath* was dispatched to His Holiness with the hope the message would be understood, bypass half-hearted supplicants and hasten a pardon. There were no further outstanding commissions and time hovered like a lark. Cecco and he lived together day and night, closer than brother and brother, as close as Mamma Lucia and Papa Fermo. Neither cared; they lived in defiance of church and supposed laws of nature. To the world, they would be regarded as merely master and assistant, their dishevelled bed, rumpled sheets and blankets concealed behind an eyeless arras. For days, they lay abed till noon, even later, until the afternoon the house was woken by the clatter of horses, then banging, cracking and splintering as the main door was broken down. Michele drew on his breeches, grabbed his sword and dagger and rushed to the hall where he encountered armed men. Fabio and Stefano appeared seconds later. "Who are you, what d'you want?"

"Which one of you is Michelangelo the painter?"

"I'm Caravaggio. These men are servants, leave them out of this." He pushed Cecco behind him and dropped his sword.

Chapter 26

Memory of Zagarolo

As days and weeks passed, I was upset on Michele's behalf that no one enquired about us, especially for his wellbeing, even though Colonna couriers frequently passed on their way to the fortress. Michele was obviously concerned he might not receive further commissions. Without comment, he announced he would paint a David and Goliath. "You'll be the David once we've shaved you."

"Not my balls again!"

"Just that excuse for a beard."

We stretched and prepared the canvas, working rhythmically and easily together. In the past, I would have helped Mario or Lorenzo but Michele worked with more urgency. When the canvas was ready, we closed all the shutters and lit candles set high up on my right. I stood in my shirt, the left sleeve off my shoulder, dangling over my breeches. I gripped Michele's favourite sword in my right fist, the point near my groin and a sack of grain in my left hand. The sack was heavy, necessary to create the right tension in my arm bearing the weight of the imagined head. Michele told me to focus attention on the sack, and I instinctively tilted my head which he liked and told me to hold.

As he worked, I glanced up occasionally. I saw his usual deep concentration, paint rapidly transferred to the canvas with absolute assurance, easing the pressure to allow underpaint to suggest subtle shadows and undulating skin over collarbone or ribs and lightened the base colour where the light caught the upper arm to project it forward. He tinted the hand red, as he had in several Baptist paintings to suggest the sunburnt skin of a working youth but, here, the red hue thrust the hand even closer to the viewer.

In the silence as he worked, no longer chatter and banter between us, or the sound of musicians practicing in rooms above, I could not help dwelling on everything Michele had suffered and lost. Always alone in a crowd but now utterly abandoned. I recalled how he wept at table describing Christ's suffering when working on the new *Supper at Emmaus*. With Michele's suffering in mind, I needed no instruction about my expression which he lovingly caught, echoing the feelings of the boy David, of sympathy and sadness, in contrast to the cold calculating poise of the white giant of Florence. My torso and clothing were painted in the shortest time I could remember and folds were suggested by brushstrokes applied rapidly and barely blended. Highlights on my flesh were augmented by chalk dust added to the lightest tones to suggest sweat from David's exertions. The handle and blade of the sword was carefully painted, and it was obviously time for the head of Goliath to go in, and I wondered who he would ask to model, Fabio or Stefano. Being the older, I thought Fabio more likely but was surprised when Michele told me to hold the large mirror upright for him to portray himself. He raked his fingers through his hair and beard to make them appear unkempt and stared slack-jawed as he painted his reflection.

When the painting was finished, I spent an hour regarding my rejuvenated self and Michele's image cut down and aged. Ranuccio's death was Michele's death by proxy and his wounds changed him as the Christ was changed in the recent version of the Supper. Apart from painting, he was less self-assured with no opportunity for high-flown debate previously shared with the cardinal but rather the action of painting became pure contemplation. My pa said painting an icon was an act of devotion, although from the shallow results and my mother's bruises, his devotion was no thicker than a layer of tempera…I sniggered. *If only Pa could see me now as David*, surely the equal of the other Michelangelo's version at which he glared with unrecognised envy at the engraving nailed to the workshop wall.

The message of the painting to His Holiness was transparent; Michele's head a trophy anyone might take for a bounty but freely surrendered in the painting in the hope of pardon. He had taken the matter into his own hands, not confident friends were working with any urgency on his behalf, suspecting certain fair-weather friends saw their commercial prospects improve so long as he was outlawed.

The lack of contact with Rome was unsettling and he even suggested we make a break for Venice. I heard he'd visited the city after his apprenticeship and described it as a mirage. He said he was about eighteen and it was there he met Lorenzo. I never knew why Lorenzo, a Sicilian, was in Venice. Michele freely admitted he had been intimidated by the paintings he saw there but now considered himself the equal and better than most of the masters whose work he remembered. He thought we might hire a wagon from Palestrina and perhaps a small carriage to leave incognito behind drawn blinds under cover of darkness but everything changed when Michele received a letter from Cardinal del Monte. He did not attempt to disguise his delight. He read the letter several times before handing it to me. I was touched the cardinal mentioned me and Michele replied immediately to ensure the courier delivered his response by return. His melancholia lifted, reassured by the cardinal's continued regard and for the first time since the killing of Ranuccio, allowed himself the luxury of stillness and calm.

I noted Michele told the cardinal he hadn't started the David and Goliath whereas in fact it was finished. I assumed he had his reasons, perhaps hoping the cardinal might plough the ground in advance of His Holiness receiving the painting. Considerations about Venice immediately evaporated and Michele concentrated on the delivery of the David and Goliath. Michele said he was sending it to the Pope with the certainty Scipione would covet it and thereby more likely to work towards a pardon. Several weeks before the cardinal's letter, we were relieved to hear from Lorenzo informing us Mario and Carla had left Rome for Syracuse, and he was about leave for Messina. It was a relief knowing our dearest friends were safe. Our mood lightened, anticipating imminent return to Rome and, taking a brush I was cleaning from my hand, he drew me close, held me tight and kissed me on the mouth. Once the new version of the Supper and the David were packed and sent to Rome, it was as though the paintings were harbingers of leaving virtual captivity as sheep are released to high pastures, young doves are fledged and flowers turn to the sun. Michele didn't paint for a week and we left Zagarolo to walk in the hills and rolled together naked in the sun. Michele said he had wanted me for a long time… or did he say he had waited for me a long time? He didn't give a reason for his reticence, and I didn't press him further but recalled a conversation with Lorenzo who suggested Michele saw me as just a boy and found shaving and painting me as Cupid disturbing. The same when I played Isaac and Ignacio pretended to… but that was the past and, for the first time in seven or eight years and much longer for Michele, we wandered in the countryside. Since arriving in Rome, I barely thought about open fields, hills and mountains, even memories of my mother were shrouded in dark shadow but supping palms full of clear spring water and the sounds of bleating sheep and twittering of a bird no more than a smudge in the sky high above us, was a return to Eden. Perhaps the distant view of Caravaggio in the Isaac painting suggested Michele might also have remembered the past as a time of innocence but peace was shattered by the sudden break-in at the farmhouse by an armed gang of bravos, undoubtably sent by the Tomassoni.

Michele pushed me behind him for protection and threw down his sword, offering himself so long as the others were spared. The lead thug swaggered forward, sneering, slowly drew a dagger, grabbed Michele by the back if his hair to expose his throat, leaned slightly back to stare Michele in the eyes. I did not see what happened but the man's head suddenly wobbled and a blade went up, tearing the man's throat, drenching Michele in blood. He stabbed his assailant with the knife he kept up his sleeve, then thrust the dagger up a second time. The man's head jolted when the blade crunched through the roof of the mouth. Michele withdrew the dagger and the man dropped to his right. Another man barged forward towards Michele but stopped in mid-stride; mouth open, he emitted a gurgled grunt, then bubbling, frothing blood seeped down his chin and dripped on the floor, his legs buckled and he fell face-forward with a two-pronged hay fork buried in his back. Emilio backed towards the door, his sparse teeth in a dreadful, wide-eyed grin. He was cut down by the third man who, as he turned away grinning, Fabio swung a spade in a wide arc and was spattered by a fountain of arterial blood. I darted to our room to fetch Michele's other sword and on returning to the hall was horrified by the carnage, blood spattered in arcs across the wall, bloody footsteps on the paving and blood-soaked clothes. Michele reeled away from a man he slashed, exposing his head to a counter thrust.

Without thinking, I raised the sword with both hands and brought it down with every ounce of strength onto the sword arm of the assailant. My feet left the ground from the impact, the man howled, his hand almost severed, and I think Michele finished him with several stabs. Seeing he was outnumbered, the fifth man fled the house.

The fight was over in ten minutes, but, to me, it seemed an hour and was horrified by the sudden arrival of other armed men which I thought was the end of us. Thankfully, they were Colonna men, one of whom finished the job, cutting the throat of the still living man felled by Emilio's pitchfork. I called out it was unnecessary and stood rigid at the sight and sounds of moans and Fabio's sobs as he grieved over his dead brother. I hadn't seen Stefano fall.

It was the first time I witnessed a seriously bloody fight at close quarters and began to shiver, rushed from the hall and vomited in the yard. I leaned trembling against the wall and noticed the body of the fourth man presumably killed by the Colonna agents.

From the distance of twenty or more years, I recall the events in the farmhouse at Zagarolo with greater clarity now than I did at the time… what I witnessed then was a blur for many weeks and more, reduced to brief glimpses of knives, gasps, stepping in puddles of blood and shuddered uncontrollably when events came into focus to haunt my dreams then and, from time-to-time, still. It was clear Emilio was probably dead before he slumped against the wall. Michele went to him as Fabio rushed to tend to his brother. "Stefano… Stefano! Sweet God, Oh Gesù…"

I will never shake off the sound of Fabio's groans. "Holy Mother, don't take him. Stefano! Brother, please don't leave me."

Two more armed men entered the hall and another pair behind supporting Lucia. She was soaked in blood and gripped a long kitchen knife to her breast. I followed them into the hall. The senior man called, "Signor Merisi… Master Caravaggio the painter? You must be ready quickly. We were sent to take you somewhere safer."

In the yard, the familiar small, battered carriage and wagon drew up beside the body of the fifth assassin.

Two of the men strode along the passage. "Where are your possessions?" I led the men along the corridor. On my return to the hall, Michele stooped beside Fabio and gently drew him away from his brother's lifeless body. One of the Colonna men whipped the cloth from the table and covered Stefano, the white sheet instantly blotted ruddy-brown.

Michele caught Fabio's face in his hands to turn him from the sight. "Fabio. Fabio, listen. Cecco and I have to leave; do you understand?" He nodded. "You will be safer here with me gone. I brought this misfortune on you, and I am truly sorry."

Fabio slipped his arms around Michele's waist and sank his head into his chest. Michele kissed his forehead and gently drew away, seeing the men carrying his paint materials towards the door and called, "Cover them carefully."

I supervised the loading and dreaded leaving what had been a haven of peace and tranquillity with a little family we came to care for deeply, a season, I later realised, was normality, something I never experienced before. When I returned to the house to make sure nothing was left behind, I saw Michele hand a note to the Colonna agent. "Deliver to His Eminence Cardinal del Monte…"

We embraced Lucia and Fabio in turn. She was in a daze and Fabio merely nodded and embraced us, tried to speak but simply stood trembling, shoulders sagging and weeping uncontrollably. Before leaving, Michele pulled off his blood-drenched shirt and threw it on the fire and washed his head and chest in a water butt of cold water in the yard. I rummaged in a bag for a fresh shirt which Michele put on as he strode to the carriage, drew me in with him and pulled down the blinds.

The carriage trundled along the rutted road, the wagon rumbled behind until we reached a crossroad. To the left, the road led east, presumably to Palestrina, the right to Rome but the one we were to take lay ahead southward. The senior agent joined us inside the carriage.

"Signor, from now you are under the protection of Duke Filippo Colonna, Prince of Paliano, senior military officer of the Court of Naples. At Naples, commissions have been arranged. I wish you well and better fortunes."

The carriage rocked as the agent left and Michele drew back the corner of the leather blind and watched the horsemen set off for Rome and the carriage rocked again as a new driver climbed up to start our journey. Two armed Colonna men escorted us and two others took turns driving the cart. Michele let the blind drop, plunging the interior in darkness except for a thin sliver of silver light that fell across the contours of his thighs.

Chapter 27

Naples

Michele said death stalked him since Ranuccio fell. As the carriage rumbled along, I embraced him. We travelled throughout the day and night with the blinds down as the sun rose on our left. The little cavalcade stopped before it was too hot at an osteria where we stretched our legs and shared a light meal with the Colonna men. The stop was brief, fresh horses were harnessed to the carriage and mules to the wagon, and we pressed further south, the landscape changing from hills to lush valleys, vineyards, olive groves and green shoots of wheat fields. Spring lambs were maturing and young men herded cattle for milking or slaughter and bells rang throughout the hours in a chain tolling the Angelus, from village to village and town to town.

I involuntarily crossed myself and occasionally, Michele grinned and did the same, whether in gentle mockery or sincerity I was unsure. I dared not sleep the first few nights, haunted by the horror of the scene at the farmhouse, tormented by ghastly dreams and, when I did briefly slumber, Michele woke me, saying I had struggled and called out. Even in daylight, I sometimes stared stupefied, reliving fragments of memory; skin peeling from the slash of the knife as the dying man's throat was cut, blood gushing in rhythmic surges, pooling on the stone floor, smeared walls and skidding bloody footprints. In time, the carriage rocked me into deep sleep that left me exhausted, my ears howling and whistling. The days became hotter and the breeze no longer cooled the carriage so we sat on the wagon and often walked for miles at the pace of the mules. After several days, the driver and escort removed their doublets and piled pieces of armour onto the wagon. Two days were lost when a wagon wheel hit a rock and shattered. The men cursed and two rode to a nearby village to find a wheelwright. We went to lie in the shade of a stand of blue-black poplar trees and became dozy in the still dry heat, lulled by the siss-siss of cicadas. A wheelwright from a village several miles from the road said the wheel was not repairable, and it was not until the next day he returned with a new wheel and recast wheel rim. When assembled, the Colonna agents helped shoulder the corner of the wagon for the wheelwright and his lad to slip the wheel onto the axle and hammer it in place with iron cleats.

Several days later, the carriage and wagon were drawn up the steep road by horse and chain to the monastery of Monte Cassino where we spent the last night before reaching Naples. Michele and I were given separate cells but, in the night, I slipped across the corridor to snuggle into the narrow cot beside him. In the morning, one of the brothers knocked. I slipped out of bed and stood naked behind the door as it opened. A brother greeted Michele and said morning service would begin when the bell stopped tolling in about a quarter hour and seemed disturbed Michele lay naked and uncovered. Without doubt, the brother heard me laugh when he left. We went to the magnificent chapel. I knelt but Michele stood throughout and did not receive. After the Mass, we were given breakfast of bread, cured ham, olives and dilute wine, then the brothers bade us good journey.

In sight of Naples, we were met by a messenger and four armed men, one younger than the others, who were to guide us into the city. The blinds were down as the carriage slowly rumbled towards the outskirts. There were many turns, the carriage rocked and moved at walking pace and often came to a standstill. The streets were a cacophony, cheerful banter and loud shouts near and far and from high above we heard much singing… sharp resonant tenors and high harsh but musical women's voices that echoed from the walls of the narrow alleys, the words in accents almost unintelligible. The air was infused with the smells of cooking food from pizza ovens, fish, meats and bread but also a sickening stench of filth, worse than the back streets of Rome. The blinds were often lifted; the first time Michele quickly blew out the candle in the lamp. *Who are they?* We imagined the curious took us for aristocrats travelling incognito.

To the ringing of church bells, we were delivered to a tall pink house where Duke Filippo's factotum greeted us. Our lodging comprised four rooms on the top floor and were informed other residents were trusted servants, retainers and pensioners of the Colonna. Although rooms were smaller, I was reminded of our lodgings at the Palazzo Madama and instantly overwhelmed by longing for Rome. Michele paced the rooms as our belongings were brought upstairs and I directed where our possessions should be placed, painting materials carried to the largest room I chose for Michele's workroom. The other rooms were sparsely furnished with wobbly chairs, scratched tables and cupboards with creaking hinges. The factotum suggested a small room with a cot, table, two chairs and a small cupboard might do. "For your serving man."

"I have no servants. When am I to meet Duke Filippo?"

"His Excellency will be informed of your arrival but is preoccupied with his duties to His Highness the Viceroy Don Juan Alonso." He handed Michele a sealed document. "An introduction to the Marchese Giovanni Battista Manso of the Confraternity of the Church of the Misericordia. I suggest you present yourself there to discuss requirements for a commission. You are expected."

"What's the subject?"

"I don't know…"

"Who is this Manso?"

"Marchese Manso is one of the seven members of the confraternity of the Pio Monte…"

"Who are…?"

"A society of noble young men of faith and devotion to the poor and needy after the model and mercy of Filippo Neri."

He gave Michele another document. "A letter of credit guaranteed by the Colonna. We are aware you have deposits here and there to redeem your credit and our agents will arrange financial matters." The factotum gave a curt nod, turned and left.

I went to the workroom and opened the shutters. Whereas Rome's streets were grander but scarred by the wars, Naples was pink and yellow and huddled, sliced by vertiginous dark narrow alleys, stacked tier on tier up steep hills, buildings five and more storeys strung with criss-crossed washing that billowed in the light breeze. From the height where Michele and I stood, the air was sweeter and less oppressive than the stench from the street, refreshed by a breeze that carried the breath of the sea mingled with the aroma of cooking. The noise from below, chatter from across the way and calls from up and down the street were unceasing. Someone coughed to attract our attention. It was the lead man who met us outside the city. Michele slipped his fingers into his purse to offer a gratuity, but it was waved away. "We're well paid for our services, Master Caravaggio."

"You know my name."

"I've heard of you and your paintings, master. All Colonna servants know about your pictures. I'm Calimero, Master… Alessio here, my brother, has a talent for drawing, and I wonder if you would consider him for an apprentice. Well, not so much an apprentice… we haven't the money… but maybe a serving man."

Michele glanced at the young man who stood with his cap in his hand, shyly glancing up at him. "Can you cook?"

"I can, signor… all my brothers cook… all Neapolitans cook."

Michele grimaced. "You really want to be a painter?"

"My family couldn't afford to pay a master to train me. Maybe I'm too old to start now anyway."

"How old are you?"

"Sixteen, master."

He turned to me. "It would be useful to have someone familiar with the city, to fetch and carry… and maybe you could teach him a little about preparation and the like."

I was not best pleased but nodded.

When the others left, Michele caught Alessio by the shoulder. "There are quills and paper in one of my bags… bring them to me, I need to get a message to Rome."

I admit I was jealous of Alessio but came to recognise he was not a rival but a friend and, in the first weeks and months, I showed him necessary basic skills and Alessio took on the more arduous, repetitive preparations. He was particularly useful in the first weeks when Michele and I had little sense of the layout of the city, except for the arc of the bay which was a helpful navigating anchor. The streets were filled with people, hawking and selling their wares of every kind and the aroma of seemingly endless varieties of savoury and sweet foods filled the air and the shadows cast by the tall buildings and sea breezes kept the city cooler than the often suffocating summer heat in Rome. Unlike Rome, Neapolitans lived their lives outdoors. High above, washing billowed like great sails from lines strung across the streets ringing with loud laughter and shouted conversations criss-crossed windows. Rich sounds matched the scents and smells and street vendors sang unfamiliar songs and musicians set up pitches on corners beside street vendors of goods and foods to entertain knots of people who congregated to hear them sing solo or small groups played lutes, guitars, tambourines, hurdy-gurdys and flutes and many joined in popular songs and clapped in time. On one occasion, Alessio joined a singer accompanied by a flute player and drummer. He had a sweet high voice, and I quickly picked up the words and joined, stamping my foot to the rhythm. I laughed and coins were tossed into the musicians' open leather pouch.

That evening, Michele asked Alessio and me to repeat the song several times.

Lascia dicea Amarilli Lascia, Damon, tua Filli E corri in braccio, corri cor mio Cuch, Cucù non odi? Egli ti invita ed io hem Mentre il cuculo il cuch cantava.

While the cuckoo his cuck-oo sang, "Leave," said Amaryllis Damon, "leave your Phyllis and run to my arms, sweetheart. Do you not hear cuck-oo, cuck-oo? He invites you, and I invite you too."

Chapter 28

Seven Acts of Mercy 1607

Alessio guided Michele and Cecco to the Pio Monte della Misericordia church along a network of narrow lanes in the shade of tall tenements under awnings of drying bed linen and clothes high above. It was an inside-out city that reflected the apparent openness and easy nature of the people although Alessio, a Neapolitan of countless generations, did not entirely agree. "I avoid the Spanish quarter. There's always trouble between Spaniards and us."

There was an edge in Alessio's voice as Spanish soldiers shouldered their way through the crowded streets. They arrived at the imposing Duomo, the cathedral of San Genero and the Assumption of Mary, then crossing the road, they turned onto a narrow street leading to the church of Pio Monte. Cecco handed Michele the letter of introduction and led the way to the church door. They were greeted by a servant who ushered them along the nave to an eight-sided chapel. From the smell of new wood, stone, mortar, plaster and paint, it was only recently completed but unadorned and the atmosphere was clammy from drying plaster. They were guided to a group of gentlemen gathered at the steps of the sanctuary and addressed the man who stood slightly ahead of the others. "Marchese Manso, may I present the painter Master Michelangelo Merisi da Caravaggio?"

"Master Michelangelo, welcome, your fame precedes you. May I introduce my confederates and brothers in Christ of the Pio Monte; Astorgio Agnese, Giovanni Battista d'Alessandro, Giovanni Gambacorta, Girolamo Lagni, Vincento Giovanni Piscielli and Cesare Sersale."

Each bowed and, in turn, Michele introduced, "My dear friend and companion, Francesco Boneri, and our assistant, Alessio."

"…Shelter the homeless, feed the hungry, refresh the thirsty, clothe the naked, visit the sick, visit the prisoner and bury the dead…" Marchese Manso's voice echoed in the empty church. "The Holy Virgin and Child must be included… and angels to support them."

"Are angels necessary?"

Manso smiled as though he knew of Michele's aversion. "Of course, they are messengers of the Almighty."

"Aren't the Virgin and Child enough?" He glanced up at the space above the altar.

"I'm thinking of the available space within the painting. Our Lady and Child are witnesses and angels mediate between heaven and earth. They embody the Grace of God." The Marchese noticed Michele pursed his lips. "But, Master Caravaggio, you painted an angel for the Contarelli chapel… two in fact."

He smiled and winked at Cecco, perhaps recognising him from the paintings.

"You've seen my work?"

"Some of the confraternity and I have seen your paintings. I especially revere the St Matthew paintings in San Luigi and also *Our Lady of Loreto.*" He laughed. "Master Caravaggio, we *do* travel beyond Naples… occasionally."

The others laughed and the Marchese's twinkling, mischievous eyes and ironic smile, which as he gently teased, brought Michele abruptly into the presence of Francesco, who also wore his deep faith lightly. Michele shyly smiled. The Marchese allowed time for reflection, then said, "Master Caravaggio, Michele…? I will be plain. Donna Costanza Sforza-Colonna mentioned your name, but I assure you there was no pressure on my colleagues and me. On the contrary, hearing of your coming to Naples, we were eager for you to put your extraordinary talents to the service and good of our mission to the poor and outcast. I will also say we are aware of rumours, but rumours are not truths."

"Slander, but not libellous." Michele grinned.

"Indeed. The confraternity wish to employ your talent for the glory of God and from what we have seen… the Almighty speaks through your work."

The commission was agreed and the contract signed, worth four hundred ducats, more for this single painting than any he had done before. He estimated the painting would be the largest to date, even larger than the *Death of the Virgin,* the cause of all his miseries and exile.

Had Alessio not guided them to the Misericordia, it would have taken much longer to find the church and were puzzled when he took them back another way. After leaving the Misericordia and entering the piazza of the Duomo, Alessio unexpectedly turned into an alley and along a further succession of alleys that led to what appeared to be a blank wall decorated with a crude painting of a Madonna with angels kneeling either side. Michele gripped the haft of his dagger until he realised Alessio had disappeared into a sharp turn to the left at the top of the stairs. Michele stopped and stared at the painting of the Madonna. Alessio returned running. "Master Michele, I thought I'd lost you."

"A moment." Michele touched the chipped picture and flakes of blue paint fluttered to the ground.

He glanced at Cecco. "I wonder where the painter found such intense colour, not lapis… surely too expensive?"

Although simply painted without hesitation, certainly without doubt or artifice, untrained nevertheless the image expressed unquestioning faith in the protection and real presence of an endlessly patient mother. Even the angels, perhaps sons or brothers of the painter, whoever they were, Michele believed they existed. Perhaps the painting was made to protect the neighbourhood, an offering for mercy and grace? Alessio was surprised the famous artist found the chipped and faded painting of interest.

After maybe ten minutes when Michele and Cecco intently stared at the painting, Michele suddenly said, "Lead on now." Along the alley, Alessio took a sharp turn to the right, and they recognised their busy street. "We didn't come this way before."

"It's quicker."

"If it's quicker, why didn't we come this way earlier?"

Alessio merely shrugged and, as they neared the house, Michele asked if he knew any local artists. "I need to buy pigments."

Alessio thought for a moment. "Carlo, Carlo Sellitto. He recently returned from Flanders and set up a studio near your place. He was born in Naples so he's sure to know where to buy materials." Alessio took them to the street where Sellitto lived. Cecco spotted *Carlo Sellitto Pittore* in fine script. He shoved open the door. On the highest landing was further script: *Carlo Sellitto.*

Michele rapped on the door and, after a long wait, a young woman answered. She wore a white shift and shawl to hide her nakedness and her hair was dishevelled. "Good afternoon, I am the painter Michelangelo Merisi da Caravaggio to see the painter Signor Carlo Sellitto."

"He's not here."

"Who is it, Martha?"

A young man in his early twenties, lacing his breeches, opened the door wide. "I am Sellitto… did you say Caravaggio?"

Michele nodded. "Michelangelo Merisi da Caravaggio and Francesco…"

"*The* Caravaggio?"

"My companion Francesco Boneri, Cecco, and our guide Alessio."

"It is an honour, signor… Master Michelangelo. My wife, Martha."

She curtsied.

Michele smiled at her embarrassment. "I prefer Caravaggio… mustn't overshadow that other fellow." They were invited into the apartment with the familiar smell of oil paint and scent of lovemaking. The workshop was in disarray, rolled canvasses in corners, unopened travelling chests. On a strainer, a new prepared canvas squared up, ready to transfer a cartoon drawing for a portrait. Propped against the far wall was a painting of St John the Baptist. "Yours?"

"It's a copy. The original was the best I painted for my first commission but you don't want to hear all that."

"You have talent, Master Sellitto."

"Carlo, please…"

"Your work has merit. I like your St John." Michele looked closely att he canvas. "Nice, very nice, solid and without mannerism… good for you."

"That's a great compliment coming from…"

"I hear you recently returned from the Low Countries; I see the influence. I'm Lombard, like da Vinci… and so is my dear Cecco, but unlike Master Leonardo, I finish whatever I start… but to business… Can you tell me where I can find quality materials, preferably ready powdered pigments? I haven't time to waste. I also need a maker of good strainers, support frames and trustworthy frame maker… and a sail cloth supplier." Carlo nodded. "I'm also in need of an assistant, a well-trained painter… perhaps you, Carlo?"

Alessio helped Carlo stretch the thirty-eight by twenty-five palmi canvas, closely supervised by Cecco to ensure even tension and the warp and weft of the canvas were at perfect right angles to one another and parallel with the edges of the frame. Expecting the first layer of gum Arabic to be dry in a day, Michele took Cecco with him to meet the priest at the Misericordia to discuss the painting in detail. Alessio had drawn a map but even so they made several wrong turns.

Approaching the church, Michele realised he had forgotten the priest's name so addressed him as *Father*. "Master Caravaggio, good day. I assume you've come to discuss the painting…?"

As they entered, the priest gave them a history of the church. "The Confraternity of the Misericordia built this church. I understand you met members of the confraternity but I don't know how much you've been told of our mission which is to the poor and to provide interest-free loans to the needy…"

"Guaranteed by…?"

"The Confraternity are our greatest patrons but naturally loans are secured by assets deposited with us, redeemed on repayment of the loan or sold to recoup any loss if unable to repay."

"From which you make a profit."

"All profit is distributed to charitable causes and to fulfil our missions, which includes the ransom of Christian slaves of the Mohammedans."

"Are there many Christian slaves of the Mohammedans?"

"Their corsairs raid Africa and the Mediterranean and further afield, whole coastal villages snatched from Greece, Sicily and Southern France… even England and Ireland, we hear. White women are particularly prized for their harems and men die slaves in their galleys."

"Am I meant to refer to that aspect of the Confraternity's mission?"

"The subject is the seven acts… unless you hear to the contrary, I suggest you concentrate on the traditional seven – shelter the homeless, feed the hungry, refresh the thirsty, clothe the naked and so on… visit the sick, visit the prisoner and bury the dead. Mother and Child must be observers of the acts…" Michele closed his eyes as images began to form, clusters of figures, four and three… perhaps five and two with the Virgin and Child above bursting into the picture in a whorl of fabric… the way Cecco as the angel appeared to Matthew in the Contarelli… He was suddenly aware the priest was speaking, "Maestro Caravaggio…"

As a major Mediterranean port city, most colours he needed were easily sourced, including a pasty yellow which resembled the colour of Neapolitan houses and which he used to lighten colours instead of lead white. Naples glowed in golden light even as the heat abated at eventide. To let him know how much he trusted his judgement, Michele put Cecco in charge of preparations. Carlo, in turn, showed Alessio the recipe to make gesso and several thin layers were laid on to prime the canvas and then layers of darkened raw umber applied in succession when each layer was thoroughly dry.

In the evenings when alone with Cecco, Michele made sepia studies for the composition to explore the organisation of groups of figures. He set the scene at night at the turn in an alley, suggested by the shortcut Alessio had taken. The priest had suggested some ideas, St Martin of Tours dividing his cloak with the naked beggar and St James the traveller, perhaps to curry favour with the Spanish overlords with an oblique reference to Santiago de Compostela pilgrimages. The priest also directed Michele to read and consider the ancient Roman legend of Pero who breast-fed her father Cimon a prisoner condemned to death by starvation.

The priest said he would loan his copy but Michele said, "My Latin's not good enough, Father, but I know the story."

The resolution for the composition was to divide the seven acts into three groups, four to the left, two on the right and one at the turn in the alley. The various groups would be illuminated from the left, as though from an open door of an inn where the innkeeper welcomes St James with a pilgrim cockleshell in his hat and St Martin beside him dividing his cloak. A figure behind would represent someone quenching his thirst and a boy squatting to the left and behind the naked beggar would stand for the sick. On the right, he would place Pero visiting her father in prison and breastfeeding him through the prison grille. Emerging from the alley in the background, a priest with a torch, lights the way for bearers carrying a body, with probably only enough space for the corps' feet. Unresolved were the Virgin and Child and angels, for which he reserved the top third of the picture. He was now adept at choreographing models like actors. The studies were burned as soon as each section of the painting was complete. Alessio was told to paint the workshop walls dark brown, the shutters were drawn and all but one window was covered with oil cloth so only two of the highest panes were clear to illuminate the scene. Cecco modelled the naked beggar, his physique now manly with a fine muscled back, hardly a starving beggar but these days when modelling he was serious and sat very still, unlike the days he posed for the Baptist. Carlo was St Martin and, when they were alone one afternoon, Michele asked if he thought Martha would consider modelling for the Pero character. "This might be impertinent but has she given birth recently?"

After a long silence, Carlo broke the pose and his shoulders sagged. "How did you know?"

"I could smell her breasts and her belly is still full." Carlo stared at the floor. "Did she lose the baby?"

"It was born… he was born, lived a few days but was feeble. We returned to Naples soon after he died. It was agonising to leave him all alone buried in a foreign country."

Michele nodded. "She's still lactating." He cringed, realising how mercenary he sounded, but Carlo was distracted by the thought of his lost son.

"She wet nurses a noble woman's child."

"Ask her if she'll model for me."

It was fortunate their rooms at the top of the house lacked ceilings, which meant the huge canvas was easily accommodated with no need to hire a larger workshop elsewhere. In any case, he preferred to live with the painting ever present, a few steps from the room where Cecco and he slept, although he often slumbered in a chair just ten feet from the canvas. It was a reminder of the time he lived at the Palazzo Madama… before the fall. Cecco often voiced Michele's loss, how he missed the cardinal, Lorenzo, Mario and Filippo too and raised Michele's spirits by prancing naked around the room, posing as a satyr. Now twenty, Cecco had grown what by dim light might pass for a goatee. Michele laughed. Balanced on one leg, his arms in profile, Cecco glanced sideways.

"Come here, piccolo capra."

"Why now, Michele?"

"What d'you mean?"

"We never did this before Zagarolo." Michele shrugged. "Is it because I'm older?"

Michele gipped Cecco's jaw and turned his head towards him and carefully scrutinised his face. "You look more like a man but still boyish, even with those thin hairy bits about your mouth."

Cecco gently tapped Michele's face, who caught him in his arms and their wrestling gradually became breathless. When not working, Cecco's sense of fun endeared him to the rest of their new Neapolitan family and it was Martha who asked if their families knew one another: You both have northern accents.

"We're both Lombardi but Michele's family wouldn't piss on us, with their connections with the la-di-da Colonna." He giggled and said in falsetto, *Buonasera Marchesa, come fa Principessa?* He glanced at Michele who smiled. Cecco laughed and continued, "I heard the Merisi boy was a painter and had gone to Rome… so I left Bergamo and tracked him down. It took a few months but we met by pure chance at a tavern in the middle of a storm."

Michele smiled at Cecco. "Il mio trovatello."

Monday, 26th of February, 1607

In less than three months, the Seven Acts neared completion. Even without lost Roman nights and days carousing and reeling home drunk and hung over all day, it was a near unbelievable achievement. The Madonna was done from a woman who looked a little like Lena, her beauty and serenity a pale memory of the original. Cecco was painted twice, clean shaven again and hanging off a table in different poses to model the tumbling angels supporting the Virgin and Child, wings and wheeling white fabric marked the threshold between the sacred and the earthly works of mercy and a subtle backward glance to the first time he used the device in the final Contarelli altarpiece. As well as the naked beggar, Cecco modelled for the figure to represent the sick, his pose vaguely delineated and only the foot painted in detail caught in the light of the open door of the inn. Michele had no idea how the figure to represent thirst might be done so sent Alessio with a note to the priest outlining what he needed to discuss. When they met, the priest suggested the story of Samson in the Book of Judges. "Samson had a great thirst and drank water from the jawbone of an ass provided by God."

"But that's divine intervention, not an act of human mercy."

"That's as maybe but God is ever merciful and that's what I suggest you paint."

Further discussion was interrupted by the clatter of footfall as a grandee and entourage entered the church, passed Michele and the priest as they went to the altar and as though choreographed, all genuflected deeply before the altar and crossed themselves before turning to Michele.

The priest bowed deeply and introduced, "Signor Tommaso de Franchis, welcome and may I introduce Master Michelangelo Merisi da Caravaggio?"

"Master Caravaggio, belated welcome to Naples. We look forward to seeing your painting for the Confraternity which I understand is almost finished."

Michele nodded. "I came to meet you because my family and I wish to commission a pair of paintings for the church of San Domenico Maggiore. The subjects are…" de Franchis glanced around the church. The light suddenly began to fade although it was near midday. Dogs howled and the church darkened until only candles gave light. Everyone strode to the door. Outside, it was twilight and eerily quiet. Everyone looked up as the sun was eaten away; eventually, it glowed pink-orange with a glittering halo. The priest crossed himself. "An eclipse."

The commissioned subjects were a *Flagellation of Christ* and Our Lord at the Column. The agreement was sealed with a handshake as the sun emerged in glory and bells rang across the city. Franchis drew on his glove, glanced up at the sky a moment, turned and said, "I look forward to a pair of masterpieces. Good day, Master Caravaggio."

The notary garbled the salient points of the contract already scribed in duplicate.

...the honoured artist, the painter Master Michelangelo Merisi of Caravaggio agrees to paint a Flagellation of Our Lord at twenty-seven by twenty-one palmi and Christ at the Column at sixteen by twenty-four palmi, each for the sum of 400 scudi. All work to be of the highest quality from the artist's own hand, to supply all decent quality materials to work with support and gilded frame, to be completed for installation by the last day of July in the year of our Lord 1607.

"Sign here and here, Master Caravaggio, and, Father, would you witness? Your copy, Master Caravaggio, and I hold Signor Franchis' copy." He closed the document folder and offered Michele a leather purse. "Forty scudi advance." He bowed to both. "Father, Master Caravaggio... Good day."

Michele's satyr played the fool to keep up his spirits as he worked into the night to finish the Seven Acts to which Michele added a rust-red sun behind the tumbling angel on the left, setting the time and date of events and even the place, Naples, on the day of the eclipse. Indeed, the painting was a paen to the city. He lay with Cecco, sweat pooled on his chest in the calm after the storm, Cecco's head nestled so the curls of his sideburns tangled with the wet hairs of Michele's armpit. Their breathing gradually slowed and they dozed until there was a light tap on the door. Cecco lifted his head. Michele got up, drew on breeches and slipped a dagger in the drawstring, pulled on a shirt, draped his cloak around him and tiptoed barefoot to the door, shot the bolt and yanked open the door six inches, his knee pressed against the door.

"Master Caravaggio?"

"Who wants him?"

"May I come in?"

"What do you want?"

He murmured, "I represent His Lordship, Luigi Carafa-Colonna." The name *Colonna* spoken hardly more than a breath. He opened his cloak, revealing the Colonna badge and to indicate he was unarmed.

Michele opened the door and the man slipped in. "Why the mystery, who is this, Luigi?"

"The Colonna is a large… clan. Many branches."

Michele smiled. "But a single column. What's the message?"

"From what I understand, the Misericordia picture is almost finished and you have been commissioned to paint two pictures for San Domenico." His eyes widened as he glanced over Michele's shoulder. Michele turned to see a little goat caper naked at the far end of the corridor by the workshop.

He turned back to face the man. "You were saying?"

"Er… San Domenico, the church of San Domenico has great prestige and the Colonna have always…"

There were increasingly heavy thuds behind as the barefoot goat pranced closer. "The Colonna have always had an interest in San Domenico."

Arms encircled Michele's shoulders. "Ignore my satyr, the only one in captivity, the product of a goat and a Milanese whore. Tomorrow, I will roast him and friends and I will eat him for our supper." He smiled. "Signor, you were saying?"

The man struggled to contain his astonishment. "It… it is believed there is an unfinished painting of the Holy Virgin and Child, Saints Dominic and Saint Peter Martyr surrounded by poor supplicants, a *Madonna of the Rosary*. One wonders if it is true?"

Michele hesitated. "If it were true… I'm not saying it is, but if it were true, how did you hear of it?"

He felt Cecco peer first over his left shoulder, then right, then left and right again. The visitor's eyes followed his appearances.

The man blinked, then stared Michele in the eye. "Let us suppose there is such a painting and if an unfinished *Madonna of the Rosary* were long overdue and the painter accepted several advances but still had not delivered."

"If that is the case, what is it to the Colonna?"

The man continued, "Let us suppose such a painting had been commissioned by say, the Duke of Modena… a random choice of name from a certain painter who accepted an advance of thirty-two scudi."

"Very specific."

"Random number…"

"The final agreed price being, let's say, four hundred scudi."

"I follow…"

"A certain gentleman, Signor Masetti, Fabio Masetti on several occasions unsuccessfully requested the advance repaid." He adjusted his eyeglasses. "Since the supposed painting has never been delivered, such a painter could not sell such a picture without damage to his professional reputation."

"Ah, reputation!"

"Yes… in tatters. Paintings by such a respected master are still in great demand, so long as his reputation for fair dealing remains intact. If I were he… such a reputation is worth saving."

The satyr kissed Michele's neck. "Ha!"

Michele turned to watch Cecco cartwheel back along the corridor, then, grinning, turned to face the bewildered visitor. "What's your proposition?"

"Three hundred ducati and Signor Masetti reimbursed his thirty-two scudi by us, in exchange for completion of the painting to be the altarpiece for San Domenico."

Michele smiled. "I must see if there is such a painting… if you will bear with me."

"Take this draft contract, and I will return after dark tomorrow evening and, if satisfied you have located the said picture, matters will be concluded."

"My thanks, Signor Nessuno."

"Good night."

Michele shut and bolted the door and, as he turned, the naked satyr reappeared at the end of the corridor in the attitude of a ham actor. Michele drew his dagger. "Now, piccolo capra…"

Michele took Cecco to tour the port, wharves and inns to find models for the flagellation painting. On the waterfront, they found characters to people the paintings, especially the lined and careworn. Having gained their confidence and by offering more than a day's pay for a day's modelling, most readily agreed. More difficult to find was a model for Jesus. Not only patrons but everyone had clear visions of how his countenance, demeanour and presence should appear.

Michele's favourite had been the model for both the Calling and the Entombment, the most handsome man he had ever seen and his body was perfect but his name... what *was* his name? It was ridiculous he couldn't recall his name when they spent so many hours and days together. His distant nude body vibrantly erotic, still potent four years or so later, his face and body remembered in every detail but his name, no longer.

Cecco and he watched the small fishing boats slowly sail into harbour, baskets of fish, lobster, crab and octopus tossed onto the jetty, stacked four, five and six high, each boat adding more to the line. The noise of bidding and bargaining echoed from the buildings near the harbour as men, mainly men, although there were a few older women who drove hard bargains, vied for the best of the catch for their household, tavern or hostelry. Nuns and monks were given special privilege and a few pretended to resist when not charged for their purchases. The men doffed their caps as the fathers nodded and made half-hearted crosses in the air. Cecco nudged him and nodded to a boat gliding up to the pier. An old man steered as the younger hand stripped to the waist, stowed the furled sail, then stacked baskets near the prow. His physique less toned than the executioner in the St Matthew and skin paler but still beautiful. Michele nodded. The boat was the last in port and only a few of the crowd now remained. The young man threw just three baskets onto the jetty, turned to the old man. "I said we left too late. You're too old, Papa; we have to find a hired hand."

"Signor, what have you caught?"

He turned, his eyes were blue-grey and he squinted. He drew on his shirt, then nodded towards the baskets. "Crayfish, a few lobsters, crab and assorted fish."

"How much for the lot?"

He glanced back at the old man who was preoccupied tying up the boat. "Give me what you think is fair."

"If you bring them to my house, I'll give you half a scudo."

"What? You're joking with me. You're after more than fish... bugger off."

Cecco nodded towards Michele. "This is the great Roman painter Master Michelangelo Merisi da Caravaggio... He wants more than fish, it's true." He grinned. "He's a fisher of men."

He stared at Michele. "What's that to me?"

"I'll be brief. I'm commissioned to paint a picture of the Flagellation of our Saviour for the church of San Domenico Maggiore... you know the church?"

"Of course."

"I need a model for our Lord. I've been looking for the right person with... someone who... I can't explain in words. If you agree to model, my assistant Francesco here will show you the way to my house, and, if you agree, bring the fish. Bring your pa too if you're nervous. I must go now. Have supper with us." He offered his hand.

The young man wiped his hand down his breeches and shook it. "I'm Rocco."

Michele knew exactly the pose he intended for the Christ. At Viterbo during his flight from Milan, he had seen a *Flagellation* by Sebastiano del Piombo. A name he recalled from his short stay in Venice. There had been little money left and he was hungry. What was worse was on the road from Arezzo near Orte, he was spooked by horsemen who drew up to see if he matched the description of someone who attacked the sergeant of police in Milan. Fortunately, for safety, he had joined a group of travellers on pilgrimage to the Holy City, who vouched for him, He was also sickening, hardly matching the description of a vicious killer. When he parted company from his travel companions who went ahead to Rome, he detoured to Viterbo where he sold the mule for a pittance but enough for a bed for the night and a decent meal. Thanks to an ague, he was forced to stay three nights which used up most of the money from the sale of the mule. By the fourth day, he was well enough to set off again for Rome and on the way back to the road going south, arrived at Santa Maria del Paradiso, an old Romanesque church. From habit, he was compelled to enter and lit a candle to thank the Holy Mother for his recovery. He mouthed a prayer and gazed up at the altar where his eyes were filled by a painting of the *Flagellation*. Christ's body was twisted, his head low as he reeled from blows. As he stared at the painting, an old monk approached and asked if he was well or wanted to make confession. He shook his head. "But, Father, who painted the picture?"

"Sebastiano Luciani." The Papa Clement made him Piombatore.

He saw Michele frown. "The bearer of the lead Papal seal."

Chapter 29

The Fraternity

He expected Rocco to be skittish about posing nude but he stripped unselfconsciously, even with Cecco, Alessio and Carlo in the workshop. He grinned. "I have five brothers." Michele made a sketch to show the staggered twist of the body, bound his arms to a nail in the wall and wrapped a length of torn sheet around his waist to barely cover his private parts. All but one of the shutters were closed and Rocco's powerful torso emerged from the gloom, glowing and burnished by afternoon light.

The *Madonna of the Rosary* miraculously came to light, rolled up among his effects. Once tacked to its reassembled stretcher, Michele sat an hour assessing what was needed to complete it. He was pleased with the seven existing figures, a group of five who raise their hands to St Dominic handing out rosaries. Two older men, Cecco, in a beige-grey cloak, a woman and child established an off-centre equilateral triangle that directed the eye to the sketched in Madonna and child. The other saint, Peter Martyr, pointed to the vision of the Madonna, revealed only to him, his colleague St Dominic and the viewer. All that was needed to complete the painting was the Madonna and Child and three hundred ducati were his. The Colonna agent returned with the contract.

Michele smacked him on the back and offered him a glass of wine. "Signor Nessuno, you have heard of the miracle of the house of the Virgin transported to that mean little town of Loreto. By coincidence, there is an extraordinary picture by a renowned painter from Rome, a certain Master *Cacchiotirare…*"

His guest frowned. "Well, my friend, there has been another miracle. A painting I never painted has miraculously appeared in my workshop, painted in my style but nevertheless I have no recollection of painting such a picture. The subject seems to be similar to the painting you mentioned, although the Madonna and Child have not yet fully materialised. I suggest the presence of St Dominic offering rosaries means only one thing…" He guided the visitor into the workshop. The painting is clearly intended to be a *Madonna of the Rosary* for the Dominican church. He laughed. "Is that not a miracle?"

His visitor slipped off his cloak, fumbled for eyeglasses and scanned the painting from close and far. "How soon could you finish it?" He walked over to the *Flagellation* painting and on to the outlined Christ at the column. "You are committed to a lot of work."

"By Lent. That's only two weeks. I only have to paint the mother and child."

The man replaced his eye glasses and turned to look again at the Rosary. "If you say so." He laid the two copies of the contract drawn up in fair hand on the table, added the agreed date for delivery, then turned the documents to face Michele for signature. The contract was short and to the point that he, Michelangelo Merisi, would *complete a Madonna of the Rosary for the sum of... said painting to be collected by the agents of the purchaser on such and such a date... the sale to be confidential... dated and signed for the purchaser... L. Finsonius.*

Michele held the quill, hovering over the contract. "Who is L Finsonius?"

"Louis Finson is the intermediary. My master wishes his purchase to remain confidential."

He put down the quill. "I smell something fishy. Are you trying to con me?" He unsheathed his dagger and stabbed it on the tabletop.

"There's no trickery, Master Caravaggio. As I say, His Excellency wishes to purchase the painting in good faith, through his trusted intermediary Signor Finson..."

Cecco murmured, "Does it matter who buys it? Get the money in cash before the painting leaves the workshop."

"He's right, no promissory notes, no letters of credit, cash on collection, ducati or scudi, hard metal."

"But that's a great deal of coin."

Michele wrote '*in coin*' over the agreed price on both documents, signed both copies and held up the papers. "Take or leave."

To complete the painting, he blocked in the Madonna and painted the child, glancing down to St Peter Martyr as though empathising with his wounded head. The prospect of so much cash could not be jeopardised so he persuaded Martha to model the Madonna. Where Lena was beautiful as a princess, Martha was earthbound but with inner beauty often lacking in the most beautiful. Sadness that she and Carlo lost their child infused her painted self as the Madonna. Now Lena's gone, her kid's an orphan... will he ever know his mother was the Mother of God, holding him safe in her arms as she gazed down with love on the pilgrims who knocked on her door? Once the mother and child were finished, his only addition to the painting was a fluted column to ensure those in the know would recognise his eternal debt to the Colonna. The finished painting was taken off the stretcher unvarnished, rolled, covered and manoeuvred down the stairs once the cash was counted. When alone, Michele and Cecco shifted a large oak armadio and hacked a deep niche in the wall where he deposited the bags of coin, threw the debris onto an old sheet and scrubbed the floor clean of tell-tale plaster dust before they heaved the armadio back into place.

He worked all hours to complete the pair of paintings for San Domenico. Rocco posed with each of the torturers in turn who were painted in shadow so Christ's suffering was illuminated by harsh light with their vented rage confined to shadows. What had Gesù done to these men that they reacted with such violent fury towards him, that they beat him so willingly? It was not revenge that fired their rage; it was Christ's innocence that cast him as victim, his innocence an affront to their miserable lives, petty sins, banal misdemeanours... the light that searched the deepest recesses of shadows and darkness of their souls had to be extinguished.

The *Flagellation* was almost finished and *Christ at the Column* well advanced. The model for this Christ was a Frenchman called Pietro, presumably Pierre in his homeland. He was married to a Neapolitan woman whose brother was a painter. Pietro modelled for his brother-in-law and other painters and was recommended by Carlo. The three-figure composition harked back to Michele's earlier Roman paintings and he employed two of the models from the *Flagellation*, one grabbing Christ's hair and raising his left sinister arm to whip him. The other, snub-nose model, a gentle young man whose forehead was prematurely creased by care lines and, had he been a little more acceptably handsome, Michele would have preferred him for the Christ. He grinned, imagining the response from the priests if he had. He painted Pietro naked and considered leaving him uncovered but was persuaded by Carlo to add a loincloth which was tied so loosely it appeared to be slipping off. A column represented the might of Rome, the scored shaft witness to countless acts of brutal torture but also a further opportunity to offer gratitude for his protection by the Colonna.

Michele met Cecco and Carlo at the church to supervise the hanging. The wagon rumbled up to the door and workmen helped the lads carry the pictures into the cool nave of the church. Tommaso Franchis arrived with his family to view the pictures and was visibly moved.

"Master Caravaggio, I have not seen anything like your painting before. It feels I could put out my hand and touch Our Lord as he…" He turned away and slowly paced between the two paintings, leaning, his face barely four fingers from the canvas. Michele left Franchis to contemplate the paintings and went along the nave and met as the priest as he reached the sanctuary.

The priest smiled. "In the past, I heard wonderful things about your paintings, Michele, but these are more than I expected."

Michele glanced over the priest's shoulder towards the altar. "The Rosary painting isn't up yet."

The priest turned and glanced at the altar. "What Rosary picture?"

Cecco slipped his arms around Michele from behind. "What are you reading?"

He only answered when Cecco kissed his neck. "The Golden Legend."

"Is this for the viceroy's commission?"

"Hm… the martyrdom of Saint Andrew."

"Tell me the story."

"Let me finish and I'll tell you. Now fetch Carlo… we need to order materials."

"I've left."

Cecco ran down the stairs. Michele was always taciturn when he began thinking a new painting into existence. The next weeks and months were going to be exceptionally busy, not only with the viceroy's painting of Saint Andrew but also a new commission from the church fathers of Sant' Anna della Lombardi. The Colonna were surely active in securing both commissions.

Rocco's father, the old fisherman Benedetto, was the ideal model for Saint Andrew, weather-beaten and wrinkled from sailing in all weathers with blinding sun from above and reflected light from the sea below. Michele made him stand on a stool with his arms loosely roped to nails hammered in the wall. Cecco stood on the ground to his left, leaning away, gripping the rope around Benedetto's right hand. The old man was naked except for a red cloth around his waist and Cecco wore his brown-beige breeches and shirt pulled down from his right arm to reveal the muscles of his back. Michele painted long sessions and both Cecco and the old man were only allowed to take breaks when their muscles went into spasm or trembled uncontrollably. Cecco had never felt such pain when the muscles in his back, legs and arms seized and was astonished how Benedetto managed to bear the agony so long, especially with all his weight bourn on his left leg.

Over supper, Michele told Cecco the story of Saint Andrew. "Martyred in Patras… Greece, because he refused to stop preaching the Gospel. The Roman pro-consul ordered his crucifixion, tied rather than nailed to the cross to prolong the agony. After three days when he constantly preached from the cross, the crowd threatened to rise up against the pro-consul but Andrew begged to die on the cross like his Lord and as soldiers tried to release him he prayed and died preaching and still tied to the cross."

Cecco was fascinated by the way Michele painted the light on Benedetto's ribs and strained shoulder and chest muscles – like the sheen of light on leather and the scorched corded neck and face sagging as the saint dies, still preaching. There was further tension from the taut X shape of the cross and Cecco's and the saint's garments tying them together but at the same time drawing them apart. Carlo posed for the pro-consul dressed in armour borrowed from the viceroy's armoury and an old woman who lived several doors from their lodgings posed as herself, representing the voice of the crowd, gazing up at the dying saint, revealing the huge goitre in her throat. Cecco wondered if the viceroy would accept so raw an interpretation of the subject but was delighted when Michele received a letter in His Excellency's own hand, congratulating him on such a fine interpretation of the martyrdom of the saint he held in special regard. The courier delivered the balance of the payment which, after paying the frame maker and gilder, was deposited with other monies in the secret recess behind the armadio.

"Michele, there you are, come quick…"

He followed Alessio who ran ahead of him up the stairs. "What is it?" Alessio reached the workroom and stopped at the door to let Michele go ahead. Entering the workshop, Carlo and Martha were sweeping the floor and Cecco stood by the worktable. He gestured with both hands to the palettes on the table which appeared uniformly grey. Michele couldn't make sense of what he saw, as though the entire room were covered in a grey silk sheet. "What is it?"

"Sand." Carlo and Martha swept sand into piles that crunched underfoot as Michele went to examine the table.

"Who would do this?"

"It's a warning… from the Neapolitan fraternity of painters."

"What have I done to them?"

"They obviously think you've taken the best commissions in the past half year."

"Who are they?"

Carlo touched his arm. "I told you…"

"Who are the ringleaders, what are their name?" He swept the palettes off the table. "Bastards!"

He turned over the table and Cecco jumped back. "Don't take it out on me…"

"Where were you… how did they get in, were you off gallivanting?"

"Don't, Michele."

"Whoring as ever. You should have been here." Michele hit Cecco hard on the head. Martha put her arm around Michele's waist to draw him away from Cecco, but he pushed her away.

"You can't blame Cecco, any of us… for God's sake, we're not your servants, Michele, and, if anyone's to blame, it's you."

He ignored her and went to the chest containing colours and flung back the lid. It was filled to the brim with sand. He picked it up and threw it at the wall. "Everything… they ruined everything."

He howled, ran and kicked the broken box across the room, colours emerging from the grey sand. "Get out… the lot of you… leave me alone."

"Michele."

"Go!" When alone, he dragged the armadio away from the wall and was relieved the money was untouched. He swept the floor, tables and shovelled the sand into sacks. Colours were ruined, impossible to separate sand from powdered hues and raged as he swept valuable materials into sacks and, even when the floor and surfaces appeared clear of sand, everywhere crunched under foot and was gritty to touch. He hauled the sacks down to the street and left them against the wall. By the time he returned to the workroom, he was hot, sweating and exhausted. He slumped onto the small cot in the spare bedroom and covered his face with his arm. He regretted treating Cecco badly, lashing out the way he used to do in Rome.

Orazio Gentileschi to Michele Caravaggio.

Michele, I was pleased to get your letter and to hear you and Cecco are well but hear this – Baglione's picture was taken down from the Gesù! Nobody knows what's been done with it. Who would want it? What price his fancy gold chain now I ask? Cardinal Giustiniani must be blushing too – so much for his connoisseurship (if there is such a word). In passing I saw a painting by a youngish painter, I think he's called Manfredi – it made me laugh – a piss-take of Baglione, showing Mars thrashing Cupid's arse red! I know you'll raise a glass or two to celebrate Baglione's come-uppance and so will I – and, at last, we are vindicated. Not only that, but it's good news to hear about your latest commission – a Resurrection no less! Gesù, you have the Devil's luck. Congratulations, my friend, and what a poke in the eye for old Giovan Baglione. I've already put the word around – Michele Caravaggio has a Resurrection commission – I'll let you know how that goes down.

Orazio.

Michele read the letter twice and grinned, handed it to Cecco who laughed and repeated several times, "*Mars thrashing Cupid's arse red.* Ha! Baglione sure has his come-uppance, and I bet there'll be no more preening and parading Benedetto Giustiniani's gold chain for a long while."

Cecco never saw Michele so elated with the opportunity to paint a resurrection after Baglione's disaster. He must have imagined the form of a resurrection many times and never doubted he, rather than Baglione, should have had the commission for the Gesù in Rome.

Rocco modelled for the resurrected Christ with his left foot on a box to represent him striding over the great stone as he left the tomb, his thigh flexed to take his weight. His right hand raised like the Christ in the Sistine Judgement, the left gripping the white banner with the red cross of the resurrection. The figure was a companion to the executioner in the Contarelli martyrdom, his body glowed in raking light which hardly illuminated the surrounding cavernous space. Michele tied a white cloth around Rocco's loins, the fabric of his shroud whirling in great swirls tacked to the wall as though caught by a rushing wind and echoed the angel modelled by Cecco for the Saint Matthew altarpiece. Below were four guards, each assumed poses Michele had worked out but their response was worse than theatrical ham-actors. He found turning and twisting them as though they were marionettes was the solution with two rushing out of the painting to the left, one screaming in terror and the other anxiously glancing back. Two other guards formed an inverted arc at the bottom of the painting, one suddenly awake, the other as though stunned, unable to move. On the ground were abandoned weapons and pieces of armour. The screaming figure was similar to the one on the left in the Taking of Christ in Gethsemane. By June, the painting was almost done. Rocco returned for a day for Michele to refine details of the head of Christ and, when finally complete, he invited Rocco and the other models with Carlo, Martha and Alessio to view the painting before it went to the church of Sant' Anna. Cecco served liberal quantities of wine.

One who modelled a sleeping soldier gasped. "It's me to the life and you've painted Christ Himself... but how could we have beaten Our Lord in the other picture?"

Michele laughed. "You didn't... you were only play-acting; we're all play-acting."

"But I feel as though I did. No other artist could paint such a thing."

Michele roared, "No Neapolitan painter could, I give you that. I've seen their work, not one can paint." His high spirits made Cecco apprehensive, especially when he picked up a large flagon, slopping each cup to overflowing, splashing dark stains on the floor. "Am I right?" The whole company fell silent. "You have to agree with me. They are so envious they are reduced to pouring sand in my pigments."

"They're not as good as you, Michele. That's true, but they're not all bad."

"You'd say that because you're Neapolitans. Name one good Neapolitan painter."

"Careful what you say, Michele..."

"Why should I be careful?"

At the end of June, the *Resurrection* was installed and blessed at Sant' Anna della Lombardi, followed in the first week in July by the blessing of the *Seven Acts of Mercy*. Michele was feted wherever he went, but he was most pleased by comments from fishwives and workmen. One woman, her reddish-brown hair tightly tied back, a bloody apron stretched over her rotund belly, sang to him as she stepped towards him, her hips swaying, hands and shoulders alternately gesturing towards him. Her voice was high and bell-like and she made up words and tune as she came closer, caught his face in her podgy hands and kissed him on the lips.

Caravaggio, Caravaggio... Caravaggio
Long live the great painter
of our Saviour and the Madonna
Bless you... Bless you, signor

Cecco hurried to the Ospedale. Inside it was dark and cool. He drew the note from his doublet. "I've come to see Master Michelangelo Merisi the painter."

"Come with me." He followed the brother.

Cecco was shocked by the sight of Michele, lying on his side, his knees to his chest, his face swollen and blotched with dried blood that also matted his hair. "I think he's awake. Signor… Master Caravaggio, can you hear me?"

Eventually, one near-black swollen eye opened a fraction. He saw Cecco and grinned, further splitting his lower lip, causing blood to seep across his cheek and stain the pillow. "Thank God, I slipped my painting hand in my armpit."

He was gently rolled onto his back. "Can you open both eyes, signor?" The lids flickered. He raised his hand and slipped his index finger in his mouth. His lips began to bleed as he ran his finger over his teeth to check those he had yesterday remained.

He glanced again at Cecco. "Where am I?"

The Father spoke, "You were brought here last night… were you brawling?"

"Ambushed."

"Do you have enemies…?"

"I think I know who they are."

The priest was abrupt. "Does that matter?"

Cecco was alarmed. "Tomassoni?"

"No, much closer."

He examined his left hand which was swollen and skinned. "I think the success of the *Resurrection* was too great a rebuke for local so-called painters."

"What did you expect when you openly insult Neapolitan artists? And how can you be sure? Throwing accusations around is likely to attract more of the same."

"Certain persons put sand in my paints… I'm told it was a warning. They haven't the guts to do this themselves… now they paid bully boys to do their dirty work."

"You should be more circumspect and respect local pride."

He spat; the spittle sprayed droplets of blood. "Local pride, my arse."

Colonna agents arranged a small carriage to bring Michele and Cecco home and it was several days before the bruising faded from black to yellow. He thought at least two ribs had been broken and expected the cuts and bruises would take weeks to heal. Cecco took care of Michele's every need during his recovery, cooking rich lamb broths, making pastas with tomato, goats' cheese and slivers of cold boar.

At night, Cecco ran his fingers lightly over the scars on his back and, when Michele drew him close, he murmured, "You're good to me, Caro." Then he gently pushed his head down.

Cecco giggled. It was their private game. "Do I have to?"

"Yes, you do."

Michele received several messages from Colonna agents but did not share the contents with Cecco who was preoccupied, tending to his recovery and attempts to smooth occasional vehement outbursts about Neapolitan painters. He was irritated Michele continued making threats, stubbornly defying the beating by the artist's confraternity bully boys and still bad-mouthed their paintings. By now, he was reasonably well but, even though he went into the workshop, Cecco noticed he wasn't working. Not since Zagarolo was there a time he did not have a major painting in progress. After the euphoria of city-wide acclaim and celebration of the *Resurrection*, he made several visits to the Colonna residence at Chiaia. Cecco imagined the Colonna were arranging fresh commissions.

Michele said nothing until, almost in passing, he said, "I'm leaving Naples."

"Where are we going?"

"Malta."

"Where's that, somewhere near Africa?"

"Not that far."

"Do you have commissions there? Is that what those Colonna letters and visits to the residence are about?"

"I suppose."

"When do we leave… what should I to pack?"

"I'm leaving with the fleet day after tomorrow. Costanza's son is commander."

"You said *you're leaving*… you mean you're going without me."

Michele turned to look out the window. "It's only for a short time."

"Why can't I come?"

"As I said, it will only be a few months… or so."

"Months! Surely, you'll need an assistant."

"I have to go alone. They say it's too dangerous for me to stay here, after what happened…"

"I don't understand… I went to Zagarolo with you, why not Malta?"

"Fabrizio and Costanza think this is a certain way to ensure a pardon from the Pope. Fabrizio committed much more serious crimes than me and thinks if I became a member of the order of the Knights of Malta, the Pope would have to accept he can't keep me outlawed forever, and, if I'm accepted by the Knights, then, according to the statutes—"

"Ha! Obviously Fabrizio Sforza speaking, how else would you know about statutes of the Knights of Malta? In any case, it won't take just a matter of weeks, it will be months and more… years even."

"I already have portrait commissions from several knights with connections to the Colonna, so it should be just a year, maybe a year and a half, and we'll be together again… but this time in Rome."

"A year and a half! But surely it would be understood you'd need an experienced assistant." Michele dropped his gaze. "I see… the Colonna think I'm a bardassa. They think those holy mercenaries wouldn't allow you in their precious order with your fuck-piece in tow to tarnish your reputation. Your reputation! No matter you killed a man but a catamite is a step too far."

"Stop, Cecco."

"Why should I? It's a crazy idea. Didn't Fabrizio Sforza have to stay three years in Malta before he was considered rehabilitated and you don't have the Lady Costanza for a mother. How do you think you will have paid your debt in just a year and a half?"

"It's not like that, Cecco. Fabrizio actually… anyway, Costanza has regard for you. She knows you come from near Caravaggio where she has domain. She thinks of you the same as she does of me."

"Bullshit! She wouldn't know me from a pig's scrotum."

Michele involuntarily laughed. "She knows I care about your welfare and is happy to be your patroness."

"I don't believe that for a moment. You probably said I was just an assistant and—" They were silenced by loud knocking on the door.

Cecco usually answered but defiantly sat staring ahead. The knocking continued until Michele went to the door. "Who is it?"

"A message for Master Caravaggio. The Lady Marchesa Sforza-Colonna sent me to ask you to attend her and her son Lord Fabrizio."

Chapter 30

Fabrizio

He laughed. "Where would you go, Cecco?"

"Don't mock. I have friends… and don't have a price on my head. Carlo and Martha say I can stay with them until…"

"There's no need, just stay here. Wait for me, Cecco, I'll be back in a year, maybe less."

"You planned this behind my back."

"It's a chance I have to take if we want to return to Rome. There's no future for me in Naples."

"Thanks to your arrogance and stupidity, bad-mouthing local painters."

He shrugged. "That may be so."

"You're incapable of staying out of trouble. You run towards it. You can't help yourself, Michele; every time you succeed, you bring yourself down."

"Nobody understands my work."

"That's shit, Michele, and you know it. A handful of your paintings were rejected, and I agree the priests are arseholes, but you're the best painter in Rome, in Naples… the whole of Italy… everyone knows that, whether they support you or not. Baglione may hate you, but he tries his hardest to copy your work. It's the same in Naples. You've made a fortune, but you had to fuck it up."

"Going to Malta will help get a pardon from the pope…"

"How will going to Malta…?" I saw there was no point in further argument.

"It worked for Fabrizio. Trust me, it's been arranged. I go to Malta, join the order and after a year…"

"A year!"

"After a year or so, we can go back to Rome. Be my good satyr and wait for me."

"It's madcap nonsense and won't succeed and… if you go, I'll never see you again."

"I'm leaving with the fleet day after tomorrow." I didn't respond. Michele turned to look out the window. "It won't be long and…"

"If that's so, why can't I come? I was the only one who stood by you… I thought you were happy I came with you."

"Of course I was, and I wanted you… but Fabrizio and Costanza think this is a certain way to ensure a pardon… if I became a knight of Malta, the pope would have to accept… and if I'm accepted by the order of the knights, then…"

"If, if, if! It won't be a matter of weeks; it will take months… years and Fabrizio was three years in Malta before he was rehabilitated, and he's a prince! Without Lady Costanza for a mother, how do you think you'll serve your time in just a year… even a year and a half?" It was hopeless. He had cleared the decks without a word, dismissing Carlo and Alessio, and I had no cards to play. We stood in silence.

I stared at him, but he avoided my gaze as he scraped paint on the palette into neat heaps. "It's worse than betrayal. I thought we were… happy or at least content… at least Isaac was reprieved." I snatched my cloak and rushed out of the house to stay the night with Carlo and Martha.

The flotilla stood out to sea and several ships appeared on the horizon. The largest, grandest and newest was decked with banners and, as it sailed into the bay, I saw it flew the cross of Malta, the banner of the Knights and Colonna and Sforza flags. When the flagship and attendant vessels anchored a longboat rowed by eight oars left the harbour returning about twenty minutes later with Fabrizio Sforza standing with his entourage sitting before him. He wore shining black dress armour and helmet with fluttering red and white plumes. As the boat approached the harbour wall, I saw Fabrizio had natural command, the grandson of Marcantonio Colonna who saved Europe from the Ottoman onslaught the year Michele was born. He acknowledged cheers from the crowd as he landed and the throng parted as he reached the top of the stairs and stepped on to the concourse.

When the crowd parted, still dazed that Michele was leaving, I was left standing in Fabrizio's path and, before I stepped aside, he looked me up and down and his gaze lingered a moment too long. I instantly divined the unspeakable crimes for which Fabrizio was convicted for which he was now absolved. Under different circumstances, I would have been approached by his lordship's servant and whisked off to his bed. I shuddered remembering how as a child Fabrizio killed Michele's mother's hens for sport. I witnessed countless chickens dispatched with an axe or cracked neck but saw no pleasure in it. I imagined Fabrizio not only sodomised bardassas and whores but beat and possibly killed for pleasure. What else could be considered an *unspeakable crime*?

Michele's battle with the world was a puzzle until I saw Fabrizio those few seconds and wondered if the pattern of Michele's behaviour started as early as playtime with Fabrizio. In retrospect, I realise we were back with the matter of the second son, the younger brother.

Staring out to sea, the sun sank towards the horizon and light was fast fading over the bay, and I became melancholic, thinking of the brief haven of peace of Zagarolo and Michele's tender attentions. I remembered watching Michele sleeping by moonlight, his skin was pale as Christ lowered to the ground, head turned towards me, his mouth slightly open, breathing lightly and his damp hair parted in the middle. I gently touched recent wounds and lightly traced old scars with my finger. His scars were the means by which he made Christ's suffering tangible, having shared the pain and torment of Christ at the column.

His instant success in Naples was a source of joy but, as ever, thoughtlessly squandered, and I was crushed hearing a recent rumour Michele encouraged friends in Rome to attack Baglione. He denied all knowledge, of course, but, even if friends in Rome acted on their own initiative, it was hardly likely to improve his chances of pardon for killing Ranuccio. The Colonna obviously calculated Michele's presence in Naples was no longer tenable and the example of Fabrizio's presumed rehabilitation must have seemed a viable solution. As the sun touched the horizon, I foresaw this fragile house of cards was based on too many assumptions and supposition that Michele was temperamentally disposed to simply concentrate on painting. The sea swallowed the purple sun, and I wondered if Lorenzo was right that Michele attracted bad fortune and humiliation because of something awful from his past for which he felt compelled to seek atonement.

The breeze from the sea was now chilly, and I had not brought a cloak. I was hungry too, quickly walked to a local tavern, sat near the ovens and ordered bread, cheese, Cervellatine salami, tomatoes, olives in oil and a cup of wine. As I supped, it was obvious there was nothing I could do to stop Michele sailing for Malta. He ignored any advice that contradicted whatever he set his mind to do and was the reason he kept his plans close to his chest until the last moment, leaving me with no options. From what he said of the marchesa, he believed she had his interests at heart and, if her son's exile in Malta expiated his crimes, it also meant Michele was back in Fabrizio's orbit and, having crossed the prince's path earlier, I wondered how sincere his rehabilitation was and what influence he might have over Michele.

By the time I heard the bells strike eleven, I was woozy and decided to spend the last night with Michele. Leaving the busy red painted tavern, I shivered. The wind was up, the sea was black and ships' lights rocked in the harbour and beyond. The buildings ahead were bathed in blue moonlight. I jogged along streets and alleys to keep warm, soon arriving at our lodgings, and I was apprehensive as I went up the stairs. I hesitated before pushing the door which was unbolted. Michele seemed genuinely relieved I had come and gently greeted me. Although reluctant, I gradually acquiesced to his enthusiastic rocking advances and woke after a sleepless night of desperate coupling and whispered assurances I didn't believe. Eventually, I slept but woke at first light to misery, anxious and distressed at the thought of not being with Michele… and already lonely.

When he woke, Michele reached for me. Seeing I was reluctant and close to tears, he drew me close. "It's only a year, twelve months, maybe a bit more."

"More like two or three years."

"Don't be pessimistic. Fabrizio said I'll be given a big altarpiece, bigger than the Seven Acts. You know how fast I work without distractions. They'll make me a knight and we'll be able to return to Rome with Colonna and the Papal Nephew's support. A knighthood and gold chain just to outdo Baglione and Cesari."

I got up and began to dress. "You're not thinking about us… we'll never be together again, here or in Rome and why should I share your sentence?"

He got up, shifted the armadio and took out a heavy leather pouch. "Every penny I made from the Misericordia commission, six hundred scudi and two hundred more to cover all your needs."

"So, now I'm a rich bardassa. Keep your money."

"Take it, Cecco, even if you just keep it until I see you again."

I threw the heavy leather pouch against the wall, expecting it to burst and scatter coins but it simply landed with a thud. We both laughed. "We had good times, Cecco."

"We did, Michele, but I have to make my own life and go on alone."

I walked slowly beside Michele to the Margellina harbour. Four Colonna men carried two chests of Michele's possessions and painting materials. Fabrizio, surrounded by his guards, waved to Michele who nodded in return. Michele went forward several paces until he realised I remained at the edge of the crowd. He turned back, hugged me, kissed my cheek and whispered, "We'll soon be together again."

I returned his kiss but his optimism rang hollow, and I was utterly miserable. Fabrizio greeted Michele as the Lady Colonna's coach arrived. Fabrizio went to offer his hand as she alighted, followed by her ladies. She stepped forward to embrace Michele. The marchesa was almost as tall as her son, Michele a little shorter and dressed in his customary back doublet, breeches and hat. Fabrizio wore black Spanish armour edged in tooled gold, his helm decorated with plumes of Colonna colours. Cecco paid particular attention to the Lady Costanza whom he guessed was almost fifty but seemed barely older than her son. Her skin was clear, pale with rosy cheeks, dark eyes and thin, determined lips that broke into smiles when she spoke. Her dress was rose and white and her cloak golden sand which caught the morning breeze.

There was a brief conversation between the three at the top of the stairs, then Fabrizio bowed low to kiss his mother's hand, and she ruffled his hair. They laughed as he rose to kiss her goodbye. He turned to Michele, tapped his cheek and strode down the stairs to the waiting boat. The crowd cheered and rowers raised oars in salute as he stepped aboard, followed by his bodyguard. Fabrizio stood and put on his helmet; the plumes fluttered as the boat was rowed towards the flagship.

Meanwhile, Lady Costanza spoke at length to Michele who responded, then tuned his head towards me. The lady followed his gaze. I was surprised and instinctively nodded. She smiled and slightly inclined her head. Michele continued to speak and nodded several times in my direction. Finally, he doffed his little black hat, kissed her hand and she hugged him a moment. He ran down the stairs to the boat loaded with his chests.

Before embarking, he turned to scan the crowd for sight of me. He waved in my general direction, but I wasn't sure he actually saw me. He stepped aboard and was rowed to one of the support vessels. I wondered if it had been decided he and Fabrizio should not sail together to prevent fraternisation and idle gossip during the journey. He heard cheers and saw the Lady Costanza turn to her coach and, as she was about to enter, glanced in my direction to regard me a moment before disappearing into the coach, followed by her ladies. The crowd slowly dispersed, but I went to the harbour steps to watch the fleet raise anchor and slowly set sail south. I scanned Michele's ship but could not see him, presuming he had gone below to his berth. The bulk of the fleet stood beyond the bay, as though squatting on the horizon and unfurled their sails when the flagship raised her colours and set sail. I stayed in the hope Michele might appear on deck but there was no sign of him as his ship tacked to follow the flagship, heading for the strait of Messina.

Chapter 31
Malta

The boy stared at Michele, unblinking and unembarrassed by his calculated lack of manners. He stared at him the way Michele stared at his subject… observer observed. Although only fourteen or fifteen, he had the assurance of someone much older, assurance founded on generations of power, alliances and unquestioned privilege. It was surely the reason the Grand Master Alof de Wignacourt wished to be portrayed with the boy, to express his near sovereign power and prestige enhanced by the presence of his high-born page, Nicholas, scion of the great house of de Paris Boissy. Wignacourt instructed he would be painted in his magnificent chased and gilded parade armour. The Grand Master and his page posed only once at the same time for Michele to plot their relative heights and position to one another. It was also the first time he saw de Wignacourt in armour; thereafter he usually wore his usual uniform when he granted sittings and a knight of similar build modelled the armour at other times in his stead. As the Grand Master stood before him for his portrait, he realised it was the first time they were entirely alone. Every other occasion he was accompanied by his entourage of secretary, page and major-domo at least and Michele was searched for weapons before Wignacourt and entourage arrived. "Remind me of the pose, Master Michelangelo."

"I would prefer you to call me, Michele, Excellency, if you please, or even Caravaggio."

De Wignacourt hesitated, unsure of the etiquette. "Of course, Master Michele."

"Turn, then look back and up at the frame of the window. A little higher, Excellency."

With a fine long handled brush, he drew his portrait in dark umber line, then broadened the edges to indicate the darkest tones and, with a clean rag, lightly rubbed those edges which would be lighter than the dark sepia background. The session lasted an hour and neither spoke. Michele observed the protocol that the higher in rank should initiate conversation and de

Wignacourt cleared his throat several times; Michele thought it was a sign of self-consciousness. When the hour bell tolled, de Wignacourt stood down. "By your favour, Master Michele…"

Michele bowed, the Grand Master nodded and left without looking at the painting. De Wignacourt's Spanish parade armour, black and gold, was exquisite. When the stand-in entered, there was hardly a sound, no creaking, each piece so perfectly shaped that overlapped layers of metal slid silently emulating the movement of the skin over muscle. When Michele ran his hand over the plates, the knight flinched as though he felt the caress and confirmed his suspicion that Michele's reputation was known among the knights. It took almost two weeks to paint the armour during which time the knight never spoke but it was not the serene silence of the Grand Master but the silence of contempt. The first day with the stand-in, he was unnerved when the response to his request to move a little this way or that was sullen silence, occasionally a sigh or grunt, but Michele accepted silence was better for concentration, unbroken by inane chatter and gossip. Indeed, the Grand Master's palace and the surrounding grounds were places of silence, except for the zizz of cicadas and hooligan birds, who came in gangs and left squabbling and quibbling finches?

The next sitting de Wignacourt granted, he suggested His Excellency might prefer to sit. "Won't the angles… perspectives, I don't know… won't it be all wrong?"

"I'll lower the painting and, with your permission, also sit."

"Would that mean a better painting?"

"It is easier to sit when painting fine detail."

Wignacourt nodded to his servant who set a chair and, when seated, he dismissed his man.

"Tell me where to look…" The second sitting was crucial when he blocked in mid-tones and bled in body colour, adding the thicker lighter tones towards the end of the session. It would normally take a day, but he was not sure how long de Wignacourt would stay.

"Master Michele, your painting of the Baptist for the Co-Cathedral is a triumph. You have received my congratulations on several occasions and responses I have heard are well deserved."

"Thank you, Excellency…"

He raised his hand. "Have I moved too much?"

"No."

"Your painting and the few others I have seen by your hand indicate to me a searching spirit, someone who unflinchingly recognises human weakness and beauty… portraying the human in the divine and the divine in humanity. I recognise the same in your illustrious namesake… whose work also echoes, though faintly, the work of the Almighty."

He sat, brush poised over the emerging features of the Grand Master. He held his breath hearing Francesco's sonorous voice from a great distance of time and space. He glanced towards de Wignacourt who disconcertedly returned his gaze. He sensed his thoughts were known.

Wignacourt smiled. "Michele, I will come to the point, I have decided to approach His Holiness for leave to offer you induction into the order in the third class. If you accept, you may choose to promise obedience to the rule or simply live according to the principles of the order without promise. What do you say?"

Overwhelmed that the offer had come so quickly and unexpected, he stood and curiously felt unworthy. "But, Excellency… I am a great sinner."

De Wignacourt turned to him, a rolled unread petition in his hand. "Who is not a sinner, Michele? Your past is known to us… the bad and, from the evidence in your paintings, the good. Have we ever raised questions about your past… have we accused you of anything?"

"You know I killed a man?"

"Rumours and other information have come to us and a list of crimes and misdemeanours." He stood and came to look at the painting for the first time. He stood aside as the Grand Master perused the emerging image.

He pointed with the petition. "So that is me." He gazed a long time at his portrait, then pointed again. "And those marks indicate where my page Nicholas will stand… good, good."

He stood close and bent slightly to examine the face. "It is indeed our self, already a good likeness." He touched the surface and quickly withdrew his finger, tipped by a smudge of paint. "Have I ruined the painting?"

"Easily repaired…" Michele smoothed the fingerprint with a touch of the brush. "Good as new."

He handed Wignacourt a clean rag and, when he rubbed off the paint, he sniffed his finger. "I find the smell of paint rather agreeable… do you use linseed oil?"

"Sometimes, Excellency, but usually walnut. Even sweeter."

He handed the rag back to Michele. "Of course, the stain of sin may be wiped away… baptism first and communion but also by true, contrite confession and absolution."

"My sins are all mortal, Excellency."

De Wignacourt did not respond, stood back to view the picture from a distance. "During the fight… did you intend to kill?"

After a long silence, he looked de Wignacourt in the eye. "The fight was about a woman. She was my model, and I believe she was a working girl in the employ of… my opponent, the man I killed. I believe she was his mistress and believe he killed her in a fit of jealousy."

"You intended to kill in revenge."

"No, Excellency… he called me out. I went unwillingly with no intent to kill. Maybe he meant to kill me… perhaps he thought Lena, my model, had become my mistress simply because I had painted her…"

"The model for the *Madonna of Loreto* painting?"

"You know it?"

De Wignacourt nodded.

"She may have been a common prostitute but she somehow… remained pure. I mean no insult to the Holy Virgin." He caught de Wignacourt's steady gaze. There was no judgement in his eyes. "The fight went on a long time. We were both exhausted. Yes, at moments, I wanted to hurt him but near the end, I believe he was determined to finish me… I stumbled and stabbed with the sword to defend myself but, as I fell, I caught him in the groin."

"Therefore, you did not intend to kill him."

"There was so much blood… it gushed like a fountain."

"As you painted the blood in the St John picture."

"So much blood. I knew he was done for, but, if I could live my life again, I would prefer to be known as a coward than to have met him for that disaster."

De Wignacourt gripped Michele's shoulder. "Since this is a moment of reflection and confession, of sorts… I joined the order when I was a youth and, within a year, the Turks attacked us. We were besieged for four months. I was at the Birgu, and we were almost overrun… we fought back and in the end were victorious." He grip was tighter. "I have killed Michele and, God forgive me, at times I raged and wished to kill every foe before me." He sat. "It is said I fought well at the Battle of Malta, the Grand Master at the time, de Valette, a great general, said I had fought well and honoured me."

He scratched his cheek. "I was honoured for killing with intent to kill but killing in the cause of defending this island… defending Christendom."

He stared ahead a long time, reliving the past. He eventually glanced up. "As I see things, Michele, you killed without intention to kill and incidental to your defence of the honour of the gentle woman I saw in your painting, a woman in whom you saw the Holy Virgin." De Wignacourt stayed three hours, ignoring occasional interruptions from his major-domo and servants. He eventually went to the door. "Who am I to judge you, Michele?" He hesitated before tapping the door for it to be opened. "I will write to His Holiness for permission to grant you the honour as knight Magistral Obedience, the St John painting will be accepted in lieu of the necessary passaggio payment." He stepped closer to the door but hesitated, then turned towards Michele. "You are closest to God when you are in the depths of despair… Think of the penitent thief dying beside Our Saviour… Today you will be with me in Paradise."

Chapter 32

The Page 1607

The portrait of de Wignacourt took only two further sittings to complete, and he accepted the Grand Master's generous offer to become a lay member of the order, straining to seem honoured but, curiously, not eager. For his first full sitting, de Wignacourt's page, Nicholas, brought the Grand Master's helmet as requested, with its red and white ostrich plumes and the Maltese banner, a white cross on a red ground. He stood the lad next to the Grand Master's chair, side on to the viewer. He wore rich brown livery with intricate lace cuffs, a Maltese cross badge, red stockings and kid leather shoes. His thick darkening blond hair, which when he was a child, would have been almost white and cut to the shape of his head with a severe fringe. Although French, he had less an accent than the master de Wignacourt; indeed, he occasionally used military slang learned from the knights and even odd words in Maltese argot.

"Shall I address you as Master Caravaggio?"

"Michele will do."

"Isn't that somewhat informal?"

"Caravaggio, if you prefer, and shall I call you Monsieur de Paris Boissy?"

He draped the banner over Nicholas' arm and swept the plumes away from his face. As he sketched the basic outline, the page stared back at him in an unblinking and haughty manner.

Today, he looked directly ahead, off to the left; his stare had no focus within the painting so Michele clicked his fingers to get his attention. "Monsieur de Paris Boissy, I wonder if you would kindly look towards me, thank you. You are most generous, Monsieur de Paris Boissy, as presumably all the de Paris Boissys have been for so many illustrious generations."

The boy turned his head, his stare hardened. Michele grinned, but there was no response. The lad was not particularly attractive, pasty-faced; in his case in-breeding bred out beauty, a face only a doting mother could love and arrogant manner that matched his looks. Because he felt no empathy with the youth, it was easy to capture his likeness at the first sitting. Nicholas stood for two hours before Michele allowed him to leave. He expected him to demand frequent rest times, but he never did. When he was gone, Michele set the helmet cushioned on the table to capture the angle at which the lad held it. As he refined the helmet, he discovered he had caught the boy's face in the reflection, with a highlight from his white collar. It was an echo of his own reflection in the flagon of wine in the *Bacchus*, which Francesco must have gifted to the Duke of Tuscany by now. Before retiring, he inspected the painting in detail and saw he had captured a different expression in the boy's face than he imagined… not the arrogance he thought he had seen but the boy's gaze was of attention, if not fascination and his pert lips were not a sneer he thought he had seen.

Nicholas de Paris Boissy to the Illustrious painter – Master Michelangelo Merisi de Caravaggio. Master Caravaggio, I believe I treated you with discourtesy which is unworthy of my rank and your enormous talent. I hope my manner is forgiven and that we may be friends.
N de Paris Boissy
When will you next require me to sit for you?

Michele laughed, drew a line under the post-script and replied:

The most humble painter, Master Caravaggio to the Illustrious and noble Lord Nicholas de Paris Boissy
Greetings Illustrious One, I thank you most graciously for your generous sentiment and I trust that what has passed between us is no impediment to our future friendship. Thank you also for your appreciation of my enormous talent.
I remain your friend, Michele Caravaggio. Come when it is convenient and when your duties permit.

Knights progressed in their red and white cloaks worn over armour, followed by Michele in his black uniform of the order, behind him, the banner of the order. Nicholas de Paris Boissy carried the Grand Master's plumed helmet, another page beside him carried the de Wignacourt emblazoned shield. The Grand Master wore his parade armour and a black hat with red and white plumes. The procession on 14th July arrived at the West door of the Co-Cathedral for Michele's investiture into the Order. He had received detailed instruction on his duties and responsibilities as a knight of the third class and had been given two Turkish slaves, both of whom he had painted behind bars as witnesses to the execution of St John.

Inside the Co-Cathedral, the procession marched slowly along the nave, turned right through the Chapel of the Sacrament, along the corridor to the Oratory where Michele's *Beheading of Saint John the Baptist* was installed with a magnificent gilded frame within a lavish decorated arched recess. Knights and retainers lined either side as he was escorted to the steps of the sanctuary. The Grand Master went to the sanctuary, and he and the whole congregation deeply genuflected to the host. He turned to the congregation and crossed himself. *In nomine Patris, Filie and Spiritus Sancti*, then went to his throne in the choir to the sound of ringing *amens*. The boys and men of the choir sang an anthem. Towards the end, Wignacourt left his seat and returned to the steps of the sanctuary where he read the Bull of Michele's investiture.

Whereas it behoves the leaders and rulers of comonweals to prove their benevolence by advancing men, not only on account of their noble birth but also on account of their art and science whatever it may be, so that human talent, hopeful of obtaining reward and honour, might apply itself to praiseworthy studies. And whereas the Honourable Michael Angelo, born in the town of Caraca, in the vernacular called Caravaggio, in Lombardy. Having been called to this city, burning with zeal for the order, has communicated to us his fervent wish to be adorned with our habit and insignia...

Michele glanced sideways at de Wignacourt's secretary Francesco dell'Antella who puckered his lips to suppress a smile. He and Michele had become close allies and it was dell'Antella who drafted the Bull for the Grand Master and included details of his origins in Caravaggio.

...as we wish to gratify the desire of this excellent painter, so that our island of Malta, and our order, may at last glory in this adopted disciple and citizen with no less pride than the island of Kos, also within our jurisdiction, extols her Apelles; and that, should we compare him to more recent artists of our age, we may not afterwards be envious of the artistic excellence of any other outstanding man of equally important name and brush...

Michele bit his lip and dare not look back at dell'Antella in case he laughed.

...and we wish to comply with the pious wish of the aforesaid Michel Angelo, we receive and admit him, by the grace of God Almighty and by papal authorisation especially granted to us for this purpose, to the rank of Brethren and Knights known as Brethren and Knights of Obedience...

The Grand Master gave a dinner *to* fete *our illustrious brother, Master Caravaggio* but Michele noticed several knights did not raise glasses or even make pretence of civility. Prominent among them were Brothers Giovanni Liscaris and Martin de Redin. The Brother Inquisitor, Fabio Chigi, sat with them but seemed not to share their disdain. Thankfully, Fabrizio Sforza sat near Michele and made polite conversation including his recollection of their boyhood friendship and commended him on his swordsmanship. The aged Ippolito Malaspina for whom Michele painted a *Saint Jerome* also engaged him in conversation, referring to his friendship with Ottavio Costa, Francesco del Monte's boyhood friend. After dinner Fra Antonio Martelli sought him out to arrange time for him to sit for his portrait. Martelli was a member of the highest order of the Grand Cross, a veteran soldier of many campaigns and close ally of de Wignacourt and Malaspina.

Nicholas came to stand for his portrait several more times, his manner became less formal and mutual liking grew between them.

"Michele, I'm told you killed a man… was it a duel?"

"Who told you such a thing?"

"I heard talk. By certain knights."

"Yes, and what do they say?"

He fiddled with the plumes and his stance became rigid, less natural. "I don't want to insult you."

"Just tell me what's been said. It's not anything you said after all." He fidgeted more, then looked at him directly. "They say you ambushed the man you killed in cold blood… is it true?" He put down the helmet. "If it's true, you are no gentleman, and we cannot be acquainted."

"Is that all you heard?"

"And that you painted filthy pictures for some of the cardinals and aristocrats… even the Pope."

"Is that what they say?"

"Is it true?"

"Do you want it to be true?"

"Why won't you answer?"

He put down his brush, wiped his hands on a rag and added a little walnut oil to the paint on the palette. "Did I kill a man? Yes. Have I painted nude figures, if that's what you mean by filthy? I have. Is there anything else you wish to know?"

"So, you *are* a murderer."

"If I killed in cold blood, indeed that's what I would be." He grinned. "Do you feel safe being here, alone with a murderer?"

"I don't feel particularly unsafe." He slightly arched his neck. "You said if… if you killed in cold blood… you admit to killing but suggest it was not cold blooded."

"If I had killed in cold blood, do you think, knowing that was the case, the Grand Master would allow me to remain in Malta, to become knight?"

"The Grand Master knows?"

"He knows everything and accepts I did not kill in cold blood and, as a good soldier, he is acquainted with the difference between self-defence and murder, and facts and slander. Does that satisfy your curiosity?"

He came to look at the near finished painting. "Tell me what happened."

"I told the Grand Master everything, but I am not prepared to repeat what I said to him or explain, excuse or defend myself further. Is that understood?"

"You don't intend to kill me in cold blood."

"Yes, I do." He raised the palette knife. "I intend to cut your throat from ear to ear, any minute now."

Nicholas laughed. "I thought so…"

As Michele ruffled his hair, Brother Martin de Redin entered, hesitated then said, "Lord Nicholas, His Excellency wishes you attend him."

"I come immediately."

He turned back to Michele and grinned. "Next time you'll have to tell me about those filthy paintings."

Approaching the Grand Master's receiving chamber, the sentry tapped the door, then pushed it open. De Wignacourt gestured he should enter. "Brother Michele." Wignacourt greeted him from his chair with brothers seated either side. "You know Inquisitor Fabio Chigi and Brother Martin de Redin and Fathers, Rodomonte Roero and Ippolito Malaspina, for whom you painted the excellent *St Jerome translating the Bible*."

Michele nodded in acknowledgement. "You wished to see me, Excellency."

"A matter of urgency..."

De Redin cut in. "A serious matter based on what I witnessed and heard... have you corrupted His Excellency's page, Lord Nicolas de Paris Boissy, have you sodomised him?"

Michele was speechless. De Wignacourt raised his hand to de Redin. "Brother Martin informed me that this morning you were seen in an intimate and compromising position with my page and heard Nicholas say you would show him filthy pictures next time he came to sit for the portrait. Is this true?"

"I witnessed what happened."

Chigi leaned forward. "Allow Brother Michelangelo to speak... Go on, Master Michelangelo."

He opened his mouth and slowly raised his hands, palms towards his accusers and laughed. "Forgive me, Excellency, Brothers... everything Brother Martin says is true."

"Condemned from his own mouth."

De Wignacourt raised his hand. "Is that all you wish to say, Master Michelangelo?"

"More or less, Excellency, except that a vile interpretation has been put on something completely innocent."

"You caressed him in my sight and God knows what else you have done with him in secret."

"I ruffled his hair when I promised not to murder him..." Both de Wignacourt and Chigi smiled. Michele continued, "Nicholas said he'd heard gossip I had murdered a man... details are known to Your Excellency..." De Wignacourt nodded.

"You not only touched the boy but you promised to show him filthy pictures..."

"Brother, I have no filthy pictures to show him... you are welcome to search my few possessions."

"How did the subject arise, and why did he mention filthy pictures in my hearing?"

Someone spoke up. "Perhaps you promised to make filthy pictures for the boy. You are an accomplished artist with great skill and a history of painting filthy pictures for... certain Roman patrons..."

"By Roman patrons, I presume you mean His Eminence the Most Reverend Cardinal del Monte? Perhaps the Marcheses Mattei and Giustiniani, His Eminence Cardinal Giustiniani, His Eminence Cardinal Nephew Scipione Borghese, the Barberini family or perhaps you are referring to His Holiness the Pope… to which do you refer, Brother?"

"I don't mean to accuse any of these illustrious…"

"Then if such illustrious persons are above accusation, how dare you accuse me… Brother in Christ."

De Redin stood and drew a folded sheet of paper from his pocket and read.

To the Illustrious and noble Nicholas de Paris Boissy, greetings… I thank you most graciously for your generous sentiment and I trust that what has passed between us is no impediment to our future friendship… Come when it is convenient and when your duties permit.

He handed the note to de Wignacourt who read and passed it to Chigi. Redin repeated, "*I trust what passed between us is no impediment to our future friendship…* Will you explain to His Excellency the nature of that *generous sentiment* and exactly what passed between you and Nicholas de Paris Boissy?"

Michele smiled. "But, Brother, you forgot to refer to the note first written by Lord Nicholas above the line which makes sense of my response. It is a jest intended to save his young lordship's embarrassment. He treated me with disdain when he first posed for the portrait with His Excellency. A miserable painter, poor artisan that I am with a bad reputation, which opinion several knights appear to share… you included, Brother de Redin. But Nicholas had the grace to see me as I am and had the nobility to apologise and even offer the hand of friendship. That is what passed between us, despite his appalling spelling, my response was intended to recognise the generous sentiment shown to me by him, by his apology."

"But an alternative interpretation suggests…"

Chigi spoke, "I have heard enough, Excellency, and am satisfied with Brother Michele's response."

De Wignacourt stood. "Indeed, so am I. Thank you, Brothers; would you kindly allow me to speak with Master Michele in private?" Once alone, de Wignacourt gestured for him to sit. "My Dear Michele, you must remember we live in a close community and many of the brothers have lived confined lives from early ages and have never lived in the world you have known. Nicholas is bound to be fascinated by your, forgive me, somewhat chequered life at the heart of Roman society, sacred and profane… indeed your past work has addressed both worlds. My life has been one of obedience in war and peace, of which we have spoken, but by comparison with what you have experienced, I recognise my way is a narrower path than yours."

"I understand, Excellency…"

"Enough of that now. Is the painting finished, or is that asking too much in the light of the several brothers who have also commissioned portraits? You are a captive painter here, Michele."

"Three more brush strokes, Excellency… Perhaps you would like to view it in say, two days?"

"I look forward to it."

He walked Michele to the door and slapped his back. "Remember, Michele, be cautious."

Next time Michele saw Nicholas in the refectory, he winked as the company filed out. The youth lingered to speak to him. "His Excellency is delighted with the picture. He told me so and intends to reward you with another special honour."

Martin de Redin overheard their conversation, touched Michele's shoulder. "I imagine that will be the Order of *Mil-ano*…"

He and several other brothers laughed.

"How original, Brother, what a wit you are… the *order of my arse*… perhaps you would like to kiss mine since you're so obviously obsessed with shit."

Redin shoved him, banging Michele's head hard against the wall. "Filthy sodomite!" Michele slipped his dagger from his sleeve and lunged at him. De Redin raised his arm, the dagger slashed the sleeve. "I'm unarmed…" De Redin squealed and ran off along the corridor.

Michele left the refectory and returned with his sword, several others joined him as he rushed along the upper corridor and banged on the door with the hilt. "Come out and face me, you miserable coward… whore's son." He kicked the door, the bolt almost gave… kicked repeatedly until, the bolt and upper hinge were torn away and the door caved in. He pushed aside the door hanging at an angle from the lower hinge and rushed into the cell. A dark figure stood against the light and slowly drew his sword, but Michele rushed him, pushed aside the blade and beat him to the floor. Kneeling on his chest, he continued to punch his face until it was smothered in blood. He was grabbed from behind and dragged away howling and kicking.

He was not permitted to see the Grand Master and was handed over to the Sguardium who manacled him and did not speak a word or barely glanced at him as he was marched to the harbour, passing brothers who stared with astonishment or smirked in disdain. He was taken to a boat to the isthmus of the Citta Victoria and up to the heavily fortified Birgu. The heat was unbearable and the silence absolute, only the footfall of Michele and four guards rang against the stark sun-bleached walls of the causeway. Two of the men peeled off and the other pair continued, then abruptly stopped beside what appeared to be a wide covered well, the wall waist height. The wooden cover was pushed aside to reveal a metal grille. Michele laughed. "Saint Lawrence… wasn't he cooked to death?" The lock was opened and the grille folded back. The guards stood down and chatted while Michele leaned against the low wall.

Certain he was about to be killed and thrown into a midden. "What are we waiting for?"

"Shut up." Eventually, the two other guards returned, one carrying a long ladder, the other a linen bag and leather water pouch. The ladder was laid on the side wall and lifted until it pivoted and dropped into the black hole. The manacles were removed, and he was handed the leather pouch and bag. "Your rations for two days… climb down."

The deep cylindrical cell over four times the height of a man reminded him of the Tor di Nona. The iron grate was half covered by the wooden cover but sunlight never reached the ground. The smell of faeces, urine and rotting straw was overpowering. In daylight hours, the sun heated the upper courses of stonework but too high to radiate down any warmth and, at night, it was cold. He had no cloak so he shivered, walked in tight circles to try to keep warm. On the third day, the grate was unlocked, clanged open and a large bag with bread and another pouch of water was lowered. He took the bread and put the empty pouch in the bag and tugged the rope.

As it ascended, he called, "It's cold down here… give me a cloak or a blanket." There was no response.

He squatted with his back against the cold wall. Each morning a sliver of silver light gradually turned gold as it broadened to a crescent which moved almost imperceptibly around the upper half of the cell eventually turning amber to red-orange and finally fading violet, then above him blue-purple, the grate halved by the black of the wooden cover. Each night the blue-black sky was pinpricked by a million points of light which wheeled slowly by. He didn't know the constellations very well but saw patterns that created geometric shapes, the way invisible geometries held his paintings together. At full moon, which never came into view, its blue-grey light was almost as bright as day but the light fell in different directions on the wall and the sickle of light pointed downwards like the horns of a bull. Food and water were sent down three more times. On the tenth day, no one came.

Bread and water were gone and, by nightfall, he became agitated. Perhaps he was to be starved to death… Would de Wignacourt allow such a thing? He was an honourable man. He had a soldier's honour… surely not. He hardly slept and, in the middle of the night, went to the opposite side of the cell to the midden to evacuate his bowels and used the cloth in which bread had been delivered to clean himself as best he could.

As he fastened his belt, he heard the lock turn, looked up and saw the grate folded open and the ladder slowly descend. Gesù, this was it…

"Come up."

"Am I to be killed?"

"Come up quick."

As he rose, the air was warmer and sweeter and, reaching the top, recognised two of the guards who goaled him over a week ago. Without a word, he was marched quickly along narrow alleyways through the castle grounds and down the blind side of the isthmus to an inlet where a small boat bobbed on the water. The boatman rowed him across the Grand Harbour in a wide arc around Valetta to eventually rendezvous with a large felucca, its sail furled with no lighted lamps. "I see I'm to be dumped at sea like Jonah!"

One of his guards climbed aboard and shook hands with the captain. "This is your charge… let's call him Signor Incognito. Are all his effects stowed?"

"They are."

"You've charted your destination?"

"I have." He turned to Michele. "You are banished for the crime of deadly assault upon the venerable Reverend Father Giovanni Rodomonte Roero… You're lucky he survived that beating…"

"Roero! I thought it was that shit de Redin."

The guard grinned. "De Redin's a slimy bastard, but it was Roero you nearly killed… but now that's unimportant. You're defrocked, stripped of your membership of the Order and of its protection. Despite everything, His

Excellency seems to hold you and your talent in high regard and specifically asked me to pass on his blessing in the hope somehow you find peace. Everything I've said is in strict confidence and the means of your supposed escape must remain a mystery and you should know that as a fugitive, warrants for your arrest will be posted at ports across Papal and Spanish territories."

Chapter 33

The Bird Woman

I stood motionless, watching the fleet slowly sail towards the straits until Michele's ship finally disappeared over the horizon, overwhelmed by certainty I would never see him again. The crowd imperceptibly broke into groups chatting, trading, arguing and further splintering into fours, threes and couples until I stood alone. The bells chimed eleven but the light breeze kept the air fresh and empty. Standing motionless so long it was an effort to take the first step to leave the harbour and to accept the reality that Michele was gone.

I wandered the streets and alleys, not hearing the calls, rasping voices and idle chatter and, although aimless, by noontime I was drawn to the Pio Monte. I sat in the shadow of the church, yearning to enter, but dreaded seeing the *Acts of Mercy*. The streets emptied as people made their ways home to dine and siesta. I hoped the doors would be bolted but, as I gently pushed, a dark cavern yawned, and I entered. It took a while to adjust to the dim light and cool of the charcoal void. I stared at the paving as I slowly walked towards the altar where I stood, arms tightly holding my chest, still gazing at the ground. I trembled and wept even before I looked up, the painting a blur of dancing light and colour. I wiped my eyes on my sleeve as my breath came in short gasps and I lay naked, begging, and my twin self-angels hugged one another as they tumbled… the sun obliterated by the shadow of the Earth. I was not only exhausted by pleading and lost hope but also sleepless nights, the last of desperate coupling and whispered assurances I didn't believe.

By first light, I was in utter misery. I stared a long time at acts of mercy but saw no hope for me. I became lost on the way home from the Pio Monte, searching for the painting of the Madonna and Angels Michele and I had seen on a wall at the top of a flight of steps, a prayer for mercy by an anonymous fisherman, baker or maybe a carpenter. My footsteps rang in the empty alleys drenched in blinding light. I sweated and was anxious until I recognised familiar streets and ran up the stairs to the apartment. Alessio roused from his siesta and simply hugged me. I tried to draw away for shame that I wept but he held me tight. He was my only friend, but I felt more alone than any time in my life and without purpose. I thought to return to Rome, but I was known to the Tomassoni and, with Michele out of reach, I might be a sacrificial lamb. The alternative was Milan or even Bergamo. It was almost a decade since I ran away and knew nothing of my family, whether Mamma was alive, or Pa and was Gennaro still curate or even now priest in charge. I had money and Michele said I should use it but returning to Bergamo would be utter defeat. I didn't leave the apartment for days, sending Alessio for food which he cooked and wine which we, or rather, I, drank copious cups. I never explained why or how I had money, because he never asked, perhaps he guessed. He put up some of the small paintings I had done in Rome and suggested I should paint.

I laughed. "Who for?"

"To sell. I could show them to Calimero, maybe he…"

I stared at the copies I had made of heads from Michele's Contarelli figures and those I painted at the Mattei palace. They seemed ghostlike, mere resemblances of what I remembered as living breathing people seen through the doorway of the gilded frames. "I'm not Michele."

Several weeks after Michele left, I was surprised when a Colonna messenger came to request my attendance at the Chiaia residence to see the Lady Costanza's steward and to bring samples of my work. I quickly removed work clothes and put on my best doublet and hose, ran fingers through my hair and smoothed my moustache and beard. I brought my sketchbook, also used for note taking, a sharpened piece of lead as well as five small paintings. The messenger led the way and, however much I tried to engage him in conversation, he remained polite but taciturn. The gates were opened as we approached the villa. We entered, and I was invited to wait in the hall. The steward soon appeared. "Welcome, Master Boneri, thank you for coming so promptly."

I stood. "Thank you, signor…?"

"To business. It is understood you are Master Michelangelo Merisi's principal assistant. He gave good reports of your talents."

I was astonished Michele even knew I had painted but why wouldn't he have caught sight of my efforts during the many times we changed residences with possessions haphazardly loaded on wagons?

"Have you heard from him?"

"We are in touch with Malta, and, if you have not yet had word from him, I'm sure you will in time. He is very preoccupied with commissions for the knights, but it is obvious he holds your talents in high regard, which is the reason we sent for you. I see you brought examples."

"I made copies of details of Michele's paintings, the heads of figures… drawings and in…"

"Good morning."

The steward turned and deeply bowed. "My lady, good morning."

Donna Costanza and her maid reached the bottom of the staircase. Cecco bowed, then glanced up, careful not to stare. She was informally dressed in simple cool white skirts, pale lilac bodice, her hair dressed but not elaborately so with a small lilac and gold cap pinned at the back creating a halo effect. She was as beautiful close to as I saw from a distance, with fine laughter lines around her eyes and her face retained its youthful bloom.

"Marchesa Costanza Sforza-Colonna, may I present Master Francesco Boneri, chief assistant to Master Michelangelo Merisi."

She nodded and smiled. "Master Boneri… Francesco." She giggled. "Cecco, I believe?" How easily she put me at ease.

I smiled. "Yes, Madam, everyone calls me Cecco."

"My dear friend His Eminence Cardinal del Monte is also Cecco." She smiled. "In private of course… I believe you know him."

"His Eminence remembered me?"

"He thought you charming and natural, wandering around his house to see Michele's paintings."

"I was too bold, Madam, and young… too young to remember my manners."

"You were naturally curious. Boys are always curious. Our dear friend Michele would not hesitate to do the same."

"You have heard from him, Madam?"

The steward coughed. "Don Antonio, are matters with Master Francesco concluded?"

"I mentioned the paintings, Madam, the copies by Master Francesco."

"I would like to see Master Cecco's pictures. I imagine you have many matters to attend to."

Don Antonio hesitated. "Will you be alone with…"

"Sofia's here and I don't think Master Francesco will attack me… would you, Cecco?"

"I am armed, Madam." I slipped my knife from my belt. "A habit... to sharpen my leads." Holding the short knife by the blade, I offered the handle to Don Antonio who gingerly took it, bowed to Lady Costanza and left.

Donna Costanza smiled. "Don Antonio is very conscientious and loyal to my family and to me."

"You are very loyal, Madam." In an instant, I realised it was not done to make observations of those high born. "I apologise for presuming..."

She simply smiled. "Tell me about yourself, Cecco. I hear you're from Caravaggio. Was Michele your only master?"

"My family come from near Bergamo, not far from Caravaggio, of course and my father was a painter. He gave me lessons, mainly drawing. He painted in the old style, devotional pictures. He never liked Michelangelo... the first I mean, not Michele. He said the hands of the David are too big and... he kept an engraving on the wall to make the point to anybody who would listen. Imagine, Madam, criticising Michelangelo. He had no shame."

Costanza laughed. "Of course, my ancestress knew Michelangelo. She was a poet. The Lady Vittoria."

"Michele mentioned her. He said your family have always been great patrons..."

"But no longer great collectors."

I realised she might have thought I was touting for work. The Lady continued, "It is true my family are friends to all arts, poetry, sculpture, painting, architecture... music." She nodded towards my paintings. "I will be interested to hear what Don Antonio thinks of your pictures."

She stood to indicate the audience was over. "I have enjoyed our conversation, Cecco."

I bowed and the maid Sofia led me to the door where Antonio handed back my knife. "Master Francesco. Good day." I walked slowly until out of sight of the villa, then jumped and skipped along the street, elated by the chance appearance of the Lady Costanza. *Hardly chance!* The encounter was contrived, and Michele really had drawn her attention to me at the harbour and whatever was said was the point of my meeting her. I dared not imagine a commission might be forthcoming and tried to fend off the idea but was too excited to go straight home so decided to find Alessio.

From tavern to osteria to tavern, I walked in a strange dream world. Excited by meeting the marchesa, perhaps one of the most renowned women in all Italy, and I had spent almost half an hour in her presence and she called me Cecco, spoken kindly and listened to my chatter. I shivered with pleasure remembering how attentive she was and how grand her villa and cool with a light breeze from the sea, tinkling music, a flute and guitar played in the background, and views across the bay. I was itching to tell Alessio but could not find him so by mid-afternoon decided to go to Carlo and Martha's, on the way buying cured ham, cheese, olives, bread, wine, peaches and black grapes to celebrate. There was no response when I arrived at their door and none of the neighbours knew where they had gone so I went home feeling deflated. I let myself in and ran up the stairs to find Alessio sitting on the top step. "I've been looking for you all afternoon."

"Good news?" I unlocked the door and told Alessio to prepare supper. "Pasta with something, we'll save what I bought for tomorrow."

"You bought a whole cask of wine…"

Fra Michelangelo Merisi da Caravaggio, Knight of Malta to Master Francesco Boneri in Naples
18th July 1608

Cecco, as I predicted, I was made knight of the third rank so it will not be long before we return to Rome. The Grand Master petitioned the Pope to permit my appointment and awarded me a gold chain which will discomfort Baglione to no end and a pardon is just a matter of time. Did I not say it would only take a year or so before I have my Cecco back again? I'm told Francesco, as well as the Gonzaga and Scipione Borghese are working to arrange a pardon – the Colonna too. I hear you are doing decent work.
M

Delivered by a Colonna servant, the note was typical of Michele, four-fifths bragging, the rest hunger for a pardon and a morsel for me. For once, he was keeping his head down, confirmed by a brief conversation with Don Antonio, indicating Michele had made several portraits of knights of the order, one with connections to the Colonna. Even more prestigious, a portrait of the Grand Master Alof de Wignacourt in parade armour attended by his page. It was said he also painted a further *Saint Jerome* and a *Sleeping Cupid*; perhaps he really was thinking of me? It was already well known the *Beheading of John the Baptist* painting in Valetta was acclaimed, but I remained anxious.

I was delighted when I was offered commissions, presumably arranged by the Colonna. The subjects were not particularly inspiring, portraits of minor officials, but realised if I made a great fuss about their best clothes and hats, I might remain in Lady Costanza's sights. Portraits were a lucrative market although early commissions barely made fifteen scudi profit after framing costs, but, by the time, I received Michele's letter, I was asking twenty and even thirty scudi. One memorable commission, I was advised would bring forty-five scudi if I were to attend a lady who lived in a grand house in the Spanish quarter. I presented myself and was led into a small salon where I was kept waiting half an hour with increasing irritation until the lady eventually appeared. She did not excuse her lateness nor did she introduce herself, although my instruction was to present myself to a Senora Eliza Colomba. From her heavy accent and sallow complexion, I assumed she was Spanish. Her grand home was surely well above her station and from her gaudy striped sleeves, I presumed she was a courtesan or mistress of some grandee.

I had seen her calculated swagger before in Rome when a street girl struck lucky, snaring some high born. I was reminded of Fillide Melandroni but Fillide had style, wit and, although she occasionally shrieked like a fishwife, if anyone moved in on her pitch… *I'll cut you bitch!* She knew how to play the lady when necessary. This pale imitation was an old tune played on a single string, and we eyed one another. Despite her assumed hauteur, she knew I had seen her for what she was, that I had seen better and was not impressed. She swished up and down the room, fanning herself, imagining she appeared a high-bred Spanish filly rather than the mule she was.

She turned to me. "I believe they speak well of your paintings."

I slightly inclined my head and, for the first time, noticed she held a black bird, a crow in her hand, barely visible against her black velvet bodice, her fingers tightly gripped its head. "I want my portrait painted with my birds."

Alessio, Martha and Carlo laughed. "She keeps birds?"

"A mangy crow and doves, at least there were pigeons flying around the house, unless there's a hole in the roof." I arranged a party to celebrate Michele's success in Malta and my commission. Alessio set up the table in the large workroom. Candles were lit around the room and dishes laid on the table dressed in Michele's Holbein rug and covered by a white cloth. There were flagons of wine and bowls of fruit for dessert and Alessio and I were in high spirits even before Martha and Carlo arrived. Alessio put up my copies of Michele's figures' heads which had certainly done their work since at least Don Antonio, who from his restrained praise hinted that maybe even

Donna Costanza was impressed. "*Yes, Master Francesco, they are rather good.*" I imagined he echoed Donna Costanza's opinion rather than his own... I was pleased my work achieved even a little appreciation although I had no illusions I came anywhere near the quality, standard and depth of Michele's paintings.

Nevertheless, the commission to paint Eliza Colomba at forty-five scudi to include a gilt frame was a decent price by any standard and allowed me to continue to live well enough without dipping too much into the money Michele left in my charge. I began to think I may have been wrong to lose faith in Michele who might well return in less time than I imagined, and we might soon return to Rome. The supper party was good humoured, we toasted Michele's success, and I raised a further toast that Baglione's *Resurrection* had been removed. I had to explain the feud between Michele and Baglione and, after perhaps too many goblets of wine, I was persuaded to recite Michele's poem mocking his adversary and declaimed like a ham actor:

> *He doubtless deserves to be called John the cunt*
> *Who undertakes to find fault with another...*

Martha gave a little shriek. I excused the swear word, but she was speechless with laughter, red faced and fanned herself with her hand, gesturing I should go on.

> *La, la, la, la, la... called John cunt*
> *Who undertakes to find fault with another*
> *Who would be his master a hundred years...*
> *La, la, la... I forget...*

Carlo re-filled my glass. "Go on, Cecco..."

> *...find fault... find fault with another*
> *Who would be his master a hundred years*
> *With my words I refer to painting...*
> *Since this man claims to be called... a painter*
> *Though he never could rank with that man...*
> *You who presume to find fault...*

"I forget..."

But yet know your own are still nailed up in your home
Because you are ashamed to show them in public.

By the early hours, the four of us were drunk and Carlo had to support Martha as they stumbled down the stairs, Martha repeating parts of the Baglione poem she could recall with *la-di-das* to fill the gaps where memory failed. Alessio and I leaned out the window, watching the pair stagger along the street. Carlo shushed Martha who became louder by the shush and each shriek of laughter rang from the walls particularly when she loudly farted.

A month almost to the day after the letter from Michele with news of his advancement, Alessio returned from his sister's house with news that Michele had been arrested and imprisoned for rioting. What was known was vague, but apparently Michele and others had been involved in a brawl and Michele had wounded a senior brother. I sat heavily at the table and buried my head in my hands. I knew it was too good to be true. Michele never has good fortune unless he overturns it fourfold.

Alessio's brother Calimero passed on what he gleaned from gossip and overheard conversations between senior Colonna servants. Information was sketchy and constantly changed, that Michele had killed a brother, then he had not killed but wounded a senior knight, that Fabrizio Sforza was helping Michele, then Fabrizio was not even in Valetta. I sank into an ever-darker mood. What seemed consistent among the rumours was that Michele was imprisoned and certainly faced a long goal sentence at best and I was alarmed not knowing if the Papal capital penalty for duelling applied in Malta or what the penalties were within the Grand Master's jurisdiction. Wherever that left Michele, the grand plan, as ever, was undermined by Michele's thin skin. I had no doubt Michele was not the instigator but was inevitably the one caught red-handed… the scapegoat. How many times had he paid the price for what Onorio Longhi or Orazio Gentileschi started and how many times had he painted *John the Baptist* but not learned the lesson that he who stands out attracts the axe?

I was unable to work, became feverish and lay hours on the bed. Alessio embraced me but his kindness was little comfort as I grew ever more miserable not knowing if Michele had been injured in the fight and, if so, how badly. Days passed with more questions about what my and our future held… if any. I was reduced to tears of anguish considering how close Michele came to achieving his aim to convince the Pope he was reformed and worthy of pardon. In the past, matters were swiftly settled by del Monte and, even after the killing of Ranuccio, the Colonna spirited us away but, this time, he was alone and beyond help. I slept dream-crowded, unable to find Michele, concealed from the light in a dark impenetrable void with uncertainty about his fate. Alessio stayed with me, cooking and tidying the rooms, cleaning and shaping brushes, mixing paint and preparing canvases in the workshop. At night, we embraced as companions and friends. "What's the harm?"

"It's between the two of us… nobody's business. You said Michele and Fabrizio were like brothers."

"That may be true, but Michele isn't Colonna blood and not all brothers remain close or loyal if they ever were… and Fabrizio is a prince and has risen to general of the Maltese fleet. He would never jeopardise his position… even for a brother."

"Couldn't you ask Donna Costanza, beg her to…?"

"What am I to her?"

"She likes you."

"I amused her for half an hour."

"She arranged commissions for you."

It was a couple of anxious weeks since the news from Malta when Alessio rushed up the stairs with news Michele had escaped the island but no one knew where he had gone. In the next week, rumours suggested Michele was in Sicily. I was sure he must have gone to Mario in Syracuse or Lorenzo in Messina but his connection to both former assistances must be known or easily discovered. It was also reported there were sightings of Maltese ships cruising the straits and the coast off Naples which appeared to confirm rumour. There was no news from the Colonna household and Calimero learned nothing from eavesdropping which suggested the Colonna were as much in the dark.

Chapter 34

Santa Lucia 1608

The felucca was rowed slowly until out of sight of the port, then lamps were lit, the sail unfurled and hoisted. The captain steered into open waters and sailed north-north-west. The crossing took all night skirting Calabria arriving off the coast of Sicily late afternoon the next day. The captain stood off several miles and dropped anchor so it was almost nightfall when they entered the harbour at Syracuse. The captain and three-man crew evaded the port master's men and carried Michele's chests to an osteria near the port. He thanked and paid them handsomely.

"Don't fret, Master… Nobody knows you're here." He grinned. "You don't exist."

He stayed the night at an osteria in the harbour and, next day, the ninth of October, set about tracking down Mario. He asked the patron if he knew Mario Minitti. He was cagey and said he didn't know the name. Michele changed tack, asking where artists were likely to congregate and was told to try several inns on Ortigia Island across the harbour. There was no luck at the first two inns, and the sun was burning hot by the time he entered the Tavern of the Four Winds where he noticed a huddle of young men at a table by the window and noticed spots and splashes of paint on their clothes.

He ordered wine, olives and bread and as he was served, listened in to their conversation. "I would say Naples. There's a strong artists guild and plenty of work."

Another said, "Florence." But the consensus was that Florence's time was past.

A third lad said, "Rome's where the money is, the churches and the cardinals… rebuilding after the wars… And aristocrats."

"You're quite right. Rome *is* where the money is." They looked across at Michele. They regarded him a moment, noted his black corduroy velvet doublet, although rather worn but high quality and elegantly tailored. In turn, he noted the young man who favoured Rome, his fingers were stained with ochre paint under his fingernails. He caught his hand and shook it. "Gentlemen, I see you must be apprentices or artists' assistants."

"And who might you be?"

"A painter."

"Would we have heard of you?"

"I doubt it. I don't exist, but I know Rome only too well, but, to the point, do you know or where I might find the painter Mario Minniti. I understand he's from these parts?"

"Yes, he lives near the church of Santa Lucia."

"Would you pass this message to him?" He removed his glove and drew out a paper from his doublet and offered a silver Maltese coin. "For your trouble."

"Who shall I say sent it?"

"On the assumption you'll open the note the moment you're out of sight... I am Cavaliere Michelangelo Merisi da Caravaggio. Good day, gentlemen." He tipped his hat.

They stood as he left. *"Caravaggio, Caravaggio, Caravaggio!"*

"Michele!" He recognised his voice immediately. They rushed to embrace and Mario held on to him until they sat opposite one another in the noisy osteria and Michele poured wine. Like Cecco, he seemed bigger, taller, and broader than he remembered.

"You look thin, Michele."

He smiled. "Prison victuals... but you look grown up. How we've changed in what, two years? It seems a lifetime. Lorenzo got a message to me at Zagarolo and said you and your wife had gone to Syracuse."

"Carla, you must remember her, before..." He pursed his lips.

Michele grimaced. "No need to be coy. I could never forgive Ranuccio what he did to..."

Mario raised his cup. "To Lena..." They drank.

"Have you seen Lorenzo? When he wrote, he said he was leaving for Messina. Is he married?"

Mario hesitated, stared Michele in the eye. "No... I think he only ever loved... someone he thought was beyond his reach. How about you? We heard you were in Naples..."

"Cecco was with me. We were there eight or nine months. Things got out of hand with the Naples guild of artists, so I went to Malta, until... things got out of hand!"

Carla must have considered him the cause of all her and Mario's woes; the carousing and the fighting in Rome and the Tomassoni killing… They were just married when Mario was dragged into that quagmire. Where he was under Colonna protection, Mario, Carla and Lorenzo were left to face the consequences, putting them in jeopardy by association. Syracuse was a welcome return to sanity after the madness of Rome. Michele imagined she must have resented that Mario lived in Michele's shadow as he became famous and, had they not been overwhelmed by the chaos of the killing, they would probably have remained in Rome, Carla's native city. They arrived in Syracuse with little more than the clothes on their backs, including Mario's painting materials and several unfinished pictures… unfinished because he was always at the beck and call of the great master Caravaggio.

Mario's family welcomed them home and gave them a house near Santa Lucia church. It was not grand but comfortable and a nest where their daughter and son were born in quick succession. Mario used a large room above the ground floor for a workshop and, after several small commissions, he was offered work by local painter Francesco Cassarino. It was assistants' work but Carla insisted he accept with the hope it might lead to future opportunities but Michele's arrival cast a shadow over those hopes. She was alarmed by how elated Mario was hearing Michele had arrived and made such haste to the tavern. She was left alone with her babies a long time and began to fret that the quiet family life they lived, the rhythm of nesting, birth, family and friends, the circle of the seasons, Nativity, Lent, Easter, Whitsun and Trinity would be disrupted and dreaded Mario missed the excitement and even danger of living in Michele's orbit.

Over several hours, they exchanged stories. Mario invited him to stay with Carla and him. Michele was unsure, not knowing how she would respond, but Mario was insistent she would love to see him again but when he entered the little house, Carla wiped her red hands on her apron and, when he removed his hat and gloves, she was startled he kissed her on each cheek and then on the lips. "Carla, it's good to see you after so long."

Two men arrived with a hand cart and Mario directed them to take several chests up to the room next to Carla and his bedroom. Michele saw she was startled and unhappy in his presence. She noted his left hand rested on the hilt of his fine wrought sword his fingers habitually twitched and remembered his violent temper was the cause of their troubles. She tilted her head and regarded him a few moments as though she saw him for the first time. He looked ghastly, his face gaunt, greasy lank hair and beautiful but shabby clothes. He seemed smaller than she remembered, noticed the healed scar on his neck from the fight that turned his and their world upside down and his right hand trembled. She could tell he was unwell. Her expression softened, having seen through his studied bravado, but, rather than a hunter, she recognised a haunted creature. She blinked and lowered her eyes; they both knew she had seen him. She glanced up. "Are you hungry, Michele?"

"You recommended him for the commission for the most prestigious painting for the city?" She hissed, "You fool, Mario, why?" Although their voices were hardly more than whispers, Michele overheard every word. "If you had to recommend anybody to the Senate, why not yourself… Why him? I don't understand, Mario. Why did you have to recommend *him*?"

"He's my friend and, in any case, I couldn't attempt anything so big. They want forty by thirty palmi. I wouldn't know how to begin. When I mentioned his name, they jumped at the chance to commission him. He is known everywhere."

"But didn't he make a botched job of his first go at the paintings for San Luigi? What was it… the Martyrdom of Mark or John? You told me so at the time."

"It was Saint Matthew, but he pulled it off and the Calling was done in three months… I modelled for one of the figures."

"Fat lot of good that did your career… and I heard his first altarpiece was turned down too."

"That's not the point, Carlita. I've nowhere near his talent."

Michele heard a slap and her voice rose. "Mario… You make me mad!"

"Shush!" The baby stirred and began to cry.

His sword was on the bed beside him as he lay fully dressed, a habit that ceased when he and Cecco were in Zagarolo but resumed since leaving Malta. It was dark and quieter even than Valetta. Something woke him. He listened hard, ears howling in the silence. Perhaps it was the church bell. He glanced at the part open door and beyond to Mario and Carla's larger, lighter room. The baby's cot stood beside his parents' bed and as Michele's eyes adjusted to the dimness, he noticed movement. It was not the child but rhythmic rocking and there were short gasps and whimpers. Carla's knees were up and Mario had pushed her nightdress above her breasts which he fondled and suckled as his rump rode up and down. Carla turned her head in Michele's direction, her eyes and parted lips mere smudges in the oval of her face.

He couldn't tell if she could see him watching from the black void beyond the doorway of his room. In the morning, Carla was breezy, fussed over the child and her manner was noticeably less cool towards him.

Mario found a large warehouse for Michele to hire near the port, big enough to house the large canvas and with few windows so Michele could control the light. Although airless, it was cooler than the workshop in Valetta. It was over two years since Mario had been his assistant, and they worked the same rhythmic pace stretching the canvas, a heavier weave than Michele was used to which required extra coats of gum Arabic and more layers of gesso to seal the fibres and then coated with several base layers of umber. Since Naples, Michele added a little melted beeswax to his favoured walnut oil to give added transparency and greater depth to the rich dark tones. Mario had established contacts with other painters, so there was a wide choice of available models, but Michele still went to the port seeking weathered, lined and careworn characters as well as the beautiful… so long as they were unaware of their beauty. Mario said the Syracuse Senate was impressed he was such an intimate friend of the famous Master Caravaggio but Michele said he was sick of both praise and opprobrium, dreaded to know what was known about him, fact or fable. Having agreed a generous fee to be his assistant, he offered Mario half as much again if would act as go-between with the Senate and the church fathers of Santa Lucia and to ask Carla if she would be his Lucia. "I'll pay her the same as you."

"There's no need to move out…"

"Mario, just find me a place, you need the room for your own work." The house Mario found was near the port and the warehouse and both suited his requirements. The only drawback was the house faced south and, when the breeze from the sea dropped, it was unbearably hot. He woke sweating, thirsty and delirious several nights in a row. His clothes reeked of sweat and body odour because he never removed them. Carla and Mario brought food to the workshop although earlier meals were untouched and live with buzzing flies. It was waste but, more important, Michele was drenched in sweat, trembling and violently shaking. Carla touched his forehead which felt cold and clammy. She was alarmed. "You should go home… you're not well."

"Carla's right. You have the sweats."

"I'm all right… just leave me alone, thanks… thanks both of you. I won't do any work today. I'll just… I need to see what I've got… what I have to do to get the painting done. I'm all right… don't fuss."

The heavier canvas caused the brush run out of paint sooner than on finer weave and, when one coat was laid over another, coverage was not always complete. Thin base coats of ochre toned down with black and subsequent layers created an uneven surface which, after days of merely staring at the canvas, he came to accept the background; well over half the painting, suggested a cavernous space.

With the recent Valetta Martyrdom of the Baptist in mind, he sketched a blind shallow arch within a larger arch, the mottled paint surface caused by the imperfect over-layering suggested mould so, rather than a prison or dark basilica, the scene appeared set in a catacomb. The nine figures mourning at the graveside were assembled from Mario's friends, models and assistants, individually posed to suggest contemplation, grief and even curiosity. A bishop with hand raised to bless the grave was partially obscured by a man in armour and Carla had lain on the ground, head thrown back, turned three-quarter to the viewer. Her lower body was obscured by one of two gravediggers painted on a larger scale to exaggerate the space between foreground and the body of the saint. He had never before worked with such radically different sizes of figures. Mario thought the decapitated corpse was too gruesome… *unseemly*. Michele was furious but, after careful thought, he asked Carla to pose again and spent half a day re-painting the neck to reduce the gory slash to a faint line with the result the neck appeared rather long and goiterish.

As he worked, Carla heard him mutter as he almost stabbed the canvas with the brush, whereas in Rome he vented his rage in the streets against rivals; here, it was directed at the canvas and, perhaps, ultimately, himself. When the light turned amber, Mario came with the baby to collect Carla and both were concerned by Michele's pallor. "You should go home, Michele… you're not well."

"Mario's right. You're very pale."

He refused to leave but agreed to rest. He sat in the chair, staring at the painting but was soon lightly snoring.

"He's very unwell."

"He had the sweats in the early days in Rome."

"It's not that… he's not well here." Carla touched her breast.

He sat opposite the painting for hours, straining to determine what the painting was trying to tell him. The heavier canvas meant a necessary change in approach and technique. Until now, the surface and finish were evenly painted with thin layers and glazes and few evident brush marks. His best work to date was done in that polished technique developed in Rome, and, in the Neapolitan paintings, the *Seven Acts of Mercy*, the Flagellation and especially the *Resurrection*. Now, however, it was the second Emmaus that came to mind, that touched something deeper and marked a change in the way he approached the subject. In this martyrdom of Lucia… his past compulsion to fill the great void above seemed unnecessary and emptiness more appropriate and suggesting the void of local great cave he was shown by local antiquarian, Vincenzo Mirabella, a friend of Mario's family.

In the morning, Carla let herself into the workshop and found Michele barely conscious, slumped in a chair, leaning against the wall. She gently rocked him. "Michele…" He slowly turned his head towards her.

She opened each eye in turn with her thumb. They were yellow-grey and his complexion pale and sallow. "You're no better… I'll fetch Mario. You need to see a doctor."

He caught her arm. "Don't. I'm fine." She watched him a few moments as he slowly unwound from the chair and stood.

"You were here all night?"

He shrugged. "The painting…"

She glanced at the canvas. "You've not worked on it for two days."

He gestured around the warehouse. "It spoke to me here." He pointed his head. "Last night… the painting…"

She squatted before him. "Michele, painting in your head is not painting; it's not the same. I think you're very unwell. Mario said you had the sweating sickness in Rome."

"I… it's not that… well, yes, I have a fever, a mild fever… It will pass, and I'm not crazy, Lucia."

"You want me to pose for Lucia today?"

"Did I say Lucia?"

She smiled. "I'm your Lucia."

"Yes, you are."

He turned to the painting as though seeing it for the first time. "My mother was Lucia."

"I didn't know."

"I don't think I ever told anyone. She was Lucia… Lucia Aratori."

"Is she…?"

"Yes."

She stood and drew him towards her. "I am so sorry, Michele…
When…"

"A long time ago."

She regarded him a moment. "You've kept this inside an awfully long time. Tell me about her."

He shrugged but dare not look her in the eye. "It was soon after I finished my apprenticeship. Master Peterzano gave me a letter from my brother saying she was in God's care. I hadn't seen her in many months."

When night came on, Michele lit candles and lamps to light the picture. He had sat almost immobile another day and as the evening wore on, random observations made in the day crystallised and details evaporated leaving two significant elements. A burial… the body and grave diggers… The boy ignudi of the past had matured into solid strapping workmen, observers but also participants. A dark rectangle in the ground suggested the grave, a deep trench to receive the body of the saint, her far arm rested on her body, the other towards the viewer, her hand over the void dug in the earth. The pose echoed the Madonna in *Death of the Virgin*. He stepped closer. The legs of the workman were not resolved; the models must come back. The legs of the gravedigger on the left were only faintly suggested and seemed to move. His figures were usually static in moments of contemplation, witnesses and participants in what has occurred. The executioner watched Matthew as he dies, the executioner in the Valetta St John pauses to grip the knife in his belt after killing the prophet, but these labourers are different. This is movement, not simply implied by pose but real movement, moments and blurs the eye cannot see, the shift from one moment to another, one pose to another, one position to the next. Movement that makes all else still… He glanced at the painted Lucia. Carla, lying still, as she lay under Mario, her arm outstretched towards the child and a silent invisible witness, eyes and mouth smudges in her pale, oval face.

He hoped she hadn't known he observed their lovemaking. He spoke aloud. "Are the eyes gouged out according to the legend?"

In the weeks she modelled, Carla and he became friends of sorts. Michele closely examined her image in the painting, her still corpse. Carla as Lucia… He stiffened as the painting delivered a sudden ferocious debilitating blow. How could he have missed… why didn't he recognise who she was, who she represented. Carla the mother raised to Lucia the saint. Lucia his mother… her light snuffed out. He was suddenly overwhelmed by the memory of his lost mamma. However hard he strained to remember his mother's face, her features remained a blur. She was reduced to a succession of glances, gestures and remembered embraces. When Master Simone gave him the letter, he knew the news was bad. He broke the seal which must have been appended by the brothers at the seminary. He remembered every word verbatim.

To Michele Merisi at the Workshop of Master Peterzano from Ordinate Giovanni Battista Merisi.

Brother, with sadness I must tell you our dear mother Lucia rests in the gentle care of God the Father, Our Blessed Lord and Saviour and the Holy Virgin by the Grace of the Holy Spirit. I know this will come as great sadness. May God Bless you, Brother, at this time of trouble – Amen

He had memorised words that were not those of Battista. His handwriting, small and tidy, but the voice was the priest who gently dictated formulaic phrases and blather no more than an exercise to enhance his clerical skills. *How to convey news of the departed in a seemly manner...*

Master Simone drew Michele's head to his chest as a gesture of comfort, but he merely stood, arms by his side inhaling the aroma of Simone clothes infused with walnut oil. He went to the workshop doors, closed them to shut out the light and, holding them tight together, leant against the frame, his body wracked by deep shuddering gasps and sobs that left him breathless and in dread his grief would never subside.

Carla and Mario arrived in the early hours and found him sitting on the floor leaning against the wall. Mario covered the painting with a cloth and they gently led him to their house. They tended him with great care as the fever worsened. After several days, he was slowly nursed back to a semblance of health as the fever ebbed. They kept the blinds down and, when the baby cried, Mario took him in his arms and walked the streets to calm him.

Carla sat on his bed. "Gesù, Michele, we were worried." She gripped his hand. Michele gently squeezed her fingers in response. "Michele, I have some news... good news. A certain Giovanni de Lazzari contacted a member of the Senate. He heard you're in Syracuse and wants to meet you to discuss a commission."

"I'm too weak... let Mario do it."

"He wouldn't take it. It's offered to you and Mario would consider it dishonourable to suggest otherwise. Even if you turned it down, he'd be afraid of committing himself to such a large picture."

"Ridiculous… he has the talent."

"He's afraid he hasn't *enough* talent. You know he's in awe of you. After everything you two suffered in Rome. Because of what happened in Rome. It's a miracle you're alive, Michele. This fever was nothing by comparison with the high price the Tomassoni put on your head."

She went to open the shutter a little. "Is that too bright?"

He shook his head. "We're astonished you were able to keep going, still painting wonderful pictures, especially the Santa Lucia."

"What do you think of it? I don't know. I can't judge any more."

"I've never seen the like. If you didn't add another dab of paint, it's the most moving picture I've ever seen by you or any painter."

She looked down, a little embarrassed. "Maybe I'm influenced by what you told me. You painted it for her… It's a great memorial and, even though you were denied a last farewell, your picture has prepared her for her journey to God."

She leaned down and held him in her arms. "God Bless you, Michele, and may your blessed mother Lucia rest in eternal peace."

The week before the festival of the Nativity, Mario appeared at the door to the workshop. Michele put down the brush and shoved a chair with his foot towards Mario and stood wiping his hands. "From your look, it's sad news."

Mario stared at the floor until Michele gripped his arm. He paused a moment, then let his shoulders sag. "There's no way to dress this up… You've been stripped of your knighthood… unfrocked. You were tried in absentia on the twenty-seventh of November. I heard this from Lorenzo and he writes Maltese fighting ships are patrolling the coast from here to Messina and some big-wig knight of Malta proclaimed there's a price on your head."

Michele smiled. "I'm not surprised and, strangely, not sure I care."

"But the ships, they must have an idea where…"

"It's for show. The Grand Master knows very well where I am… I could run naked along the beach, waving my arms, but no one on board any Maltese ship would see me."

Chapter 35

Flagellation

Master Mario Minniti in Sicily to Master Francesco Boneri in Naples
12th February 1608

Cecco Caro, it's been some time since we were all in Rome and I hear you're painting in Naples with good reports of your portraits and still lives. Bravo from me and Carlita. You'll be interested to know an old friend of our acquaintance is staying with us. He's working on a big commission and asked us to send his greetings. Lorenzo also sends good wishes and hopes you might visit us soon.

Mario

The letter was delivered via the Colonna, probably opened and re-sealed. Rather than calm my fears, I became increasingly anxious for Michele's safety. Perhaps the letter confirmed what the Colonna already knew and certainly confirmed rumour. The presence of Maltese ships in the vicinity suggested they were closing in and a swift raid would soon have him in chains. In the afternoon, two Colonna men arrived to request my attendance on the Lady Costanza. Without ceremony, I was ushered into her presence.

I bowed and was pleased she smiled. "Welcome, Master Francesco… Cecco. I hear your paintings are well received."

"Thank you, Madam, you're most gracious."

"I am given to believe you received a letter from Sicily in our care. I hope our messengers have safely delivered it to you?"

"They have, Madam, this morning."

"I'm sure you heard the rumours about our friend and reports of Maltese ships offshore and wonder if the contents of your letter might enlighten us… about our friend?"

I was certain she and Don Antonio already knew the contents, so what was she fishing for? I answered immediately since any delay would indicate I was calculating. "The letter is from my friend Mario Minniti, our friend's main assistant when I first met him. He and his wife live in Syracuse and believe our friend is staying there and, thanks be to God, he's safe but, Madam, I am afraid for our friend's safety, as you say the Maltese ships… Do you think the knights know where Michele is?"

She barely whispered, "I believe they do."

"Then why haven't they taken him? Did his Lordship, Captain Fabrizio, help?"

She pressed her finger to my lips and spoke sotto voce. "My son is patrolling the seas to the east of Malta shadowing Ottoman vessels."

Hearing Fabrizio was still at sea in the Eastern Mediterranean meant I judged him badly.

"So, who… helped? Who do you think helped our friend to escape a dungeon on an island?"

"I suppose, Madam, whoever had most to gain by having Michele out of the way. It must have been someone of high rank, if not the highest."

Costanza gestured to Antonio to come close. I hesitated. "There's only one person with the authority to order and enable Michele's escape."

Antonio spluttered. "Preposterous."

The marchesa raised her voice. "Let him reason."

I continued, "The Grand Master Wignacourt accepted Michele."

The Lady Costanza raised her hand. "Let us continue the conversation on the terrace where, let's hope, there is a breeze. Sofia, I would like fresh flowers."

On the terrace, she said, "We must be circumspect but please continue."

"Since the affair in Rome, our friend has been much chastened. He seems to have found favour with the Grand Master which probably provoked envy among military men…"

"A society of men, divided by languages into separate confraternities, yes."

Antonio was irritable. "I don't see where this is leading."

"The Grand Master favoured our friend because he painted his portrait and, from what is known, the painting of John the Baptist was well received but caused jealousy among other brothers."

Antonio cut in. "Our reports say our friend did not start the ruckus but was the most violent."

"But he is easily provoked." Antonio didn't respond. "Our friend has a keen sense of what is right and if he felt the attack that caused the riot was unjust or directed at him… he would not be able to control his temper."

"I thought we were trying to decide who helped the man escape?"

"Patience, Don Antonio. Go on, Cecco."

"I thought Captain General Fabrizio was the obvious person to help our friend but since he is at sea... and I'm sure he would do nothing to undermine the authority of the Grand Master and suspect no one else would take the same risk, and that is why I believe the Grand Master decided that to imprison our friend, perhaps for years, it would be better he was released by some miracle. Who else would have the authority to arrange an escape and the means to get him away from Malta to Sicily?" I glanced out to sea. "Madam, I believe what your Ladyship said, that our friend's whereabouts are known in Malta." My anxieties ebbed. "The Maltese ships are simply for appearance's sake."

"Yes." Costanza's hands were pressed together as if in prayer and tight against her lips. "Out of the mouths of babes..."

Antonio was unimpressed. "Is it really likely the Grand Master would permit the escape of a criminal?"

The marchesa crossed to the balcony to look out to sea a moment, then turned. "The Grand Master is an excellent soldier, a veteran general, has great understanding of the human soul and is a kind judge."

"They say from Calabria it's possible to see Sicily."

I looked up from painting. "What?"

"You can see Sicily from Calabria."

"I believe so."

Alessio poured a little oil in a jar of ochre. "Not too much."

He stretched a piece of leather, suede side up and fixed it with cord to the neck of the jar and turned it upside down on the shelf. I sensed he glanced at me but continued painting without further response.

"I thought you might go to Sicily."

"Why would I do that?"

"To see Michele."

"Shut up, Lessio, and prepare supper."

"There's nothing to eat."

"Then go to the market."

"I've no money."

I sighed. "There's denari in the purse, just go."

Alessio bowed. "Highness." In the silence after Alessio left, I concentrated on the work before me, astonished by how clearly I deduced it was the Grand Master who arranged Michele's escape from Malta, a reasonable assumption that seemed to have eluded Lady Costanza and Don Antonio. I had no idea how Michele had got away until the question arose… As for going to Syracuse… Basta! This time I won't come running. Basta certo! I went to the window to catch sight of the bay. *So what if you can see Sicily from Calabria?*

Concentrating on the portrait of Eliza Colomba, I made drawings of her over-elaborate sleeves and the crow gripped tight in her hand. "When will it be finished?"

"It may take some time; I have many other commissions."

"Be as quick as you can."

"If I did that, your portrait will not be so good."

She was visibly irritated but remained silent as I continued drawing. Her irritation soon dissipated as she stared at me with curiosity, her head slightly inclined to the left. I stared at her ten seconds in advance of making a line that developed into a tone before returning my gaze to her again for another ten seconds. *Look ten times longer than the time you spend painting.* It was a lesson Michele taught me well, fixing what I saw in my mind before drawing, often without looking at the paper to ensure the hand followed the eye rather than take its own path. *Paint the apple before you, not how you think an apple should look… think of all those saints you see in churches, no one ever looked the way they are painted, they could never piss or shit… I paint what I see and as close to nature as possible.* Eliza blinked, returning me to the present to find she still regarded me with curiosity and saw she craved attention. Before leaving, I allowed her to see the drawings and, although she made no comment, I knew she was impressed. "I'll try to finish the portrait as soon as I can."

"With doves."

"Doves?"

"My favourite birds." I gave a slight bow and was surprised she accompanied me to the door. It was strange we were both changed in the time we spent staring at one another, me warming to her need to be seen and she, seeing herself perhaps the first time, through another's eyes. I would not be able to paint her the way I imagined, mocking her pretentious hauteur, but, having seen her as she was, I had more sympathy for her. As Michele brought God down to earth in order to make Him believable, I felt kinder towards her, even touched by her little vanities.

I continued with the drawings for the portrait with particular attention to the striped sleeves of her dress and capturing the way the crow gently nipped her thumb which appeared to cause her no discomfort. I considered the matter of her fascination with birds in general and especially doves. I was not sure whether her name was the one she was born with, her married name or a conceit but, in any case, she was attached to doves. Michele adopted his hometown as the way he preferred to be known and the reason I added *del Caravaggio* to my name… Michele loathed the idea he might be considered the second Michelangelo, whereas I wanted my name to be always associated with him as women take their husband's name in marriage. However, Eliza's portrait was abruptly put aside when I received a commission to paint an altarpiece to depict Christ at the column for an oratory in a village between Naples and Monte Cassino monastery. I presumed the subject indicated an indirect commission from the Colonna since the fee was seventy-five scudo, half as much again as the portrait for Eliza. I hired mules to ride out with Alessio to meet the priest but, when we found the scattering of houses and small chapel, the priest was not waiting for them as expected. Instead, an old man hailed them. "Are you a bit of an artist come to see the church?"

"I'm Master Boneri del Caravaggio, the painter, and this is my assistant Alessio and I suggest you are more respectful to a servant of the Colonna."

Chastened, he doffed his cap, mumbled apologies and led us to the small west door which he unlocked. "Father Raffaele sends his regrets. He was called away to give last rites." We ducked into the church which was old style with round arches, only three bays long and the altar seemed crammed into the shallow apse. The wall behind the altar was bare and other pictures on the side walls, a crucifix and pictures of Christ and Our Lady reminded me of my father's work with most of the gilding worn down to the red boule and the sheen of the images cracked, creating a mosaic effect as the light caught the picture surfaces at different angles. "It's to go here." The old man slipped behind the altar to point above his head. When I stepped into the sanctuary, the old man shouted, "You mustn't…"

"How else can I measure the dimensions, let me pass. Lessio, hand me the measure."

I held the measure divided into hand-spans and called out, "Twelve by… nineteen palmi."

Alessio noted the dimensions and I nodded to the old man. "We're finished, give our regards to Father Raffaele."

Ambling back to the city, I was aware Alessio hardly spoke. I glanced sideways as he rode staring ahead, unaware he was observed. He was taciturn since he mentioned Sicily was within sight of Calabria. Perhaps he thought I would soon leave to be with Michele. Our increasingly fraternal friendship raised questions in my mind about my feelings for both Michele and Alessio. Ever since Michele decided to leave for Malta, I felt aggrieved and, thanks to his reckless lack of control, betrayed by his selfishness and even more now everything was in tatters… At least Alessio was loyal, and, even if not available as a lover, a good companion. I glanced at him again and he smiled suggesting his silence was contemplative rather than apprehensive.

Alessio stood naked, scratched his head, however often he modelled, the moment of revealed nudity without immediate purpose; to wash, to strip for bed or occasionally to fall into my embrace made him self-conscious. I was business-like, draped a long strip of grey-white fabric around his waist and tied his wrists and hooked the rope to a nail high up on the wall, adjusted the turn of the body and positions of his arms and rather than a study drawing I decided to follow Michele's method of drawing direct on the prepared canvas. I measured from the edge of the canvas to a vertical chalk line about a third from the right edge of the strainer and, using hand spans to determine the size of Christ's head, I had Alessio pose, head turned to the left almost facing the viewer, eyes closed, head lifted, face wincing in pain, his near shoulder hunched and body leaning to the right. I marked the head and torso to the junction of the legs. Where Michele had his scourged Christ turning to one side as though staggering, I painted Alessio as though lurching from the dark towards the viewer. I covered windows as Michele did to delay what was revealed emerging from shadow. I wouldn't let Alessio see the painting until I had almost finished the Christ figure which took over a week. When I let him see, I was surprised by his reaction. "It looks just like a Michele painting."

"No, it bloody doesn't!" Although dismissive, I was secretly pleased by his response. I needed other models and asked Alessio if his brother Calimero might wear his Colonna uniform as an officer supervising the torture and was pleased he agreed, turning up in part armour, quilted sleeves and a large red hat with a white feather. He also brought expensive brown leather gloves matching his under-jerkin which I suspected was also borrowed. Calimero could only model short times between his duties at the Colonna residence but short, concentrated periods suited me well, and he enjoyed swaggering around the workshop aping his capo and barking orders. "What are you laughing at you, lazy fuckers? Get to work." He caught

Alessio by the neck and rubbed the back of his head with his knuckles. I made drawings in order to work longer periods when Calimero was not available. I positioned the officer to the left, supervising the torment, gesturing to the recoiling body of Christ in front of a column to underscore the presumed Colonna involvement in the commission but equally to make a link to Michele's paintings of the same subject.

As the painting progressed, Calimero introduced comrades to model for other characters. I was intrigued by one man in particular, a strapping trooper with the head of a Roman emperor whose presence filled the room. He had the easy-going nature of a big man, undoubtedly lethal in a skirmish.

Alessio teased me mercilessly. "I know which one you favour, and I bet you can't wait to see him stripped down to nothing but his boots."

I also chose a bald older man and both came to the workshop for me to draw them. The big man, Bruno, came twice and I drew him from the back, his head turned to the left, glancing up to Alessio as Christ. The bald man posed behind Alessio, holding him by the hair, which took several more sessions to resolve the interplay of his left hand and Alessio's raised right arm. When the drawings were finished, I sent a generous amount of money for Calimero to share but was surprised when half was returned with the message that the lads were quite happy with a few drinks and a meal.

News from Sicily was sporadic. I awaited a response from Michele or Mario but none was forthcoming for several months. We heard Michele painted a *Burial of Santa Lucia* for the cathedral at Syracuse and had gone on to Messina to paint a Lazarus. I guessed he stayed with Lorenzo. My spirit rose when I received a message even though I didn't recognise the handwriting.

I have heard nothing from you for months about the state of the portrait and when I should expect it to be delivered to me in a gilt frame as agreed at no extra charge. I expect a swift reply with no excuses.

Eliza had not secured the commission with an advance so all costs, materials and labour were found by me. I completed several portraits and still lives under the same conditions simply to get my name about. Perhaps Eliza knew this and assumed that was the way painters worked. I was irritated by her manner.

Francesco Boneri del Caravaggio to Eliza Colomba

Madamina, I regret I have not advised you of progress with the portrait but I received several commissions with customary advances in payment to defray the cost of materials, assistants etc… The drawings are complete and the painting progresses well. I am unable to paint for the next week because of other commitments but you are welcome to view progress on the portrait the week after. If your servant would return with a date convenient to us both, perhaps you will bring an advance of five scudi. Francesco Boneri, Painter.

There was no written reply, simply a visit from her boy servant with a date in the middle of the following week. Alessio grinned. "That gives you nine days. D'you think you can finish the portrait in the available time?"

"I've no intention of finishing the portrait before the commission for the church. I will do a week's work, and she will see how well I have done. If she doesn't bring the advance, it will never be finished."

By the time Eliza arrived, I had painted the face, hands and bodice and the sleeves were roughed in with patches of colour. The crow was blocked in and the painting gave an indication of how the finished image would look. When she entered the workroom, I was surprised how differently she presented herself. She wore the usual black bodice but with pale yellow sleeves attached. Her hair was dressed tumbling low on one side, the other pinned under a large, plumed hat. I almost said how stylish but merely nodded and mumbled welcome. She bobbed a shallow courtesy and we laughed. Her sudden movement startled her crow which raised its wings and trampled her sleeve. It blinked several times and gradually became calm. I noticed a fine silver chain attached to the bird's leg, wound around her arm and lightly held in her left gloved hand. "This is where you work… I smell paint and… something musty."

"Canvas smells like sacking."

She examined the jars of colour and sniffed the oils and tapped the large pot holding my brushes, bristles up. "So many brushes… and why a kitchen bowl?"

"Mortice and pestle. It's for grinding colours to powder, a tiring job, isn't it, Alessio?"

"Yes, master." He handed Eliza a glass of wine.

"Does he work you hard?"

"When he's under pressure to fulfil commissions, he's on top of me all the time."

When Alessio removed the cloth, she was startled. "Is that all you've done? I expected it would be finished."

"As I said in my note, I have urgent commissions from important families and advances have been paid and dates for delivery agreed. Our arrangement is less formal, less legal… a favour if you like, and if you cancelled the painting, I would have made a loss in materials and time spent drawing and painting."

She tapped her lip with her fan and, after several moments, snapped, "So, if I pay an advance, how soon will you finish the painting?"

"That's difficult. It depends on what you think, any changes, additions and so on…"

"Additions?" She stared at the painting. "I thought I mentioned I wanted a dove in the picture. Were you thinking of charging extra?"

"I never thought to charge extra but still need to make drawings."

"Why d'you need to draw first, couldn't…?"

"It's necessary to draw if the subject is unfamiliar; you wouldn't build a house without first making plans; painting is the same; otherwise, unforeseen problems occur." I encouraged Eliza to leaf through the drawings I had made of her face, upper body, detailed studies of the striped sleeves and a small page of studies of the crow.

"I see your drawings are good, but I heard your master Caravaggio never made drawings."

I hesitated but came down on the side of loyalty. "That's true, but he is the greatest living painter and what is given to genius is not given to cattle."

She smiled. "Then he would have finished my portrait by now."

"But wouldn't have started without an advance, let's say five scudi."

"Five scudi is a little high. Let's agree on three."

She agreed to send the advance but, until she did, I continued working on the altarpiece, painting Calimero as the captain of Pilate's guard working up the sheen of the armour in contrast to the duller suede gloves and under-tunic, concentrating on the light catching the facets of the diamond quilting of the sleeve. Although not Spanish, I made Calimero's features darker to suggest Israel's oppression by the Roman occupier. I also painted the bald man behind the column with a thick stick in his right hand.

Before continuing, I allowed the paint to dry and, even though the advance payment was not forthcoming in the several weeks since our meeting, I worked on the portrait of Eliza… After painting Calimero's sleeve, I was keen to work up Eliza's even more elaborate slashed and striped sleeves, having carefully noted the colours, white and dusty carmine pink with a slightly orange tint. Taking my time, I worked several days before the sleeves were finished, and I was pleased my drawings accurately depicted the details of folds, creases and tones and realised the portrait and the Christ at the column were better painted and with greater confidence than anything I had done to date. If not masterpieces, they were certainly nothing to be ashamed of and Alessio was moved to say how wonderful both paintings were and, without flattery, said they were much better than anything he had seen me paint before. "We should find the pigeon seller at the market near the harbour and buy a bird for you to draw… and then we'll eat it."

I laughed. "I'm not sure I fancy eating my models."

"You don't mind swallowing me."

Chapter 36

Raising Lazarus 1609

Giovanni Lazzari insisted he would only deal with Michele directly. In turn, Michele invited Lazzari to his workshop. Carla was annoyed. "You can't expect him to come from Messina."

"If he wants a Caravaggio, he'll come."

"You're being unreasonable, throwing the commission away… Is it to force Mario to take it?"

"He could do it."

"Please don't, Michele."

"Whose side are you on, Carla?"

"It's not a matter of sides. I don't want him to fail… It's too soon for such a big commission."

"I was his age when I did the Contarelli paintings and you said he shouldn't have recommended me for the Lucia picture."

"You heard?"

She was flustered and blushed. "You're his loving wife. Why wouldn't you want advancement for him, and why not now…?"

"Mario's not…" She lowered her voice. "He's not a shooting star like you, and, although he's talented and ambitious, when you arrived, I saw how it is between you. If he'd taken the Santa Lucia commission, he would have been looking over his shoulder, wondering how you would have done it. For that reason alone, it would have been a failure." She wiped her eyes. "Is that betrayal?"

"You're a good woman, Carla, and always have his best interest at heart."

"Lazzari's offering a thousand scudi… Even you admitted you never made that much from a single commission."

"True… almost twice as much as I've ever made for a painting but, if he wants my work, this Lazzari fellow must come to Syracuse to agree terms and sign a contract. It's all about vanity… not mine but his."

Mario and Carla stood at the door of the workshop. Michele covered the Santa Lucia picture. The morning light was bright for December and quite warm. Rome will be freezing... Mario confirmed Lazzari arrived the night before... "He's looking forward to meeting you. Look at you, Michele, you might have worn the black doublet I repaired and the clean shirt I pressed for you."

He grinned. "Michelangelo, the other fellow, used to greet the pope in his work clothes... Ha! But I bet he never made a thousand scudi for a single piece of work."

"Gesù, Michele, you talk shite sometimes."

Mario spluttered. "Carla!"

"No, Michele, do you really still feel the need to compete with a painter who's been dead half a century and more?"

Michele laughed. "He was a sculptor, not a painter."

"You know what I mean." She gently pushed him. He caught her in his arms and swung her around until they were both dizzy.

She giggled. "Put me down, Pazzo!"

Michele let her down, unsteady on his feet, white as a sheet and coughed until he was red in the face and the veins in his temple bulged. A clatter of hooves and a small travelling coach arrived at the door. Mario and Carla went to greet the visitor. The magnate had two armed guards who dismounted and opened the coach door and handed down a pretty young woman, followed by a man dressed in formal rather than travelling clothes.

Mario stepped towards them. "Welcome, Signor Lazzari, Madamina..."

"Is he here?"

"He will welcome you inside, signor... you should know he's not been well this past month."

The couple and bodyguards passed from light into dark and, as Lazzari doffed his hat, Michele stepped forward, held out his hand as though he expected Lazzari to kiss it and, in a booming voice, said, "Welcome to my humble workshop, Signor Lazzari... and my lady..."

Taken aback by Michele's presumed senior status, Lazzari slightly bowed. "You are most gracious, Master Miche... Caravaggio..."

"Cavaliere Caravaggio of the Order of the Knights of Malta."

"Cavaliere? But I thought..."

"Rumour, signor. What God grants, as you know, no man may cast aside."

"Er, indeed."

"My former associate Master Cesari was elevated to Cavaliere, but he is not half the painter I am and, as for Baglione… a brass chain." He laughed. "But to business, signor." He nodded to Mario who served a good Sicilian wine. "Your health."

Lazzari dismissed his men and responded to the toast.

Michele smiled. "Excuse me, Signor Lazzari, I have forgotten. What is the subject of the painting you wish to commission?"

Lazzari turned to Mario. "I thought your agent—"

"Signor Minniti did tell me, but I have forgotten."

Lazzari held out his hands. "Lazarus… the raising of Lazarus for the church of the…"

"Ah, yes… Lazarus… a little self-aggrandizement, Signor Lazzari." He laughed and slapped his back. After a slight hesitation, Lazzari also laughed. "Please say you don't want angels… otherwise, the deal's off."

"Cavaliere, no, I don't expect angels."

"The fathers at San Luigi wanted angels and that bastard at the Misericordia in Naples. I painted an angel for Francesco though, but he deserved it. He was surrounded by goodness."

Lazzari was confused.

Mario cut in. "Cavaliere Caravaggio refers to His Most Reverend Eminence, Cardinal Francisco del Monte…"

"Yes, I heard His Eminence was…"

"If it's Lazarus and no angels…" He held out his hand. Lazzari shook.

"Good, have your man bring the contract tomorrow, and I'll sign… Oh yes, one third in advance… in cash. Once that's deposited with my agent… I'll get started."

"Will you work here or in Messina?"

"As soon as the painting of Santa Lucia is finished."

"How long will that take?"

"A few days, or weeks but when it's installed, I'll come to Messina. I need to see where it will hang…"

"May I see the Lucia painting?"

"I'm sorry, signor. She remains private until consecrated and on display."

From Messina port, Calabria was a ghostly powder-grey sliver of land across a dark blue-green channel. A little over two years ago on his way to Malta, he passed through the same channel between what appeared to be two islands. It was his first journey by sea, which reared up towards the horizon and he was uneasy when the waters became choppy, especially passing through the narrow straights which from dry land now seemed calm. Gazing across the water, he once again thought about Cecco and hoped... He received several letters from him but had barely responded. It was difficult to say anything specific with uncertainty whether friends and patrons could secure a pardon and impossible to say anything intimate, assuming correspondences via the Colonna were almost certainly scrutinised in transit... The city of Messina stretched along the coast in a narrow ribbon with the church of The Fathers who Carry the Cross, set back from the port. He hoped the commission was for the Duomo but a thousand scudi tempered disappointment. Lazzari wanted the altarpiece to measure forty-eight by thirty-six palmi, larger than even the Baptist for Valetta and the Resurrection in Naples. "Tell him, Mario, thirty-nine by twenty-eight is the largest I'll do."

"But he's paying a..."

"Flatter him, Mario. Say Cavaliere Caravaggio would expect him to agree that artistically the painting should fit comfortably in the space above the altar, not crowd the space as a mere artisan would make the mistake of doing."

A priest rushed over to them. "Master Caravaggio, please don't stand on the altar, come down."

He shifted his weight onto one leg and held the measuring stick in the manner of a saint; the stick held between the thumb and first two fingers, the others fanning outward. "Brother, we are doing God's work here."

He jumped down and tapped the priest's chest with the stick. "You deal with your duties, and I'll attend to mine." Michele made Lazzari pay for materials ordered from Syracuse.

He dictated the list to Mario. "A strainer for a thirty-seven by twenty-seven palmi canvas, with overlap and a frame of that size..."

"But you said the painting would be thirty-nine by..."

"With the frame, it *will* be thirty-nine by twenty-eight... The usual colours, you know what I need... and extra azurite and vermillion, walnut oil and beeswax... Lazzari must also agree to pay for models and their lodgings... you know the ones I want you to bring from Syracuse."

Michele kissed Carla but the child flinched, turned away and buried her head in her mother's hair. He could see from her reaction Carla was as shocked as the child by his appearance, unkempt hair, longer, greasy and hanging in rats' tails. He was aware his face was still pale and eyes dark ringed. She handed him two letters Mario had brought from Syracuse, one addressed in beautiful script, the other written in a familiar, careful hand to Master Michelangelo Merisi da Caravaggio at the house of Signor Minniti, painter in Syracuse. He smiled. *Cecco.*

M, I hope this letter reaches you. I heard you're in Sicily and guessed you'd go to Mario or Lorenzo. I wish we'd parted friends but I always keep your best interests at heart. I came back to Rome – keeping my head down. Things have died down a bit but the Tomassoni still bad-mouth you. Rumour has it some important people are trying to get you a pardon but don't know much for certain. I heard some gossip – somebody called Finsonius or Finson – Luigi Finson? You'll remember the name from the contract signed in Naples. He's trying to flog a picture he claims he painted – a Madonna with the Rosary. It was put up at the Dominican church, and I got sight of it. I can tell it's yours, the one you started in Rome and finished in Naples but a big red hanging cloth was added, like the one you did in the Death of the Madonna but a bit stiff looking and whoever painted it tried to copy the drape in the death of the Virgin.

I hope when you're pardoned, we can be friends again.
Cecco

He was elated to hear from Cecco and regretted he had treated him badly… He gambled Cecco would keep faith with him but that hope was strained by the grand Maltese plan that failed. From Cecco's letter, it seemed he considered the state of their friendship uncertain. He desperately wanted to see him and, when pardoned, they could finally return to Rome together… once the Lazarus painting was finished. Cecco's reticence unnerved him, but he was surprisingly unconcerned about the *Madonna of the Rosary* and the mysterious Finson. There was no doubt anyone who knew his work would never be fooled but mention of the Tomassoni was alarming and he was anxious for Cecco's safety.

They embraced. "You're more handsome than ever Renzo."

"You've changed."

"Uglier?"

"I mean, you never offered compliments in the past." He hesitated. "But you don't look well, Michele." He touched his chest. "I think you're heartsick." He was surprised how well Lorenzo understood him. He was his longest friend since they met in Venice and the only person he knew when he arrived in Rome. He knew Renzo loved him, and they once shared intimate interludes but Michele was too preoccupied with work and ambition… and then Spada, whom he allowed to dominate and leech from him. Cecco was the only one who stayed with him and, despite everything, perhaps still waited for him… and may have thrown away the most loyal of lovers.

"How've you been, Renzo?" He rubbed his neck. "I miss friendships we had in Rome… Mario and Carla, and the lads at that awful tenement in the early days, Filippo, especially Cecco and you."

"Have you heard from Spada, or any of the others, Onorio… His Eminence?"

"None of them."

"All false friends except for you, Mario and Francesco, who might have innocently tipped off the Tomassoni by writing…"

"I sent my letter via Andrea Rufetti… I never heard of Zagarolo, but you say the Tomassoni found you."

"It was a nasty affair when their men turned up. Very bloody… two of our friends lost…" After a moment, he smiled. "By chance, I had a letter from Cecco… and His Eminence today, which is an extraordinary coincidence." He took out the cardinal's letter and handed it to Lorenzo.

His Eminence Cardinal Francesco del Monte to the most renowned Painter Master Michelangelo da Caravaggio,

My dear Michele, I write to you direct in the abiding faith in the Holy Trinity that He will direct this communication to you safely and without interception. Matters concerning you, my son, have reached my ears, particularly the triumph of the commissions for the church of the Misericordia and other houses of God in Naples and also the now famous St John for the Knights of Malta. I am aware of the circumstances of your leaving Valetta and that you now reside in Sicily with Master Minniti and family. Convey my blessings and prayers for him and his family. You may also have seen my namesake. If he is with you, tell him I send my blessing. On the important matter, intercessions have been made on your behalf to the Curia by SB who is optimistic for a pardon. Do not despair, Caro, and be assured of my unswerving trust and faith in you.

May Christ always be with you and Amen.

He stroked Lorenzo's face. "You wrote to me at Zagarolo saying you were going to Messina... Mario remembered you gave him an address near the Tavern of the Two Fishes. In you came and here you are."

"Thankfully, I did and what a chance. I spend little time here these days. I live like a monk."

Michele looked around his room. There were a few paintings, a small box of materials. "You have commissions."

"Very few. Simple stuff, a portrait, a Madonna or local saint. Always small, devotional..." Michele could see his technique was good but his subjects were pedestrian and was sorry he had to work to order, following formulas and conventions.

"Come be my assistant. I have a big painting—"

"That's kind, Michele, but I have work I must finish."

After a long silence, he asked, "Apart from paintings, what have you been doing since you arrived here?"

Lorenzo was hesitant. Eventually, he said, "I soon realised there was little future for me as a painter. Even in a backwater like this. I missed Rome, helping you and being at the centre of... everything. Knowing I painted the ground for this or that of your paintings. The Contarelli, the Cerasi... the others, with Mario and Cecco. We willingly... let go your own ambitions. I don't regret that but coming back to my home country I was exposed to the truth..." He gestured around him at several unfinished paintings. In the silence broken only by distant gulls, he looked directly at Michele. "I considered becoming a religious."

"A priest."

"No, a friar."

Michele almost laughed but realised he was sincere. "Why?"

"Because I was lost. I considered the priesthood and even becoming a monk but had no vocation for either... but a friar lives halfway between... I suppose, unlike you, Michele, I had no vocation for painting either."

"What d'you mean unlike me you had no vocation?"

"Michele, through your paintings, you touch people's souls."

"I don't follow."

"God speaks through you... the rest of us paint what we see or the way things should be seen but you..."

"That's shit, Renzo. I killed Ranuccio and the only soul I have is..."

"God kills... Sodom and Gomorrah, razes cities to the ground, drowned Pharaohs' army... crucified his own son... But then, He was raised from the dead."

"Renzo, do you believe Christ was resurrected? I don't."

"I think you do... you bring everything you paint to life."

At the church of the Fathers who Carry the Cross, he stared at the large space above the altar and tried to imagine what form the painting should take. He was confused and disturbed seeing Lorenzo and alarmed he considered a religious life. Lorenzo had spoken without self-pity, even though the love and devotion he had shown over years was never returned... I paid back Francesco's love with deceit and abandoned Cecco without a second thought. He sat a long time until an old priest shuffled up to him. "Good day, my son." Even though Michele didn't respond, he sat beside him. Once settled, he continued, "From the time you've sat here, you must be contemplating mighty matters."

"Must you bother me?"

The old man folded his arms, slightly rocked and smiled. "I suppose I mustn't but something's bothering you enough to grip your attention so tight." Michele looked at him a moment, then turned back to stare at the space over the altar. The old man shrugged. "I'll leave you in peace and pray for your troubles."

"Father, tell me the story of Lazarus."

"Lazarus. Lazarus you say...? Lazarus. Well... let's think." He closed his eyes a moment. "There are two stories of Lazarus, one in St John and another in Luke."

"I only know of one but tell me both."

"I think I know the one you mean but I'll start with the parable told by Our Lord in Luke about the poor beggar Lazarus at the door of the rich man. When Lazarus dies, he reposes in the bosom of Abraham but, when the rich man dies, he finds he is in Hell."

"Yes, I recall... the chance of a rich man entering the kingdom of heaven is as impossible for a camel to pass through the eye of a needle."

"Not impossible." He smiled. "The eye of the needle was a low narrow gate into Jerusalem kept open after curfew... a camel might pass through if its burdens were laid down outside the city."

Michele smiled and turned to the old man. "Signor Lazzari wants to unburden himself of some of his wealth."

"I should confess, Master Caravaggio, I knew who you are."

Michele nodded. "Go on, Father."

"Yes, the story. The rich man sees Lazarus in heaven and calls to Abraham to permit Lazarus to dip his finger in water to give him some relief from the flames." He turned to Michele. "But Abraham said the distance was too great."

Michele looked back at the blank wall. "Why would Abraham not allow the rich man some relief from his torments?"

"Because the distance between Heaven and Hell is too great."

"Hell is cruel. Why would God demand such terrible revenge… eternal fire and suffering."

The old man raised his hand. "We shouldn't think of it that way. God's love for us is unwavering and eternal. Hell is not of God's devising, the soul is spirit so cannot burn, the idea is ridiculous, but sin… the remembrance of sin, guilt… is such a burden the soul could not bear to be in the presence of such perfect love."

"You're saying that it is we who put ourselves in Hell… but, if that's the case, why are there venal and mortal sins?"

"All nonsense!" He laughed. "Pure invention, but please don't say I told you so… or I'll be burned… in body." He laughed again.

Michele could not help smiling. "You're a Protestant, Father."

He chuckled. "I'm too old to be a heretic… but then old enough to read between the lines."

"So, Father, where is the rich man in Jesus' parable?"

"He cannot divest himself of the burdens which weigh down the soul but, painfully, perhaps pitifully, he can see a reflection of God's glory in Abraham and Lazarus and pines to join them."

"Lazarus, in your interpretation, cannot come to the beggar but he, the rich man, must somehow find a way to unburden his soul?"

"Who am I to say?"

"Isn't what you describe a kind of purgatory?"

"You must be thinking of Dante's vision. I find it difficult to imagine God permitting external punishment… centuries, millennia… eternal agonising pain. Remember Gesù said we should forgive our brother not seven times… but seventy times seven. In other words, every time and, if necessary, to infinity. There are no limits to love and forgiveness, and we should not even keep record because God always forgives a penitent and contrite heart. So, I believe the soul is offered eternity to unburden itself and make its way to God."

"God kills indiscriminately. What about Sodom and Gomorrah?"

" Couldn't the story equally describe a volcano or earthquake, natural phenomena."

Michele was intrigued. The priest was an older, decrepit, gap-toothed version of Francesco, brother to Filippo Neri and expected any moment his flesh would fall away to reveal Francesco, his dearest mentor and he was homesick. As he mused, he became aware the old man was speaking.

"…but Lazarus in St John is a different matter. It is not a parable but a particular miracle of Our Lord." He smiled. "But before that, are you hungry, Master?"

"Are you, Father?"

"Thank you, I could take a little sustenance and there's a tavern near the port…"

"The Tavern of the Fishes no doubt. Be my guest."

"As I intended, of course." He leaned on Michele's shoulder to get up. "As we go, tell me the story of Lazarus or whatever you remember from childhood."

Late afternoon, light was golden as they made their way towards the port. In daylight, he noticed the old man's black soutane was frayed, stained, worn grey and shiny around the collar, cuffs and elbows. His grey hair was so thin the blotched skin of his skull was visible beneath. "I recall the story well enough… Lazarus was the brother of Martha and Mary… She who anointed Our Lord's feet with perfume and dried them with her hair…"

"That always seemed so extravagant to me… but go on."

"Lazarus became ill, so the sisters sent for Jesus… who came too late to heal him so he raised him from the dead."

"After four days… Our Lord waited two days before setting off for Bethany."

"I understand the story… as a prefiguration of Christ's death and resurrection, but I don't understand what it means."

"Ah, so you realise there's deeper meaning in the story… good." He linked Michele's arm. "Yes, the raising of Lazarus anticipated Our Lord's sanctification of the tomb, emphasised by what his disciples said when he set out, that at Bethany his life was at risk. But still he went, as he later went up to Jerusalem where his life was again in mortal danger."

"Why did he wait two days… to arrive four days after Lazarus died… after all, didn't he cure the centurion's servant from a distance, without ever meeting him?"

"That's right and is the very point. It was believed the soul remains near the body for three days, with the hope of resuscitation but by the fourth day it departs so there was no doubt that Lazarus was dead and, of course, the sisters said that after four days the body stank."

"Remember, Father, we are about to eat."

The old man stopped and laughed aloud. "The great Master Caravaggio is squeamish." They entered the tavern and the old priest was greeted by all and sundry and a table was cleared for them near a glowing fire. They were served sardines in pulped spiced tomatoes with half a loaf of bread and a flagon of wine which the old man had no trouble quaffing copious amounts despite its throat-scouring acidity.

When Michele gagged at the first sip, the priest smiled. "You'll get used to it."

"Gesù, what is this?"

"Local… I grew up on it."

"Now I know what keeps Etna alight… you'll never die drinking this."

"Northerners are so soft." The old man ate quickly and mopped his platter with bread and drank three cups of wine to Michele's one… half of which he left. He tapped Michele's arm. "Returning to Lazarus… by raising Lazarus from the dead, Christ anticipated his death and resurrection. In part that's true, but the delay in Christ's raising Lazarus is the lesson that we must accord with God's time and not our urging, as Martha and Mary found but also that the nature of Lazarus' raising from the dead was different from the resurrection of Our Lord. Lazarus was resuscitated and was destined to die again. Why else would he remain in his funeral shroud? When Christ rose from the dead, he conquered death for us all and there would be no second death and therefore Our Lord left his shroud behind. He had no further need of it." Michele was silenced by the power of the faith of this ordinary priest, thin, age bent, fingers contorted by arthritis and no stranger to eating and drinking. "I hope I haven't bored you, Master Caravaggio?"

"It's Michele, Father."

He smiled. "I'm Father Benedict but my former name was Pierre Luigi."

"Thank you, Pierre Luigi, such enlightenment is rare."

"My dear Michele, it's rare anyone listens to this ancient ghost. I often think I preach to deaf stones, but I must finish. The Gospel tells us that Gesù wept and groaned at Lazarus' grave, but, surely, you say, if he had the power to raise him, why such emotion?"

Michele shrugged. "We often forget Our Lord shared every one of our human emotions and feelings and at the grave he was overcome by pity for our mortal condition but as God breathed life into Adam, so the second Adam, the Logos; remember how St John's Gospel begins: *In the beginning was the Word and the Word was with God…* It was the Logos who commanded Lazarus to come forth and return from the dead."

"And Adam was saved when Christ descended into Hell."

"Quite right. So, you did sometimes pay attention to your lessons as a schoolboy… But, finally, perhaps we may deduce that salvation is offered to both the living and the dead, and isn't that where our conversation began?"

As he escorted Pierre Luigi back to the church, the old man stopped. "I should tell you that Fra Antonio Martelli of the knights of Malta is in Messina and Maltese galleys patrol the channel."

Michele squeezed the old man's puny arm. "That's kind, Father, but I believe I am not at risk of capture."

"Ah, you know more than you will say."

Having expected demands to refine the gravediggers, Michele was surprised to hear the Santa Lucia painting was installed and blessed. Carla sent a message from Syracuse to confirm she had seen the Santa Lucia in place. The painting caused him a great deal reflection, being his memorial to Lucia his mother. Parting with the picture was particularly difficult, he even considered returning the fee. The painting profoundly touched him and allowed him to witness and be present in spirit at his mamma's burial. Had he not been in Venice plotting vendetta, he might have been with her at the end to arrange her funeral rites. Perhaps it was the reason he simply left the painting behind for it to find its own way.

Mario and Lorenzo were once again his assistants, and they worked together with the same methodical rhythm as though it was only yesterday they were in Rome. Lads no more, they understood him well and were so experienced he hardly needed to explain the proportion of hues to mix a particular colour; *reddish-brown, a more golden version, subdued orange, that greenish yellow for Lazarus' flesh…* so that Michele barely needed to modulate colours as he applied them.

Lorenzo said, "If only Cecco were here." Michele flinched.

The frieze of figures was painted in less than a month. He hired four strapping workmen to hold up the model for Lazarus. Where the body of Christ had been gently lowered in the *Entombment*, here Lazarus was being raised from the ground. The models worked in two-hour shifts; beyond that they began trembling, causing the model to slip. Lazarus was painted nude in a cruciform rigour mortis, arms stiff outstretched, the lower hung lifeless but the upper arm and hand raised as though hailing the Logos as he was returned to life. The arms foreshadowed Christ's stretched arms during the crucifixion. Once the figures of Mary and Martha were painted huddled close to Lazarus' head, he paid and sent the models away. There was no further progress for ten or more days because he could not find a model for Christ.

"Father Pierre Luigi… I'm searching for Jesus."

"Aren't we all, Master Michele?"

"He must be handsome but not…"

"Pretty?"

"Not pretty, no… but…"

"Blessed with that something that makes it impossible to portray…"

"Exactly that… You understand."

He fell onto the cot in the workshop. Having worked the entire day without pausing to eat. He supped cups of wine but trembled from exhaustion rather than alcohol. He fell into a light doze, hearing Mario and Lorenzo cleaning and quietly tidying. Their murmured conversation was barely audible, but he could not help overhearing occasional snippets.

"I'm worried about him… Did you notice he mutters to himself under his breath… I heard him say something that sounded like: Lazarus to dip his finger in water to quench my thirst… He twitches when he paints and just drops his brush when he's done with it…"

"I've never seen him this way before. And where does he go at night and why won't he let us go with him…? I suppose he's still looking for Jesus." They laughed. "At the docks. Fishing for men…" Michele could not supress a smile but, thankfully, they were not paying attention to his corpse.

Lorenzo whispered, "I thought he would be calmer once he gets down to work, but this painting seems to have the opposite effect."

"Carla thought the same about the Santa Lucia…"

"Haven't seen it… but why would it affect him?"

"She thought it reminded him of his mother. Her name was Lucia; her funeral was over before he heard she had died."

"I don't remember him mentioning anything about her."

"Me neither but I think Carla's right, the painting seem…"

"…memories… back to him…"

"She thinks he's haunted… past months…"

He tried to follow their whispered conversation, but they moved away to the far end of the workshop…

"This is different… his strange behaviour…"

"D'you think he's losing his mind?"

Lorenzo shook him. "Mario's prepared supper."

It was a while before he knew where he was as Cecco's ghostly presence in a long incoherent dream slowly faded. He saw him as he was in Zagarolo with the whisp of upper lip and chin-fluff. More than the way he looked was the more tangible memory of his scent and silky touch of his skin, his waist, belly and hips. He was groggy and ached, barely ate a morsel. "I have to get to bed."

"Michele, before you go, the Messina Senate want you to paint an Adoration of the Shepherds for the Capuchin church… and a Nativity with patron saints for the church of San Lorenzo in Palermo."

"I suppose both are required for Nativity."

"That gives you five months… you've easily done that before."

"If they cut me in half I suppose."

He climbed the stairs and lowered himself onto bed and slept intermittently with further broken dreams of Cecco who appeared with an earthenware jug, stooping to inspect a small rose bush. He glanced up and smiled as he watered the plant, then walked towards a doorway, the earth turned black and the leaves withered. He bitterly wept within and without the dream.

June 21ˢᵗ, 1609, Cara Carlita, I miss you, dear wife, and our darlings and send my love and blessings. As for the Lazarus, Michele couldn't find the right model for Our Lord. An old priest suggested a young deacon who looks a bit like the Gesù in the Calling of St Matthew. The pose is the reverse – from the back – and Michele left the Gesù to me and Lorenzo. He sketched the figure and left it to us to complete. The face is too small and the sleeve of the red garment poorly done. I'm not proud of our efforts. Lazzari turned up unannounced to see the painting – Michele was not pleased when the niece said the naked Lazarus should be covered. I leave to your imagination his reaction. Lazzari is desperate for the finished painting. Michele promised before Lazzari's name day in December. Michele's health is no better. I send kisses to you and our darlings.

Mario

Chapter 37

Naples – Last Days

I lost count of the weeks before receiving a letter from Sicily. After such a long silence, I was irritated and left it unopened for hours, dreading the worst, the handwriting being neither Michele's nor Mario's. I worked a long day and, when Alessio started supper, I eventually broke the seal and opened the paper.

Lorenzo Carlo in Messina to Cecco Boneri in Naples. 17 August AD 1609

Cecco, I heard from Mario you didn't come to visit our friend who said I should write because he, Mario and I, are finishing a painting for the church of Padri Crociferi. It's a big picture of the raising of Lazarus and it reminds me of the Christ in the Calling of Saint Matthew in San Luigi. M let Mario and me help, which is unusual – once he finished the Lazarus and those holding up his body, he left Christ and other figures just sketched in. He was in haste to finish since receiving two other commissions for Nativity paintings – one for here and the other in Palermo. He wants both finished for the feast of the Nativity. There's been no news of a pardon but he received a couple of messages from Naples so friends must be working on his behalf. I know you must be concerned Michele hasn't written but he's exhausted, works every hour morning to night and he's not well. He rambles and mutters to himself. I know he thinks about you because he painted another Saint John with a ram. I think he might have started it some time ago. Mario posed to get the body finished but the face is certainly a memory of you. I hope this letter is some consolation for your separation and hope a pardon will soon be granted. Don't despair, Cecco. Mario, Carla and I send our love. Believe me, you remain M's dearest companion.

Renso

I handed the letter to Alessio to give me time to take in what I read. "What d'you make of that... Do you believe what he says about me *remaining* Michele's dearest companion?"

"I would say yes."

Folding the letter, I put it in a small box with other papers, contracts and such but didn't speak of the matter further. Fortunately, I received another commission to paint a man with a rabbit. Alessio asked where the commission originated, but I didn't respond guessing it was the Colonna. The only clue to the identity of the person who actually offered commission was the name at the bottom of the paper: Rugiero Coniglio. It was obviously not intended to be a portrait, so I had Alessio model, encouraging him to try ideas for the composition as he held the rabbit in his arms or allowed it to sit on the table.

I groaned, "This place is a fucking menagerie, a dove in a cage and a rabbit on the table with shit everywhere."

Alessio was relieved by my lighter mood after several days brooding over the Messina letter. The next few days were spent making drawings of Alessio in a fancy doublet and feathered hat and detailed studies of the rabbit and the dove. The dove was surprisingly docile and squatted on the table for prolonged periods.

The rabbit fidgeted and occasionally hopped around the table or jumped to the floor to explore the room, dropping pellets everywhere. "I'm going to kill the rabbit, use it for a still life, then cook and eat it, the bones rendered down for gesso and glue."

To Cecco Boneri – 24 August.

Caro, I believe the pardon will soon be forthcoming. I want you to go to Rome, where I will join you when I receive the pardon. Take everything I may have left in Naples. When matters are settled, the Colonna will send you soldi and arrange a wagon to get you to Rome. I will repay the Colonna.

Go to Rufetti. He expects you. I will join you as soon as the pardon arrives.

M

Brief to the point of terse, I recognised his low, insistent voice prompting, *Get that canvas prepared... go to the framer, tell the lazy bastard to finish the fucking job today...* His urgency always arousing. There was no time to lose, I must speak to Don Antonio to agree a date to leave. I also needed to decide what I should take to Rome and what to leave, but I was also determined to finish my commissions. There were few of Michele's effects left in Naples, perhaps the large mirror being the most valuable and the concave glass too but my initial excitement was gradually tempered by unease.

In the time since he left for Malta and this latest note, he offered little assurance matters would be the same between us or that our return to Rome would be any different from before. The Tomassoni will not have forgotten, much less forgiven the death of Ranuccio and the same competitors and rivals remained. Returning to Rome was likely to be just as great a disaster as the Malta adventure and, according to rumour, he was once again on the run in Sicily concerning a boy… and, from what Mario and Lorenzo wrote, his health and mental state was uncertain. Would I recognise the man I came to know in Zagarolo and the early days in Naples when we were close and when he was preoccupied with simply painting without distractions, making paintings the equal and perhaps surpassing his Roman pictures but, as ever, could not help provoking hostility? I had changed but Michele appeared unchanged. I would have been happy to be his Ganymede but the curt instruction to return to Rome reduced me to little more than a servant. I was also concerned he might expect me to put aside my commissions and return to prepare canvasses and grind pigments at my master's bidding. After all, Mario neglected his paintings, and I don't recall he was mentioned among Michele's list of good painters during the Baglione trial.

Alessio and I were up early in the cool morning air as we cantered towards the church with ghostly Monte Cassino in the far distance. The old priest must have heard the thud of the hooves from a distance and stood at the church doorway and raised his hand in greeting. I jumped down from the saddle and stepped towards the priest. "Father Raffaele, it's me, Francesco Boneri the painter."

The priest dressed in a shabby cassock barely acknowledged my greeting. "Ah, the painting."

"Yes, Father." I turned to Alessio who unstrapped the painting, stretcher and frame pieces from his saddle. "We have to assemble the stretcher and frame…"

"Let me see the painting." I led the way into the church, feeling excited at the prospect of seeing my first altarpiece about to go on display. I glanced around at the old-style paintings, devotional images, stiff, icon-like, austere and dark as though Giotto or Duccio, never mind Michelangelo, the other… had never lived. My hands trembled as I unfurled the painting and Alessio helped hold down the corners. The light was dim which enhanced the naturalism of the figures looming out of the dark. The old man stared down at the painting, his hands raised and a look of astonishment. I was pleased he appeared overawed, contemplating something way beyond his experience. His voice was hoarse when he spoke, "Take this filthy thing out of the house of God. It is blasphemy."

"What? Father, it's painted with due devotion, every brushstroke a prayer. It's a new way of painting in the style of my master, Michele da Caravaggio…"

"Caravaggio! I know very well who created this depraved way of painting. I may be old but I'm no hayseed. I've seen this Caravaggio's paintings in Naples and heard he is a murderer and, worse, a sodomite and what are you, his catamite… bardassa?"

"I have never…"

"Get out of this holy sanctuary and take this…" He shoved the canvas aside with his slipper.

"Don't you touch my painting with your foot, Priest. I've laboured long and hard and with sincerity…"

"You dare answer a holy priest?"

"Holy priest, my arse… I know all about holy men, so give me my money, and I'll take the painting where it will be appreciated."

"You mean you're taking it to Hell?" He smirked.

"You're an excuse for a man and a priest."

"Get out."

"Not without my money."

"Money? No. You return the advance."

"You didn't pay the advance, *truffatore!*"

"Not a penny."

"Then go to Hell yourself, boy-fucker *ladro!*"

I rolled up the painting and rushed to the door; before leaving, I turned. "I curse you, old man." I gave him the horns and snarled, "I curse you to suffer the fires of Hell before and after you die. May your belly swell, eaten alive by maggots, and die in agony." Alessio was as visibly shocked as the priest. The old man turned away and fell to his knees before the altar.

Alessio was silent more than half an hour as we returned to Naples until he glanced sideways. "You didn't really curse the priest; you didn't mean it." My fury had ebbed, leaving me bilious, having repeatedly re-imagined the confrontation, wishing I had tortured the priest more but, by the time Alessio spoke, I had returned to myself.

I regretted losing my temper. "I suppose I didn't mean all I said… in any case, curses are meaningless."

"Not in Naples."

Carlo and Martha were amused when Alessio related the tale. "I've never heard anyone curse a priest before." I was too upset to play up to the scene which Alessio embroidered. I now shared rejection Michele suffered each time his work was depreciated and understood the powerlessness and nausea. As the others chattered, I decided to take the portrait to Eliza next day.

Naturally, she kept me waiting but, the moment I decided to leave and was at the door, she appeared at the top of the staircase. "Where are you going?"

"You've detained me long enough. You have no manners, those with true nobility know how to behave."

I saw her baulk but managed to restrain her ire and in a strangulated voice, she said, "I want to see my portrait." I hesitated, then returned to the salon and unfurled the painting. She paced up and down, glancing at the painting, swishing her dress as she turned. "It's not what I expected."

"You saw it in the early stages and you liked it."

"I don't like the sleeves. You have to repaint them; I have better ones."

"I'm pleased to hear that but I have no intention of repainting anything."

"Let me show you my new sleeves. They're much more fashionable. I'm sure you'll like to paint them."

"I'm not a seamstress and have important commissions, so please pay me now."

"Not until you repaint the sleeves."

"That would mean further materials and labour, removing the varnish and I cannot afford to waste any more precious time, so pay me the forty-five scudi you owe me."

"Not unless you change the sleeves."

"In that case, the price will be ninety scudi to include the costs of alteration, call it seamstress' fee."

"Even if you repaint the sleeves, I will only pay twenty-five scudi."

I rolled up the painting. "Good day."

Eliza laughed. "What use to you is a portrait of me?"

Alessio asked the same when I returned with the painting unsold. "I'll scrape off the face and reuse the canvas for another painting and no one will ever know she existed. I'll paint black patches on the dove's feathers to indicate the portrait of an untrustworthy bitch. I'll call it the bird seller… and birds are the least she sells."

"Paint out the dove and put in a stinking fish and call it the fishwife's…"

I pinched Alessio's nose. "As I say, I'll change the dove's wings, add dark patches to indicate she's a piebald whore and title it *Woman with a Dove*. Anyone will know what her wares really are. I'll bring it to Rome with the *Man with a Rabbit* picture and I'm sure both will fetch more there."

315

Chapter 38

Nativities

He used the backs of his studies for the Lucia and Lazarus pictures to explore ideas in ink and sepia for the two nativity paintings. The one for the Capuchin church of Santa Maria degli Angeli in Messina was to be over thirty by eighteen palmi with the title *Adoration of the Shepherds*. The second with Saints Lawrence and Francis of Assisi for the church of San Lorenzo in Palermo, slightly smaller at twenty-seven by nineteen palmi. He had both canvasses stretched and prepared at the Messina workshop and rapidly blocked in the Adoration, leaving much of the rich burnt umber base showing through. He consulted Father Pierre Luigi several times about the theology of the incarnation.

"The Capuchins are very austere… I heard they drink only water and eat their own shit… although I may have confused them with some other… I should look over my shoulder before I accuse them of fanaticism, we are all brothers in Christ." He gave a gap tooth smile. "I know that amuses you."

"You remind me of someone – Pierre Luigi – although he was much more diplomatic than you."

He cackled. "Much younger and less raddled than me no doubt."

"Rogue… you enjoy teasing everyone."

"Only you, dear Michele… I think, perhaps you take life too seriously." Despite Pierre Luigi's caustic view of the Capuchins, Michele decided the Madonna and new born clutched close to her breast should lay on the bare earth lower than Joseph and the three shepherds who loom over them and lower even than the ass and ox, the humblest of the humble and poorest of the poor. In the left foreground, he painted a basket with carpenters' tools in reference to the nobility of common labour and the profession of Saint Joseph, passed on to his son and the tools that would make his cross. *Had Pierre Luigi thought about the cruel irony that Gesù worked with wood and nails most of his life?* Even closer to the viewer, he painted a rock to represent the rejected stone, Gesù himself whose ministry was the cornerstone of his church. He had in mind the composition of Titian's

Bacchus and Ariadne he had seen in the Aldobrandini Palace soon after its transfer to Rome. Francesco arranged for him to view it and, when they later discussed the painting, he said he was impressed the way Titian drove a triangular wedge of warm colours into the otherwise cool blues of the background. Michele applied a similar device in the Adoration with hot red, orange and gold entering the painting from the right, into a dark background rendered in mid- and dark browns: *The people that lived in darkness have seen a great light...* When the Adoration of the Shepherds was almost finished, he left Lorenzo with careful instruction on how he wanted the final glazes to be laid on.

"I'm going to Palermo tomorrow, Father, so, before I leave, tell me about San Lorenzo."

"Dear Lord, Michele, I'm sure you know all you need to about San Lorenzo. You're just teasing me to make me work for my supper."

"Would you like me to take you for supper, Father?"

"That's a kind offer; it would be discourteous to refuse." The old man leant on his arm as they slowly made their way again to the Tavern of the Two Fishes. "I imagine you expect me to tell you Lorenzo was slow-cooked to death. *Turn me over, I'm done this side.*"

"Isn't that the story? Michelangelo painted him with a gridiron in the Judgement fresco."

"Sheer nonsense, pure mistranslation; not '*assus est*' but '*passus est*'. Not *he was roasted*, but *he was martyred*. And why, you will ask... why would such a dreadful death become so popular?" He stopped and turned to look up at him. Michele shrugged. "Because we love to torture our martyrs."

Michele hired a waggoner to take the prepared canvas and support frame ready for assembly on arrival in Palermo. The summer air was hot and still, and Mario and he ambled along the coast road for two days, arriving at Bagheria where they spent the last night before cutting cross-country to Palermo. It was an affluent town which had grown up around the palatial villa of one of the Spanish viceroys. They stayed at an inn near the harbour in the hope of a cool breeze from the sea. They rose early next morning and took a walk before setting off. "My arse aches and my thighs are sore riding so far." Beyond the harbour wall, there was a small cove where a teacher was encouraging his pupils to learn to swim.

The teacher gestured with his arms and one leg. "This way, boys... like a frog."

The boys stood naked up to their knees in the water and one shouted, "But it's bad luck to swim, our families have been fishermen forever… we never learn."

"But you must, especially if you will be fishermen… otherwise you'll drown."

"Our fathers, grandfathers and uncles tell us if we know how to swim, we'll become careless. We must respect the water."

Michele laughed. "See how they stand naked and defiant without an ounce of false shame."

Mario nodded.

"I say you must learn to swim. What your families say is silly superstition."

Michele called, "Who are you to say? You're not their family."

The teacher turned, surprised by their presence. "This is no business of yours."

Michele grinned. "Let them be… don't they have Latin and Greek to learn?" As they mounted, Michele pointed to one of the boys who emerged from the sea. "My God, he could be Cecco when he was younger." Michele turned to look back at the boys as they left, illuminated gold in the bright morning light. The teacher stared back at him. "Pity I hadn't seen the teacher sooner; he would have been a better model for Gesù in the Lazarus."

The oratory was on the south side of the church of San Francesco d'Assisi and the Franciscan monk, Father Lorenzo, welcomed them and was the obvious model for his saintly namesake. "Welcome, Master Caravaggio, and you, signor, it is a great honour you are to paint the nativity." He led them to the altar and genuflected. "I sent the measure of the area and hope I was accurate."

"I'm sure you were."

"Master, you already have the contract for the painting… the Nativity with mother, Child, St Joseph, some shepherds and saints Lawrence and Francis. There must also be angels to glorify the event and animals if you wish."

"Angels?"

"It is recorded in the Gospels that angels announced the birth of Our Lord first to the shepherds, so if they were granted that grace, we must afford them the same honour… don't you think?"

"Will one do?"

"Perhaps… so long as he's prominent."

"One prominent angel then."

The monk smiled. "Good, a prominent angel with the legend Gloria in Excelsis Deo."

"In fine script."

"Naturally."

Standing well back to scan the painting, he was pleased it had gone well, no unforeseen problems. The figures were larger and closer than the Messina nativity and, apart from the Madonna's dusty orange-pink dress, the entire painting was done in earth colours, browns and ochres. Since the Santa Lucia painting, he habitually preserved much of the under-painting, which meant the paint dried sooner, and he could work even faster. He arranged for Father Lorenzo to play San Lorenzo and his colleague, San Francesco. A local man was recommended for one of the shepherds and Michele painted him as only a slight caricature of Pierre Luigi, the wide brim hat he always wore outdoors suggested a halo, which would have amused him enormously. The young shepherd was Mario, turning away from the viewer towards the shepherd but Michele changed his hair from dark to thick white-blonde in the style and colour he remembered of Nicholas de Paris Boissy to emphasise the intense light flooding the scene. The Madonna was a serving maid from a local tavern who had given birth just weeks earlier so her belly was still distended. He reduced the size of the baby but anyone paying attention would notice it was still too big for a newborn. The child lay on a cloth on the bare earth, a premonition of the Pieta, the body laid on the shroud and separated from the Madonna by the dark garment drawn over her belly. The Franciscan ideal of the humility and poverty of Christ was taken further than the Messina Nativity and all that was lacking was the angel.

Gloria in Excelsis Deo. He smiled. Master Simone, God bless him, taught me little painting but script writing very well. The angel was finished and the acclimation on the fluttering ribbon looped around his pointing hand was the final detail. The monk insisted the instrument of San Lorenzo's martyrdom must be included, whatever Father Pierre Luigi said. In response, he painted the saint's close hand gripping a metal bar and beyond he left an ambiguous vertical dark slab to suggest the gridiron end on, more a prie Dieu than an instrument of torture. He left Lorenzo and Mario to remove the canvas from the strainer and nail it to the frame and cart it to the Oratory. It had been arranged for the frame to be delivered to the church and, once dropped in and wedged, workmen raised the painting and fixed it to the altar wall.

"Master Caravaggio, you have exceeded expectations. The painting is more than a painting; it's an expression of deep faith." The priest handed Michele a purse with payment in coin and signed the contract completed. They were about to leave the sacristy when they heard a commotion in the church.

"Where is the bugger… Where is everybody? Come out, you bastard."

"Dirty swine."

Father Lorenzo left the sacristy, the door slightly ajar. "What is this shouting and cursing in the house of God… Be still."

"Where is he, Father, where's he hiding?"

"Shameful filthy bastard."

"Stop this profanity. Be quiet in the house of God. What do you want?"

Through the narrow slit between the door and frame, Michele saw several men, a woman and the master he had seen teaching his boys to swim who raised his hand and spoke, "Father, I am sorry we have broken the peace of this place, but we are here because a serious matter has come to our attention. A certain man, who claimed he was making a painting for the church, debauched this boy." Michele moved his head a fraction to see the boy who modelled for the angel standing beside his mother and an older boy. Murmuring and muttering preceded more shouting. The monk raised both hands until silence was restored. "This is a serious accusation… what evidence do you have?"

"He took my son to a barn and made him take his clothes off… What more evidence do you want?"

"Is this true, my son?"

The boy clung to his mother. "It wasn't like he said…"

"Did you take your clothes off for this man?"

"Some… not all." He looked up and, after staring several seconds, he pointed. "I was dressed like that." His smile was radiant. "That's me… it's me! Look, Mamma…" Everyone looked up at the painting.

The mother led the group to the steps of the sanctuary, as close as she dare, then genuflected to the host and crossed herself. "My son… it's him to the life, and he's an angel." She fumbled for her rosary beads and knelt in awe.

"There! That proves he took the boy's clothes off."

"All I did was pull my arm out of my shirt sleeve and point up… like that." He nodded towards the painting and copied the gesture.

The teacher caught the boy's chin. "He took you to a barn, alone. You admit that and your brother here said he saw you go with him and he told you to take off your clothes."

"I took my doublet off, and he asked me to lie on a pile of straw and slip my arm from my shirt sleeve."

"Then what did he do?"

"He made drawings of me."

The boy's mother knelt before her son. "Did he touch you… do things to you?"

"What things?" His father smacked his head.

The monk stepped forward to shield the boy from further blows. "Is this how you treat him?"

"I'll beat the truth out of him. It's the only way."

"Not here in God's house."

The mother gestured to the boy to join her at the altar rail and caught his hand. "Kneel down, Son, cross yourself and before God, Gesù and the Holy Mother, tell us the truth. Just tell us what happened and if it was something bad… if it was bad, it is not your fault… Isn't that right, Father?"

The priest nodded. "Tell me, Dom, what happened?"

"As I said, the man came up to me. He said he was making a painting for the church of San Lorenzo and would I pose for an angel. I asked if he would pay, and he said he would. He gave me four of these coins from Malta." He showed the coins in the palm of his hand.

"That's a lot of money just to model for him."

The mother glared at the teacher. "Master Pepe, let him finish."

"He said the light was too bright and I showed him the old barn, the one near the strand. He showed me how he wanted me to pose. I lay across a straw bale and he sat on the floor and made drawings. That's all that happened."

"Are you sure, Son? There's nothing you should be ashamed of if he… did anything bad."

"Dom, he must have threatened you."

"He didn't."

"But I saw him about a month ago when I was teaching the boys to swim…"

Dom's father turned to the master. "None of us swim, Master Pepe. It's unlucky."

"But they must learn to swim. It's safer, but what's important here: I saw the man the one Dom described, dressed in black. I saw him staring at the boys. It was an unhealthy interest. The boys were naked and…"

"They were naked?"

"As I said, I was teaching them to swim and the man in black, the painter, stared at them. I think we should call the authorities."

Michele slipped the dagger from his sleeve, stepped to the door and gripped the latch.

"No!" The boy's father's voice reverberated around the church. "We don't need the law; the family will deal with this… This is our concern." Michele slowly released the latch and stayed behind the door.

"No vendetta, not here in Holy Church."

"The Father's right, husband. Dom swears nothing happened and look— look at that angel. Our boy… an angel. Have you ever caught him telling a lie? Look at that face, look at that angel's face. Our son will live forever in this painting. No evil person could have painted such a beautiful face and then debauch him."

The boy's father spat, "I curse this painting and the devil who painted it. I swear and the one who made it will disappear forever without trace."

Mario slept and Michele kept watch. The farmhouse was little more than a ruin, perhaps the monk's family owned it before he went to the seminary. Mario began to snore. Michele gently rocked him with his foot until he turned on his side. He recalled the clamour in the church and his return to the cove where he had seen the school master teaching the boys to swim. No one was around. He went towards the town; there were few people abroad and thought it unwise to ask if anyone knew the beautiful boy he had seen standing naked in the water. It was a ridiculous quest, a waste of half a day. At an inn near the beach, he sat at a table in the shade overlooking the sea. A waiter served olives in oil, garlic and vinegar, cured ham, bread and wine. He closed his eyes and the sound of cicadas filled the air, along with the occasional call of gulls. He jolted awake, glanced up and saw a boy lying on his side, straining down from the pier, his hand stretched towards something in the water. *Cecco!*

"There's a barn; it's very shady. If you need to work out of the sun, would that suit you?"

He nodded. "What's your name?"

"Dom… Dominic, after the saint… You did say four silver Maltese coins? Let me see."

He pressed two coins in his palm. "You'll have the other two when I'm done."

"They're heavy." He tossed the coins in the air. "What d'you want me to do?"

"Take off your doublet, unloose your shirt and slip your right arm out and point downwards like this."

"Don't you want me to take all my clothes off? I heard that's what artists ask you to do." He grinned like Cecco. "Our teacher, Master Carlo:… Carlo Pepe likes us to run naked on the beach. He says he wants us to learn to swim." He laughed. "I think he likes to see us naked."

"That's not necessary." He made several drawings in ink and wash and a detailed study of the boy's head.

A monk brought horses, a mule and provisions for several days and, on hearing Michele's decision to return to Syracuse rather than Messina, suggested they skirt Palermo, go south and, on reaching the sea at Sciacca, they should make their way along the coast to Agrigento, then inland to Catania and south to Syracuse. "Be on the lookout for brigands and, with God's protection, you'll have a good few days' start by the time they realise you're not on the road to Messina."

Michele offered money but the monk refused. He pressed a small purse in his hand. "Alms for the poor, use it as you see fit." They waved the monk goodbye and, keeping the setting sun on their right, cantered a half hour and walked the horses an hour. By alternating the pace, they estimated they covered maybe twenty-five miles by daybreak. They slept in the open and, by nightfall the second day, they arrived at Sciacca. They stayed the night at a tavern near the sea and set off early next morning for Agrigento. The sea breeze was refreshing and the coast road seemed less threatening than the bridle paths when they travelled cross country from Palermo, with the anxiety they might run into robbers. By mid-afternoon, they reached Agrigento and thought better of setting off again cross-country to Catania. Mount Etna eventually reared up to the north, its ghostly south face with the summit shrouded by vapours of thin cloud tinted red orange and the ground shuddered. It was impossible not to feel awe and dread as they slowly trod the trembling earth. In sight of the belching cauldron, Michele involuntarily crossed himself. He stared at the rumbling mountain, surely the legend it was the mouth of Hell was true. It was a relief to turn south towards Syracuse.

When they arrived at the house, Michele was shocked to see how unwell Carla seemed. In turn, she was annoyed hearing Michele was on the run again. She said she had seen or heard nothing to indicate anyone was looking for him in Syracuse but, for safety, Mario sent Carla and the children to her parents' house and he and Mario boarded at an inn near the port and made discreet enquiries about boats to Naples. In the days before leaving Sicily, Carla's health worsened. Michele visited her at her parents' house, surprised how feverish she was. She confided she had miscarried soon after Mario and he left for Messina and had not been well since. She was furious when Mario told her about the boy Dom. "In the name of God, Michele, why would you take a boy into a barn and tell him to strip?"

"It's not the way it was."

"But, surely, you knew you were taking a terrible risk. Why didn't you speak to his parents?"

"I was in a hurry. He was the perfect model... I didn't think."

"You never have, Michele."

Visiting the Santa Lucia painting in situ further threw his world out of kilter, the sudden remembrance of his mother dying beyond the horizon when he was in Venice. The cold letter from Battista received the day he left Milan an outlaw... then there was no time for tears, and grief was overtaken by rage towards Battista. But her loss was part of the skin he shed on leaving. Of course he thought about her from time to time but the Lucia he concentrated on bringing to life was more real than the pale, insubstantial apparition that occasionally wafted through his dreams... the shock seeing Carla as Santa Lucia, his sanctified mother, he could not bear to finish the painting, to paint the trench of her grave in which her body now lay corrupted. Even more dreadful was the Lazarus, the horror of a man returned from the dead, brought back to face death a second time... The remembrance of pain of the first death made more dreadful with the certainty of further pain at the inevitable second death. A hand twitching in the light... Ranuccio... don't come back, please rest in peace.

Mario, Carla and Lorenzo embraced him on the quay, then Michele quickly went aboard. Lorenzo brought the materials from Messina and offered to accompany him, but Michele said he must stay and follow whatever path he chose. The gangplank was raised, hawsers tossed aboard and the boat slowly parted from the quay. Having checked the baggage was safely stowed, he returned to the deck. Carla leaned heavily on Mario. She should never have come to see him off but had insisted. The boat was now a few hundred yards from the quay and he murmured, *Dear Carla, Bless you... you're not long for this world.* Lorenzo and Mario waved from time to time but, when the boat reached the point of the harbour, he saw four mounted men gallop onto the quay. Mario turned Carla away and gestured to Lorenzo to follow. He seemed puzzled at first until Mario nodded in the direction of the four horsemen. Michele was relieved the trio left unnoticed and was certain he would never see them again. The four men dismounted and went to speak to the harbour master. Thankfully, the boat was soon out of sight of the harbour and the sails snapped and billowed unfurled as they reached the open sea. It was his third journey by sea and found it as foreboding as ever. It was the darkest blue-turquoise with white crested waves. *One day*, he thought, *I will paint the Styx, black water with Charon beating the terrified dead with the oar, a horse skull on the prow.* He wanted to sleep. His bones ached and he trembled but the heaving boat made him nauseous, the only way to keep from spilling his guts in the wind was to fix his eyes on the distant smudge of land sitting on the horizon.

Chapter 39

The Instrument Maker

Arriving at the outskirts of Rome, Alessio and I walked the horses to a small livery stable not far from the Piazza Colonna where they were fed, watered and groomed until they looked presentable. Alessio was amused. "Why the fuss? They're pack horses, not thoroughbreds."

We had ridden most of the past week and sweated and trembled with fatigue. The horses' hides were sodden with sweat and sharp as needles. I didn't want Rufetti to see Alessio and me dishevelled and Colonna horses in a state. The heat had been unbearable, even riding short distances in the cooler morning and at night, sleeping during the day from late morning to evening. At each town, there was always a small fountain or pool where we dismounted, unsaddled the horses and threw hands full of cool water over them. I wasn't entirely sure why I felt compelled to present myself in a good light. No one of any importance would hear that Francesco Boneri had broken two horses in a mad dash from Naples. An aristocrat might wind a horse, even ride it to death without a second thought, but I'm a journeyman, a painter with pride in my work and in myself. My answer was unbidden and probably close to the truth. I grinned. "Pride."

Andrea Rufetti expected us, and we were warmly welcomed but he knew nothing of Michele's whereabouts, presuming he was still in Sicily. Time passed slowly and there was no news of the elusive pardon. Certain materials were running low so Alessio and I went to the Corso to buy colours, umber, carmine, ochre and lead white and on to Via dei Chiavari to buy paper. On the way, we passed a narrow alley leading to a small workshop and heard the mellow sound of a lute and tapping in time to the lilt of the tune. I caught Alessio's arm. We stood a moment to listen to the melancholic theme which abruptly stopped, then restarted with little embellishments and double taps. I led Alessio into the alley and entered a small workroom. A young man stopped playing and looked up. He sat at a workbench strewn with tools and part-assembled instruments and finished guitars, lutes and tambourines hanging on the wall behind him. The room was rich with the scent of woods, glue and scented wax and tumbled curly wood shavings were swept into the corner. He stood. "Good day, gentlemen… you wish to buy…?"

"Yes, that wonderful tune you were playing."

He smiled. "That was just an idea that came to mind, hardly for sale."

"I'm no musician, signor, although my friend, Alessio, sings well, Neapolitan songs mainly, but I'm looking for subjects for new paintings. I am Francesco Boneri… Cecco del Caravaggio. My master painted musicians and it occurs to me it would be amusing to paint someone who makes instruments."

"I'm sorry, signor… as you're no musician, likewise I'm no artist's model."

I laughed. "Perhaps you think artists only paint nudes or bardassas…"

His face flushed, as he crossed his arms. "I… I thought no such thing."

"Tell me, signor…?"

"Faunus."

"Tell me, Faunus, do you prefer making instruments or playing them?"

"I don't understand."

"Could you make an instrument unless you could play it?"

"I suppose not, but I don't follow…"

"I can't paint without a subject. All I need is to make drawings of you as you were when we entered your workshop. I would pay you a full scudo to sit in that chair for six days."

Returning to Faunus' workshop, I was upset he'd tidied the work desk and imagined, wore his finest clothes, a leather waistcoat and elaborate diamond shaped layered sleeves with red-brown cuffs. Even more startling was his black hat with an impressive ostrich feather and, above his right ear, he wore a small pink flower. I persuaded him to alter the tidy arrangement of instruments, tools, manuscript paper, a capped bottle of fortified wine and a glass meshed with fine rope; otherwise, the still life was too obviously formal. I also pulled out the tool drawer closer to the viewer who would be intrigued to know what might be inside. I explained the strung frame Alessio assembled was a device artists used to capture the shapes and proportions of objects.

Once the frame was set up, I directed Faunus to sit in the leather backed chair with brass studs, turn and look three-quarters towards me and hold an instrument. He chose a tambourine which he held shoulder high, and I noticed he instinctively clenched his other hand. I sensed he was tense at first but relaxed as I plotted the image using the grid of the frame to make outlines and shapes on a corresponding grid lightly drawn on paper. In an hour or so, I'd drawn basic outlines to ensure accuracy and precise perspectives of rolled paper and various instruments. I then began a freehand drawing of Faunus, his head tilted slightly back and since his features became rigid, I suggested he sing. His voice was high tenor, sweet and melancholic as he sang the words of a familiar madrigal to the tune he had composed the first time we heard him play.

Grows a flower, the town goes wild
Isabella
She's a perfect golden child
Luisa! Luisa! Luisa! Luisa!
And Luisa's strong
The beauty and the strength do no wrong.

He repeated the song several times rather than move on to another. "Does the song remind you of someone, perhaps a lady?"

He smiled. "A lady, yes… two in fact."

"I take it you're popular with the ladies."

"These two especially. One is Luisa. I wrote the tune to the words for her when we were married, and Isabella is our daughter. She's three."

"You love them dearly. Sing the song as often as you please."

As he continued to reprise the song, he began to ornament with glissandi and trills until the sounds were as layered as his sleeves and noticed the drawing began to emulate the textures of the music in the animated fabric and the fronds of the feather. I worked through the day and expected by next day there would be enough material to begin the painting but, when we returned, I was surprised he wore an elaborate ruff and rather than the plain black hat he wore one of fur with the same ostrich feather attached. The change was startling and, rather than sing, he shook the tambourine which now rather than seen end-on, it formed a perfect circle. In his mouth, he had something small spherical white or ivory which he hardly blew to make whistling sounds, pitched to the thin brass jingles of the tambourine. He hummed the tune of *Isabella,* haunted by the gentle dissonance of the whistle. The sound was mesmerising.

To deflect attention from his good looks, I drew Faunus less handsome and younger than he was; nevertheless, he thought it was a good likeness and was flattered. I traced the drawing onto the prepared canvas and blocked in the basic forms, returning to Faunus' workshop with the painting to mix true colours. I used the material from the first drawing, without the ruff, and wondered if he would ask why but he didn't comment. The painting progressed rapidly, and I was pleased, not only with the figure but also the jumble of the still life in the foreground painted with care and attention to fine detail. When finished, I was delighted that, although my painting reflected Michele's original *low life* subject matter, my interpretation was different, more *Commedia dell'arte* than *Musica da Camera*.

Chapter 40

Cerriglio

Michele was invited to stay at Costanza Colonna's residence at Chiaia. From the terrace, he stared at the whisps of smoke drifting from the crater of Vesuvius, less active and seemingly less threatening than Etna. The memory of Costanza's generosity to his mother was comforting, but he avoided raising memories of Caravaggio. Since painting the Lucia, even mention of her name was painful. Returning to Naples, his health broken and Cecco gone with the last of his belongings for safe keeping. He longed to see him again but was unsure whether he would be welcome. Cecco predicted the house of cards would collapse and was right. What was given to Fabrizio did not hold for a rebel painter with a price on his head in a society of high aristocratic knights. He cursed himself for staying in Sicily rather than returning as soon as the Lazarus was installed. He sought out Carlo and Martha to sound out Cecco's mood and feelings towards him. Martha was a little guarded but said he seemed excited about the prospect of returning to Rome and mentioned he had commissions for several paintings. Carlo said his portraits were excellent and had painted an altarpiece. Michele was almost tearful hearing his Cecco was successful – an altarpiece at that. Martha gently added that the altarpiece had been rejected for lack of decorum. At that, Michele was overjoyed. "His painting must be exceptional… I know lack of decorum means he's not painting airy-fairy shit. When I get back to Rome, I'll make damned sure Vincenzo Giustiniani buys his work… and Borghese, at a decent price too."

My dear friend, I cannot make the blow easier except to say that Carla is gone. I think you knew how ill she was. My only hope is she is in the arms of Our Blessed Lady and that my sins and misdemeanours are not counted against her. She received extreme unction and made her final confession so I pray God she is in Heaven. She was always loyal, a good wife and mother, but I brought so much trouble to her door. God help me, Michele, how will I cope without her? We – me and the children – are staying with her family. She said I should marry again for the children's sake – but how could I? She remembered you in her final hours and asked me to send you her blessing and that you should take better care of yourself; otherwise, she said, you would soon follow her. In Carla's words, be well, my friend.

Mario

He had known she was dying... when he returned to Syracuse and certain the day she waved from the harbour as he embarked for Naples. He wept, remembering Carla lying on the ground as Lucia. She embodied his lost mother buried before he knew she was dead and now Carla was buried before he knew she was gone. He felt no need to have been there to mourn her burial, having recorded her internment in the painting. Poor Mario... so long as he knew he and Carla were in Sicily... and Lorenzo, too, he had a family of sorts. Even after the Malta disaster, he believed he could overcome all odds in the knowledge he, Caravaggio the painter, was always in demand from the highest even to the Cardinal Nephew... but that was then. Martha and Carlo invited Michele to stay for supper but he excused himself, saying he was expected at the Colonna villa but dined alone at an inn near the harbour, then left to return to the workshop, making a detour to the Osteria del Cerriglio.

A line of men leant against the wall of the short passage leading to the tavern. Each man stood silently alone and stared as he passed. Youths standing on the left wore heavy makeup and pursed their lips; older bravos stood on the opposite side, legs apart with folded arms leaning against the wall. The Cerriglio was not busy when he arrived at about nine o'clock. He had worked every day since his return to finish the St John for Scipione Borghese and started commissions, a martyrdom of Saint Ursula for Marc Paulo Doria via his agent Lanfranco Massa and a three-quarter Denial of Peter. The canvases were stretched and prepared and models arranged. He stumbled on the Cerriglio when he and Cecco first arrived in Naples, and this was the first time he visited the bar since his return. It afforded uncomplicated opportunities for companionship of every imaginable kind, at least until the first light of dawn. It was a quiet night. He went to a table in the dark corner and ordered wine. A young man approached. Michele grinned. "You must be Giovanni?"

The youth smiled. "If you like."

He was nice looking, reminded Michele of Cecco with his luxuriant dark hair and wry smile, but he lacked something undefinable from the original… Cecco's unique… self. "Well, Giovan, under other circumstances, it would be pleasant to spend time with you." He watched the youth sashay away, surprised he turned down such an attractive offer but, since the conversation with Martha and returning to Naples, he only thought about Cecco… wishing he…

"Are you Michelangelo Merisi… Caravaggio?"

"Who wants to know?"

He glanced over his shoulder. Four figures loomed over him. The oldest came close and removed his wide brimmed hat. Even in the half-light, he recognised Rodomonte Roero. "I wanted to be absolutely sure…"

"Roero. You're far from home, old man."

"Remember your place and address me as Your Excellency Conte della Vezza."

"Conte or cunt?"

Roero smiled, sat and watched as his three bravos wearing part armour threw Michele to the ground and began beating, punching and kicking. He rolled into a foetal position which invited several vicious kicks to his back and anus. He twisted and glanced up. Roero toasted him with his own cup of wine and jerked his head to the youth who scuttled away, joining the half dozen who left at the first sign of trouble. The waiter stood stock still, his hand resting on a flagon of wine, mouth open as the beating intensified and continued unremittingly. Michele instinctively jammed his right hand into his left armpit to protect his painting hand and, as his body was jolted by punches and kicks, tried to focus his mind elsewhere.

Lucia turned in the doorway… Mamma… Mamma! She gathered him up in her arms and turned to show him poor Gesù bound to the column and beaten. Holy Mary Mother of God blessed art thou and blessed is the Fruit of thy womb, Jesus. Be with me now and at the hour of my death…

"I believe that's enough, gentlemen." Roero leaned close. "Are you in pain, my son? You have certainly lost a great deal of blood and bruises, red and blackening already. You will be a terrible sight in the morning, black and blue… if you live that long. I think this will be the lesson owed to you for many years and certainly a warning that you must never… ever, insult your betters." He downed the last of the wine, stood, replaced his hat and, as he drew on his gloves, paused. "I do hope I interrupted your evening of sodomy… after all, Brother de Redin was proved right." He gestured to his henchmen to leave but held the third back and stooped over Michele. "It occurs to me, Master Caravaggio, that you might survive, your wounds might heal in time, perhaps it will take a long time but heal they might. If that were to be the case, I believe it is my duty to ensure a permanent reminder to you and the entire world of tonight's lesson." He drew his dagger and handed it to the third man.

His Excellency Francesco Maria II Duke of Urbino
To His Most Reverend Eminence Cardinal Francesco del Monte.
Cecco, my dearest friend and companion of our boyhood, it is with deepest regret I write to inform you the Papal legate advises me the painter Master Michele Caravaggio is dead. I am aware that Michele was a protégé of yours and dare I say, from all accounts, a friend. I am sure it will not offend you if I say that he was a volatile character but his paintings are beyond compare…

The deep wound from the searing gash to his face was infected, his face swelled and it was necessary to repeatedly apply poultices once the worst of the pus was squeezed from the gash. Between bouts of lost consciousness, he heard an older brother suggest applying maggots to clean the wound. His eyes were so swollen he could hardly open them. His face was criss-crossed with bandages, so was his chest and, as he emerged from the dark, blinding light and pain hit like a bolt of lightning. The slightest movement was acutely painful and, even lying as still as possible, there was pain. His face burned and, when he raised his hand to touch it, the monk caught his wrist. "You are much scarred, my son. It will take some time to heal."

"Where?" His lip cracked. He touched his lower lip which stung and tasted of blood. "Where am I?"

"The Ospedale degli Incurabili. You might have died. You're lucky to be alive. You were attacked… as you passed a rather disreputable tavern." Weakened by the infection, he became delirious as the sweating sickness returned.

Mamma! Mamma! She turned at the door and smiled as he ran across the field towards her. The beautiful Lucia smiled as he leapt into her arms. She kissed his forehead. Mamma! Perhaps he was too heavy now; she let him slip slowly and kissed the top of his head. She led him into the farmhouse, a cavernous dark room with a sooty arched fireplace, the big table covered with a rich patterned rug, white tablecloth and laden with fruit and a flagon of blood red wine. The tabletop was at his eye level and he stared at the vine leaves, green, gold and red, curling slightly, holed and powdered by blight. It had been a good crop this year, or so Papa said. His father was not in the room nor his uncle who had priestly duties to attend. Papa must be supervising the building of another house... another grand residence. His brother Battista was not around either, but he preferred being alone with Mamma, enjoying her sole attention, her caresses and smiles. The way she popped olives into his mouth and laughed when he chewed and gaped to show the mush on his tongue... You are a vile creature, Michele... He swung around. A dark silhouette, a man in black stood just inside the doorway. Mamma!

Chapter 41

Fallen Christ

"You have grown since we last met." He stroked my chin. "A nice little beard I see. How old are you now, Cecco?"

"Twenty-two, Eminence. Almost twenty-three."

"My word, twenty-two. Michele wasn't much older than you are now when he painted the Bacchus. But to business, in your letter you said you have painted commissions." I nodded. "Your work must have merit." He smiled. "With Michele as your model, that's not surprising. Tell me what you have painted and who tutored you before Michele."

"My father was a painter. He taught me to draw and paint but it was in Michele's workshop I learned everything I know, but he saw nothing I painted before... Malta." After a brief silence, the cardinal touched my hand encouraging me to continue. "It was only after Michele went to Malta I received a couple of commissions."

"I notice you style yourself del Caravaggio, did you or your family know Michele... might you be related?"

"No, Eminence, I am not another long-lost kin... I knew of the Merisi and came to Rome to find Michele, hoping to be an assistant, perhaps even an apprentice, although I had no money to pay him but he took me in."

"And you were his Cupid."

I laughed. "A few angels, here and in Naples."

"He painted you as quite a rascal... eat up, my dear. Try the cake with preserved fruit and almonds, quite delicious." He smiled. "But, again, we are forgetting the reason we asked you to come. Have you brought some of your paintings as I asked?"

"Yes, Eminence, my assistant has some pictures; I believe he's in the corridor."

"Bring him in, let's see." Alessio and I unrolled the paintings and flattened them; the three smaller paintings lay on top of the Sebastian.

The cardinal stood and gazed intently from the altarpiece to the portrait of Eliza, Man with a Rabbit and the latest Instrument Maker. "But, Cecco..."

He paused to examine the paintings in detail. "I am carried back to when I first saw Michele's early paintings." He bent to look close at each painting in turn. "Who commissioned the Saint Sebastian?"

"It was originally Christ at the Column but was rejected. I altered it to a Saint Sebastian. It was arranged soon after I met the Lady Costanza Colonna who was truly kind to me."

"As she is to all."

The cardinal bought the painting of Faunus singing to the rhythm of a tambourine, but I was horrified it might hang within sight of Michele's but relieved His Eminence mentioned it was a gift for a dear friend. Alessio was even more delighted than me. "But you don't seem at all happy."

"I am, truly, but seeing Michele's painting again…"

"You miss him."

We tacked the canvas to the stretcher and delivered the painting to the framer Michele used in the past. On the delivery day, the framed painting arrived, I drew off the cloth and Andrea Rufetti stepped forward to carefully examine the painting. "I'm impressed, Cecco… wonderful."

One of the framer's men said, "You could pick up that viol and play it."

I smiled. "Except it isn't strung." The man gathered up the cloth, I paid the balance due and they left with appreciative backward glances.

Andrea again looked closely at the painting. "You have real talent, Cecco."

Andrea waited until the framers left before suggesting Cecco sit. "Actually, I came to say there's news of Michele."

It was a while before I dare speak. So long as I didn't ask, nothing had happened. Eventually, I mumbled, "I take it… not good news?"

"He has been wounded."

"Another fight?"

"So far as I know, it was an ambush… in a tavern."

I slumped into a chair. "The Cerriglio?"

"I don't know the name of the tavern." Of course, Andrea would never have heard of such a dive but Michele knew it well and was the likeliest rat hole he would go for a cheap knee-trembler. I was quickly over the shock and soon reduced to cynicism. "How bad is it?"

"The beating was serious, but it is the cut to the face that caused concern."

"A vendetta wound." Andrea shrugged. "Where is he?"

"At the Colonna villa."

"I'll go to Naples…"

Andrea gripped my arm. "He's well cared for and will recover in time; there's no need for you to go."

"Is that what you were told?"

Andrea's hesitation was the answer. "There's little you can do, Cecco. Colonna doctors attend him. He's in the best place and you can do more for him by looking after his interests here until he's well enough to return when he's pardoned by His Holiness." I recognised Michele's and my interests were best served by my continued dependability and loyalty, so I merely nodded. Andrea squeezed my shoulder. "You will not be forgotten."

When Alessio and I were alone, I dropped the pretence. "Not forgotten, my arse. I could kill Michele with my bare hands. If the Colonna hadn't persuaded him to go to Malta, he would probably have been pardoned by now and back here a year or more."

"It must have been more trouble from Neapolitan painters…"

"No, Lessio, it wasn't Neapolitans; it wasn't a grudge by a few pissed off painters; it was the Knights. They cut his face, the mark of Cain. It was vendetta."

Alessio received the commission for *Christ's Fall on the way to Calvary* in the proportions twelve by seventeen palmi for one hundred ducati to be completed for Lent 1611. He forgot the patron's name but fortunately details were written down although the scribbled signature was indecipherable and might have been the agent's name. Alessio was not sure if it was an altarpiece for a chapel or chamber for private contemplation. I shrugged. "I'm sure whoever it is will be back after leaving a five scudo deposit."

On balance, I thought it was more likely the cardinal's recommendation; otherwise, Andrea would more likely have approached me. I began with small studies to explore the composition and rather than the traditional calm expression of resignation, I would show Christ in distress to draw sympathy. Although under life size, it was an opportunity to work with full length figures for the first time and to show what I could do. In the following weeks, I found models and made detailed drawings. Longinus the centurion was based on the drawing of Alessio's brother made in Naples, seen from the back wearing armour and a red hat with feathers. To his left, I also reused drawings of the bald man in studies for Christ at the column and Alessio posed for other figures, the fallen Christ – the two malefactors on their way to their deaths. I made drawings in the taverns for Simon of

Cyrene and a rapid sketch of a waitress I noticed folding a cloth for my Veronica.

The cartoon was almost ready for transfer to the canvas by the end of May. About the same time, Andrea advised me Michele was recovered but remained weak and a pardon was thought imminent. We heard the Gonzaga were publicly supporting Michele's case, but I guessed they were acting as proxy for del Monte. Despite his supposed weakened condition, I was surprised to hear Michele was working on two commissions he intended to finish in June. Andrea suggested that was when he would need my assistance to bring him back to Rome. "But remember, Cecco, the pardon is not yet in our hands and, until it is, his head is still on the block."

Older people said they had never known such a heatwave in their lifetimes. Intolerable heat lasted months with no sign of respite. Many joked Hell would be cooler, but I was in high spirits despite general anxiety as Alessio and I rode slowly south. We wore wide brimmed hats and linen scarves to protect our necks and set out for Naples early in the morning on the tenth of July when there was some relief in the pre-dawn hours but, well before midday, we were forced to shelter at a tavern, the horses watered and tethered in the shade of the building. We slumbered at the table and only set off again about five in the afternoon, arriving at an osteria late evening where we had supper. We spent the night under the eaves of the airless hot roof. We lay naked, under wet cloths, sleepless and sweating until the sky turned pearl when we set off early at walking pace. The pattern was repeated almost a week until we reached Naples where at least there was a light sea breeze to stir and freshen the stifling air and tall buildings offered shade from the burning sun. Returning to Naples, I was anxious as much as excited by the prospect of seeing Michele again. It was difficult to imagine his reaction and I was increasingly anxious as we approached the Colonna residence at Chiaia. I trembled with anticipation when I waved to the guard at the gate. "I'm Francesco Boneri. I've come to help Master Michele organise matters for his departure for Rome."

"But, Master Boneri, Caravaggio is gone. He left by boat."

"For Rome?"

"Let me speak to Don Antonio."

Antonio came to the gate a little out of breath. "Cecco, Master Caravaggio left for Rome. Go to the harbour, you may be in time… the felucca, Santa Maria di Porto Salvo, go, go!"

We galloped to the harbour and arrived drenched in sweat. Alessio held the horses as I ran along the moored boats, asking for the Santa Maria di Porto Salvo. Someone pointed beyond the bay. She had reached open sea and, although sailing slowly with little wind in her sails, the distance was too far to be caught by rowing boat. I considered hiring a small light felucca to catch up with the Santa Maria but money was running low and almost all my and Michele's funds were hidden in Andrea's house in Rome. I ran back to Alessio. "We have to get back to Rome."

Chapter 42

Scipione Borghese

1607

H-AS-OS The Cardinal Nephew stepped close to the painting to decode the inscription on the sword blade – *Humilitas Occidit Superbiam*. He smiled, then returned to his chair to contemplate the picture delivered by courier earlier that day. It had been difficult not to cancel appointments and duties, itching to return to his private chamber where servants unpacked the painting Michele had sent. He dined with Stefano who was disappointed when Scipione retired alone to his chamber to examine the Caravaggio. At first sight, he shivered with delight and smiled. "You send me your head, rascal, in exchange for keeping your own."

He laughed and refilled his glass. *You see it all, Michele. Everything inverted, as in a looking glass, the weak overcomes the strong, the lover kills the beloved, humility kills pride. Am I too literal? Uncle Camillo assumes I am. Perhaps we should think of the painting in terms of reflection, a double self-portrait perhaps, the younger ruffian in crime, your crimes, returns to destroy the older Michele. Your reputation for lawlessness... I never saw that side of you, but you were never two-faced.*

He paced the room, topped up his glass and again stood close to the painting and peered even closer at the severed head. "It is certainly you to the life, Michele."

He smiled and peered closer. *There is still life in the face; streams of hot blood pour down, life ebbing, vision fading from the eyes. I see the imprint of the stone that brought you down, the sword that finished you off, the boy grips the handle as though holding his stiff cock, the blade aimed at his groin. I see your gasping, gaping mouth, blood in the mouth, nose and eyes, gurgling blood choking howling horror...* The cardinal reeled away from the painting and sat heavily, slopping wine. He wiped the foot of the glass on his sleeve and filled it again almost to the rim.

He toasted the picture. "I know what you're saying. Michele, you rogue. You desperately want forgiveness, a pardon to return to Rome." *To return home, to friends and lovers and this mirror image, your gaping mouth offers reward in kind, not just the painting. I know, of course, and remember your gasps and moans when on my knees...*

Standing again, close to the painting, he squinted at the face of David. "That's not really you, Michele." *It's that pretty boy, the one who posed for Vincenzo's Cupid. I remember him, one of your boys, Michele. Ah! My Saint John the Baptist, he was at the reveal when Vincenzo arranged that ridiculous theatrical charade, the green cloth swished away. The boy stood in the shadows, but I noticed him. Michele spoke your name... was it Cherubino? Peachy buttocks. I wonder if he's still in Rome, and available?* He unbuttoned his soutane and pulled down his breeches and grasped his erection but was distracted by a piece of paper just visible under the painting. He drew up his breeches and shuffled across the room to pick up the paper. It was addressed to His Holiness. He broke the seal.

I send you this painting, Holiness. It is I as I am now. You can see here the pain and anguish for my crime for which I desperately repent. That which I committed has destroyed me, and you can see it in my face, Holy Father. If it is your wish to save me, please pardon me; otherwise, I will be like this head, suspended in darkness. In this painting, I send you the head of Caravaggio who offers Your Holiness his life.

The cardinal smashed the glass on the floor, hesitated a moment, then folded the letter and slipped it in his pocket, turned from the painting and grimaced. He thought a moment, then drew the note from his pocket, held it over a candle flame until it caught light and shrivelled to wafer thin ash which he dropped an instant before burning his fingers.

1610

Scipione bowed to His Holiness, stepped close to his chair, genuflected and kissed hands, then lips. The Pope touched the cardinal's face, then dismissed all attendants and gestured Scipione to walk with him. They left the papal apartments and stepped into the blinding light of the formal garden. Gardeners bowed and scattered leaving the pope and Cardinal Nephew alone. The still heat was almost unbearable so they crossed to the shade of the trees. "This is about Caravaggio."

"Yes, the petition for clemency."

"Gonzaga raised the matter with me several times, prompted by the Colonna I suspect."

"In turn prompted by del Monte no doubt, but I too urge you to consider, Uncle."

"But not pressed as vigorously as the others and more diplomatically." The pope walked several paces in silence, then said, "Michele Caravaggio is a problem. A great painter, no doubt, but how close he sails to the wind with his interpretations of holy images, indecorous to say the least and what a terrible reputation."

"Without doubt his past is a dreadful catalogue of petty crimes and the Tomassoni killing... A family we must remember, not unknown to criminality, but I believe Merisi is chastened and his character reformed."

"Not so chastened, Scipione, if reports from Malta are to be believed. You realise certain knights petitioned me to refuse a pardon. Michele had his chance; I granted de Wignacourt permission for his entry to the order and how was he repaid? He beat a fellow brother and provoked a riot."

"I hadn't heard that."

"Rodomonte Roero was seriously injured, and we have heard of further indiscretion in Sicily... something about a boy."

"My information suggests he's innocent."

"But he has a history of... let's say, interest in boys."

"Surely, Michele merely caters for the tastes of his patrons."

The pope stopped and turned smiling. "I believe *you* also collect his paintings and God forbid that was not the reason you had me ruin Cesari."

"My Caravaggios are all religious. Vincenzo Giustiniani has more of his paintings than me. Cesari had three, and I offered him a fair price to save him from bankruptcy, but he was stubborn. And del Monte! I find it hard to believe Caravaggio could make the images he does unless he shares his patrons' tastes, but there is the more serious matter... Holiness, he is the greatest living painter... his work, surely you must feel... you must recognise how his pictures move so many."

"I accept they do... but he causes as much offense as devotion. I am not unsensitive to his brilliance, Scipione, the way he touches the human heart and, although I believe he is sincere, his paintings pose dangerous questions. His work encourages the commons to believe they have direct access to Our Lady which might be considered a challenge to the unique dispensation and authority of Holy Mother Church."

"With respect, Uncle, I don't see his paintings that way. It is the subtlety of his genius, think of his interpretation of *Our Lady of Loreto*... I know you have seen it, an astonishing image of a peasant couple kneeling before Our

Blessed Lady and Child and an old woman and her son have knocked on the door and are granted a holy apparition."

"Are we to accept a comparison between the Madonna and Child with a peasant woman and her whelp? It might be considered a subtle insult to the status of Our Lady and Our Lord and, if such grace is offered, a vision granted to the lowest of the low, does that not blatantly undermine Holy Church, Peter's commission and that of his successors?"

"But, surely, everyone deserves hope?"

"Hope is one thing, Scipione, but only Holy Church guarantees hope of heaven." They continued walking. "The question is… what do we do about Caravaggio? My latest information from Sicily…"

"He's been back in Naples these past months. In hope of a pardon. If I may, Holiness, Michele's in terrible straits. He has been seriously wounded; it's a miracle he survived."

"The Tomassoni… the Knights?"

"It's not certain… would the Tomassoni have the reach? I'm not sure. More likely the Knights, and rumours suggest Michele named Roero."

"If Roero took matters into his own hands, that's vendetta and contrary to my ordinance." The pope strode from the garden towards his apartments. "The matter must be resolved. We cannot allow the man to suffer." When they reached his study, the pope stood in silence a long time, then touched his nephew's shoulder. "Let him know he should return to Rome and a pardon is imminent."

Stefano sprawled naked, face down on the bed as Scipione gently ran his hands over his well-toned back and small hard buttocks with golden down illuminated by the narrow shaft of light from the gap in the shutters. Bells rang and Scipione gently shook his companion. "Stefano, Stefano Caro… you must leave, servants will soon be about."

After a while he stirred, eyes half open, black hair tousled, rolled over and stretched. He yawned, his penis rigid. He swung his legs over the side of the bed and staggered as he went to piss in the night pot. Scipione watched fascinated by every movement, from the twitch and flex of the buttocks to the sound of the final ring of piss, the unselfconscious arrangement of his prick and balls when drawing on his small pants. He searched under the bed for his shirt with which he gradually concealed his exquisite body in contrast to the muscular thighs and buttocks enhanced by his white hose. "Caro, remember to send the letter to Michele Caravaggio, you remember the content?" Stefano nodded, then drew his fingers through his shiny blue-black hair. "It is quite urgent… so don't let it slip your mind… and sign for me."

Stefano nodded again. "I won't forget." He pulled up his breeches, buckled his shoes and put on his doublet. "Shall I see you tonight?"

"I'm dining with del Monte and Giustiniani. They're desperate to know Camillo's… His Holiness' decision but I should be home early; they're both devout, del Monte at least. Then I shall see my Caro." They embraced and Stefano slipped out the door. As he reached the stair to his rooms above, he heard a serving woman murmur to a page, "That's Signor Stefano Pignatelli… you have never seen him on this floor."

His Reverend Eminence Cardinal Nephew Scipione Borghese to Master Michelangelo Merisi da Caravaggio in Naples

His Eminence has instructed me to advise you that in response to His Eminence's petition on your behalf and assurance of your true penitence and contrition, His Holiness is graciously minded to grant pardon. His Eminence suggests you may return to Rome with that expectation.

His Eminence thanks you for your generous gift of the David and Goliath picture and looks forward to thanking you in person at the proper time.

S Pignatelli,
Secretary to His Eminence Cardinal Scipione Borghese

Chapter 43

To Porto Ercole July 1610

It was almost six months before he was able to work. The fever gradually subsided, leaving his face less swollen but grey. Once the bandages were removed, he couldn't bear to look at his reflection. The scar felt lumpen, sutures pulled the skin very tight, the flesh felt heavy and numb. His sight was blurred and one eyelid continually twitched. The first moment he looked at his scarred reflection, he shuddered. Stitches had bunched the lips of the scar so the skin either side of the wound was sore and creased. It was worse than expected. He went to lie down and gingerly ran fingers over the scar, the rippling sensation turned his stomach. He retched, leaned over the side of the bed and vomited. He wiped his mouth on the sheet, hands trembling as he rolled onto his back and stared at the ceiling. *I am one with the fraternity of the damaged, branded by birth or circumstance and from whom people turn away in disgust. I share the mark of Cain. What I am, whatever I am, my scars hereafter will be assumed to testify all that I am.*

His eyes unfocussed as he laid on paint, rubbed his eyes and squinted. The brushwork was less refined and, when he compared his colours with the St John, they appeared garish, the reds harsh and Ursula's flesh grey. He had in mind the *Taking of Christ* picture in which he used rich colour and like the Taking, put in a self-portrait as a ruffian on tiptoe, only the upper half of the face illuminated, a silent witness to the arrest. There was no one to ask what they thought of the colour and was bothered by the incongruity of the composition, with St Ursula in profile, clutching her breast in disbelief, the arrow sunk deep but the king of the Huns who fired the arrow was at right angles to the martyr. Whatever his concerns, he was surprised by the enthusiasm for the picture by Lanfranco Massa, Prince Doria's agent. "A great painting, Master Caravaggio, but when will I be able to tell my master the painting is finished?"

"It only needs varnishing." He wore a wide brim hat to ensure his face was in deep shadow as he handed over the painting and received payment. Rather than doff, he touched the brim of the hat in salute. Lanfranco took the painting with the varnish still wet and stood it in the sun to speed up the drying in order to send the painting to his master but the varnish crackled. He wrote to the prince, "It dried too quick in the sun, dear God, it is so hot, the temperature so far above normal but the good news is that Caravaggio says he can repair it."

Francesco del Monte to Michele Caravaggio.
My dear, you cannot imagine my distress when I had dreadful reports of your death. I was informed by my dear namesake Francesco – M della Revere – who received an avviso from the Papal legate; erroneously – DG. However, I was alarmed to hear the truth of the matter was an attack in the street. I am sure you took my caution whatever the insult to be slow to anger, in emulation of Our Saviour, turn the other cheek. I hear from Cardinal Borromeo and the Gonzaga – His Holiness is disposed in your favour. The Cardinal Nephew is somewhat evasive on the matter, but I imagine he is not at liberty to disclose confidential information to which he may be party. The prospect of your imminent return to Rome fills my heart with gladness and I look forward to receiving your embrace once again.
Bless you and may God be with you.
Francesco

12th July 1610

The captain, Alessandro Caramano, greeted him on the quay and ordered the hands to stow his possessions below. "Take special care with the three paintings."

He breathed the fresh air deeply and gazed up at the sky. *I thought this day would never come… the sea's calm, the sun's up, an auspicious start to the end of my journey.* There was so little wind the hands rowed the felucca Santa Maria di Porto Salvo, out of the port and, as they stood off the coast, the heavily patched sails sagged as the captain tacked north. Pink and yellow Naples stayed in view for hours and, by midday, the hands joined Michele and the captain under the awning on deck for respite from the burning sun. By evening, the sky and sea to the west was orange and lights glimmered in the violet haze on shore. Vesuvius was the only recognisable feature on land, its caved summit caught the last golden light of the sinking sun. The lamps were lit and the captain navigated by the stars. Even at midnight, it remained hot, and he was unable to sleep and volunteered to take turn on watch.

As the sky began to lighten, pearl grey and the horizon glowed pale yellow, the youngest hand came to sit next to him near the tiller. "It's my turn to relieve you, signor." He nodded. The last hour before sunrise was refreshingly cooler and the wind was up so the boat glided faster over the water. He glanced back for the last time to be sure the rudder was still securely lashed down to keep them on course. "The captain's awake. He'll trim our course if necessary."

"How long have you been at sea?"

"All my life. The captain's my uncle. Papa drowned when I was little. It was a freak storm, an act of God." He unwound a spool of twine, attached a wriggling worm for bait and cast it over the side. He smiled. "Breakfast."

"You say an act of God… do you believe God would take your father away from you and your mamma and brothers or sisters?"

"Yes, of course, if it's his will. People die every day and babies are born every day; some live long lives, some short. I had a baby sister; she died before she was a year old."

"But why?"

"We won't know until we meet God, and he shows us the pattern which is invisible to us now."

"Did the priests tell you this?"

"No, what do they know?" Michele laughed. "I hope I didn't offend you, signor."

"What's your name?"

"Pietro."

"You've not offended me, Master Pietro… but tell me, is it true sailors and fishermen never learn to swim?"

"Of course, why else would we save respect for the sea?"

"And you trust in God to keep you safe?"

"And the Lord Gesù and Our Lady." The lad crossed himself and Michele couldn't help copying.

"Pietro the fisherman; the fisher of men."

"Fisher of men!" Pietro stared a moment. "How did you come by that scar?"

He touched his forehead and traced the still tender lumps between his eyes and down his nose and cheek. "It was a gift, a reminder that acts have consequences… as you well know, Pietro… since you cannot swim."

14th July

He shouted through the bars. "Tell them I am Michele Merisi da Caravaggio, the painter."

"Calm down, signor, if it's mistaken identity, the matter will be quickly resolved."

"If you don't believe me… look at the paintings, unroll them and see. There's a painting of Salome with the head of the Baptist, a St John with a ram and a young St John drinking at a spring… Just look. D'you want me to paint your portrait? Gesù!"

"As soon as we hear from Rome…"

"Why Rome?"

"Because the warrant for the arrest was issued there… you fit the description of a wanted man. You say you're someone else. Well, if you were the suspect, we'd expect you to change your name, wouldn't we? Put yourself in our shoes."

"But if you think I fit the description of the man you want, how will they know I'm someone else?"

"Well, you said you're a painter, and I've gone through your possessions; there's paint on almost every item of clothing, and I found colours and brushes, so I'm convinced what you say is true, and I've appraised the prosecutor's office in Rome I'm satisfied you're not the man we're looking for."

"So why not let me go on my way?"

"I can't until authorised by Rome."

"How long will that be?"

"The courier should be back tomorrow… or the day after."

"The day after!" he shouted at the gaoler as he walked away from the cell. "Where are my possessions, the paintings, chests… my materials?"

"Safely stored, so you needn't fret."

16th July

"Scipione." The Pope offered his hand and the Cardinal Nephew kissed the Papal ring. "We heard Michele Caravaggio has landed at Palo and is under arrest."

"Arrested? Mistaken identity."

"When?"

"Yesterday. He will be released tomorrow… but will be kept under close surveillance… for his protection."

Seven a.m. 17th July

"You said my possessions were put ashore."

"I assumed they had but there's no point shouting and raving."

"You were responsible to take care of my things." He broke into a howl. Two port officials caught his arms. "Let me go… let me go, bastards."

"Calm down or you'll be arrested proper this time and then your things will be even further away and maybe lost for good."

He leaned forward, panting, too weak to resist the two men gripping his arms. "What d'you mean they'll be further away?"

"The captain said he was going north to Civitavecchia, that's only twenty-odd miles…"

"You knew they were my possessions, so why did you load them back on the boat?" The man merely shrugged. "Where can I hire a horse?"

Eleven thirty a.m. 17th July

"Let him approach, Stefano."

"The Cardinal Nephew will see you." The courier crossed to the cardinal's seat, genuflected and kissed his hand.

"You rode hard I see… covered in dust."

"Excuse my appearance, Eminence, but I was told to get the message to Rome and the gentleman we released rode north towards Civitavecchia."

"He's not on his way to Rome? Why?"

"The boat left with his paintings aboard."

"I see." He clenched and unclenched his fist. "But the paintings are on the boat for sure?"

"Yes, Eminence."

"No doubt the Port Master will advise the gentlemen from Rome of Master Caravaggio's intentions."

"I imagine so."

Unlike the golden candlelight in his paintings, the light was blinding white. Sparse trees wilted, only black poplars stood sentinel against the landscape scorched brown and dull orange-yellow. Even the slight breeze off the sea was hot, dry, airless and offered no respite from the merciless sun. Galloping from Palo, the horse slowed after a few miles and would go no faster than a canter no matter how hard he slapped its rump. He guessed he had covered less distance than hoped so dismounted to rest the horse and walked a few miles. His legs trembled and sweat trickled down his face, stinging the scar.

His took off his doublet, drenched in sweat and slung it over the saddle. The horse was skittish when he remounted and, even though he jabbed its flanks, it merely trotted a few paces until it stood stock still and, however hard he urged, it would go no faster than a jolting trot. After a couple of hours at walking pace, the horse's head hung low and Michele dozed and twice slid from the saddle. He guessed he was barely halfway so dismounted, cut a thin branch to make a whip. He struggled to sit upright and whipped the horse's rump hard to force it to move, jabbing with his heels and cutting its hide with the switch but it would go no faster than walk, the sting of the switch more tolerable than the heat. The light was fading by the time he reached the outskirts of Civitavecchia, the horse wobbled and its throat rasped as it coughed and limped towards the harbour. Arriving at the port, he sweated and shivered, the horse coughed and its mouth dripped foam. He dismounted and led the horse to the wharves where he found stables.

"Gesù, the creature's thraped… you've almost killed it."

"Never mind that. Did a boat come in from Palo sometime today?"

"You callous bastard… you left Palo…"

"What time?"

"Does it matter… afternoon, I suppose."

"You rode in this heat, no wonder the creature's…"

"If it means so much to you, you can have it."

There was no sight of the boat and the harbour master was nowhere to be found. At a tavern overlooking the wharves, he collapsed at a table, buried his head in his arms on the board littered with empty platters, goblets and spilled wine.

A waiter nudged him. "Food and drink?"

He didn't raise his head. "What d'you have?"

"Fish, pasta, squid, olives, bread… local wine… the usual."

"Has the Santa Maria di Porto Salvo arrived? The master is about forty… Alessandro Caramano and his nephew… Pietro, he's about sixteen with a couple of other hands."

"That's the one. Yeah, the youngster, Pietro, they come here often. I remember him when he was just a boy."

Michele sat up. "She's here?"

"Sailed about an hour ago."

He banged his head on the table. "Shit! D'you know where they're headed."

"Livorno, I guess… then Genoa, but I heard one of them mention they were pulling in at Porto Ercole."

"How far?"

"About thirty-odd miles, I should say."

Morning 18th July

"Signor… Signor!" His head lolled at a crazy angle.

The innkeeper loomed above him. "What time is it?"

"Ten o'clock."

"Gesù. I slept the whole night here." He slowly uncoiled his aching body and muscles cracked as he stood. "I should have been away by now."

"We tried to waken you last night and this morning. You're exhausted. You should stay and rest properly. You asked for a room but fell asleep in the corner here. We couldn't rouse you so decided to leave you to sleep."

"I have to get to Porto Ercole."

"You're unwell."

"It's just the heat."

"I think it's fever, signor. You should be careful." He paid for the unused room and uneaten food and a large gratuity to the innkeeper. His shirt was stiffened by dry sweat as he staggered to the door. The sun blazed and burned. He slung his doublet over one shoulder, saddle bag over the other and made his way to the stables. "Where's my horse?"

"You can't have him; you rode him to death yesterday… see…" He led him to a stall. The horse lay still on the ground and, as it looked up at him, the white of its eye gave the impression of terror.

"It'll live, you can have it. I'll pay for another."

"Not from this stable, piss off."

"I have to get to Porto Ercole."

"Then walk. You won't have any of these creatures."

"It's my horse…"

The ostler threw coins at him. "Go."

It was half an hour before he bought a mount from another stable, the price was outrageous, but there was no time to haggle. As he mounted up, the ostler said, "Surely, thar's not riding in this heat?"

As he left the outskirts of Civitavecchia, he noticed four men arriving from the east; without doubt, they were following him. Why else was he detained two days at Palo? He stood the horse in the shade of a stand of poplar trees to be sure he was not seen and, when they moved towards the port, he whipped his fresh mount to a gallop and set off north. He estimated he should be at Porto Ercole by early afternoon if he kept up a decent pace but the horse, like the other, was not capable of a sustained canter, never mind gallop in the intense heat. He had to let the horse amble at walking pace. Eventually, he dismounted and leaned against the horse's wet flank as he led it the next mile or so. The horse reared when he mounted so dug in his heels to force it to canter but, after just a few hundred yards, it slowed to a walk and would go no faster. He slumped forward onto the horse's neck and lost consciousness for seconds, maybe minutes. The horse stood shivering. He grimaced. *If only you were Pegasus.*

He slipped from the saddle onto the strand which arced westward towards the town. He lay helpless on his back from where he watched the Santa Maria slip out of Porto Ercole harbour to the open sea and slowly disappear beyond the isthmus. Gasping for breath, he stared up at the bleached sky, the pitiless sun scorched his face and burned the scar. His head pounded, he heard blood surging through the veins in his neck and temple and his skull felt as though it had shrunk and crushed his brain. He turned his head to the sea and the hump of land beyond the port… *the boat's gone… It's gone…*

Chapter 44
Camillo Borghese: Pope Paul V

His Excellency Francesco Maria II Duke of Urbino To His Most Reverend Eminence Cardinal Francesco del Monte

28th July AD 1610

Cecco, my dear,

You must be prepared to pray Our Lady will sustain you. With great sadness, this time it is true the painter Michele da Caravaggio is dead. The Papal legate wrote to me that the avviso was not issued until the facts were fully established. I believe the Knights of Malta petitioned the Pope not to pardon Caravaggio. Poor Borromeo and Gonzaga were led to believe a genuine pardon was imminent which, in my opinion, was a ruse. Scipione has ridden two horses as a pretend friend to Michele, desperate to get his hands on every painting. You recall the Cesari affair and I expect he's after paintings Michele brought with him from Naples. With Caravaggio out of the way, there's nothing to stop him acquiring them. In passing, I'm not sure I trust the Papal legate here in Urbino, as you know, the ultimate objective to bring us under Papal jurisdiction. Be careful in your dealings with Scipione, Cecco, and entre nous, my dearest friend, with our interests at heart, I trust you will destroy all correspondence on the matter.

I remain your friend,

Francesco

His Excellency Francesco Maria II Duke of Urbino To His Most Reverend Eminence Cardinal Francesco Maria Bourbon del Monte

31st July AD 1610

My dear Cecco,

I received a further avviso from the Legate to confirm Michele Caravaggio died on or about the 18[h] July at Porto Ercole on the beach but transferred to the Conzolatione hospice in the town. Because of the extreme heat, the body was quickly interred in sacred ground somewhere in or near

Porto Ercole. A local priest confirmed that, apart from the evidence of extreme physical exhaustion, he probably died of the sweating sickness or heat stroke. Otherwise, the corpse suffered several ancient wounds with a visible recent wound to the face but was not the cause of death. From investigations by my agents, it appears the Knights of Malta were in the vicinity. I understand the felucca returned Caravaggio's paintings to Naples where they were lodged at the Sforza-Colonna residence at Chiaia. However, the Knights entered the residence and seized three paintings, claiming Caravaggio was a member of their order and, thus, the pictures belonged to them. However, I understand the Spanish authorities have intervened and took the three pictures into their custody in the name of the viceroy. You may know better than I, but, from reports, the Curia claims a pardon was granted and Michele is considered a true son of Holy Church.

Cecco, I hope this goes some way to clarify some of the facts and that you find some solace in it.

The exact wording of the Avviso I received today reads: Michelangelo Caravaggio, the famous painter, died at Port' Ercole, while he was on the way from Naples to Rome because a pardon had been granted him by His Holiness from the sentence of banishment which he was under for a capital crime.

May Our Good Lady Bless him and you
Francesco

Cardinal Francesco Maria del Monte To His Excellency Francesco Maria II Duke of Urbino
IV.VIII.MDCX

My dear Francesco, your letter calmed some of the more dreadful imaginings that haunted my imagination. I began to compose a reply to your earlier communication but, with so many dreads and unanswered questions, I found it too difficult to put into words. Since leaving my household, I have prayed incessantly that Our Lord Christ and the Holy Mother keep Michele under their protection. Despite his waywardness, many times he called on my protection when he crossed the boundaries of the law. I genuinely believe he was an honest soul as his incomparable paintings attest – whether sacred or profane. Some might find such a statement from a priest curious but, as we learned as boys, in Platonic terms, truth is beauty and therefore beauty must be truth and Michele had that capacity to find beauty even in the corrupt – as you will have seen in my inconsequential gift of his Basket of

Fruit. The perfection of God's fruitful creation corrupted by original sin yet under the acute eye of a lesser yet worthy sub-creator, corruption honestly and truthfully rendered becomes beautiful and a worthy offering to the Almighty. Are we not all broken imperfect creatures? That Michele was laid to eternal rest in hallowed ground came as grateful relief and though his final suffering was from natural causes, there was ever the dread he might meet an unnatural, violent end. He was recovering from malarial sickness when he first entered my household which recurred several times, so it is no surprise he died of fever. The presence of the Knights of Malta was cause for alarm but if, as you suggest, their intention was to take the paintings, I am thankful the viceroy's agents recovered his effects. If you have any idea what the subjects of the paintings are, I would be grateful to learn, in strict confidence of course.

You are always in my thoughts and Our Lord's Blessing and mine upon you, my dear friend.

Francesco.

19ᵗʰ August 1610

To the judge of Military Affairs in the Garrisons of Tuscany.

Honoured Signor, I have been informed that the painter Michelangelo di Caravaggio has died at Port' Ercole and that you have in your possession all his property, especially the items in the inventory which accompanies this letter, the property having been taken over as a spolium under the pretext that the deceased was a member of the Order of St John and that it belonged to the Prior of Capua who has declared that he has no right to this spolium inasmuch as the deceased was not a Knight of Malta; and thus I charge as soon as you receive this letter, you send me the aforesaid property by the first felucca available and especially the painting of St John the Baptist, and, if by chance, it has been disposed of or removed from the property for whatever reason, you shall endeavour by all means to see that it is found and recovered in order to send it well packed with the other property and deliver it here to the proper authority, and you shall carry this out unconditionally, informing me of the receipt of this letter.

From my desk in Naples

Under the seal of Viceroy Don Pedro Fernandez de Castro Seventh Conde de Lemos

Vatican, August 1610

"Scipione, there is nothing more to be said, the viceroy has the paintings and that ends the matter."

"But, Holiness…"

"Enough." The Pope rose from his chair and gestured the Papal Nephew to follow him to his private chamber. "Was he murdered?"

"Not so far as I can ascertain. The knights were nearby. They had no need to kill a dying man. The viceroy's seizure of the paintings makes it obvious the knights took the pictures."

The Pope stood before the window. "Too many were after his pictures. We are troubled by this affair. I am in two minds. Were our instructions too ambiguous? Were we perhaps jealous of our reputation and determined to enforce strict discipline when evidence was unclear?"

"I don't follow, Uncle."

"Motives, Scipione. What did we intend? Was I too quick to condemn before knowing the facts of the Tomassoni matter? We know you were desperate to have the paintings but what were our true intentions? What about the man, did we abandon him?" He crossed the room to his prie-dieu set before a large crucifix. "He was a nuisance without doubt but his paintings, are they not…visions from God?"

"But many are profane, Holiness."

"Indeed, and there was vulgarity in many of his sacred works… but beyond that, whatever the subject, did he not always raise moral matters and the challenge to see beyond the profane to what is sacred?"

"I've never known you so pious, Uncle." He smiled but the Pope remained distracted.

"Perhaps we misjudged the man."

"Come, Holiness, he was a criminal after all."

"That was not your position when you pressed for a pardon." He tapped his finger on the table. "In the grand scheme of things were his crimes so great? His actions now seem petty."

"But the Tomassoni murder…"

"Murder? Murder is doubtful, more than doubtful. I saw the record and, reading between the lines, I believe Tomassoni had murder in his heart but Michele, from what I have read never stabbed anyone, always the flat of his sword, not defensible, of course, but up against the Tomassoni brothers he was out of his depth." He scratched his forehead. "The painting he sent to you, *David with the Head of Goliath*… he painted his own features for

Goliath. If I remember, the wound from the stone is visible? The mark of Cain."

"What?"

"Don't you see, Scipione? It is a confession. He killed not just Tomassoni in a literal sense but metaphorically his true brother of flesh and blood by denying him. It was the talk of Rome and del Monte was mortified. The painting speaks of remorse."

"And Roero?"

"He beat Roero… savagely. We don't know the circumstances; De Wignacourt was vague in his report and Roero took his revenge in Naples, a premeditated vendetta extracted in cold blood and still he went after the paintings."

"And the boy in Palermo?"

"Hearsay and gossip probably put about by Roero." He clasped his hands, raised them to his lips and paced the room. "How clearly I see matters now." Returning to Scipione, he touched his arm. "Have the Triple Crown, my cope and crozier brought to me."

In the fading light, he dismissed attendants. "Stay, Scipione, we need you as witness." When robed and crowned and candles were lit, he turned to the crucifix and knelt at the prie-dieu: *In nomine Patris et Filli et Spiritus Sancti.* He stood, took the crozier from Scipione in his left hand and raised his right hand in the Trinitarian blessing: *Ut successor Sanctus Petrus, Dominus noster Gesù Christus de omnibus peccatis absolvimus Michaeli Merisius da Caravaggio. Amen.*

Scipione crossed himself and stood. The Pope handed back the crozier. "Uncle, you have absolved him of every sin." The Pope removed the Triple Crown and set it on a table. "We have merely dipped our finger in a drop of water in the hope perhaps he might finally find peace."

Chapter 45

The Cardinal

I ran along the façade of the Palazzo Madama and darted into the building before the guards could stop me. I took the stairs two at a time to the piano nobile calling, "Eminence… Eminence!" I heard the guards behind as I reached the top of the stairs. "Eminence!" I ran along the corridor, looking left and right, servants flinched and parted as I darted past.

A priest emerged from one of the rooms, his arms outstretched to catch me. "I must see His Eminence." I was grabbed from behind and dragged backwards. "Eminence! Please, let me see him…"

A thick leather gloved hand covered my mouth, my voice strangulated as I screamed, "Eminence!" I struggled but was lifted shoulder height and carried towards the stairs by four hefty men. "Please put the young man down." It was the gentle voice I knew and strained my neck to see the upside-down cardinal walking towards me along a carpeted ceiling. The guards lowered me to the floor and bowed. As he approached, I knelt and touched my forehead to the back of the cardinal's hand. I felt my hair ruffled and the cardinal turned over his hand, caught me gently under the chin and lifted my head. With his thumb, he wiped tears from my cheek.

He glanced up and nodded to the guards. "Thank you, gentlemen, you have done your duty well."

Once they were gone, the cardinal gestured to me to rise, put his arm around my shoulder and led me along the corridor and touched his finger to his lips when the priest stepped forward. "Everything is as it should be, Father." In his private salon, the cardinal stood a moment for me to become accustomed once again to the surroundings. Beyond him, I saw the open door to the private chapel, then turned my gaze on a painting in the anteroom of a youth playing a lute. I had not seen the picture before but knew it was by Michele.

"An early painting by our dear friend. The subject is a great castrato Pietro Montoya. Take your time, Cecco… enjoy such an exquisite image, made real by our friend." Simply looking at the painting cast an atmosphere of calm as the cardinal no doubt intended. I wondered if I really heard musicians singing to the sound of a lute as they did when Michele and I lived in the rooms far above, or whether the sound emanated from the painting. It was impossible to be sure. The cardinal spoke, but I did not catch what he said. I turned to face him and noticed the wrinkles around his eyes were deeper and, perhaps, he was a little fuller in the face but as slim a figure as ever, and I guessed his soutane was one of those I remembered in the past with shiny elbows and worn cuffs.

"I'm sorry, Eminence..."

"You have grown into a handsome young man, Cecco." He smiled. "That cheeky Cupid." We fell silent. Eventually, he said, "Please sit." I waited for him to sit first. "Of course, I know why you came and why you're distressed."

"Is it true?"

He leaned forward and gripped my hand. "It is, my son."

I jammed my free hand between my thighs and leaned forward in short jolts as I sobbed, mouth gaping. It was a while before I brought myself under control and the cardinal handed me a kerchief. His image was blurred as I glanced up. "Do you know how?"

"I have seen several reports... Be calm. I understand he died of natural causes, probably heat stroke. His health deteriorated since the horrible attack in Naples and suspect he was only partially recovered... and, apparently, he was ill well before that."

"Then it wasn't the Tomassoni, thanks be to God."

"I doubt they knew he had returned."

"He was in Rome?"

"No, he landed on the coast to the north and died at Porto Ercole." I slumped in the chair and covered my face. The cardinal leaned towards me and squeezed my arm. "Poor boy, you must have suffered agonies not knowing whether he was alive or in the arms of the Almighty. Be sure he was always in my prayers and intercessions and always will and we must believe that core of goodness we see in his wonderful paintings, think of the *Madonna of the Pilgrims*... that they outweigh his transgressions."

"Even Ranuccio?"

"I believe murder was not in his heart and the Papal pardon exonerates him." It was a while before I was able to wipe my eyes and glance up at the cardinal who tapped my shoulder. "Let us pray a moment." He led me into his private chapel and we knelt side by side before the tiny altar with an ancient crucifix and unlit candles.

"We pray in the name of the Father, Son and Holy Spirit and to the Holy Virgin to intercede with her Blessed Son to look kindly on the soul of our dear departed son, Michele Caravaggio. Also bless our brother Francesco here, both of us in our time of grief." I tried to rise but he gently pressed down my shoulders to keep me on my knees and made the sign of the cross on my forehead. "Bless you, my dear Cecco."

In mid-September, the heatwave finally broke with a succession of thunderstorms that drove Alessio to my bed. He was highly superstitious, afraid of thunder and lightning and covered the mirror with a cloth. The first storms merely increased humidity but eventually the sky cleared and, although the sun dominated again, it was pleasantly warm and the air was fresh. It was three weeks since I trespassed on the cardinal's kindness to hear the news confirming Michele's death. The cardinal said Michele was buried at Porto Ercole in an unmarked grave but decided not to torment myself further weeping over bare earth. Although I confessed my anger with Michele to the cardinal and had been absolved, nevertheless, guilt remained. Words would never wash away regret and my confession was not entirely sincere since I harboured a further grudge that Michele once again and finally left without a word. Alessio was kind and understanding, saying, in time, I would remember better times. "After all you were amato of the greatest painter in the world. No one will forget that."

"I doubt that. I will be forgotten, but not Michele... he casts a long shadow."

I lived in a world seen from behind the weave and weft of raw canvas, perhaps the hanging hovering before myself as Cupid and imagined taking a sharp blade to slash the fabric top to bottom to escape the unreality in which I lived day to day. I strode aimless miles along streets, alleys and crossed piazzas, barely aware of where I was and without destination. Loud muttering and screeching but no one took notice because the jabbering and screaming was in my head. I stood rigid. People pushed past me, turning to see why I didn't move, some scowled but others laughed. Someone touched my shoulder.

"Cecco..." Alessio must have followed and gently guided me home where several days and nights I lay abed, Alessio beside me as I relived the years with Michele, especially the special time at Zagarolo. I laughed and cried and raged and swore, dwelling hours on the day Michele killed Ranuccio and the first weeks we spent in Zagarolo, repeated time and again, adding further detail as further memories resurfaced. Alessio simply listened as the dam burst and the monologue only paused when I needed to piss or when Alessio prepared food which I barely touched. I couldn't paint when crushed by thoughts of Michele's body rendered to dust and bone seeping fat into the dirt – the same materials with which he no longer breathed life into Christs and Madonnas. Standing before the prepared canvas, I was reduced to inactivity, facing the impossibility of turning paint into flesh and blood the way Michele had with such apparent ease. More than that, the crazy thought he might rise like Lazarus since there were no eye witness accounts of his death, supposedly alone on a beach near a small port town I never heard of. I had a mad idea his ghost might return to torment me for my continual anger. It was an insane superstition that made us sleep in the presence of Lena's corpse to hold her in the present world to prevent her haunting us from another, even though he was innocent of her murder and me his death.

With Alessio's help, I pushed the large bed into the workshop and, without comment, he resumed sleeping with me for companionship, understanding my unspoken dreads. I could only work in short bursts before nagging voices shrieked *not good enough* and mocked whatever I attempted to do. The fallen Christ became my sole preoccupation as finally, thankfully, the heatwave broke, thunder and drenching rain brought further anguish remembering the night Michele rescued me from the pimp under the weight of his sodden sagging cloak.

In time, I noticed I was best able to paint when Alessio chatted to me or silence was broken by passers-by gossiping outside the window or a neighbour singing as she swept that part of the street before her door. Eventually, I paid a young lad called Maurizio to sing songs of unrequited love, accompanying himself on a lute. He and Alessio often sang in unison and Lessio taught Maurizio the Neapolitan songs he learned as a boy. By paying attention to the singing and tunelessly humming along, I found solace by drowning out the chaos of memories, regrets and guilt and, in time, thoughts about the Fallen Christ coalesced.

Alessio posed for the head of Christ, but I added something of my own features and eventually modelled through the looking glass. I recalled during the last days of Lent when I was a boy, the priest encouraged contemplation of the suffering of Christ and the Holy Mother in the depths of despair at the foot of the cross, and we were to remember that every sin we committed added to Our Lord's agony as he paid our debt. Modelling Christ, I hoped the painting might bear the weight of my grief and loss, as Veronica's cloth was imprinted with the bloodied face of Gesù. The head was my sole preoccupation for days as I struggled to make the paint carry layers of grief, exhaustion and pain in a single expression. Rather than finished, the head was simply abandoned and I turned my attention to the hands, the fingers gripping the timber of the cross. The entwined fingers were a memory of the hands of Christ in Michele's Gethsemane painting but I could not come near the elegant fingers he painted, entwined in resignation. By contrast, the hands I painted were thick, sausage-like and ungainly. I threw down the brush and slumped in the chair opposite the painting. I groaned and covered my eyes. Alessio came to kneel beside me. I wailed. "Look… ugly… ugly. I'll have to scrape them out and start again."

"But why?"

"They're fat… ungainly."

Alessio went to the painting and stared at the hands a while. "Wasn't Gesù a carpenter most of his life?"

"What do you mean?"

"I doubt he'd have the hands of a cardinal. He worked all hours summer and winter, cuts, scars and blisters. Surely you don't want to paint like Baglione or his like. Gesù was a journeyman, making a living like the rest of us."

Completing the Fall was a torturous path with many false starts and changes of mind. Mario told me Michele struggled to organise the large group of figures in the *Martyrdom of Matthew*, but I witnessed the seemingly effortless painting of the huge crowded *Seven Acts of Mercy* and intimidatingly resolved the way the giant of Florence overawed my father affronted by the ambition and innovation that compelled him to find fault to justify his envy. My dread was that had I inherited the same limitations of my father or lacked the talent and insight to transcend earthbound materials of pigment suspended in oil? Perhaps I was no better than Baglione and others in Rome and Naples that the brilliance of Michele's paintings cast blinding light on our weakness and the realisation that intense industry counted for nothing. None could emulate the way he transcended his worthy early paintings and with industry and dedication to become… Caravaggio. His very being offended those unable to follow where he led, bringing to life, true visions of the sacred and profane by the transubstantiation of paint into flesh, blood and soul. Tragically, his thin skin was God's curse for his aspiration to become co-creator, as the first Michelangelo's overreaching ambition for Julius II's tomb was impossible to complete in a single lifetime. Like my father, all I could do was the best I could in the hope I might make just one painting as good as the *Boy Peeling Fruit* painted by Michele in his youth. I was pleased I achieved the metallic surface of the centurion's armour and the two thieves for which Alessio posed, but it was the face and hands of Christ that were the most satisfying because, at Alessio's insistence, I let them be, ungainly as they were, rather than depicted the way they ought to look. Once finished, the Fallen Christ somehow echoed Michele's martyrdom and my own loss reflected in the anguish of Christ's expression and the tangled fingers desperately grasping the wood of the cross in anticipation of the coming agony, the drawing of lots for his clothes as perhaps Michele felt as he lay dying, stripped of possessions, his paintings gone and circled by metallic crows.

Marchese Giustiniani invited the cardinal to bless the *Fallen Christ* and was highly complementary but, like Michele, I would have preferred it to be installed in a church. Giustiniani had a wide circle of aristocratic friends and senior clergy but few, if any of the populace, apart from cleaners and servants, were likely to see the painting.

Perhaps it was coincidence that, within days of our move from Andrea Rufetti's to a small house in Vicolo del Divino Amore near the Palazzo Farnese, I received an anonymous commission for a *Cupid at the Spring*. The client's agent made it clear his patron demanded absolute anonymity and discretion from which I deduced an erotic interpretation was required, perhaps by a marchese, an archbishop or cardinal, possibly one of those invited to see Michele's Cupid, coveted it and even knew it was me who was the model.

What was particularly intriguing was how appropriate for me to paint a version of Cupid and impossible to ignore the memory of my personation of the god of love, notwithstanding the sacrifice of my pubic hair. At twenty-three, I was taller and adolescent puppy fat toned to fine musculature by stretching and preparing canvasses throughout my adolescence.

Perhaps an older Cupid might fulfil my patron's desires. I set up the large mirror to explore poses for the painting and stripped naked to pose the first time in several years to examine my reflected self, turning this way and that, full frontal, profile and straining to glance over my shoulder to examine my back. I put my hand out to touch the mirror, then stepped close to regard my face, turning slowly left to right, then flicking my attention from eyes, nose and mouth and pressed my lips to my reflected mouth, feeling the cold glass between me and my other self.

When decided on the pose, I had Alessio model. He was about my build and once the body was drawn, by using two mirrors I substituted my own face in profile, compelled to sustain the link between my younger self portrayed by Michele and my present self-image. I painted the background in dark monochrome to suggest an outcrop of rock with water flowing from a cleft cascading to a pool with Cupid's attributes of arrows and quiver in the foreground. Wings borrowed from Orazio Gentileschi were in a sorry state and bigger than I remembered but, once Alessio was naked and winged, I attached strings and fixed them spread to a frame as though Cupid had just landed. I spent a week painting every feather with Lombard detail and Alessio had to take frequent breaks because of cramps. "I can't go on any longer."

He slipped out of the straps and stood with the muscles of his calves bulging. Working directly on the canvas as Michele did, I realised Cupid was placed too far to the left. An easy solution was to cut away a quarter of the right side but I was intrigued by the puzzle. It also occurred to me Cupid's head was too far from the source of water so, after some thought, I decided to paint a spout, which made me smile. *Beccuccio* sounded rather like my name. The problem was solved, ensuring water flowed into Cupid's mouth. The close proximity of the beccuccio to his lips recalled the times I knelt before Michele who cradled the back of my head, pressing it back and forth in a steady rhythm.

The wanton boy who created chaos among gods and mortals was undoubtably my younger self, whereas this present Cupid was subject to the same desires formerly unleashed on all without mercy. Giustiniani was right to veil his Cupid, an image as dangerous as the uncovered face of Medusa. More import, the memory of Giustiniani's occasionally revealed painting resolved my problem. When we left Andrea Rufetti's house, he invited me to take anything in the attic I might find useful and, among other items, I took a large orange brocade drape with elaborate tassels. When unfurled, a snail shell fell out of the folds. I turned the shell in my hand, marvelling at the sheer beauty of the swirling rings and wondered how it got there. At the Vicolo, I arranged the heavy fabric over the corner of the frame leaning against the wall and drew back the heavy brocade to reveal the silky gold colour lining against the velvet sheen. I arranged the edge of the drape to echo the shape of Cupid's wings and spent two weeks painting the fabrics and tassels, lovingly recreating the various textures. The result was disturbing because Cupid and the drape inhabited different worlds but shared the same space. It was as though Cupid suddenly appeared on stage; his wings not yet folded as he eagerly quenched his thirst. His presence and the drawn drape reversed Giustiniani's control over when Cupid was revealed or hidden.

Alessio was intrigued by the stark realism and as we stood staring at the finished painting and drinking wine. He eventually broke the silence. "I have never seen anything like this before… a painting inside a painting… and I see you added a penis…"

"What?"

"They say oysters are like a woman's… and a snail's like a prick." He put out his curled tongue… round and bloated with a crease, his lips taut, resembling a withdrawn foreskin. He slipped his tongue between two fingers. I rarely made suggestive jokes and gestures these days and merely shrugged. I added a dove as an allusion to Cupid's mother Venus, using the drawings made for Eliza Colomba's portrait. When the Cupid was close to completion, I received an unexpected commission for a painting of the cleansing of the temple, an incident in the passion story when Christ threw out the money changers from the Temple in Jerusalem. The size was the same as the Fall of Christ, the way Michele's arrest of Christ in Gethsemane was companion to the supper at Emmaus. The commission was from Marchese Giustiniani, surely thanks to Cardinal del Monte which confirmed the anonymous commission for the Cupid was not Giustiniani who was certainly unafraid of controversy.

Chapter 46
Resurrection

In 1620, ten years since my return to Rome and the dashed hope to be reunited with Michele, I received a steady stream of commissions, sacred and so-called low life, my speciality of half figures, musicians and the like with detailed still lives. I painted private altarpieces, the *Cleansing of the Temple* and the *Beheading of John the Baptist* and often made saleable copies of popular subjects including two penitent Magdalenes. I considered marrying the model but it was not to be. I think perhaps she knew my past and did not wish to live with the ghost of Michele between us. I had different friends from those in the old days… or rather, friendly acquaintances. I heard little from Mario and Lorenzo and it was said Onorio Longhi died of the pox and, towards the end, he raved. I was pleased with a *San Lorenzo* painting, essentially a portrait of an acquaintance, a scholar of humanities at the Studium Urbis near the Piazza Navona.

Don Massimo was an entertaining avuncular youthful fifty-something who held court at a taverna where he gently coaxed students and regulars to discuss any and all matters. He invariably sat on a bench, leaning close to the fire, wearing a deep wine red gown and, when he considered a proposition, he clasped his hands and gazed at the ceiling a moment as he analysed the statement before responding, usually with a series of brief questions to assess the validity of ideas raised. He saw the *Cleansing of the Temple* before it went to the framer but liked the *Cupid at the Spring* better which he considered original and inventive. When I was commissioned to paint a San Lorenzo, he was naturally my first choice and he agreed without hesitation. I painted him as I first saw him, clasped hands, glancing up, warming himself by a fire. When he saw the finished painting, he nodded with appreciation. "It's a wonderful portrait, but, Caro, Lorenzo wasn't martyred on a grill…"

My love for Michele mellowed over the years. I once counted the time we were lovers that amounted to just ten months and a handful of days but preferred to count the years I knew him from our meeting that stormy night before the turn of the century. My anger and frustration abated over time and saddened that gradually the name Caravaggio, formerly centre of adulation, envy, speculation and gossip about his wandering the seas and islands like a modern Ulysses was gradually, if not forgotten, at least diminished… except by those who knew him. Not only friends but also adversaries, his genius was meat for carrion who gorged on his talent and hated him because they never came near the scintillating brilliance and truth of his paintings.

The greatest irony was Baglione who wrote a brief biography of Michele. He was surprisingly generous and even-handed, which was easy, given his adversary was long buried. Now I simply concentrate on painting with ever greater diligence and fine technique, conscious I will never live beyond Michele's shadow, content to be known as his assistant, pale reflection and even demeaned as his bardassa for all I cared. However, when all hope for future important commissions faded, in 1619, the wheel turned when I was approached by the secretary of Piero Guicciardini the Tuscan Ambassador to Rome to discuss a commission for an altarpiece. The ambassador wanted a large painting for his family chapel in Florence. I saw Cardinal del Monte's hand, a lifelong friend of the Grand Duke. The secretary arranged a meeting at the ambassador's residence, and I was astonished to be told the subject was the Resurrection. The exquisite irony of the subject made me woozy and, although the Guicciardini chapel was in Florence, to paint a Resurrection, a companion to Michele's Resurrection in Naples, might lift my reputation and certainly represent a further slap in the face for Baglione whose poor version was removed from the Gesù and disappeared without trace a decade past.

I persuaded Alessio to help once more since the altarpiece was the largest commissioned at thirty-three by twenty palmi and, most valuable, at two hundred scudi. I largely abandoned the traditional method of stretching canvas on a separate strainer. Once the canvas was stretched, a near black base coat was applied in three layers and was ready by the time I returned from a brief dash to Naples to see Michele's *Resurrection* and the *Seven Acts of Mercy*. After a decade, it became an act of remembrance and, as a kind of memorial, I decided to follow Michele's form and composition, with Christ stepping over the slab of the tomb with guards in various states of shock and incomprehension. I made ink and wash studies in broad tonal strokes and, before returning to Rome, persuaded Alessio's brother Calimero to model in armour and drew some of his colleagues for soldiers for the lower part of the painting. At the Vicolo, the prepared canvas was propped against the wall just three fingers short of the ceiling and wider than a man lying full length on the floor. I stood on a trestle to paint the Christ and, with Alessio occasionally modelling, the figure was completed in a month. The great slab hovering above the yawning void of the tomb was my homage to Michele's *Entombment*. In the foreground, I drew the guards in various states of wakefulness and shock, transferring the drawing of Calimero leaning back, slumbering against a rock in the right foreground, close to the viewer, his legs stretched forward and his shield on the ground to the left. The trestle was dismantled when I worked on the middle and lower sections and lay on the floor to paint the lowest sections. My elbows ached and my breath was short, shocking realisation I was in my forties and older than Michele when he died.

The *Resurrection* took longer than anticipated. Other small commissions interrupted progress but equally I spent inordinate amount of time on details, particularly armour and the dress of the four other guards and their startled expressions. I was obsessed by the sound of the event. Would there be rumbling earthquake, cymbals, trumpets and drums or would the resurrection have been as silent as the moment of Christ's birth... his birth in a cave echoed by his emergence from a cave at his resurrection? I considered my Christ powerful, illuminated by raking light from the upper left, the foreshortened arm as convincing as that of Michele's David. I dared to think it was the best painting I had done and hoped it would be a success and considered suggesting to the Guicciardini agent it might be displayed in Rome before it went to Florence, perhaps in San Luigi or even the Gesù as a gesture of the horns to the academy. Like Michele, I had not been invited to join the academy but, likewise, could care less. What I considered particularly successful was the void at the heart of the painting, the contrast between two elements of the dynamic Christ above the empty tomb, the triumph of life over the gaping maw of death and the sheer boldness of the composition worthy of Michele. The figures of the guards were seen as from above, drawing the viewer into the scene. I was pleased enough to invite a few artists, including Orazio Gentileschi, now almost sixty, his daughter Artemisia, recently returned from Florence, and whose interpretation of *Judith killing Holofernes* was even bloodier than Michele's version. I was pleased Andrea Rufetti came and I also invited the Guicciardini agent in advance of a formal presentation to the ambassador. The response from painters was more than encouraging. Artemisia was particularly impressed by how daring I had been with the emphasis of the empty tomb at the core of the painting. Orazio was stunned, hardly aware of me beyond being Michele's boy and unknowing I had painted in the fourteen or so years since Michele and I left Rome.

However, the Guicciardini agent cast a shadow over the reception. "Don't you think there's a huge gap at the centre of the picture?" He pointed to the cave.

I smiled. "That's the point. Christ descended into Hell, then rose from the dead."

"So, why isn't Our Lord shown coming out of the tomb to fill the space?"

"Because he ascended from the grave… it's a metaphor."

Andrea spoke up. "The cave is a crucial element of the painting. It signifies…"

The agent smirked. "So, my master is expected to pay for a gaping hole in his painting…"

The following day, the Guicciardini agent returned. "I spoke to His Excellency the Ambassador who agreed there cannot be a hole in the middle of his picture and suggests you add an angel pointing to Our Lord above."

"But shouldn't His Excellency see the finished painting first?"

"He accepts my judgement."

"Are you a painter?"

"I will ignore your impertinence and repeat His Excellency requires you to make the adjustment I mentioned and, furthermore, wants his son to be painted as the angel. I wish you good day." He mounted his bay gelding and cantered along the Vicolo. I wrote to the ambassador, explaining His Excellency would see the relevance of the cave if he would graciously visit the workshop but without success. Andrea worked on my behalf but the only response was a request about when the Guicciardini boy was to be expected with his bodyguard. It was obvious the agent was in command of the situation.

Ignoring my appeal, the boy arrived with a priest's white Alb, perhaps loaned by the ambassador's confessor. The agent demonstrated the pose he decided the boy should adopt… I paid one of Orazio's assistants to make a set of wings painted white and chalked. I made a study of the boy as he posed and a detailed drawing of the boy's head and said I had no further need to delay him. It was several weeks before the angel was finished during which time I was reduced to despair.

Being so pale, the angel drew attention from the rest of the painting and seemed flat and the gesture ridiculous, especially the index finger pointing at nothing. Several times, I became tearful seeing the painting reduced to buffoonery by ignorance. The agent sent frequent messages, demanding to know when the painting would be finished, with increasingly insulting asides. "It's only a boy you have to paint. Any competent journeyman would have finished weeks ago. You're not Leonardo da Vinci."

Eventually I had enough. I repainted the figure on the left, turning to look back, overlapping the angel to try to push it back into the picture. In response to the agent's final note, I replied, *The painting is finished with the addition you required. It is ready to go to the framer unless His Excellency would prefer to view it unframed. If His Excellency would prefer not to view the painting in my humble workshop, perhaps you would arrange a suitable venue.*

Without warning, a wagon arrived to collect the painting but, the following day, I was shocked when it was returned with a note affixed to the stretcher in the agent's handwriting.

His Excellency the Ambassador is not pleased with the painting and is returned. Although the picture does not meet His Excellency's favour, he generously permits F Boneri to retain earlier payments to the value of two hundred scudi and further monies for his labours and other disbursements.

The following day, the Guicciardini agent arrived with a purse and clearly enjoyed my embarrassment. "I have brought the monies despite the painting being a disappointment…"

Choked with anger, I trembled and swallowed bile as the agent preened and strutted, enjoying his modicum of power. Now I truly understood why Michele attempted to stab the painting of the *Death of the Virgin*. If those who commissioned it lacked insight and were blind to what was before their eyes, they didn't deserve the outpouring of contemplation, creative imagination, transcendent craft and sheer industry to produce such unique work and, therefore, distorted by rejection, it should no longer exist. I watched Michele held writhing by three or four priests, his face contorted, gritted teeth, snarling, unable to catch his breath, delirious, impotent, the vision obscured, caked in shit and misdirected expectation. His work was not for the high and mighty with rarefied taste and grandeur but those without illusion and delusion. My laboured breathing gradually calmed, pounding blood in my ears slowed as I focussed on the agent, unnerved by my long silence and left standing in an effete pose with the purse dangling heavy on his finger.

He smirked. "Master Boneri, you understand?"

I stepped close to the agent who flinched, his eyelids fluttered, suddenly apprehensive. My fists were clenched and, after a moment, I responded in a low voice, "Your amateur, uneducated, ignorant, uninformed opinion destroyed a near masterpiece. I should have thrown you out of the workshop the moment you embarrassed yourself in the presence of those who have the means, talent, judgement and experience to make serious appraisals of the painting. Now take your master's money and shove it up your arse…"

I swiped the purse with the back of my hand, scattering the coins across the ground. The agent stared, expecting me to apologise and pick up the coins but, seeing I shook with rage, he turned and stooped to collect the money. Blinded by rage, I rushed forward and kicked his arse. The agent staggered forward and almost fell. A crowd had gathered, neighbours emerged from houses and passers-by stopped, ever keen to enjoy a public spat. When the agent almost fell to the ground, his horse reared and the crowd broke into applause and laughter.

Somehow reports of the incident got out of hand, becoming public gossip. The high-ups clucked about the insult to their caste but many painters and those who met in the taverns and osterias loved repeating what the painter, Cecco del Caravaggio, called the Tuscan ambassador's agent: *Vaffanculo, inutile bastardo.* I expected to be arrested any day but nothing happened. Andrea arrived, saying there had been an offer for the painting on the strength of reports from painters who had seen it. The rumour that the Guicciardini agent had been humiliated drew large crowds in the Vicolo to see the painting which was probably the reason the authorities were dissuaded from acting against me. People lined the street, chattering and joking about the now infamous arse-kick, waiting their turn to view the painting and it was touching how many people left gifts of fruit, flowers and spicy sausages among other items, including several rosaries. I had created a delicate diplomatic situation by my indirect insult to the ambassador but Guicciardini chose not to respond. My only concern was how Cardinal del Monte might take the insult to his friend, but, for the first time, I decided not to make excuses or apologies.

Within a week, the painting was collected from the workshop before I could paint out the angel and payment was delivered. I had no idea who bought it, speculating it might be Giustiniani or possibly the Colonna but, whatever the case, I never saw it again. As time passed, I was convinced the Colonna spirited the painting away to prevent it from attracting further attention from painters and the commons who, ignoring fashion, still went to kneel and focus their devotions before Michele's *Entombment* or the *Madonna of the Pilgrims*: *their* Saviour, *their* Madonna and *their* Child. Andrea Rufetti denied knowledge of Colonna involvement and, despite the incident, remained a close friend and supporter but, apart from low-life style paintings, musicians and half figures and saints, there were no further important commissions. Even though the *Resurrection* had been bought, I was depressed my interpretation was never likely to be seen again in public and, like the Baglione version, probably destroyed.

Chapter 47

Return to Bergamo 1620

I imagined my mother in grey rags, a Magdalene, her hands and feet purple, shoulders slumped, grey hair unkempt and her frail bony body crushed. It was unbearable, and I was torn between wishing her alive and widowed or dead and beyond further torment. Not knowing whether she or my father survived or relatives still lived in or around Bergamo, in poverty or wealth, played on my mind.

Most of my friends in Rome had moved on or become estranged and I was engulfed by an overpowering sense of loneliness and longing to see again the place where I was born and spent the early years of my life. The distant pale blue smudge of the Alps against the clear sky to the north and the cold blasts that swept down on bitterly cold days that whistled through the shutters in an unknown tongue. It was impossible to ignore the harsh brutality of my father's tempers and my half-brother's bullying but now I was relatively well off, if not extravagantly wealthy and my tormenters diminished. The small town with open countryside just a few short paces away was increasingly attractive when compared with the crowded streets and stinking alleys of Rome.

The memories of sweet Lombard air were now more alluring than what seemed exciting and exotic about Rome in the early days. The bustle and grandeur, street music, friends from every corner of Italy and further afield and the latest paintings in new and redecorated churches barely masked the stench and unremitting summer heat, choking smoke and occasional freezing winters. I had no illusions my memory of Bergamo was as insubstantial as Michele's idealised Caravaggio in the Isaac painting. My younger self still squatted naked behind a green brocade arras in the Giustiniani palace whereas I had naturally aged, my luscious hair ribbed grey and thinning, perhaps in the last quarter of my life, no longer the beautiful boy, riotous Cupid or angel of death dangling Michele's bleeding head by the hair. I yearned to see my homeland again. For days, I contemplated making a visit to seek the truth, whether grief or joy, regret or contentment. Even the unlikely possibility Father Gennaro remained a priest at Bergamo was inconsequential… What could he do to me now?

When the time for departure arrived, I was suddenly loathe to leave what had become my home for the past near quarter century, two years short to be precise. My work remained in private collections, several medium size altarpieces in private chapels but not one in a church, even a small side chapel, and the prospect of such a prize was now remote. Giovan Battista, my first friend in Rome, tried to raise my spirits, saying my life had not been in vain and insisted I let Michele go. I believe he meant I should not compare my paintings with his as my only yardstick. I knew he was right. As much as I had worked long hours with diligence over decades, perhaps rather than trying to emulate Michele, I should have found the courage to step out of his shadow, with the dread I replicated my father's narrow path. Giovan squeezed my arm. "Never think that, Cecco. Yours is a fine body of work and, if not appreciated as it should, future generations will respect you." I was not so certain.

The morning of my departure, Alessio, Andrea and Giovan Battista came to help load the cart and wish me well. The carter slapped the reins and we jerked forward, trundling along familiar streets, sights and noises and eventually crossed the Tiber as we made our way north. I dare not look back but glanced down at the sluggish brown river with boats passing under us and flotsam slowly dragged along by the westward flow. I shuddered, reminded of Lena fished out of the stream, her sodden grey cocoon delivered to Michele's door and cringed, remembering his rage and struggles when he was restrained from stabbing the painting. I simply stared ahead to suppress further memories which, like a cloak snagged on a door nail, might draw me back. I glanced at the finally completed great dome of Saint Peter's under which the *Madonna of the Serpent* rightfully should hang but whatever was in its place would remain a void by comparison. I instructed the driver I intended to spend a few days in Florence to see again the giant David and wondered if the creased and faded engraving was still pinned to the wall of Pa's workshop, if he lived, which I doubted… The workshop now probably an empty shed with the musty smell of hens and mules.

The cardinal invited me to visit him days before I left for Lombardy. We had not met for several years, and he seemed suddenly aged; unusually, he wore a biretta, perhaps to hide lost hair. It was the only time I saw a little vanity, but his beard almost white, fuller in figure and face but his easy smile, barely veiled mock-seriousness, and his lively twinkling eyes never changed. He told me my *Resurrection* painting had been bought by the

Cardinal Nephew, which he said was a triumph. I was delighted it had not been destroyed and elated it was one of two surviving versions, one by Michele, the other by me, with the third by Baglione consigned to the fire. I mentioned I was still haunted, not knowing how Michele died and had not been at his side. His Eminence gently chided me, saying I must not torture myself and leave Michele to Gesù's tender mercies.

The bells faded in the loosening distance as Rome was left behind, and I suddenly remembered Andrea Rufetti had given me a letter, almost forgotten in my haste to leave. I drew the paper from my doublet and ran my fingers over the smooth red seal imprinted with a cypher I recognised.

Cecco, my dear,

I write to remind you: the stone rejected by the builders has become the headstone of the corner. Be strong, my son, and regard this as a new beginning rather than an end and be assured your paintings will not be forgotten and you will always be known as Caravaggio's boy.

You are in my prayers.

del Monte

Epilogue

Porto Ercole 18th July 1610

Blue… endless blue – a brazen affront to the unities of earth, fire, flesh, bone and blood. Carmine, tin-yellow, lead-white and black. Not lapis from across the water that makes voids that shrink, slip and recede. Robe the Madonna in red or purple, unless the client insists. But if it must be blue, however costly, adulterate with black, even Umber… Come down, Holy Mother, be near to raise our hope and quell our fear and be present and not swathed in distant blue. I painted light-searched dark rooms, back-rooms of taverns, alleys, caves, and voids. Light that reveals and gives form but not this… light-bleached figures and washed-out forms that make ghosts of both, mere whisps of smoke, not angels. Scalding tears burn my eyes. No tears of shame mind. Never shame. Eyes stung by sweat pooled in the creased flesh pouting scar, a cruel stigmata like Cain's. This hottest summer, they say in living memory, lips sea-air salty, parched and cracked. A flat black sea ruled by a scorching sun, exhausted waves slap wet sand, boundless blue scarred by the screech of gulls, giggling and mocking high above the strand.

A boy discovered the stranger on the beach sprawled among purple-brown seaweed, bleached scraps of wood worn by timeless rocking seas and storms sanding strange skeletal shapes and pebbles holed and smooth as ivory, mere flotsam and jetsam like the stranger. The boy stood and stared a moment, then ran calling, *Mamma, a man… come quick.*

Barely conscious, shivering in the blistering heat, tongue cleft to his palate with the taste of acid and lead. Every sound heard with the clarity of a searching light. The woman's footsteps crunched as she rushed towards him, caught hold of her son, pushed him behind her, hesitated before stooping. Might he suddenly jump up and… She withdrew her hand to her breast, held her breath, then cautiously prodded the man's chest and felt for a pulse. He was barely alive, his breathing hollow, shallow. Sitting back on her haunches, her forefinger traced the crinkled raw scar across the forehead and into the crease between the eyes. She stood. "Give me…"

She pulled and pushed the trembling brown and white patched horse to stand between the sun and the man to cast a cool shadow. Shielded from the blinding light, he opened his eyes to a dancing blur and spider-legs tangle of eyelashes. He saw the dark silhouette of the horse's head reach down to sniff him; the long hairs of its muzzle lightly scraped his neck. It delicately raised its foreleg to avoid trampling him. The woman pushed the horse's head away and dabbed the man's face with a cloth. She gave the reins to the curly black-haired angel who wiped tears on his forearm as his mother dripped water on the man's lips from a leather skin. Although warm, the water was sweet and he licked his cracked lips. Turning his head to the sea and the hump of land beyond the port. *The boat's gone… It's gone…* He breathed in short shallow gasps and, when his vision cleared, staring down at him was the most beautiful angel since… since his Cupid, his little faun. The boy trembled and sobbed. *Poor lad's never seen anyone die before.*

The earth shuddered to the dull thud of approaching horses. Hooves crunched on the beach as riders dismounted. He recognised the rasping voice. "There you are."

Roero laughed. "In time to see you die." His dark silhouette loomed over the man's body. He drew his sword and, with the flat of the blade, turned Michele's head to examine his features. "A nice wound…"

"Don't kill him, Father."

"Kill him…Woman, why would I kill a dead man? I'm simply here to torment him."

"Why torment him, Father?"

"Torment, my good woman, comes in many forms. You may think of hellfire and demons but there are more exquisite forms. This gentleman, I use the term loosely, this creature, in the hour of his death will take with him the certain knowledge that he and all his works will be forgotten."

The man silently mouthed words. His breath was too weak to speak.

The boy's voice cracked. "Please don't kill him, don't kill him, Excellency, and us as well."

"Shhh… Be still, child, we're not here to kill anyone." He stooped to speak in the dying man's ear. "Did you think we were chasing you to kill you? Ha! You're of no consequence. What we are chasing is the same as you… the paintings." He had barely the strength to lift his hand. Roero whispered, "And not for the Order, the Grand Master neither and certainly not for the Cardinal Nephew." He chuckled. "Scipione Borghese has insatiable greed for your work. He'd do anything to get hold of as many of your pictures as he can. He made sure you were separated from your pictures when you were held at Palo. He cares nothing about you. Did you really think he would intercede on your behalf with His Holiness? Of course not." He chuckled. "We will find the boat and destroy the paintings but that's only the beginning. Once the Grand Master dies, brothers are sworn to destroy your impious paintings, all of them. We have given the family at Bagheria permission to destroy the Nativity in Palermo. The Messina paintings and the Santa Lucia will go the same way, however long it takes, however many generations – centuries, if necessary – they will all be burned. Some may take longer, especially those held by those sodomites del Monte and Borghese and their friends. Giustiniani will always sell for a profit but from Germany to Sicily and Madrid to Malta, we will call on earthquake and fire to destroy every trace of your work. In a matter of hours, perhaps less, you will be dead and every trace of you and your paintings in time will disappear forever."

The mother dabbed his lips with a damp cloth. Roero no longer taunted him. He and his men muttered together some way off and even the woman's soothing voice was lost in the rhythmic sigh of waves and call-call-call of the gulls.

My final painting is done in my mind, not in paint but in my imagination. A Pieta with Christ lowered from the cross into the arms of a beautiful Saint John the Apostle, perhaps Rocco the Neapolitan fisherman, against the cavernous dark of the eclipsed sky, soldiers play dice for my raiment and cloak... Roero and crew will do. Lena, the Madonna, laments the loss of her child, red eyed in silent contemplation, consoled by Fillide as the Magdalene...

The mother stroked her son's arm. "Go fetch the priest."

Carla must be the second Mary...

"He's beyond redemption."

"You're cruel, Father; everybody deserves Our Lady's intercession and Christ's forgiveness."

I am the body of Christ tormented.

"Not this creature."

"What's his name?"

"They call him Caravaggio."

I am laid on the slab...

"What's his Christian name?"

"To call him a Christian..."

"His name, Father!"

"Michelangelo… Michele."

"Michele… Son, you're not alone. Be at peace with God and may he bless you." He felt the woman put a rosary in his painting hand and heard her pray. "Hail Mary, full of grace, the Lord is with thee; blessed art thou amongst women…"

Cecco… my weeping angel… My bones crushed for gesso, my decayed corpse, sperm and viscera mixed with earth and blood, and seeping fatty fluids to bind, applied to the patched sailcloth of the Santa Maria di Porto Salvo. He mouthed *Mamma…* although his lips moved and the woman bent her ear to his mouth, she could hear no sound.

A door opened. By raking light, he saw a woman holding a small child. She glanced down, her gaze was gentle as she leaned against the doorframe. She smiled. The boy-child leaned towards him, his pointing finger blackened with charcoal…

Cecco l'Angelo… mi solleva…

+

MIC . ANGEL .MERISIUS DE CARAVAGGIO
EQUES HIEROSOLIMITANUS
NATURAE AEMULATOR EXIMIUS
VIX . ANN . XXXVI . M . IX D . XX
MORITUR XVIII JULIS MDCX

Author's Essay

Apart from brief accounts of Caravaggio's life by Giulio Mancini in 1617, his arch competitor Giovani Baglione in 1642 and a more measured life by Giovanni Pietro Bellori in 1672, there were few serious researched biographies until Walter Friedlaender's 1955 *Caravaggio Studies*. Friedlaender presented all known and attributed paintings and documents with translations, researched with the aid of students at New York University Institute of Fine Arts. *Caravaggio Studies* is academically disinterested, whereas recent biographies, blogs and newspaper articles are preoccupied with revisionist agendas and exaggerated sensationalism. Characterising Caravaggio as irredeemably violent is a lazy means to advance lurid *murdering artist* tropes to sell shedloads of biographies and magazine articles. Revisionists, such as *Caravaggio A Life* (1998) by Helen Langdon, suggest that apart from the odd misdemeanour and misunderstanding, Caravaggio was a good Catholic boy and straight as Chuck Heston.

However, *Caravaggio's Boy* is based on known biographical events with invented material and characters where there are gaps or unexplained incidents where it is necessary to explore what might have influenced Caravaggio's thinking. It is an attempt to repair biographical lacunae as a fragmentary mosaic might be restored to suggest how the complete picture may have appeared. Novel form also avoids the sterile academic mantra – *not enough evidence in the literature*. Gaps in the life story are not black holes or absolute but gaps and scraps offer opportunities for informed speculation, particularly where fragments align with known personality characteristics and motivations. It is not good enough to fall back on an attack on a Milanese law officer as evidence of an underlying violent personality without asking why would a seventeen-year-old attack anyone without cause or reason? Taking extreme positions does Caravaggio no favours and indicates certain authors' inability to see, read and understand nuances in his paintings and his life.

Apart from documents recording Caravaggio's family and short apprenticeship, there is a dearth of hard data for the four years between leaving Master Simone Peterzano's workshop about 1588 and his arrival in

Rome about 1592. It is rumoured he went to Venice, then fled Milan as an outlaw. How likely are either scenario? Peterzano claimed to be a pupil of Titian therefore, although tenuous, the Venice suggestion is plausible. The attack on the law officer is mentioned in various biographies without detail and, on balance probably happened; why else would he flee Milan? That the attack was serious suggests revenge supported by Caravaggio's response to the unwelcome appearance some thirteen years later of his brother, the Jesuit Giovanni Battista Merisi.

The recorded meeting sprung on Caravaggio by his patron Cardinal del Monte reveals a close relationship with the cardinal in contrast to a dysfunctional sibling relationship. Caravaggio was clearly disturbed not only by long held sibling rivalry but also the probability Battista had privileged information about Michele's pre-Roman life. The brother's blatant reference to *normalising* Caravaggio's life by arranging a marriage may be interpreted socially as well as sexually but, in the context of the meeting, the remark is double edged. Battista's agenda in presenting himself to the cardinal was obviously in the hope for preferment, expecting his brother's support in exchange for silence about something in Caravaggio's past. Battista must have known of the attack and perhaps the motive, hence my characterisation of Battista as a sly, bullying zealot, who, although a year younger than Caravaggio, signed the contract with Peterzano, implying his position as a seminarian destined for the priesthood gave him precedence in the Merisi household. From the date of Caravaggio's denial of his brother, there is a sudden change in his patterns of behaviour.

The nature of the relationship between Cardinal del Monte and Caravaggio is well documented but enigmatic. I suggest del Monte was a humanist with true vocation and represented a lost father figure and mentor with infinite patience. Until the arrival of his brother, in parallel with his rising fame, there are no recorded brushes with the law in Rome but thereafter his crime sheet documents escalating hooliganism, petty crime and worse. In the four years after leaving the cardinal's household, del Monte continued supporting and protecting Caravaggio, although his guidance diminished as his former protégée became increasingly reckless, leading to the killing of Ranuccio Tomassoni. However, most criminal episodes were calculated paybacks and he never used weapons in a manner to seriously wound and certainly not to kill, that is, until the fight with Tomassoni. The fatal brawl is one occasion he faced a serious, even more brutal adversary. I believe Tomassoni's death was certainly accidental and, thereafter, with the exception of the misdirected attack on Father Rodomonto Roero in Malta, Caravaggio was usually on the receiving end of attacks and at the mercy of events rather than instigator.

The question of Caravaggio's sexuality supposedly remains in doubt with several recent biographies taking a view the case for homosexuality is *not proven*. This is in line with similar revisionist positions that suggest a near Victorian prejudice that great genius may not be 'tainted' by homosexuality. Both Friedlaender and Bernard Berenson conclude Caravaggio was homosexual but Helen Langdon supports Creighton Gilbert's view that *the historical evidence for Caravaggio's homosexuality* is *extremely flimsy,* although Gilbert focuses on only three paintings and brief period in Caravaggio's career. Furthermore, when Langdon discusses *Amor Vincit Omnia*, she writes, *He (Cupid / Amor) displays himself on the rumpled sheets of the bedroom, and both pose and expression are provocative, enticing... With one hand behind his back, he points suggestively to his buttocks, while displaying the softness of his thighs, and the V between his legs, to the spectator.* Langdon cannot or will not draw the obvious conclusion that the painting is homo- rather than hetero-sexually erotic. Why else the reference to Cupid's buttocks?

To his credit, Friedlaender suggests probability in favour of homosexual without moral judgement. Berenson in his under-researched, dire critique, *Caravaggio and his Anomalies (1953)*, is categorical that Caravaggio was homosexual but intended as a negative character judgement, echoing Baglione's pictorial accusation of sodomy. Berenson and others take the same view to support tenuous arguments that Caravaggio's work was flawed by 'anomalies' which he infers a character 'anomaly' must mean correspondingly anomalous paintings. It is not surprising that someone who traded artworks with the integrity of a used car salesman would venture from his field of expertise to pontificate about a painter whose work he obviously critiqued from faulty remembrances and, as he admitted, from black and white photographs. How else would he make a fundamental blunder mislabelling the *St John the Baptist* as *Ganymede*, having mistakenly seen an eagle in the background of a monochrome photograph rather than what is actually there – the branch of a tree. Andrew Graham-Dixon believes Caravaggio *probably swung both ways*, with which I agree – to a point. In the seventeenth century, the act of sodomy attracted potential social, corporal, even capital penalties and no surprise there is little evidence in the literature and therefore *not proven* to the satisfaction of certain pedantic art historians is preposterous. In itself, that brings into question the validity of art historians who lack the ability to *read* pictures without the crutch of received art historical documentation, dogma, orthodoxy and opinion acquired by rote and unable or unwilling to recognise the pictorial evidence in the paintings.

Everyone understood Baglione's pictorial attack on Caravaggio in his second version of *Sacred and Profane Love* where Caravaggio is portrayed as a satanic paedophile. Furthermore, in Caravaggio's paintings, there is not a single female nude or portrayal of a woman that compares erotically with female nudes by Giorgione, Titian, Raphael, Rubens. Rembrandt, Ingres and Picasso et al. Furthermore, his women are invariably depicted with detached regard, affection and respect due to maternal or sororal paradigms, objectively beautiful but without desire. On the other hand, Caravaggio's nude and semi-naked males are unvarnished objects of desire, sexually available and undoubtedly erotic in intent and fact. Blather about serving patrons' tastes is undermined by Caravaggio's obvious sensual attraction to men and youths and not merely a young man's fancy or passing phase since within months of the end of his life, age thirty-nine, he was accused by a Sicilian teacher of *too much interest towards his (boy) pupils*.

There is evidence of close physical relationships with Lionello Spada, Francesco Boneri known as Cecco and the bardassa Giovanni Battista, the latter mentioned in the Baglione trial. There was also evident mutual affection for – and reciprocated by – Cardinal del Monte which suggests another characteristic of homo-erotic friendship that a common homosexual orientation often bypasses social, economic and ethnic barriers. Contemporaries presumed Francesco del Monte to be homosexual which, as much as his support for the French faction, probably contributed to his being discounted as Papabile. Furthermore, Graham-Dixon's case for a bisexual swinger does not correspond with known psychological patterns of behaviour. From extensive conversations with an American clinical psychologist who (respecting client anonymity) described to me case studies of bisexual clients. He concluded bisexuality to be a rare condition, whereby the subject embarks upon relationships with successive but not contemporaneous partners, leading to chronic, often destructive, patterns of behaviour. In his experience, young males claim bisexuality as a socially acceptable state in the initial stages of transition from a perceived heterosexual 'norm' to acceptance of homosexual nature. In Caravaggio's case, his sexuality appears predominantly homosexual rather than bisexual in the modern sense so that his relationships with women, affectionate and even sexual, was necessary protective camouflage, calculated to preserve a public *bella figura*. Indeed, Caravaggio's exaggerated macho posture or male impersonation (coined by Mark Simpson *Male Impersonators: Men Performing Masculinity 1994*) seems over-compensation to mask his true nature.

I began researching the life and paintings of Francesco Boneri, known as Cecco del Caravaggio, having read the catalogue raisonnè of his paintings compiled by Professor Gianni Papi: *Cecco del Caravaggio* (Nuova Memoria, Florence 1992). I had seen the painting *Instrument Maker* by Cecco at Apsley House, London, and *Musician* at the Ashmolean, Oxford, and consider him the best painter among Caravaggio's closest friends and imitators. A literature search and re-reading certain documents revealed an interesting character who, like Mercury to the Sun, is almost obliterated by the blinding light from the star.

Cecco was the only one to stay with Caravaggio after the death of Tomassoni, going with him to Zagarolo and on to Naples. Thereafter, he is only documented by his paintings, most with little provenance and even important collections have sparce documentation. The paintings suggest not only direct influences but also personal developments that took him some way beyond Caravaggio's influence. Suggested dates for paintings abruptly begin in 1607 when he was with Caravaggio in Naples. From the skill and confidence of his presumed earliest paintings, *Lady with a Dove, Man with a Rabbit* and still lives, it is obvious Cecco had learned to paint much earlier, perhaps with his father or under the influence and even guidance from Caravaggio, which over six or seven years would constitute an apprenticeship. Throughout the time Caravaggio was in Malta, Sicily and on his return to Naples, Cecco made a series of genre paintings of musicians, still lives and altarpieces and continued a further decade after Michele's death. About 1620, Cecco returned to his native Lombardy, presumably to Bergamo or environs where he disappears from view, although there are frescos and a curious crucifixion which looks like a carved figure inlaid in a trompe l'oeil *'wooden'* cross.

I speculate about Cecco's life as a means to comment from a tangent on Caravaggio's life splicing chapters of imagined episodes from Cecco's life with those of Michele in the hope of adding perspective to Caravaggio's career. I believe Cecco was the single long term amorous relationship Caravaggio enjoyed and was reciprocated. That Cecco went with Caravaggio to Zagarolo after the fight and the death sentence is documented and, in my view, the most likely time the relationship became sexually intimate. Sexual mores at the time were less concerned with child welfare, paedophilia and safety than in the modern world, particularly among the underclass of street urchins, bardassas and probably assistants and apprentices, but I am not prepared to engage in, imagine or describe such activity.

The character, Alessio, is wholly invented to be Michele's guide to Naples, later becoming Cecco's assistant, necessary as Cecco emerged as a professional painter. Likewise, the Darius character was solely invented to highlight the confessional aspect of the Uffizi Bacchus painting, with the dark visitor seen in the reflection in the flagon on the table with the black hat… Caravaggio's calling card. The Neapolitan painter Carlo Sellitto 1581–1614 knew Caravaggio but whether he collaborated is unknown.

On the issue of Faith, Caravaggio was born into a Lombard family of some means, Catholic religious faith was ubiquitous. From infancy, he was steeped in orthodox Catholic tradition and, in Rome, it is known he attended sermons by Filippo Neri who preached the dignity, worth and humanity of the poor and downtrodden. In Rome, he lived in the household of a prince of the church, cultured and urbane yet a great humanist and pastor who, even though he lived within a louche aristocratic milieu of power and wealth, his private life was recorded relatively austere, his clothes, although of quality, were noted to be well worn. Empathy with the poor and downtrodden underpinned Caravaggio's paintings and raking light exposed both human dignity and cruelty and after painting the secular *Amor Vincit Omnia*, never again strayed beyond Catholic imagery. However, his interpretation of biblical events is seen not solely through the fervour of Father Filippo Neri but equally in modernist quasi-political forms, combining the sacred and the secular. He is recorded saying *all my sins are mortal* pays ironic lip service to the orthodox belief that salvation was solely mediated by the Catholic Church.

Death of the Virgin – an apocryphal story suggested the model for the Madonna in the Death of the Virgin was a drowned prostitute. Although unsupported by hard evidence, I chose Maddalena 'Lena' Antognetti, the accepted model for the *Madonna of Loreto* to be the murdered Virgin. Primarily to link Ranuccio Tomassoni more closely with both Lena and Caravaggio, also to add drama and to close the circle.

Caravaggio's imprisonment in Malta for the attack on Fr Rodomonto Roero is partially documented but the mystery of his implausible solo escape from the cell in Malta and subsequent arrival in Syracuse clearly indicates high level collusion. I propose the Grand Master de Wignacourt was the only person with the authority to permit and arrange Caravaggio's escape with his belongings and a convenient rowing boat and felucca at his disposal. Finally, there is the mystery of the sequence of events of Caravaggio's last days and hours. Ambiguities around the pardon only make sense when seen in the context of Scipione Borghese's motives, ever eager to acquire as many Caravaggio paintings as possible. Scipione had form, having arranged his uncle Paul V to bankrupt Cesari d'Arpino in order to acquire three of Caravaggio paintings. He also had means to have Caravaggio detained long enough to separate paintings from painter but miscalculated when the captain of the felucca took the initiative to return them to the Lady Costanza's villa in Naples for safety.

Caravaggio's apprenticeship started comparatively late and lasted half the average eight years. X-ray evidence indicates he worked in direct method, drawing into the base dark layer, often with the handle of his brush, applying dark, middle and lighter tones in succession. The assumption that by working direct on the canvas he did not make preparatory drawings is difficult to believe. There is at least one attributed sepia study, (San Francisco) that suggests there may have been others indicating that, rationally, he must have pre-planned some of his compositions but no *presentation* drawings à la Michelangelo or Leonardo exist. There is evidence he was noted for drawing at an early age which leads me to believe he made exploratory exercises but did not bother to keep, indeed, may have deliberately destroyed them to disguise his methods and to enhance his prestige. David Hockney suggests Caravaggio used lenses to project images onto his canvasses, citing the *Cardsharps*, where the older rogue appears to focus his glance beyond the dupe's hand. I believe Hockney is somewhat self-serving, given his well recorded method of projecting images onto canvasses but anyone teaching a life class knows how difficult it is for a model to recapture the precise same pose after rest breaks.

Although he worked meticulously, Caravaggio's early Roman paintings are mechanical and somewhat stilted. However, progress was rapid and exponential and by the Contarelli commission was approaching a mature style but the *Entombment* and the *Madonna of Loreto* of 1602 / 03 mark the beginning of his truly mature work. Great art is the product of drives and tensions in the personality of the artist which are sublimated and integrated through the creative process. Caravaggio's early work is driven by his preoccupation with the male figure, evident from the early naked St Johns, *Amor Vincit Omnia* and the Contarelli Martyrdom in which the near-nude executioner and attendant *ignudi* are erotically highly charged but by the time of the *Entombment*, the nude Christ, although achingly beautiful and poignant, is sensual rather than erotic and resolved through creative sublimation and objective distance in tune with the subject. Thereafter, there are fewer overtly erotic figures in his work and whereas Michelangelo's ignudi are observed, the foreground ignudi in the Contarelli Martyrdom join the viewer as observers of the action.

Conclusions

The fourteen years from 1592 to 1606 in Rome, Michelangelo Merisi rose from obscurity to celebrity, becoming the most pivotal artist of his generation who changed the direction of art for over two and a half centuries and whose work resonates to the present. In the manner of his near contemporary Shakespeare, Caravaggio gave his characters inner lives and made the divine human and the human divine. Like Shakespeare, Caravaggio blurred the distinction between good and evil, sacred and profane and is the first visual artist to speak to the modern era in its own language. It is too easy to see events in Caravaggio's life directly reflected in his paintings but his realisations of beatings, martyrdoms and death exhibit something dark from his past and known to history in the record of escalating criminal behaviour.

Certainly, something from his pre-Roman career had an impact upon his youthful character, perhaps glimpsed through the unwelcome appearance of his Jesuit brother Battista. There were also rejections – the first St Matthew altarpiece and, successively, *Madonna of the Serpent* and *Death of the Virgin* – public disappointments compounded by losing the libel trial brought by Baglione and, even more so, the close supportive friendship and guidance of Francesco del Monte; Caravaggio cut himself adrift from his most loyal mentor in what was to become an increasingly hostile environment. Thereafter, his work turns darker, more serious and no longer overtly erotic but the image of a volatile, aggressive hooligan is only half the picture.

At core, he was religious, humanist and empathetic but tormented by something in his past but veiled for posterity by his early obscurity. 1606 to 1610, the last four years of Caravaggio's life, are less well documented by both his earliest biographers and contributed to the mystery of his death. He yearned to return to Rome, the scene of his first triumph, a hothouse of artistic and cultural stimuli. Naples was a thriving, bustling city but artistically predominantly mannerist. Nevertheless, with the support of the Colonna, his work was in demand, reflected in the sudden rise in what he could financially command. Although Cecco shared his exile, when Caravaggio was alone in Malta, Caravaggio lived in a society with whom he had no shared past, except his distant boyhood friend Fabrizio Sforza-Colonna, but faced hostility from certain knights who no doubt were aware of his past.

Arriving in Sicily, he re-established friendships from his earliest days in Rome – Mario Minniti and his wife in Syracuse and Lorenzo Carlo in Messina. A smaller circle of acquaintances was less demanding on his time, hence his large output of some twenty paintings during his last four years, including some of the largest pictures he ever produced. His pattern of behaviour appeared more subdued, chastened and certainly less riotous, with the exception of his attack in Valetta on the senior knight Rodomonte Roero. The only other incident recorded by Susinni was the denunciation by the Sicilian school master Carlo Pepe, for too great an interest in his boy pupils. The effect of his itinerant lifestyle is evident in his paintings, technique, colour and meaning. Whereas the *Martyrdom of St John the Baptist* for Valetta, technically and compositionally falls within his Roman style, his Sicilian paintings exhibit a stylistic change, technically looser and less finished. Furthermore, paintings he completed on his return to Naples are less assured and colour occasionally harsh, perhaps a consequence of the wound to his forehead and possible effect on his sight.

This book is faithful to documentary evidence with leaps of faith to interpret data to bring personalities to life and present truths through gaps in the weave and weft of the tapestry of Caravaggio's life.

Finally, the novel form is inspired by Memoirs of Hadrian (*Mémoires d'Hadrien* Librairie Plon, France 1951) by Marguerite Yourcenar, her goal – *to reinterpret the past but also strive for historical authenticity.*

Caravaggio paintings mentioned by date, which may contradict orthodox dates.

Title	Date/s	Commissioned by	Present location
Rome			
Boy Peeling Fruit	1592	1 Cesari – d'Arpino 2 Scipione Borghese	Longhi Collection, Florence
Sick Little Bacchus	1593	1 Cesari – d'Arpino 2 Scipione Borghese	Galleria Borghese, Rome
Boy with a Basket of Fruit	c1593	1 Cesari – d'Arpino 2 Scipione Borghese	Galleria Borghese, Rome
Fortune Teller (first version)	c1594	Marchese Vincento Giustiniani	Museo Capitolino, Rome
Cardsharps	c1594	1 Cardinal Francesco del Monte	Kimbell Art Museum Fort Worth, Texas
Concert of Musicians	c1595	C F del Monte	Metropolitan Museum. New York
St Francis in Ecstacy	c1595	1 C F del Monte gift to Ottavio Costa of Genoa	1 Genoa 2 Wadsworth Atheneum, Hertford Conn
Boy Bitten by a Lizard	c1596	Possibly for CF del Monte	National Gallery, London
Bacchus	c1596	1 CF del Monte 2 Grand Duke of Florence	Uffizi. Florence
The Gods Jupiter Neptune Pluto	c1597	C F del Monte	Fresco: Casino Porta Pinciana, Rome
Sacrifice of Isaac	c1598	Hospital of the Consolation	Barbara Plasecka-Johnson, Princeton NJ
St John the Baptist (1)	c1598	Hospital of the Consolation	Cathedral Museum, Toledo
St John the Baptist	c1598	Principe Corsini	Palazzo Corsini, Rome
Judith Beheading Holofernes	c1598	Signor Vincenzo Coppi	Galleria Nazionale d'Arte Antica, Rome
Basket of Fruit	c1599	1 Cesari – d'Arpino 2 Scipione Borghese	Biblioteca Ambrosiana, Milan
Calling of St Matthew	1599 / 1600	Contarelli Chapel - San Luigi dei Francesi, Rome	
Martyrdom of Sr Matthew	1600	Contarelli Chapel - San Luigi dei Francesi, Rome	
Conversion of St Paul	1600	Commissioned Tiberio Cerasi - Cerasi Chapel, Sta Maria del Popolo, Rome	
Crucifixion of St Peter	1601	Commissioned Tiberio Cerasi - Cerasi Chapel, Sta Maria del Popolo, Rome	
Supper at Emmaus	1601	Marchese Ciriaco Mattei	National Gallery, London
Amor Vincit Omnia	1602	Marchese Vincenzo Giustiniani	Gemäldegalerie, Berlin
St Matthew and the	1602	1 Contarelli –	Kaiser Friedrich / Bode

Angel		rejected 2 Vincenzo Guistiniani	Museum, Berlin. Destroyed 1945
Inspiration of St Matthew	1602	Contarelli Chapel - San Luigi dei Francesi, Rome	
St John the Baptist with the Ram	1602	1st version M Ciriaco Mattei	Capitoline Museum, Rome
St John the Baptist with the Ram	c1602	2nd version Prince Doria Pamphilj	Doria Pamphilj Gallery, Rome
Taking of Christ	1602	M Ciriaco Mattei	National Gallery of Ireland, Dublin
Sacrifice of Isaac	1602 / 1603	Cardinal Maffeo Barberini – later Pope Urban VIII	Uffizi, Florence
Entombment	1603	Fathers Oratorio Chiesa Nuova	Vatican, Rome
Madonna di Loreto or the Pilgrims	1604	Sant' Agostino, Rome	
St John the Baptist	1604	Ottavio Costa, Genoa	Nelson-Atkins Museum of Art, Kansas
John the Baptist	c1604	Principe Corsini?	Galleria Nazionale d'Arte Antica, Rome
Ecce Homo	c1605	Signori Masimi	Palazzo Rosso, Genoa
St Jerome Writing	c1605	Cardinal Scipione Borghese	Borghese Gallery, Rome
Pope Paul V (Camillo Borghese)	1605	Borghese Family	Prince Borghese, Rome
Madonna del Serpe (Madonna and Child with St Anne)	1606	1 Palafrenieri 2 C Scipione Borghese	Borghese Gallery, Rome
Death of the Virgin	1606	Laertio Cherubini Chapel – Sta Maria della Scala Zagarolo	Louvre, Paris
Mary Magdalene in Ecstacy	1606	1 Held by the Colonna 2 CN Scipio Borghese	Private Collection, Rome
2nd version Supper at Emmaus	1606	Marchese Patrizi	Brera Fine Arts Academy, Milan
David with the Head of Goliath Naples	1606	For Pope Paul V	Borghese Gallery, Rome
Seven Acts of Mercy	1607	Confraternity of Pio Monte della Misericordia, Naples	
Crucifixion of St Andrew	1607	Spanish Viceroy Naples	Cleveland Museum, Ohio
Madonna of the Rosary Not completed by	1607	1 Duke of Modena 2 Completed by	Kunsthistorisches Museum, Vienna

Caravaggio		Luigi Finson?	
Flagellation of Christ	1607	San Domenico Maggiore	Museo Capodimonte, Naples
Christ at the Column	1607	San Domenico Maggiore	Musee des Beaux-Arts, Rouen

Malta

Title	Date	Commissioned by	Present
Saint Jerome Writing	1607	Fra Ippolito Malaspina	St John's Co-Cathedral, Valetta
Alof de Wignacourt with his Page	1608	Alof de Wignacourt	Louvre, Paris
Beheading of Saint John the Baptist	1608	Alof de Wignacourt	St John's Co-Cathedral, Valetta
Sleeping Cupid	1608	Fra Francesco dell'Antella Secretary to Wignacourt	Pitti Palace, Florence 2nd version in the Royal Collection, London

Sicily

Title	Date	Commissioned by	Present
Burial of Santa Lucia	1608	Church of Santa Lucia, Syracuse	Bellomo Palace Museum, Syracuse
Raising of Lazarus	1609	Giovanni Lazzari for Church of Padri Crociferi	Museo Regionale, Messina
Adoration of the Shepherds	1609	Santa Maria degli Angeli	Museo Regionale, Messina
Nativity with Sts Francis and Lawrence	1609	San Lorenzo, Palermo	Stolen 1969, presumed destroyed. 2015 a digital replica was made.

Naples

Title	Date	Commissioned by	Present
John the Baptist	1610	CN Scipione Borghese	Galleria Borghese, Rome
Martyrdom of St Ursula	1610	1 Marcantonio Doria 2 Nicolo, Prince of Angri & Duke of Eboli	Palazzo Doria d'Angri Palazzo Zevallos Stigliano, Naples

Francesco Boneri, called **Cecco del Caravaggio** paintings mentioned by assumed date

Title	*Date*	*Commissioned by*	*Present*
Woman with a Dove	c1607	Unknown	Museo Nacional del Prado, Madrid
Man with a Rabbit	c1607	Unknown	Galeria Colecciones Reales, Madrid
Christ at the Column	c1607	Unknown	From Xray evidence, repainted as St Sebastian
Angel with Sts Ursula and Thomas	1607 / 1608	Unknown	Private collection, New York

Martyrdom of St Sebastian	c1608	Unknown	Museo Nazionale, Varsavia
Christ on the way to Calvary	c1609	Unknown	Slovenská Národná Galéría, Bratislava
Christ cleansing the Temple	After 1610	Unknown	Kaiser Friedrich / Bode Museum, Berlin
Cupid at the Spring	c1615	Unknown	Vitij Collection, Rome
Flute Player	Pre-1620	Unknown	Ashmolean Museum, Oxford
Instrument Maker	Pre-1620	Unknown	Wellington Museum, London
San Lorenzo	Pre-1620	Unknown	Santa Maria in Vallicella, Rome
Penitent Magdalene	Pre-1620	Unknown	National Museum, Stockholm
Resurrection	1619 / 1620	1 Rejected commission by Piero Guicciardini, Tuscan Ambassador to Rome 2 Scipione Borghese	1 Borghese collection, Rome 2 Art Institute of Chicago
Crucifixion	After 1620	Unknown	Bergamo